VERMILION DRIFT

ALSO BY WILLIAM KENT KRUEGER

VERMILION DRIFT

A NOVEL

WILLIAM KENT KRUEGER

ATRIA BOOKS
New York London Toronto Sydney

ATRIA BOOKS

A Division of Simon & Schuster, Inc.
1230 Avenue of the Americas
New York, NY 10020

First Atria Books hardcover edition September 2010

ATRIA BOOKS and colophon are trademarks of Simon & Schuster, Inc.

For information about special discounts for bulk purchases,
please contact Simon & Schuster Special Sales at 1-866-506-1949
or business@simonandschuster.com.

The Simon & Schuster Speakers Bureau can bring authors to your live event.
For more information or to book an event contact the Simon & Schuster Speakers
Bureau at 1-866-248-3049 or visit our website at www.simonspeakers.com.

Designed by Davina Mock-Maniscalco

Manufactured in the United States of America

10   9   8   7   6   5   4   3   2

Library of Congress Cataloging-in-Publication Data

Krueger, William Kent.
    Vermilion Drift : a novel / by William Kent Krueger. — 1st Atria Books hardcover ed.
       p.   cm.
1. O'Connor, Cork (Fictitious character)—Fiction.   2. Private investigators—
Minnesota—Fiction.   3. Murder—Investigation—Fiction.   4. Cold cases (Criminal
investigation)—Fiction.   5. Minnesota—Fiction.   I. Title.
    PS3561.R766V47 2010
    813'.54—dc22

                                                                2010013258

ISBN 978-1-4391-5384-0
ISBN 978-1-4391-7215-5 (ebook)

For Sarah Branham, my champion

In terms of the despiritualization of the universe, the mental process works so that it becomes virtuous to destroy the planet.

—Russell Means

ACKNOWLEDGMENTS

The Vermilion One Mine and the Ladyslipper Mine, which appear in this work, are fictitious. There are, however, real mines that are very similar in their design, scope, and history, and I've used elements of these actual places in the construction of this story. But I want to stress to anyone familiar with the remarkable area we call the Iron Range that I have taken liberties with fact in both geography and geology.

I'm extremely grateful to James Pointer of the Soudan Underground Mine State Park for the gift of his time and his knowledge. The morning I spent with him half a mile underground continues to be a remarkable memory for me. I've done my best to give readers the same sense of admiration that he gave me for the enterprise of the men who spent their lives working in near dark conditions to wrest iron from the earth. If you're ever in northern Minnesota, I can't recommend highly enough a tour of the Soudan Mine, which is operated by the state of Minnesota. I guarantee you'll never take fresh air and sunlight for granted again.

I also want to thank the staff of the Minnesota Discovery Center (formerly known as Ironworld), particularly those in the Research Center, who helped me locate a wealth of information in the archives. This resource is invaluable to all of us for a continued understanding and appreciation of the rich culture and history of the Iron Range.

I'm indebted to Dr. Garry Peterson, Chief Medical Examiner Emeritus of Hennepin County, Minnesota, for his help in understanding death, its aftermath, and the clues that bodies, no matter how ancient, can offer in unraveling the mystery of murder.

Finally, for their warm hospitality, a big thanks to all the staff at the wonderful little coffee shop called The Java Train, where the bulk of this novel was written.

Vermilion Drift

PROLOGUE

S ome nights, Corcoran O'Connor dreams his father's death.

Although the dream differs in the details, it always follows the same general pattern: His father falls from a great height. Sometimes he stumbles backward over a precipice, his face an explosion of surprise. Or he's climbing a high, flat face of rock and, just as he reaches for the top, loses his grip and, in falling, appears both perplexed and angry. Or he steps into an empty elevator shaft, expecting a floor that is not there, and looks skyward with astonishment as the darkness swallows him.

In the dream Cork is always a boy. He's always very near and reaches out to save his father, but his arm is too short, his hand too small. Always, his father is lost to him, and Cork stands alone and heartbroken.

If that was all of it, if that was the end of the nightmare, it probably wouldn't haunt him in quite the way that it does. But the true end is a horrific vision that jars Cork awake every time. In the dream, he relives the dream, and in that dream revisited something changes. Not only is he near his father as the end occurs but he also stands outside the dream watching it unfold, a distanced witness to himself and to all that unfolds. And what he sees from that uninvolved perspective delivers a horrible shock. For his hand, in reaching out, not only fails to save his father. It is his small hand, in fact, that shoves him to his death.

ONE

That early June day began with one of the worst wounds Cork O'Connor had ever seen. It was nearly three miles long, a mile wide, and more than five hundred feet deep. It bled iron.

From behind the window glass of the fourth-floor conference room in the Great North Mining Company's office complex, Cork looked down at the Ladyslipper Mine, one of the largest open-pit iron ore excavations in the world. It was a landscape of devastation, of wide plateaus and steep terraces and broad canyons, all of it the color of coagulating blood. He watched as far below him the jaws of an electric power shovel gobbled eighty tons of rock and spit the rubble into a dump truck the size of a house and with wheels twice as tall as a man. The gargantuan machine crawled away up an incline that cut along the side of the pit, and immediately another just like it took its place, waiting to be filled. The work reminded him of insects feeding on the cavity of a dead body.

At the distant end of the mine, poised at the very lip of the pit itself, stood the town of Granger. The new town of Granger. Thirty years earlier, Great North had moved the entire community, buildings and all, a mile south in order to take the ore from beneath the original town site. Just outside Granger stood the immense structures of the taconite plant, where the rock was crushed and processed into iron pellets for shipping. Clouds of steam billowed upward hundreds of feet, huge white pillars holding up the gray overcast of the sky.

Although he'd viewed the mine and the work that went on deep inside many times, the sight never ceased to amaze and sadden him.

The Ojibwe part of his thinking couldn't help but look on the enterprise as a great injury delivered to Grandmother Earth.

"Cork. Good. You're here."

Cork turned as Max Cavanaugh closed the door. Cavanaugh was tall and agreeable, a man who easily caught a lady's eye. In his early forties, he was younger than Cork by a decade. He was almost the last of the Cavanaughs, a family whose name had been associated with mining since 1887, when Richard Frankton Cavanaugh, a railroad man from St. Paul, had founded the Great North Mining Company and had sunk one of the first shafts in Minnesota's great Iron Range. Cork saw Max Cavanaugh at Mass every Sunday, and in winter they both played basketball for St. Agnes Catholic Church—the team was officially called the St. Agnes Saints, but all the players referred to themselves as "the old martyrs"—so they knew each other pretty well. Cavanaugh was normally a guy with an easy smile, but not today. Today his face was troubled, and with good reason. One of his holdings, the Vermilion One Mine, was at the center of a controversy that threatened at any moment to break into violence.

The two men shook hands.

"Where are the others?" Cork asked.

"They're already headed to Vermilion One. I wanted to talk to you alone first. Have a seat?"

Cork took a chair at the conference table, and Cavanaugh took another.

"Do you find missing people, Cork?"

The question caught him by surprise. Cork had been expecting some discussion about Vermilion One. But it was also a question with some sting to it, because the most important missing person case he'd ever handled had been the disappearance of his own wife, and that had ended tragically.

"On occasion I've been hired to do just that," he replied cautiously.

"Can you find someone for me?"

"I could try. Who is it?"

The window at Cavanaugh's back framed his face, which seemed as gray as the sky above the mine that morning. "My sister."

Lauren Cavanaugh. Well known in Tamarack County for her unflagging efforts to bring artistic enlightenment to the North Country. Two years earlier, she'd founded the Northern Lights Center for the Arts, an artists' retreat in Aurora that had, in a very short time, acquired a national reputation.

"I thought I read in the *Sentinel* that Lauren was in Chicago," Cork said.

"She might be. I don't know. Or she might be in New York or San Francisco or Paris."

"I'm not sure I understand."

"Is what I tell you confidential?"

"I consider it so, Max."

Cavanaugh folded his hands atop his reflection in the shiny tabletop. "My sister does this sometimes. Just takes off. But she's always kept in touch with me, let me know where she's gone."

"Not this time?"

"Not a word."

"Nothing before she left?"

"No. But that's not unusual. When she gets it into her head to go, she's gone, just like that."

"What about Chicago?"

He shook his head. "A smoke screen. I put that story out there."

"Is her car gone?"

"Yes."

"When did you last hear from her?"

"A week ago. We spoke on the phone."

"How did she sound?"

"Like she always sounds. Like sunshine if it had a voice."

Cork took out the little notebook and pen that he generally carried in his shirt pocket when he was working a case. He flipped the cover and found the first empty page.

"She drives a Mercedes, right?"

"A CLK coupe, two-door. Silver-gray."

"Do you know the license plate number?"

"No, but I can get it."

"So can I. Don't bother."

"She hasn't charged any gas since she left."

"How do you know?"

"I oversee all her finances. She also hasn't charged any hotel rooms, any meals, anything."

"Any substantial withdrawals from her bank account before she left?"

"Nothing extraordinary."

"Is it possible she's staying with a friend?"

"I've checked with everyone I can think of."

"Have you talked to the police?"

"No. I'd rather handle this quietly."

"You said she does this periodically. Why?"

Cavanaugh looked at Cork, his eyes staring out of a mist of confusion. "I don't know exactly. She claims she needs to get away from her life."

As far as Cork knew, her life consisted of lots of money and lots of adulation. What was there to run from?

"Is there someplace she usually goes?"

"Since she moved here, it's generally the Twin Cities or Chicago. In the past, it's been New York City, Sydney, London, Buenos Aires, Rome."

"For the museums?"

He frowned. "Not amusing, Cork."

"My point is what does she do there?"

"I don't know. I don't ask. Can you find her?"

"From what you've told me, she could be anywhere in the world."

He shook his head. "She left her passport."

"Well, that narrows it down to a couple of million square miles here in the U.S."

"I don't need your sarcasm, Cork. I need your help."

"Does she have a cell phone?"

"Of course. I've been calling her number since she left."

"We can get her cell phone records, see if she's called anyone or taken calls from anyone. Did she pack a suitcase?"

"No, but sometimes when she takes off, she just goes and buys whatever she needs along the way."

"According to her credit card records, not this time?"

"Not this time."

"Does she use a computer? Have an e-mail account?"

"Yes."

"Any way to check her e-mails?"

"I already have. There's been no activity since last Sunday, and nothing in the communication before that that seems relevant."

"Is it possible she has an account you don't know about?"

"It's possible but not probable."

"How did you manage to get her e-mail password?"

"We're close," he said, and left it at that.

"Look, Max, there's something I need to say."

"Say it."

"I have two grown daughters and a teenage son. It strikes me that I have less control, less access to their private lives than you have with your sister. Frankly, it seems odd."

Cavanaugh stared at him. His eyes were the hard green-brown of turtle shells. Cork waited.

"My sister is flamboyant," Cavanaugh finally said. "She inspires. She walks into a room and the place becomes electric, brighter and more exciting. People fall in love with her easily, and they'll follow her anywhere. In this way, she's charmed. But she has no concept of how to handle money. The truth is that financially she's a walking disaster. Consequently, for most of her life, I've overseen her finances. It hasn't been easy. There have been issues."

"Recently?"

He hesitated. "This arts center of hers. She gifted it significantly from her own resources—our resources. The idea was that other avenues of financing would then be found. They haven't materialized. I've been bleeding money into this project for some time now."

"Do you have the ability to bleed?"

"There's plenty of money. That's not the point."

"The point is her unreliability?"

He considered Cork's question, as if searching for a better answer, then reluctantly nodded.

"One more question. Has your sister received any threats related to the situation at Vermilion One?"

"No. She's not associated with this at all. The mine is my business."

"All right." Cork quoted his usual daily rate, then added, "A five-thousand-dollar bonus if I find her."

"I don't care what it takes. Will this interfere with your investigation of the mine threats?"

"I'm sure I can handle them both. I'll prepare the paperwork. Will you be around this afternoon?"

"I have a meeting until four, but I'll be at my home this evening." Cork said, "I'll drop by. Say around six?"

"Thanks, Cork. But I'm hoping you'll begin this investigation immediately."

"I'm already on the clock."

TWO

Corcoran Liam O'Connor had lived in Tamarack County, Minnesota, most of his life. He'd grown up there, had gone away for a while and been a cop in Chicago, then returned to the great Northwoods to raise his family. Several years earlier he'd been the county's sheriff, but hard things had happened and he'd left official law enforcement and now ran what he called "a confidential investigation and security consulting business." He was a PI. He operated his business alone, which was pretty much the way he did everything these days. He'd been a widower for a little over a year, recently enough still to feel the loss deeply; a father, but that summer his children were gone; what was left to him at the moment was the big, empty house on Gooseberry Lane and a family dog constantly in need of walking.

He followed Cavanaugh's black Escalade east ten miles to Aurora, then along the shoreline of Iron Lake. Rain had begun to fall, and the lake was pewter gray and empty. It was Monday, June 13. Spring had come late that year, and so far June had been cool enough that it had everyone in Tamarack County talking about summers they swore they remembered snow clear into July. Cavanaugh turned off Highway 1 and headed south into a low range of wooded hills capped with clouds and dripping with rainwater. Fifteen minutes later, they entered Gresham, a small town that had been built in the early days of mining on the Iron Range. The Vermilion One Mine had been the town's economic base, and, until the mine closed in the mid-1960s, Gresham had bustled. Now the streets were deserted; the buildings looked old and ignored. Every other storefront on the single block of the business district seemed long vacant, and yellowed signs bearing the names of realty companies leaned against the glass in otherwise empty windows. Lucy's, which was a small café, was brightly lit inside, and as Cork passed, he could see a couple of customers at the counter and Lucy Knutson at the grill, but no one seemed to be talking. It reminded him of an Edward Hopper work, *Nighthawks*, and he felt the way he always did whenever he looked at that painting: sad and alone.

Which brought back to him the dream he'd had the night before: his father's death. He could never predict when the nightmare would visit him, but it inevitably left him feeling broken and empty and unsure. He looked through the windshield streaked with rain and wondered, *Christ, could the day get any worse?*

Cavanaugh had sped through Gresham and was so far ahead that Cork couldn't see the Escalade anymore. Less than a mile outside town, he began to encounter the protesters. They wore ponchos and rain slickers and sat on canvas chairs and held their placards up as he passed.

No Nukes Here!

Stop the Madness!

Not in Our Backyards!

Washington—Go Radiate Yourself!

At the moment, there were maybe twenty protesters, which, considering the rain, seemed like a lot. They were an earnest and committed body.

A legal order restrained anyone from interfering with entry to the Vermilion One Mine, but as Cork approached the gate, a tall, broad figure in a green poncho stepped into the road and blocked his way. Cork was going slowly enough that it was no problem to brake, but he wasn't happy with the aggressiveness of the move. When the Land Rover had stopped, the figure came around to the driver's side, lifted a hand, and drew back the poncho hood, revealing the scowl of Isaiah Broom.

Cork rolled his window down. With as much cheer as he could muster, he said, "Morning, Isaiah."

Broom looked at him, then at the closed gate of the mine entrance, then at Cork again. He had eyes like pecans, and he had the high, proud cheekbones that were characteristic of the Anishinaabeg. He was roughly Cork's age, just past fifty. Cork had known him all his life. They'd traveled many of the same roads, though never together. They were not at all what anyone would call friends.

"You going in there?" Broom asked.

"That's my intent, Isaiah."

"You know, a lot of us Shinnobs are wondering about your allegiance these days."

"My allegiance, Isaiah, is to my own conscience. So far, I haven't done anything that worries me in that regard."

"These people," he said, nodding toward the mine operation, "they don't worry you?"

"These people are my neighbors. Yours, too, Isaiah."

"They're *chimook*, Cork," he said, using the Ojibwe slang for white people. "Are you *chimook*, too? Or are you one of The People?"

Broom had called himself Shinnob. That was shorthand for Anishinaabe, which was the true name of the Ojibwe nation. Roughly translated, it meant The People, or The Original People. Cork supposed that in this way the Anishinaabeg—as they were known collectively—like every human community, thought of themselves as special. Broom and the others were there because the southern boundary of the Iron Lake Reservation abutted the land holdings of the Vermilion One Mine.

"At the moment, Isaiah, I'm just a man trying to do a job. I'd be obliged if you'd step back and let me be on my way."

"'In terms of the despiritualization of the universe, the mental process works so that it becomes virtuous to destroy the planet.' Russell Means said that."

Broom was fond of quoting Russell Means, who was Lakota, and also Dennis Banks, who was a Shinnob. In the early seventies, these men had been among the founders of the American Indian Movement. Broom had known them both and had himself been present at the 1972 Trail of Broken Treaties march in Washington, D.C., which had ended in the occupation of the Bureau of Indian Affairs office. He'd continued to be a voice for activism in the Ojibwe community. He'd run several times for the position of chair of the Iron Lake tribal council but never won. He spoke hard truths frankly, but for most Shinnobs on the rez, his voice was too loud and too harsh to lead them.

"I'm not here to destroy the planet, Isaiah, that's a promise."

Broom looked skeptical but stepped back. Cork rolled up his window and went ahead.

At the gate, he signed in with Tommy Martelli. Martelli's family had been in mining for generations, and Tommy had himself worked the Vermilion One straight out of high school and after that the Ladyslipper until his age and hip problems made him become, as he put it, "a damn desk jockey." He wore a short-sleeve khaki shirt and nothing on his head, and, as he stood at the window of the Land Rover, warm summer rain dripped down his face from the silver bristle on the crown of his skull.

"Mr. Cavanaugh said you'd be right behind him," he told Cork. "Got us a real puzzler here. Haddad chewed our asses good, like it was our fault."

"What's going on, Tommy?"

"Nobody told you?"

"When he called me, Lou said some threats had been made."

"There's more to it than that, Cork. But if the boss didn't tell you, I'd best keep my mouth shut." He reached out for the clipboard Cork had signed, flashed a smile not altogether friendly, and said, "Love to see you figure this one out." He moved back to his little guardhouse, and Cork drove through the gate.

For a hundred yards, the pavement cut through a stand of aspen mixed with mature spruce. The road climbed up a steep slope, rounded a curve, broke from the trees, and suddenly the old mine buildings stood before him. They were dominated by the headframe, a steel tower a hundred feet high and covered with rust, which stood above shaft Number Six and supported the hoist for the mine elevator. The largest of the buildings, Cork knew, was the engine house. The other buildings, most in disrepair, had served other functions during the sixty years the mine had been in operation: a single-story office complex; the wet room, where the miners had peeled off their muddy clothing at the end of their shifts; the dry house; the drill shop; the crusher house. The buildings were backed by a towering ridge of loose glacial drift where a small forest of pines had taken root. To one side of the office building entrance stood a tall flagpole that pointed like an accusing finger at the dripping summer sky, and from which a soaked Old Glory fluttered limply in the breeze.

The potholed parking lot was nearly empty. Cork pulled next to Cavanaugh's Escalade, killed the engine, and got out. The air was an odd mix of scents: rainwater and sharp spruce and the flat mineral smell that came up from deep in the mine. He walked to the front door of the office and went inside, where he found a small reception desk, sans receptionist. There was a corridor running lengthwise, lined with closed doors. The place had the feel of one of those storefronts he'd passed in Gresham, a business long abandoned. He listened for the sound of activity or voices. Except for a newly mounted wall clock that noted the passing of each second with a brittle little tick, the place was dead quiet.

The phone at the reception desk rang. No one came running to answer it. Finally Cork leaned over and lifted the receiver.

"Hello," he said.

"Margie?"

Cork recognized Lou Haddad's voice. "Nope. It's O'Connor."

"Cork? Where's Margie?"

"Got me, Lou."

"Well, come on down. We're waiting for you."

"Where?"

"End of the hallway, last office on your right."

As he hung up, Cork heard the flush of a toilet, and a door halfway down the hall swung open and Margie Renn hurried toward him.

"Just powdering my nose," she said, smoothing her silver hair and her blue skirt. "Tommy was supposed to call and let me know you'd arrived."

"Ta-da," Cork said with a little dance step. Margie didn't seem to appreciate his humor.

"Let me call Mr. Haddad," she said.

"I already talked to him, Margie. I'm on my way there now."

"Let me show you."

"End of the hall, last door on the right. Right?"

She seemed disappointed that he didn't need her assistance, and Cork figured that, in the limbo that was the Vermilion One Mine these days, there must not be much for her to do except sit in the empty corridor and listen to the damn wall clock chopping seconds off her day.

THREE

The Iron Range was a great melting pot of humanity, and Lou Haddad's Lebanese family was not at all unusual. They'd come to the Range several generations back and had, for as long as Cork could remember, run a grocery store on the corner of Oak and Seventh Street. Lou's father had been different from the rest of his family, however. He'd chosen to work in the mine, the Vermilion One.

When they were kids, Cork—and just about everybody else—had called Lou Haddad Louie Potatoes. This because the guys who delivered the store's produce and who were reputed to have had mob connections once spotted Lou munching on a slice of raw potato. They'd given him the name jokingly—everyone in the mob had a nickname—but it had stuck. Growing up, Cork and Louie Potatoes had been good friends. They went to the same church—St. Agnes—were in the same grade, and their families' houses were only two blocks apart. They both loved fishing, ran around with the same group of kids, double-dated. After graduation, Haddad had gone to a Jesuit college, Fairfield University in Connecticut, and become an engineer. Cork had gone to Chicago and become a cop. And when they were ready to raise families, they'd both come back home. They'd often done things together with their wives as couples—gone to movies, played bridge, picnicked on the lake. But after his wife died, Cork found himself turning down the overtures and spending his time alone.

Haddad stood at the open door. He was Cork's height, missing six feet by an inch, with thin gray-brown hair and, normally, a ready grin. At the moment, however, he looked like a man chewing ground glass.

He shook Cork's hand, said, "Thanks for coming," and stood back so that Cork could enter.

It was a small conference room and smelled musty with disuse. It held a central table surrounded by half a dozen folding chairs. There were already three other people waiting. Two of them Cork knew: Marsha Dross, sheriff of Tamarack County, and Max Cavanaugh. The stranger was a woman in jeans and a light blue sweater. Cork greeted Dross, and Haddad introduced him to the woman.

"Genie, this is Cork O'Connor. Cork, Genie Kufus, from the Department of Energy."

"Actually I'm a consultant for the Office of Civilian Radioactive Waste Management," Kufus clarified.

Eugenia Kufus was lovely and small, and her eyes sparkled in a way that reminded Cork of the bounce of sunlight off water. Her smile was delightful and disarming, and, because it seemed very personally directed at him, Cork was momentarily flustered. Was she flirting? He thought it ridiculous that he even wondered, and absurd that he couldn't tell, but since Jo had died, he'd found himself on very uncertain ground where women were involved.

"Long time since this place saw any business," Cork said, trying to regain composure.

Max Cavanaugh said, "For the last year, we've been focusing mostly on getting the mine prepared for inspection. A lot of work necessary in the power house and lift operation. Lou has overseen most of that process. We opened the offices here just a couple of weeks ago to accommodate Genie and her people. Lou has an office down the hall, and so do I. And we've upped security, of course."

"Any trouble getting through the gate?" Haddad asked.

"Nothing I couldn't handle," Cork said.

"Good."

They gathered around the table, and Dross passed Cork three sheets of paper, each with creases showing that the sheets had been folded into thirds, as if to fit into envelopes. Centered on each sheet was a single line of text, the same line: *We die. U die.* All the notes had been printed using a red font that made the words look as if they dripped blood.

"I received one," Haddad said, "Max received one, and Genie received one."

"Mailed?" Cork asked.

"No," Haddad replied. "We found them in various places. Mine was on my car seat when I came out of Nestor's hardware store in Aurora. I never lock my door when I'm in town."

Cavanaugh said, "Mine was inside my morning paper."

"And mine had been slipped under the door of my hotel room," Kufus said.

"No fingerprints on them or on the envelopes," Dross told him. "We've checked."

"When did you get them?" Cork asked.

"Two days ago," Lou said.

Cork looked at the woman from the DOE. "You're here to survey the mine, is that right, Ms. Kufus?"

"It's Genie, and yes. I'm heading up the team that's been sent to assess the geologic integrity of the Vermilion One site."

"Geologic integrity?"

"Its suitability for long-term storage of nuclear waste."

"Ah." Cork studied the sheets. "Ink-jet printed." He held one of them to the light, checking for a watermark. There was none. He shook his head at the bloody-looking print. "I don't think I have this particular font on my computer."

"It's called 'From Hell.' Free download off the Internet," Dross said. "Big around Halloween, I understand."

"Have any of you received any other threats?"

"No," Haddad said, then looked to the others for confirmation. No one contradicted him.

"Has anyone else received one of these?"

"Not that we know of," Haddad replied. "Just us lucky three."

"Did anyone see the envelopes being delivered?"

Dross shook her head. "My guys canvassed the areas, came up with nothing."

"Is there any reason to believe that it's not just part of the general anger that the DOE's proposal has generated, that it's not some crackpot letting off steam?"

"Do you want to take that chance?" Dross asked.

Cavanaugh said, "Cork, if you wouldn't mind accompanying Lou, there's something else you need to see."

It was raining harder now, coming down in warm, gray sheets. Haddad, Dross, and Cork huddled in the old Mine Rescue Room next to the headframe. There was a guard on duty in the Rescue Room, a big guy who wasn't familiar to Cork. The name tag on his company uniform read "Plott." He sat in front of a bank of monitors, each showing a view of a different area of the property: the front gate, the mine office, the engine house, the other mine shaft openings. He had an FM radio going, but he'd turned it low when they came in so that it was barely audible. He watched the screens with a dedication that Cork was pretty certain was mostly show for those who'd intruded on his territory.

"What do you know about Vermilion One?" Haddad asked his companions.

"Among the oldest and deepest of the underground mines on the Iron Range," Cork replied. "Closed when we were both kids. What, thirteen?"

"Thirteen," Haddad confirmed with a nod. "Summer of nineteen sixty-four. My father was laid off. Sad day for a lot of folks. Do either of you understand Vermilion One, geologically?"

"I'm not from the North Country, Lou," Dross replied. "All I know is that there's iron in them thar hills."

"That's okay. Most people who aren't Rangers don't know much beyond that." He pronounced the word "Ranger" as "Rain-cher," which was how the old-timers on the Iron Range often referred to themselves.

While they waited for the cage to be lifted to the surface, Haddad explained a few things. The area in northern Minnesota known generally as the Iron Range was actually composed of three distinct ranges: the Vermilion, the Mesabi, and the Cuyuna. Because the Vermilion Range contained hematite, iron in nearly perfect concentration, it was the first area to be mined. The Vermilion One had begun as a pit mine—several pit mines, actually—then had gone to underground excavation. The first shaft had been sunk in 1900. By the time the mine was abandoned, it had reached a depth of nearly half a mile.

"Why abandoned?" Dross asked.

"New methods of mining and processing made taconite—that's the low-grade form of iron ore that runs like a great river through the range—more profitable, and digging enormous pits became the way. The Hull Rust Mine outside Hibbing is the largest open-pit iron mine in the world."

"Grand Canyon of the North," Cork said.

"That's what they call it," Haddad confirmed.

"The depth of Vermilion One, is that the reason the DOE is interested in storing nuclear waste here?" Dross asked.

"One of the reasons. The other is the geologic stability. We're standing on an extension of the Canadian Shield, the oldest exposed rock formation in the Northern Hemisphere and one of the most stable. The chance of seismic activity here is next to nothing. Compared with the Yucca Mountain nuclear storage site, which experiences several hundred seismic events every year, this place is about as dull as a nun's sex life. When you're thinking long-term safety of the nuclear waste we've generated, this is an attractive site. Plus the fact that there's fifty miles of tunnel already excavated, so the storage areas have pretty much already been created. A significant cost reduction."

"But if it does leak, it could contaminate the headwaters of a couple of the largest river systems in North America," Cork pointed out.

Haddad said, "There's that."

"What do you think of all this, Lou?" Dross asked.

Haddad glanced toward the security guard, whose eyes were glued to the monitors, and didn't reply.

Through the open window of the Rescue Room came the sound of the cage rattling up. They stepped outside, put on the hard hats Haddad had distributed, and stood next to the shaft. The cage arrived in a rush of cool air that smelled of deep, wet rock. Haddad threw back the gate. After they were in, Haddad reached to a button mounted on the framework and gave it three rings.

"Connects to the hoist operator in the engine house," he explained. "We communicate everything with the rings."

"What if we get stuck down there and the ringer fails?" Cork asked.

"The shaft has an antenna that runs from the lowest level all the way to the top. I just give a signal with this." He tapped a pager that hung on his belt.

They began a rattling descend. There was a single lightbulb in a fixture at the top of the cage, and, as they dropped, Cork could see the hard face of the rock that had been cut for the shaft. The walls were streaked red, as if a great flow of blood had run there.

"You never answered Marsha's question, Lou," Cork said above the noise of the cage rattle. "What do you think about using Vermilion One to store nuclear waste?"

"A while back, Germany went with the idea of a waste isolation facility, which they created in a deep abandoned salt mine," Haddad said. "They've discovered that it leaks. It's been leaking for years." He shook his head dismally. "The plan at the moment is to use the Yucca Mountain facility, but because of some of the potential difficulties there, other sites need to be considered. The question remains: What do we do with the nuclear waste we've created? Nobody in their right mind wants it in their backyard."

It took a couple of minutes to reach the third level. When the cage stopped, Haddad threw back the gate and led Cork and Dross out. They were in a large excavation where two tunnels, each ten feet high and ten feet wide, led off to the left and to the right. The area around the cage station was lit with electric lights strung along the ceiling, but the tunnels were black. Up top the temperature was in the low seventies, but in the mine the air was twenty degrees cooler and Cork wished he'd brought a sweater. Dross was hugging herself for warmth.

"Over here," Haddad said. He moved to a wall not far from the cage. Spray-painted in red across the old mining scars were the words "We die. U die." The message had been carefully done so that it looked very much like the printed messages Haddad and the others had received. The words seemed to drip blood.

"When did you discover this?" Cork asked.

"I didn't," Haddad replied. "It was Genie Kufus, yesterday. She came down to inspect this level, and there it was."

"She was alone?"

"Yes."

"When was the last time anyone was down here before that?"

"On this level specifically, a week ago. I sent a couple of men down to make sure the pumps were working. They checked every level except the last five."

"Pumps?"

"Water. It leaks into the mine and has to be removed. The lowest levels are still flooded. It'll be a while before we get those cleared for inspection."

"They didn't report anything?" Dross asked.

"No."

"Could they have simply missed it?"

"Would you miss that?" Haddad replied.

Cork said, "So this was done sometime between last Sunday and yesterday. How would they have gotten access to this level?"

"Coming down the Number Six shaft is the only way."

"There are seven other shafts, though, right?"

"All of them have been capped and sealed. I checked them myself yesterday after Genie reported what she'd found. None of them have been monkeyed with. Besides, none of the other shafts connect with the drifts that run off Number Six."

"Was anyone else in the mine at all during that time, on any level?"

"Yes. Mike Chernokov and Freddie Brink. They've been working on the ventilation and the water pumps. And we had a small tour group in from the state legislature on Friday. They wanted to see for themselves what the DOE found so attractive about this site. I led it myself."

"Did you visit Level Three?"

"No, I confined the tour to Level One, the Vermilion Drift."

"Vermilion Drift?"

"In a mine, a vertical excavation is called a sink. An excavation that runs horizontally off a sink is called a drift."

"So mine shafts are sinks and tunnels are drifts?" Cork said.

"That's right. The Vermilion Drift was the first underground mining done in this location, and I thought it was appropriate for the group."

"Your two guys and the legislature group, that's it?"

"And Genie."

"Did you talk to your guys?" Dross asked.

"Believe me, I talked."

"What did they say?"

"That they went down, completed their work, came back up. They didn't do anything, they didn't see anything."

"Do you trust them?" Cork asked.

"Listen, good-paying jobs on the Range aren't that plentiful. Those guys are family men. They'd have to be stupid, which they're not, or ideologically fanatic, which they also are not, to jeopardize their employment that way."

"Okay," Cork said. "I saw a ladder running down the framework on the side of the shaft. Is it possible somebody from your tour group slipped away and climbed down here?"

"There were only five in the group. All of them were in my sight the entire time."

"What about Kufus?" Dross threw out.

Haddad looked surprised, then looked as if he was about to laugh. "Why would she do it?"

"I don't know. That's why I'm asking. You said she was alone when she found this. When she reported it, how did she seem?"

"Disturbed. If you're looking at storing nuclear waste in Vermilion One, the issue of security is going to be huge. She seemed genuinely surprised and upset."

"Okay, let's work on the premise that no one who was down here legitimately is responsible," Cork said. "That would mean someone was here who wasn't supposed to be."

"No way someone who wasn't authorized could get down here," Haddad replied.

"If you accept my premise, that's not true."

"Which means what?" Haddad asked.

Dross eyed Cork and smiled with perfect understanding. "There's got to be another way in."

FOUR

U p top, Haddad separated and went to his office, while Cork and Dross returned to the conference room. Cavanaugh and Kufus were deep in a conversation that stopped the moment Cork and the sheriff walked in. From the looks on their faces and the abruptness with which the conversation ended, Cork had the distinct impression that it wasn't business they were discussing.

Haddad came in a few moments later and dropped a book in the middle of the table. The tome—nearly a foot wide, eighteen inches long, eight inches thick, and bound in heavy material that looked a lot like leather—hit with the thump of a fallen body.

He said, "These are the schematics for every level of the mine, all twenty-seven. Every shaft, every drift, every foot of the fifty-four miles of excavation. I've gone over them so many times they visit me in my nightmares. I'm telling you, aside from Number Six, which is the only shaft still open, there is no other way in. Why would there be?"

"I don't know," Cork said. "Enlighten me."

"I just did. Another entrance would mean another sink, and, believe me, cutting a shaft into rock is no Sunday drive in the country. It requires equipment, explosives, time, money. We'd know if someone did that. For one thing, they'd make a hell of a racket."

Cork opened the book. The pages were made of a thin, waxy material. The drawings on them reminded Cork of town plats, precise lines and corridors with lots of numbers indicating sizes and distances. All this was laid against a background that showed the county section lines for the ground above. In the lower right-hand corner was a legend that contained the scale and explained the markings on the map:

stopes, raises, drifts, shafts, drill holes. Under the legend was a nota-
tion: "Prepared by Engineers Office, Granger, MN." Beneath that was
a date.

"These are recent," he said.

"I requested them as soon as I knew about the DOE inspection,"
Cavanaugh said. He nodded toward Kufus. "I wanted Genie and her
people to have the most accurate information possible."

"How were they prepared?"

Haddad said, "I took the last full set of schematics—they're in
pretty bad shape—and had them redone."

"When was the last set created?"

"Just before the mine closed in the sixties."

"Any chance something was missed in the update?"

Haddad shook his head. "I checked the old schematics against the
new set myself. They're identical."

Cork thought a moment. "Do you have anything before the sixties?"

"Yes. Archived at the Ladyslipper Mine. When Vermilion One
closed, everything was moved there for storage."

"Were they the basis for the schematics done when the mine
closed?"

"No. A complete and independent survey was carried out at that
time. They wanted an accurate blueprint of the mine as it existed
then."

"Have you looked at the earlier schematics?"

"What would be the point?"

"To be thorough," Cork said. "It seems to me that there are three
obvious possibilities for how someone managed to put graffiti on
Level Three. One, it was someone who was down there officially and
did something unofficial. But you tell me you're certain that didn't
happen. Two, it was someone who accessed the mine unofficially
through one of the known entrances, but you also say that's impossible. And three, someone came into the mine another way, a way un-
known to you and that doesn't show on the recent schematics. Because
there are earlier schematics that still haven't been checked, this strikes
me as the best possibility at the moment. I think it would be prudent

to go over them, just to be thorough. You want to be thorough, don't you, Lou?"

"And if this possibility doesn't pan out?"

"Let's cross that bridge when we come to it."

They stepped back from the table, and Haddad said, "I'll head to Ladyslipper right now. If I find something, I'll let everyone know, and we can decide how we want to proceed. In the meantime, Marsha, what about the threats?"

Dross looked a little uneasy. "The truth is that they're rather vague and unspecific. They don't threaten you by name. And the graffiti in the mine tends to support the general nature of the statement. It could be argued that 'we' is the population at large, and if storage of radioactive waste here results in the death of that population, you, as a part of that population, die too."

"You sound like a lawyer," Cavanaugh said.

Dross shrugged. "I'm not sure what more I can do at this point, especially because, as I say, the threat is so vague. And, Max, most people in Tamarack County aren't thrilled with the idea of Vermilion One being used for nuclear waste storage, so the pool of suspects is rather large. But until we know how someone got into the mine, my recommendation is that no one goes down there alone."

"We'll make sure that doesn't happen," Haddad assured her.

Dross said, "Let me know what you come up with after looking at the old schematics, Lou, and maybe we can figure something then. I'll stay in touch."

The sheriff bid them good-bye and left.

"I have work I can do back at my hotel room," Kufus said. "Then I think I'll do a mile in the lake."

She looks like a swimmer, Cork thought, *nicely toned.* "The water's still pretty cold," he cautioned.

"I warm up easily." She gave Cork that disarming smile, and he thought, *Christ, she is flirting?* But she turned the same smile immediately on Cavanaugh. "Still on for lunch, Max?"

"Looking forward to it," he replied.

She left the room and left Cork feeling awkward and uncertain, stupid in his understanding of women.

After Genie Kufus had gone, Haddad said, "Thanks for agreeing to help, Cork. As soon as I've had a chance to go over the old schematics, I'll let you know what I've found."

They shook hands, and Cork turned to Max Cavanaugh to take his leave.

"Sure you can handle . . . everything?" Cavanaugh asked.

"I'm sure. And I'll stay in touch."

Outside the gate to the Vermilion One Mine, the number of protesters didn't appear to have increased. Only the hard-core dedicated were willing to endure the discomfort of the steady rain. He understood and sympathized with their cause. Tamarack County was his home, too, and he didn't want a radioactive dump there any more than they did. Isaiah Broom was still a hulking presence, along with a number of other Shinnobs Cork knew from the rez. Broom flipped him the bird as he passed. The others just eyed him with looks of betrayal.

He'd almost reached the end of the gathering when he saw a photographer's tripod up at the side of the road and covered with a rain hood. Bent to the eyepiece was an old woman with long, black hair, wet as a well-used mop. Cork pulled off the asphalt and stopped. He got out and walked to the photographer, who was so intent on her work that she didn't realize she had company.

"*Boozhoo*, Hattie," Cork said, using the familiar Ojibwe greeting.

She rose slowly from her camera, not because of her age, which was well over seven decades, but because she was a woman unconcerned with time. She smiled, sunshine in the middle of the rain. Her eyes were light almond and warm when she saw him.

"*Anin*, Corkie," she replied. She was one of only a few people who ever called him Corkie. She and all the others who used the name had been his mother's good friends. There were few of them still alive. She glanced down the line of protesters, many of whom were eyeing the exchange suspiciously. "Taking a chance, aren't you?"

"I don't think they'll jump me, Hattie. But I expect they won't be including me in their prayers tonight."

She reached inside her yellow rain jacket, pulled out a pack of Newports, plucked a cigarette, and fed it to the corner of her mouth, where it dangled while she struck a match.

"Love the gray of this day," she said. "The pall it casts. My film's going to love it, too. Just look at that composition."

She pointed toward the stretch of road that led to the gate: the protesters huddled on one side, the mine fence on the other, and between them the no-man's-land of wet asphalt. To Cork it was just a dreary scene, but to Hattie Stillday it was dramatic composition. Hers was the eye to trust. For longer than Cork had been alive, she'd been framing the nation in black-and-white stills. The main thrust of her work had been those moments when cultures collide. She'd photographed steelworkers' strikes in Pennsylvania in the early fifties. She'd been on all three marches from Selma to Montgomery in the sixties. She'd chronicled on film the White Night gay riots in San Francisco in '79. Every November, she was a part of the peace vigil held before the gates of Fort Benning, Georgia, to protest the training of Latin American soldiers by the Western Hemisphere Institute for Security Cooperation, the organization that for years had been known as the notorious School of the Americas. This was one activity that moved her to do more than snap photos. She'd been arrested a couple of times, fingerprinted, booked. Only her age and reputation had saved her from actual prosecution. Her work hung in the Guggenheim and the Getty and the Art Institute, and had been reproduced in beautifully bound volumes. Hattie Stillday was famous, but to look at her on that wet morning, an old woman with black strands of hair plastered to her cheeks and mud caking her hiking boots and a cigarette dancing in the corner of her mouth as she talked, you'd never know it.

"So the poop is true? You're working for the mine people?"

"'Fraid so, Hattie."

She plucked the cigarette from her mouth and flicked ash onto the wet ground. "I think your grandmother just turned in her grave, Corkie. But I suppose everybody's got to make their buck."

There was a great deal more to it than that. Like the power of the composition Cork didn't quite see, there were elements of this situation to which Hattie was undoubtedly blind. He could have tried to explain, but Corkie didn't feel like arguing with this fine, old woman.

"Care to pose for a famous photo?" she asked.

"Infamous you mean. And no thanks. I've got business to attend to. Actually, I'm on my way to talk to your granddaughter."

"Ophelia?" Her eyes turned cold. "What the hell for?"

"I can't say."

"This mine business? She's got nothing to do with it. You go dragging her name into this, Corkie, and get her into trouble, you'll answer to me, do you understand?"

"I'm always discreet, Hattie."

"Discreet like brass knuckles. You're just like your father."

Cork spotted Isaiah Broom coming their way. He'd already had all the conversation with the man that he wanted for the day. He leaned and kissed the old woman on her cheek and tasted the rain there. "I'll be gentle with her, Hattie. I give you my word." He turned, crossed the road, got back into his Land Rover, and drove away. Behind him the protest vanished into the gray curtain of the rain.

FIVE

He headed first to Sam's Place, the burger stand he owned in Aurora.

Sam's Place was, in a way, the vault of his heart. It held good memories, treasures that reached back over forty years. It had been bequeathed to him by the man who'd built the business, a Shinnob named Sam Winter Moon, who'd been his father's good friend and then Cork's. With the help of his children and their friends, Cork had managed the business by himself for years. But his older daughter, Jenny, was gone now, maybe for good. She'd graduated from the University of Iowa and had been accepted in the Writers' Workshop, the graduate program there. In Iowa City, she'd met a young man who was both a poet and a farmer. No matter how Cork looked at Jenny's future, coming back to Aurora didn't seem part of it.

His second daughter, Anne, was in El Salvador, on a mission program sponsored by St. Ansgar College, where she'd just finished her sophomore year. After St. Ansgar, it was his daughter's intention to become a preaffiliate with the Sisters of Notre Dame de Namur and to prepare to become a nun, a path Cork was pretty certain would not lead back to the North Country of Minnesota.

His youngest child, Stephen, who was fourteen, had gone away for the summer to work on a cattle operation, courtesy of Hugh Parmer, an exorbitantly wealthy man from West Texas whom Cork had befriended and who had, in return, befriended the O'Connors. In the infrequent communications Cork had received from his son, Stephen's response to the world outside Aurora was nothing short of an intoxicating romance. Cork could see the writing on the wall.

His wife, Jo, had died—been murdered—a little over a year and a half earlier, and it seemed to Cork that more and more the time he'd spent as husband and father had begun to recede from him, a train departing the station, leaving him alone on the platform.

Financially, Cork was set these days. He'd sold land along the lakeshore to Hugh Parmer, who'd intended to build a tasteful condominium community surrounding Sam's Place. But Parmer had chosen instead to donate the land to the town of Aurora, with the stipulation that the area be kept in its natural state in perpetuity. He'd done this in honor of Jo O'Connor. Cork was grateful to his friend, because every time he looked from Sam's Place down the wild and beautiful shoreline of Iron Lake, in a way, he saw Jo.

His PI business had succeeded beyond all his expectations and took up so much of his time that he couldn't effectively operate Sam's Place on his own. So he'd hired a woman named Judy Madsen, a retired school administrator who knew how to handle kids, to run the business.

He parked in the gravel lot, went inside, and opened the door to the serving area. "How's it going, Judy?"

Without turning from the prep table where she was slicing tomatoes, Madsen said, "We need change. And we're low on chips. Driesbach"—the route man who delivered most of the packaged food items—"called and said he's sick as a dog and won't be by today."

"All right. I'll hit the IGA and pick up some chips. Anything else?"

"Yeah. When are you going to sell me this place?"

A chronic question. And not asked in jest. Judy wanted Sam's Place, and she wanted it bad.

"It's my legacy to my children, Judy."

"I'm the one wearing an apron."

"They'll be back," he said.

She straightened up from the prep table and gave him a level look. "If you say so."

It wasn't until a few minutes before noon that Cork walked into the Northern Lights Center for the Arts. The organization occupied the old Parrant estate on North Point Road, a prime piece of property situated just outside the town limits, at the end of a pine-covered peninsula that stuck like a crooked thumb into Iron Lake. The house was an enormous brick affair with two wings, mullioned windows, and dark wood framing, which gave it the look of a country place an English baron might have maintained. It was separated from the road by a tall wall constructed of the same brick as the house. The lawn was a football field of manicured grass that sloped down to the lakeshore, where a boathouse stood. A sailboat was tied to the boathouse dock, its mast a bare white cross against the deep blue of the lake.

Judge Robert Parrant was long dead. There had been other occupants before and after the judge, but because of the man's infamy and unseemly demise, the people of Tamarack County still tied his name to the property.

Cork had an unpleasant history with the place. Ten years earlier, he'd found Judge Parrant dead in his office there, brains splattered across the wall, the victim of a murder that had been made to look like a suicide. In that same office four years later, Cork had found two more dead men, a murder-suicide committed with a shotgun. There were other deaths, and although they occurred elsewhere, they occurred somehow in the shadow cast over Tamarack County by that cursed place.

There was a word in the language of the Ojibwe. *Mudjimush-keeki.* It meant "bad medicine." To Cork's mind, that acre at the end of North Point Road, regardless of its beauty, was a place of *mudjimush-keeki.*

He walked in without knocking and found himself in the foyer of what had once been a living room but was now a large common area for the artists in residence at the center. A lot of clatter came from the dining room, where Emma Crane, the cook, was setting the table for lunch. Cork went to the center's office, which was the same room where, years before, all the blood had been spilled. The door was open, and Ophelia Stillday was at her desk. She looked up, and, like everyone else Cork had seen that day, she looked gray.

"Hey, kiddo, why the long face?" he asked.

He'd known Ophelia her whole life. She'd been raised by her grandmother Hattie after her own mother had died of a drug overdose in a crack house in L.A. Ophelia and his daughter Jenny had been best friends, and there'd been so many sleepovers at the O'Connor house that she'd become like another member of the family. She'd gone on camping trips with them and joined them for a long cross-country drive one year to Disneyland. Hattie Stillday needn't have warned him about treating her kindly; he felt almost as much affection for her as he did for his own children.

"Business." It was clear that was all she would say on the subject.

"Running the place alone since Lauren's gone, that's got to be tough."

"What are you doing here, Mr. O.C.?"

It was what she'd always called him. O.C. for O'Connor.

Ophelia was full-blood Ojibwe, a young woman with intense eyes and graceful movements. All her life she'd been a dancer, both traditional and modern. She'd performed the Jingle Dance at powwows and knew many dances from other tribes. She'd also studied dance at the University of Minnesota in the Twin Cities, and her dream had been to create original choreography that combined the elements of native dance with more modern movement. Unfortunately, her dream had been cut short by a car that had run a stoplight in Minneapolis, broadsided Ophelia's little Vespa, and crushed her right leg. Ophelia, the doctors predicted with surety, would never dance again.

"Actually I came about Lauren."

"She's gone."

"She's not just gone, Ophelia. She's gone missing."

"What do you mean?"

"Mind if I sit?"

She gestured toward a chair near her desk, a piece that looked like it had been made in the days of Louis XIV.

"It appears that no one knows her true whereabouts," he said, after he was seated. "When did you last see her?"

Ophelia sat back, folded her arms across her chest in a move that Cork, as a trained observer, might have taken as unconsciously defensive. He chose to ignore it.

"A cocktail gathering," she said. "Sunday, a week ago yesterday. The center was empty, and we met late into the evening with some of our volunteers in her private dining room to go over the roster of new artists and instructors coming Monday morning for the next residency."

"How does that work?"

"Most of our artists come for a week. With each group we try to focus on the medium they're most interested in. Watercolor, for example, or multimedia or photography. We bring in well-known working artists as instructors. It's an intense program. We have room enough here for only seven artists and two instructors. Admission is very competitive. We do have one residency that's different. It's longer for one thing, anywhere from one month to three months, and it's designed to highlight an artist Lauren feels is on the verge of a big career breakout and to help with that process. Currently, our long-term resident artist is Derek Huff. Very talented."

"How did Lauren seem that last night?"

"Excited. She's always excited at the prospect of a new group. She was positively ecstatic."

"Ecstatic?"

"Effervescent. Ebullient," she added.

Which made Cork smile. Being around artists, he decided, was bound to rub off on you.

Above the fireplace mantel hung a painting of Lauren Cavanaugh. It showed a beautiful woman in her early forties, with ash blond hair, green eyes, and flawless skin carefully drawn over the fine bones of a narrow face. Her lips seemed to hint at a smile, very Mona Lisaesque. She was stunning, but it was hard to tell what lay behind that beauty.

When Cork was young, the Cavanaugh name had been synonymous with iron mining and with wealth. Both Max and his sister, Lauren, had been born in Aurora, but neither had been raised there. Their father had taken them away when they were quite young. When her brother returned to Aurora two years earlier, Lauren had followed. Because Max attended St. Agnes regularly, Cork knew him pretty well. But Lauren Cavanaugh didn't go to church, and to Cork she was an enigma. She'd bought the Parrant estate, which had been empty for some time, and had established the Northern Lights Center for the Arts. She came with a cultural vision, a whirlwind of ideas that swept up a lot of people in Tamarack County. She proved to be a true patron of the arts. She'd organized and funded a lecture series that had brought in artists and thinkers with a broad range of interests. From what Cork understood, the size of the audiences that turned out for the events had been remarkable. According to things he'd read in the local paper, plans were being drawn for a complex that would include lofts, a gallery, and a theater for performing arts. Lauren Cavanaugh's passion and conviction regarding the importance of art, even in a wilderness outpost like Aurora, was inspiring to a lot of Cork's fellow citizens, and clearly to Ophelia.

But what Cork saw in the painting above the mantel was a woman who looked down on him, and her hinted smile could easily have been one of contempt.

"Did she ever talk to you about why she came back to Aurora?" he asked.

"Simplicity," Ophelia replied.

"Where was she before?"

"Where wasn't she? Europe, Australia, India, South America."

"And now Aurora. For the sake of simplicity. It seems to me that what she's set out to accomplish here is far from simple."

Ophelia gave a brief laugh. "Lauren isn't a woman who can sit still. She's a fountain of ideas and inspiration. She keeps a tape recorder with her all the time so that, whenever a new idea strikes her, she can record it and not risk forgetting. I'd love to listen to one of her tapes."

"So would I. Is that possible?"

Ophelia looked taken aback. Offended even. "Absolutely not."

A delicate bell rang in the dining room.

"Lunch," Ophelia said. She stood up and reached for the cane that hung from the back of her chair.

"Just a few more questions," Cork said.

"Why are you asking?"

"I've been hired."

"Who?" Then it became clear to her. "Max."

"I'm not confirming that," Cork said.

She sat back down.

"When you last spoke with Lauren, did she mention a trip at all?"

"No," Ophelia replied.

"Did she talk about visiting someone, a friend?"

"Not that I recall."

"Does she have friends? A special friend maybe?"

"She has lots of friends." She'd answered the last few questions with a look of impatience, but now she frowned and thought carefully. "No, she has lots of acquaintances. Her life is filled with people, but she doesn't seem to have anyone especially close. At least not that she's ever talked about."

"What about men?"

"You mean like dating?"

"Or whatever it's called these days."

Ophelia laughed. "She's beautiful, she's smart, she's funny, she's rich. Men make fools of themselves over her all the time."

"But does she date?"

"Mr. O.C., I'm her colleague. Actually, I'm her employee. She doesn't share every intimate detail of her life with me."

"Just asking." Cork heard footsteps, lots of them, outside Ophelia's office. Artists who'd worked up an appetite. "It's my understanding that she hasn't contacted anyone since she left. No e-mails from her personal account. Does she have an e-mail account she uses for business?"

"Yes, but if you're hoping to look at it, you're out of luck. It's password protected, and I don't have the password. Are you always this pushy?"

Cork smiled. "This is just inquisitive, kiddo. When I'm pushy, believe me, you'll know it. Could I see her living quarters?"

"Living quarters? This isn't a barracks, Mr. O.C. But I suppose it wouldn't be a problem for you to see her residence."

Ophelia's cane was of beautiful design, polished hickory with an eagle's head carved into the handle. She leaned on it heavily as they left her office and turned down the hallway, which was blocked by a door that hadn't been there the last time Cork was in the house. Ophelia used the crook handle of her cane to knock. She tried the knob, which turned, and she pushed the door open. Beyond lay the first floor of the north wing, several rooms that had become the private residence

of Lauren Cavanaugh: a study, a parlor, a small dining room, a bedroom, a bathroom. She hadn't carved out a lot of the house for her own
use, but what she occupied she'd done in style. Every room was beautifully furnished and impeccably cleaned. The parlor was decorated with
stunning artwork—paintings and photographs—of the area, taken by a
variety of the North Country's finest artists.

"Your grandmother's work," Cork said, pointing toward a series
of framed photographs.

"And mine, too," Ophelia said proudly, pointing to some images
that hung near her grandmother's.

Fate having taken away from her the chance to dance, Ophelia had
turned to her grandmother's art. Cork didn't know a lot about photography as an art form, but he thought—and did not say—that Ophelia
had a distance to go before her work approached the quality of her
grandmother's.

The bedroom looked in perfect order, the bed neatly made.

"Does someone clean for her, make up her bed?" he asked.

"Our housekeeper, yes. But Joyce hasn't been in here for several
days. There's been no need."

The closet was a large walk-in hung with so many outfits that it
was impossible to tell if anything was missing.

"She likes shoes," Cork said, noting what seemed to him to be an
inordinate number of pairs.

"She has a weakness for expensive Italian footwear," ~~Lauren~~ Ophelia said,
with only the slightest note of censure.

Cork checked her dresser. Sachet in the drawer that held her delicates, and everything was neatly—obsessively—folded.

"Who does her laundry?" he asked.

"Joyce."

"Does Joyce fold the laundry?"

"Lauren is particular."

"Clearly."

Outside the rain had stopped and the clouds were beginning to
break. Through the broad bedroom window, Cork could see Iron Lake.
Here and there, the gray surface was splashed with pools of glittering
sunlight.

"I heard that she had the boathouse remodeled," he said.

"Yes. A little retreat where she can get away from all that goes on in the big house here."

"May I take a look?"

Ophelia glanced at her watch.

"It'll take just a minute," Cork said. "Promise."

She accompanied him out a side door and along a path constructed of flagstone. She walked awkwardly, relying heavily on her cane. It was a painful thing to see, especially when Cork recalled the grace with which she'd moved before her accident. Ophelia knocked on the boathouse door. No one answered and she tried the knob. The door was unlocked and she opened it.

"Lauren?" she called, but clearly only for the sake of propriety.

It was a comfortable little nest Lauren Cavanaugh had created for herself, one very large room that included a small sitting area and a bed. Through an opened door in the far corner, Cork saw a tidy little bathroom with a shower. The place was done in rustic tones and had a very intimate feel to it, even more so than her private residence in the large house. It struck Cork as the kind of retreat that might be perfect for trysting.

"Look, Mr. O.C., I'm really uncomfortable with this."

Cork walked to the bed and pushed down on the mattress. His hand sunk into the bedding and disappeared.

"God, I can't believe I'm saying this," Ophelia said, "but I'd like you to leave."

"Why? I haven't taken any of her silver." Cork gave her his most serious look. "The woman is missing, Ophelia. I've been hired to find her. If I'm going to do that, I'll need your help. And your discretion. It would be best if everything we've discussed here today stays between us." Cork started for the boathouse door. "I think I saw a computer in her study back in the house. I'd like to have a look at it."

"No. I think it's time you left."

He smiled, pleased, despite himself, at the iron in her will. Before he could move or speak, someone outside called, "Lauren!"

A moment later, a young man stepped into the doorway.

"What is it, Derek?" Ophelia said.

"I saw the open door and thought maybe. . . . Any word from Lauren when she might be back from Chicago?"

Derek was tall, athletic, good looking. His blond hair was sun bleached nearly white. He had a tan, too deep to have come from the North Country, and carried himself with the easy grace Cork associated with California surfers. Cork's and Ophelia's presence in Lauren Cavanaugh's little retreat was obviously a surprise to him.

Ophelia said, "No word yet."

He looked Cork over, his ocean blue eyes lazy and sure. "If you hear anything, will you let me know?"

"Of course," Ophelia said.

Derek flashed them a smile made of perfect white teeth and left.

"One of the new residents?" Cork asked.

"One of the old ones. Derek is here for three months. He's nearing the end of his residency."

"Nice looking kid."

"I suppose."

"He seemed pretty familiar with the boathouse."

"He's a little relaxed with protocol. It's a California thing, I think."

"Maybe."

But Cork, ever the detective, wondered if there might be more to it than that.

SIX

Ophelia saw Cork to the front gate, where she said, "I got an e-mail from Jenny yesterday. She sounds happy."

"Ecstatic? Effervescent? Ebullient?"

She laughed. "Aaron seems like a nice guy." She was speaking of the farmer-poet whom Jenny was dating. "I'm envious."

"There are good men here, too," Cork said.

Her eyes dropped briefly to her ruined leg. "Guys here want a girl who can dance at the wedding."

Cork's cell phone rang. He pulled it from the belt holster and checked the display to see who was calling. It was Lou Haddad.

"Gotta go, Ophelia," he said. "Thanks for your help."

"If I get into trouble, Mr. O.C., there will be hell to pay." She shook her finger at him playfully, waved good-bye, and closed the gate behind him.

Cork took the call on the way to his Land Rover.

"I've had a chance to look at the old schematics," Haddad said. "I've found something."

"What?"

"Can you meet me at the Vermilion One Mine in an hour?"

"I'll be there."

It was two o'clock when Cork drove through Gresham again, and the sky overhead had cleared. The clouds had drifted east toward the Sawbill Mountains, beyond which lay the vast, icy blue of Lake Superior. A few chairs had been placed on the sidewalk outside Lucy's. They were all occupied by folks drinking coffee or Cokes in the shade of a green awning. A couple of protest placards leaned against the wall, and Cork recognized a few of the faces from the gathering out-side Vermilion One that morning. As he passed, several pairs of eyes turned his way, and he felt the hostility directed at him as solidly as if they'd thrown rocks.

He knew the sentiments of the residents of Gresham, knew that, despite the money that might come their way from a new mine enter-prise, the townspeople were no more eager than the Iron Lake Ojibwe or anyone else in Tamarack County to have a nuclear waste dump in their backyard.

When he approached Vermilion One, he saw that Isaiah Broom and most of the other protesters were still there, but Hattie Stillday had gone. Tommy Martelli logged him in, and Cork headed to the of-fice building. Haddad's Explorer wasn't in the lot. Cork walked inside, gave Margie Renn at the reception desk a brief wave in passing, and went immediately to the conference room, which was empty.

In a corner near one of the windows sat a small easy chair, an end table, and a standing lamp. On the table lay a large book titled *Vermil-ion One: The Rise of Iron on the Range*, written by a man named Dar-ius Holmes. Cork sat in the chair and took up the book. A good deal of text filled the pages, the history of Vermilion One and of mining on the Range in general, but Holmes had included a lot of photographs. Cork knew roughly the history and geology of the area. It was taught proudly to every kid in school in Minnesota. Although a large stretch of the North Country was referred to as the Iron Range, there were, as Haddad had pointed out earlier that day, three ranges: the Vermil-ion, the Mesabi, and the Cuyuna. Aurora lay hard against the Vermil-ion, the easternmost of the ranges, where the earliest mining had taken place.

In the book, the photographs of the early years showed tough lit-tle men in shirts and overalls caked with mud, wearing leather mining caps, pushing ore cars. These, Cork knew, were muckers, the unskilled workers. They were Welsh or Slavic or Irish or Finn or Swede or Ger-man and came, many of them, directly from their homelands to work the mines. Others had come earlier, lured by the wealth of timber in the great north wilderness, and, as the forests retreated, had turned to mining. The towns they built—Chisholm, Hibbing, Eveleth, Coler-

aine, Winton, Kinney, Crosby, Mountain Iron, Bovey—were a patch-
work of immigrant neighborhoods: Swedes on one side of the street,
Finns on the other, Italians a block to the south, Welsh a block to the
north. They were friendly in their work together, but in their neighborhoods, in their marriages, in their religions, they clung to the language and traditions of their own homelands and were suspicious of
the others.

The mines grew in number and wealth, and the towns grew with
them. Ore from the Range was carried by rail to harbors on Lake Superior and shipped all over the world. The Range became famous, the
greatest supplier of iron ore on earth. The money from the mines
built excellent hospitals in the communities and fine civic structures,
and the Iron Range was known to have some of the best school systems in the nation.

To every blessing there was, Cork supposed, a dark side. The mine
pits ate at the earth, ugly as cancers, and the tailings rose in red
mountains that sullied the rivers and streams. And in the end, the de-
mand for ore declined and the mines began to close one by one, leaving a population without recourse. The men were miners, bred from
generations of miners, and the work they'd prepared for all their lives
had vanished, with nothing at all promising on the horizon. A lot of
people simply left, and life went out of the towns. Aurora had gone
through this. When Cork was a teenager, after the Vermilion One
closed, the town struggled to redefine itself. Iron Lake and the prox-
imity of the Boundary Waters Canoe Area Wilderness helped. The
town began to court and to cater to the tourist trade and slowly re-
shaped itself around the heart of that new economy. Other towns
didn't fare as well and stood nearly deserted in the shadow of the
great red mountains of ore tailings.

Cork closed the book and stared out the window. He could see the
rugged, forested hills of the North Country stretching away like a
beautiful, turbulent sea. With all his heart, he loved that place, which
had been his home for most of his life. Although he couldn't see the
protesters beyond the trees that walled off the Vermilion One complex, his heart was with them. He told himself that what he was doing
wasn't about helping the mine become a nuclear waste dump. It was

about ensuring the safety of the people who worked there, people he knew, and so was a different issue. Still, a part of him felt like a traitor.

He heard footfalls in the hallway, and Lou Haddad walked in, carrying a briefcase, which he set on the conference table and opened. He slid from it a single schematic, very old looking, drawn on material that had the feel of canvas.

"What did you find?" Cork asked, joining him.

Haddad said, "This is a map for Level One. This"—he put his finger on a tunnel outlined on the page—"is the Vermilion Drift, the first of the excavations dug when the mine went underground, in 1900. Everything looks normal until you get here." His finger followed the lines of the tunnel drawing until it came to a place where the solid lines ended and were replaced with dotted lines.

"Why the change in how the lines are drawn?"

"Officially, the Vermilion Drift was closed back in the early part of the last century. A cave-in. The dotted lines show where the tunnel used to run."

"So the tunnel's blocked?"

"That's what the map says, but I've been thinking about that. Some of the underground mines had real problems with cave-ins, but not Vermilion One. The rock here is simply too stable, one of the reasons for the DOE's interest. And something else isn't right, this drift beyond the cave-in. According to the schematic, it takes a sharp turn and heads east."

"So?"

"The ore deposit runs the other way."

"So the drift goes away from the iron?"

"That's what the map shows."

"You don't buy it?"

"Not for a minute. Take a look at this, right here." Haddad tapped the paper at a point a short distance beyond where the tunnel veered east. "That's where the Iron Lake Reservation begins. The ore deposit runs directly under reservation land, I'd stake my reputation on it."

"What are you saying?"

"I think that, in those early years, they mined ore that didn't belong to them."

"How could they get away with it?"

"Probably just went about it quietly."

"And when they were finished, they sealed the tunnel to hide what they'd done, claimed there'd been a cave-in, and altered the maps?"

"That's my speculation."

"This extension doesn't appear on any of the more recent schematics?"

Haddad shook his head. "When the last survey was done, just before the mine shut down, the tunnel had been sealed for years."

"Sealed how?" Cork asked.

"Timbered off. Which would explain why the newer maps simply show the tunnel ending. As far as anyone knew, it did."

"But maybe it doesn't?"

Haddad straightened up. "Let's go see."

On his way to Vermilion One, Cork had stopped at his house and picked up a sweater to wear in the mine, a cardigan his kids had given him for Christmas six or seven years earlier. It was red, with a white reindeer embroidered on the left side. He put it on in the cage as they descended. When Haddad saw it, he laughed and said, "Ho, ho, ho." He wore a fleece-lined windbreaker. They both wore hard hats, each with a light mounted in front. For backup, Cork had brought the Maglite he kept in his Land Rover. Plott, the security guard on duty in the Rescue Room next to the framehead, had given Haddad a Coleman electric lantern.

It took no time at all to reach Level One. They stepped into the cage station area, which was only dimly lit. Haddad indicated the dark tunnel directly ahead. "The Vermilion Drift," he said.

Bright sun, blue sky, green trees, sweet air, abundant life—all this was only a hundred feet above his head—but the solidness of the chill rock around him made Cork feel completely cut off from the world he knew. As he stood facing the dark throat of the Vermilion Drift, everything human in him cried out to back away, to return to the light, and for a moment he couldn't make himself go forward.

"Claustrophobic?" Haddad asked with real concern.

"No," Cork said. "It's not that."

"Alien, isn't it?"

"Like I'm on another planet."

"Imagine spending your whole life in a place like this, Cork. A lot of men did, my old man among them."

In that moment, Cork felt a greater respect for Lou's father and the men like him than he ever had before.

"You okay going on?" Haddad asked.

"Yeah. I'm right behind you."

They walked slowly into a dark that, if their lights failed, would swallow them completely. The floor was flat, the tunnel itself a ten-by-ten-foot bore whose walls showed every scar of its creation. Cork had expected the rock to be red here, but it was dull gray-green.

"Ely greenstone," Haddad explained. "Waste rock. They had to get through this to reach the ore. That's what this drift is for. And see that?" Haddad pointed toward a short tunnel that cut off to their right. "A crosscut. The ore deposits didn't flow in neat fingers. Sometimes there were offshoots, and crosscuts were used to get to them. Here, let me show you something."

Haddad turned off the Vermilion Drift into the crosscut tunnel. Near the end of the crosscut, which was only a dozen yards long, he stopped and shined a light toward the ceiling, illuminating a wide hole there.

"This is a raise," he told Cork. "In the mining here, they used a technique called undercutting. They tunneled beneath the deposits and blasted raises, these short upward accesses into the ore itself. They'd mine the ore, creating rooms called stopes, and send the ore down the raises into cars waiting on the rails below here in the drift. The cars would take the ore back to the main shaft, where it was lifted up to the framehead and dumped for crushing."

Cork looked down at the bare rock under his feet. "What happened to the rails?"

"Recycled," Haddad said. "Whenever they finished mining a drift, they pulled up the rails and used them somewhere else." He stared upward into the raise above his head, and, when he spoke, his voice was full of admiration. "The men in charge of a crew, they were called captains. These were guys who'd spent their lives in mines in Wales and Slovakia and Germany. They were tough cusses, proud men. They knew rock and how to mine it."

"What did your father do?"

"He started out as a mucker, worked his way up until he had his own crew. Damn near broke his heart when they closed the mine."

Cork knew that afterward Haddad's father had gone to work in the family grocery store, but his heart was never in it.

"I don't know," Lou said. "Maybe it was a good thing, having to leave the mine. A lot of miners at the end were suffering. Arthritis, lung problems. Hell, in the old days, because of the ungodly noise in the stopes, most of the miners were hard of hearing."

Cork remembered something his own father used to tell him: You always knew when you were passing the house of a guy who'd worked the Vermilion One. You could hear his radio or television blasting all the way out to the street.

They returned to the main drift and kept going.

A few minutes later, their headlamps illuminated a sudden wall ahead, the official end of the tunnel, a construct of dark timbers that completely blocked the passage.

"Do all tunnels end this way?" Cork asked.

"Normally they just end in rock. This is unusual."

"Has Genie Kufus finished her survey of Level One?"

"Yes."

"She say anything about this to you?"

"She hasn't shared any of her thoughts yet. She probably won't until she's completed the survey of the entire mine."

They stood before the wall, which had been constructed of six-by-six timbers laid horizontally, one atop the other. They'd been secured to the wall of the tunnel with bolted metal L plates. The wood had fared well in the dry cool of the mine. Then Cork noticed something.

"Look here." He knelt and ran his hand along a seam cut into several of the timbers a couple of feet from the right side of the wall.

There was another seam cut two feet nearer the center. "These are fresh."

"Yeah," Haddad agreed. He knelt beside Cork and gave the top cut section a push. It yielded and fell back into the dark on the other side of the timbers. He reached in and pulled the next section toward him, and, when it was out, Cork saw that an eyebolt had been screwed into the backside, which would allow it to be removed easily from the other side of the wall. One by one, Haddad cleared the next four sections of cut timber, which created an opening two feet high and two feet wide, large enough for a man to crawl through.

Cork shot the beam of his Maglite into the dark on the other side, revealing a continuation of the Vermilion Drift. He saw no indication of a cave-in. He looked at Haddad. "You were right. Somebody lied in that official report a long time ago."

"Somebody who didn't want it known that ore belonging to the Ojibwe had been taken."

"You game?"

"Are you kidding?" Haddad crawled ahead through the gap.

Cork followed and almost immediately wished he hadn't. The air on the other side reeked of animal decay. He stood up and shot his light into the darkness ahead. "Something died in here, Lou. And not long ago."

"Probably some animal came in and couldn't find its way out. Which means you're right. There's another entrance. And do you feel that?"

"What?" Cork said.

"The temperature. It's much warmer here than on the other side of that timbered wall. There's air coming in from somewhere up ahead."

Haddad went forward with the Coleman lantern. They had to walk carefully because on this side of the wall the tunnel floor was littered with blocks of stone big as an ice chest.

Cork glanced uneasily at the ceiling above him. "Any chance of a cave-in?"

"I wouldn't worry."

"What about all these rocks on the floor?"

Haddad shook his head. "Should have been cleared during the mining. Poor workmanship."

They seemed to have walked forever in the dark, and Cork was uncomfortably aware how far behind them was the way out. He'd never been claustrophobic before, but now he felt as if the walls were closing in on him. Maybe it was just the utter black around them and the fact that he didn't really know where they were headed. The foulness of the air he breathed might also have had something to do with it.

Haddad stopped suddenly, and Cork nearly ran into him. Haddad turned off his Coleman. "Kill your light," he said.

"Are you kidding?"

"No. Turn it off, Cork. And your headlamp, too."

"I don't think so."

"Just do it."

Cork didn't like the idea. But when the lights were off, he understood what Haddad was getting at. It was pitch dark around them but not absolute, as it should have been. Far ahead, the dark was broken by a diffuse paleness.

Haddad switched his lantern on again, and for a moment the light was a knife in Cork's eyes. "Come on," Haddad said and started ahead, this time walking much faster despite the great stones littering the way.

Before Cork could follow, he heard something scurry to his right. He swung the beam of his Maglite in that direction, but whatever critter had been there had vanished. It gave him the creeps knowing that there were living things that could see him but that he could not see.

The tunnel ahead grew brighter, though still dark enough that artificial light was needed to navigate. At last they came to a jumble of what looked to Cork to be dynamite-blasted rock. There was a ragged passage into the tumble of debris where light came through. Haddad put down the lantern, knelt, and crawled into the opening.

"Well, I'll be damned," he said.

"What is this?"

"My guess would be a bit of wildcat mining. It happened in the early days on the Range, when no one was paying enough attention to property and mineral rights. The problem with open pits in this particular area was that the loose glacial deposits on the surface kept collapsing into the pit. That's one of the reasons mining went underground on this part of the Range. I'd bet whoever blasted this sink finally said to hell with it. But I'd also bet that the guys in charge of the Vermilion One back then knew exactly where the ore was that the wildcatters were trying to get at and ran the Vermilion Drift all the way to the pit. Then maybe they had another landslide, or maybe they even blasted the side of the pit themselves to try to hide what they'd done. But they didn't quite succeed. Come on, let's see what's up top."

He didn't wait for Cork to weigh in on the plan's advisability but quickly disappeared into the mouth of the passage, which angled upward and was easily wide enough for his body to squeeze into. Cork didn't follow right away, thinking it prudent to wait a bit to be sure they both didn't get stuck somewhere they couldn't get out of.

As he waited, he heard something move behind him. He spun and searched the darkness, sensing a watcher he couldn't see. He stabbed the flashlight beam into the black throat of the tunnel. Deep inside the Vermilion Drift, two yellow eyes glowed back at him.

"You coming?" Haddad shouted down.

"Just a minute!"

Cork crept toward the eyes, which didn't move. He reached down and picked up a rock from the tunnel floor. As he approached, a hiss came from the darkness, then an angry snort. Cork kept moving, the rock firmly in his grip. When he was fifteen feet away, the creature turned to flee and, in turning, showed its fat, furry body and bushy tail. A raccoon. Cork figured the tunnel would be a pretty good place to make a den for the winter months, and probably the coon had young somewhere. He was just about to return to the rock mess at the bottom of the test pit when the Maglite beam swept across a broken area in the wall that he'd overlooked as he'd passed through earlier. It appeared as if rocks had been loosely piled to close off a crosscut tunnel. He stepped around the rubble on the floor and worked one of the stones away from the makeshift wall. Behind was a well of darkness, and from that well flowed the stench that fouled the air in the tunnel. He shined his Maglite inside.

Cork had always thought that as a cop he'd seen the worst of everything. When his flashlight revealed what the stone wall had hidden, he realized how wrong he'd been.

SEVEN

The sink, which Haddad had identified as most probably a wildcat operation, was in the middle of a small clearing a quarter mile north of the headframe for the Number Six shaft of the Vermilion One Mine. The sheriff's people had been able to reach it by driving carefully among the pines that lay between the sink and the mine buildings.

It was nearing seven in the evening, and Cork stood with Sheriff Marsha Dross and Captain Ed Larson near the edge of the sink. Dross had put in a call to the Bureau of Criminal Apprehension office in Bemidji, and they were waiting for the agents to arrive. The drive would have taken a good three hours, and enough time had already passed that Cork and the others were watching their watches. Alf Murray, the chief of the Aurora Volunteer Fire Department, stood with Cork and the others, using a walkie-talkie to communicate with his men below. The firemen had brought out mobile lights and a generator, and a power cable snaked out of sight down the passage that led eventually to the Vermilion Drift. They'd set up the lights in the tunnel, but only as far as the gruesome discovery Cork had made. Ed Larson, who was in charge of major crimes for the Tamarack County Sheriff's Department, had overseen the dismantling of the makeshift stone wall. Some of Dross's people had done a flashlight search of the tunnel from that point to the timber construction where Haddad and Cork had crawled through. Dross had put others to work doing a quadrant search of the area surrounding the surface opening of the sink for anything that might prove to be evidence. She'd hoped for maybe a footprint or tire track, but the ground had yielded nothing.

Someone had gone to Lucy's in Gresham and brought back a big container of coffee, and Cork stood sipping from a white foam cup as he waited. The sun had shifted to the far west, and the shadows of the pines had begun to creep across the clearing.

"Ever deal with anything like this when you were sheriff?" Dross asked.

"Nope," Cork replied. "I can't imagine many sheriffs do."

"Jesus, I hope not."

Cork heard the sound of a vehicle engine approaching gradually through the pines. The sun was in his eyes, and it was hard to see into the deep shade among the evergreens. A minute later, a white Suburban entered the clearing and rolled slowly toward them. It stopped beside the sheriff's pickup truck, and the two occupants got out. One of them Cork knew well: Simon Rutledge, with whom he'd worked in the past, both when he was sheriff of Tamarack County and in the time since. Cork liked him immensely and had great respect for his ability. Rutledge's companion was a stranger. She was of medium height, early fifties, hair the color of a cirrus cloud and with the same wispy appeal.

"Marsha, Ed, Cork," Rutledge said in greeting, and they all shook hands.

"Thanks for coming, Simon," Dross replied.

Rutledge gestured to his companion. "Agent Susan Upchurch. Her specialty is forensic anthropology."

"The truth is we're so short-staffed these days that I do everything." Upchurch laughed. "Damn budget cuts." Her accent was southern.

"Alabama?" Cork guessed.

"Birmingham," she said.

"Long way from home."

"I went to graduate school at the U of M. Found I didn't mind the snow, and then the BCA made me an offer I couldn't refuse. Here I am."

"And we're lucky to have her," Rutledge threw in. "Fill me in. What have you done so far?"

Dross replied, "We've dismantled the wall that blocked off the crosscut tunnel. We've gone over the main tunnel all the way to the timbers. Not easy. Most of the drift is still without lights, so it's pitch dark."

"Did you videotape the dismantling?"

"Yes."

"Good. Anything else?"

"We shot video and stills of everything inside the crosscut, but haven't gone in yet. Our M.E.'s the only one who's been inside, and just to certify death."

"Is he still here?"

"No, he left to prepare for the autopsy."

"He didn't disturb anything down there?"

"No."

"Who else has been in the tunnel?"

"Besides Ed's crime scene team, only Lou Haddad, one of the officials from the mine. He was with Cork."

"Where is he now?"

"At the mine office. We can bring him back if you want him."

"Not necessary at the moment." Rutledge glanced around the perimeter of the sink. "Did you go over the area up here?"

"Yeah. Nothing."

"Okay. Let's see what we've got."

They gathered at the edge of the sink. It was a five-foot drop to the opening in the rubble where the passage began. Although there were natural hand- and footholds in the side of the pit that could have been used to climb in and out, the firemen had placed an aluminum ladder against the wall. Dross went first, Rutledge next, Upchurch after him, and finally Larson. Cork brought up the rear. He wasn't eager to return to the hardness and the darkness of the Vermilion Drift, but the tunnel was full of questions, horrifying questions, and he was a man trained his whole life in mining answers. He hesitated in the evening light, watched Larson disappear into the narrow throat of the opening in the rubble, took a good, deep breath of pine-scented air, and descended.

The passage was a snaking affair, lit by daylight that slipped through gaps in the blasted rock. It was big enough throughout its length to accommodate the body of even a large person, but the ragged rock edges and the constant twisting made the journey a slow one. Those who reached the bottom first waited for the others to arrive. In the passage itself, the air was fine, but in the tunnel where the cool mine air pooled, the nauseating smell of rotting flesh was overwhelming.

Lights supplied by the fire department illuminated the drift. Cork and the others walked a path cleared and marked with yellow tape by the crime scene team. The nearer they came to the room, the stronger became the putrid odor of decomposition. Mingled with the foulness of the air was the aroma of eucalyptus, which some of the deputies and firemen had applied to the area below their noses to deal with the stench.

The place where the wall had been dismantled was guarded by a couple of deputies. The crosscut tunnel that had been revealed was not at all deep, less than ten feet. The striations from the drill bits made the walls look like rust-colored corduroy.

There were six bodies in all. Five were nothing more than skeletal remains with a few rotted, parchment-like remnants of clothing still clinging to the bones. Four of the skeletons were arranged in a sitting position against the walls, placed in a way that put their backs to each of the four points of a compass—north, south, east, and west. A fifth skeleton lay in the center, and next to it the sixth body had been placed. That body was fully clothed. It hadn't been there long enough to be skeletal, but it had been there long enough so that the bloat of the gases from decomposition had distended the abdominal cavity, and the thin material of the black cocktail dress the corpse wore had been stretched and ripped along the seams. The neck and face were swollen like those of an overfilled blow-up doll. The corpse's tongue had turned black and grown huge, and it protruded between puffed lips. The skin was a sickly yellow-orange and translucent so that the vessels that ran beneath were visible. Cork had seen all this earlier with Dross and Larson, and they stood back while Rutledge and Upchurch both knelt and studied the scene.

"How long you figure the skeletons have been here?" Rutledge asked his colleague.

"I won't have any idea until I examine the remains," she replied.

"Well, this one," Rutledge said, pointing toward the corpse prostrate in the center, "hasn't been here more than a week." Over his shoulder, he said, "Has anyone reported a missing woman, Marsha?"

"No," she answered.

"Yes," Cork said.

Dross shot him a puzzled look. Rutledge turned and eyed him as well.

"I think the corpse might be Lauren Cavanaugh," Cork said. "She's been missing since last Sunday."

"How do you know that?" Dross asked.

"Because I was hired this morning to find her."

George Azevedo, one of the deputies guarding the scene, said, "Fast work, Cork." He laughed, but no one else joined him.

"How come you didn't tell me this earlier?" Dross said.

"Because I wasn't sure."

"What makes you sure now?"

"Two things. Those shoes on her feet. They're expensive Italian jobs. There's a whole closet full of their cousins at her residence in the old Parrant estate. And that big ring on her left hand. She's wearing it in a portrait I saw today."

"Who hired you to find her?"

"Her brother."

"Did he say when she'd gone missing?"

"A week ago."

"And he didn't report it?"

"He wanted the matter looked into discreetly," Cork said.

"If it is her, there won't be anything discreet about this now," Rutledge said.

Dross said to no one in particular, "How did she come to be here with these older remains?"

"Maybe when we identify the remains we'll have our answer," Ed Larson responded.

"How soon might that be?" Dross addressed her question to Upchurch.

"I'd like everything in here documented in detail with photographs and video," the BCA agent replied. "Once that's done, I'll examine each of the remains in situ, then remove them to my lab in Bemidji, where I can study them more carefully."

"That'll take a while."

"Quite a while," Upchurch said.

"When will you have results?"

"I'll get started as soon as the first remains are in the lab. Tomorrow maybe, and then I'll have something preliminary to offer."

"What about the new body?" Rutledge asked Dross.

"I told Tom Conklin that I'll need the autopsy done ASAP." Dross was speaking of the medical examiner.

"Handle the corpse carefully," Rutledge advised. "It's at a delicate stage. The skin'll shift around. And be especially vigilant with the head. The hair will come off easily."

"We'll be careful, Simon."

During all this exchange, Cork had noticed something in the crosscut—small metal cones that littered the floor around one of the skeletons—and his mind made a very old connection. "Agent Upchurch, is there any possibility that these corpses are over forty years old?"

"They may well be. I can't really tell yet. Why do you ask?"

"The remains in the corner to the right. See those items littering the floor around it?"

"The things that look like little rusted cones?"

"Yeah, those. I think they're jingles."

"Jingles?"

"From a jingle dress. It's traditionally worn for a healing dance."

"Jingles," Larson said. He gave Cork a pointed look. "The Vanishings, you think?"

"That's exactly what I think," Cork said. "The Vanishings."

EIGHT

Naomi Stonedeer was the first to vanish. Cork had known her well. She was seventeen, with black hair that hung to her waist and hazel eyes. She was bright and lovely and an accomplished Jingle Dancer.

The Jingle Dance was an Ojibwe healing ritual performed by women in long dresses adorned with a couple of hundred jingles sewn closely together and attached in rows. The jingles were traditionally made from snuff can lids or tin can lids rolled into cones. When the dancers performed their steps, the jingles brushed together and created the unique sound that gave the ritual its name. Though it continued to be one of the most esteemed and sacred of the Ojibwe ceremonies, it was also a dance performed competitively at powwows.

In the summer of 1964, Naomi lived near Cork's grandmother in Allouette, the larger of the two communities on the Iron Lake Reservation. Cork was thirteen and had a terrible crush on her. Whenever he visited Grandma Dilsey, he always found a way to pass the little BIA-built house where Naomi lived with her mother and her aunt. He concocted scenarios in which he played the hero and saved her from a dozen iterations of doom. But when the real thing occurred, he was powerless.

She disappeared in late June. She'd gone to the old community center in Allouette, which had once been the schoolhouse where Cork's grandfather and his grandma Dilsey taught the children of the rez. Naomi had joined a lot of other women to practice the Jingle Dance in preparation for a powwow that was to be held in Winnipeg in July. She left the community center around 9:00 P.M., wearing her jingle dress. It was still daylight, and her house was only a quarter mile away, but she never made it home. Her mother called everyone in Allouette, and, when no one knew Naomi's whereabouts, she called Cork's mother, who was her good friend. Cork's mother enlisted his father, who was sheriff of Tamarack County.

His father's first reaction was that probably the girl had simply run away, something a lot of Ojibwe kids did. Poverty was not an unusual circumstance on the rez, nor were the unpleasant domestic situations that frequently resulted. Kids often took off, heading to the safety of a relative who lived somewhere else, or to Duluth or the Twin Cities, looking for a different—they hoped better—life. Naomi's home life was just fine, Cork's mother insisted. The young woman had no reason to run.

Cork's father went to Allouette and that night began a fruitless investigation, which lasted for weeks. He contacted relatives, authorities on other reservations and in the Indian communities in Duluth and the Twin Cities. Word went out to teen shelters all across the Upper Midwest.

Naomi's father, who'd long ago abandoned his family, lived in Crosby, a good eighty miles from Aurora, where he worked as an auto mechanic. Cork's father questioned him repeatedly. Although the man couldn't supply a decent alibi for the night Naomi went missing, there was no evidence that he'd been anywhere near Allouette at the time, and eventually Cork's father stopped badgering him.

In the end, the search was abandoned, and no trace of Naomi Stonedeer was ever found.

The next vanishing occurred later that summer, in August. Cork remembered it well because it was a great tragedy in his family.

His mother's sister, Ellie Grand, lived with Grandma Dilsey. Ellie had two daughters. Marais, the elder daughter, had already left home to seek her fortune in country music. That left Fawn at home, and Fawn was special. She was a gentle spirit, a girl who smiled all the time and would probably never grow sophisticated in her understanding of the world. Cork's grandmother once told him that Fawn offered the Iron Lake Ojibwe a gift. The gift was her simplicity. It was her acceptance, with inexhaustible delight, of the everyday blessings that Kitchimanidoo showered on The People. Fawn laughed at snowflakes, was delighted when a dandelion puff exploded on the wind, cried with excitement when a fish leaped from Iron Lake and sent a spray of water into the air like pearls thrown against the sky. The Ojibwe on the rez watched over her. But even their protectiveness failed to keep her safe that summer day.

Shortly after lunch, she'd told her mother that she was going for a swim in Iron Lake. Fawn was a good swimmer and often went into the lake alone. She left in her swimsuit, carrying a towel, and her feet were bare.

Allouette had a small beach area next to the old dock where men who gillnetted and spearfished kept their boats. Jon Bruneau was at the dock that day, working on his Evinrude outboard. He swore that he never saw Fawn at the beach the whole afternoon.

Fawn's disappearance was a blow that knocked the breath out of Cork's family. Over the next few weeks, his mother spent much of her time with Aunt Ellie and Grandma Dilsey. Other Ojibwe women visited as well. As had often been the case in its turbulent history, the reservation came together around tragedy.

His father exhausted himself in the search for Fawn. He sent divers into the lake off the shore at Allouette, just in case Jon Bruneau had been wrong. He also had divers in the water at Sunset Cove, which was south of Allouette and a place that Shinnobs sometimes went for a swim. He grilled Bruneau mercilessly. He pressed his own good friend Sam Winter Moon to question the whole Ojibwe community. He thought maybe the Anishinaabeg would be more responsive to questions coming from one of their own than from a uniformed white man, even though he was considered a friend of the rez. No one saw anything. No one knew anything. Fawn, like Naomi Stonedeer, had simply dropped off the face of the earth.

The last vanishing was different. It was a white woman. A rich white woman. A woman who attended Mass at St. Agnes. Who volunteered her time on the library board. Who saw to it that her husband contributed lavishly to the campaign to build a new community hospital in Aurora. Who walked down the streets of town recognized, admired, and envied.

She disappeared on Labor Day weekend, when the sumac in Tamarack County had turned blood red and gold was beginning to drive out green along the branches of the aspen trees, and the air of late evening and early morning carried a chill bite. That Monday morning her husband reported to the sheriff's office that she was missing. She'd been missing nearly two days by then. Her husband said she'd driven to Duluth for a fund-raiser. She'd intended to come home directly, but she'd been gone two nights. This wasn't unusual. Sometimes she got it in her head to drive places, a kind of wanderlust, but he hadn't heard from her, and he'd grown worried. The search went on until almost October, but no trace of her could be found, not even her car. Like the other women, she seemed to have been swallowed by the air itself.

Her name was Monique Cavanaugh. She was the mother of the woman who, forty years later, lay decomposing on the cool stone floor of the Vermilion Drift.

When Cork finished his story, Dross said, "But if these are the women who vanished in nineteen sixty-four, that would account for only three of the older victims. What about the other two here?"

"I don't know," Cork said. He looked to Upchurch. "How soon can you tell the age of the bones?"

"Not until after I get them into the lab to examine them."

"Will you be able to tell if they're white or Ojibwe?" he asked.

"Once I've done scans of the skulls, my computer ought to give me pretty accurate facial reconstructions. But I'll tell you this right now. I'm pretty sure they're all female."

Larson asked, "How do you know?"

"The pelvis. Much larger in the female. Also some of the cranial features. The ridge above the brow, for example. It's much larger in males. Same with the jawbone. Sometimes race can make a sexual determination difficult; from what I'm seeing, that's not a problem."

"Ed, do you think it's possible whoever put the other bodies here also dumped Lauren Cavanaugh's?" Dross asked.

Larson shrugged. "Anything's possible. We'll know a lot more after we've processed the scene."

"Then we should get started," Rutledge said.

Cork stepped back. He'd forced himself to return to that wretched place, and he'd stood it as long as he could, and now he felt desperate to get out. "This will take you a while," he said. "I'm headed up top."

Dross said, "I'll go with you. Ed, keep me informed."

"Will do," Larson replied.

Dross and Cork walked back to the sink and crawled their way up the passage to the clearing. As they approached the top, Cork heard a loud, familiar voice, clearly in the midst of an argument. When he pulled himself out of the sink, there stood Isaiah Broom looming like an angry bear over Guy Simpson, one of Dross's smaller deputies. As soon as Broom saw Dross emerge from the hole in the ground, he stormed in her direction.

"I want to know what you're doing on our land," he said.

Dross planted herself between Broom and the sink and gave him an iron reply. "We're here conducting a lawful investigation, Mr. Broom."

"You're on Ojibwe land."

"This is a crime scene, and we're the law, even on the rez."

Which was true. Public Law 280, passed in 1953, gave all reservations in the United States the right to choose the agency that would provide them with law enforcement regarding major crimes. Many reservations had gone with federal law enforcement. The Iron Lake Ojibwe had chosen the Tamarack County Sheriff's Department.

Broom pointed toward the sink. "Whatever that is, it's on our land. I have the right to go down there."

"When it's no longer a crime scene, you may do so. I don't know when that will be."

"The People have a right to know what's going on."

"They will. In due time."

He glared at Cork. "*Chimook*," he said, as if he was spitting phlegm. He turned and stormed away across the clearing.

Dross said to Cork, "I think we'll need a twenty-four-hour watch on this scene until we're finished processing it."

Cork stared at the huge retreating form of Broom and said, "I think what you'll need is a bazooka."

NINE

Marsha Dross offered Cork a ride to his Land Rover, which was still parked in the lot at the mine office. The traffic from all the official vehicles had broken a clear path through the underbrush, which Dross followed to the perimeter fence. She drove the fence line to a gate that opened onto an old mining road on the west side of the complex and that was guarded by one of the Vermilion One security guys, who gave a two-finger salute as they passed through.

When they reached the Land Rover, Dross killed the engine of her pickup and sat a moment staring through her windshield.

"We'll need a positive ID of the body," she said without looking at him.

"Max Cavanaugh," Cork said. "I was supposed to see him tonight, have him sign an agreement for my investigation."

"Where?"

"His place."

"What time?"

"Six."

She looked at her watch. "It's almost six now."

"Guess I won't make it."

"I hate this part of the job."

"What? Talking to me?"

She smiled. Finally.

"Have one of your deputies do it," he suggested.

"Is that how you handled things?"

"No." He stared through the windshield, too. "So I guess you don't want me talking to Max until after you're finished with him?"

"Yeah," she said. Then: "Have you ever dealt with anything like this?"

"Possible multiple homicides spread over nearly half a century? Hell, probably nobody has."

"Five women and now a sixth."

"If it is the Vanishings, only four are female for sure."

"Agent Upchurch seemed pretty certain they're all women, Cork. I'm sure she's right."

"And you know this how?"

Instead of answering, she said, "That sink you found is on Ojibwe land." She swung her gaze toward him, and he knew without her saying a word what she wanted and why she'd offered him the lift. "I'll need to talk to folks on the reservation," she said. "I could use your help."

Although he'd helped with investigations in the past, had done so ever since leaving the department, this time he balked, and for reasons he couldn't quite articulate. There was something about the situation beyond its complete bizarreness that dug at him, and he wasn't sure at all what that was.

"I'll think about it and give you a call. Right now, I need to get something to eat."

"Two of those women were Ojibwe," she said.

"Probably more," he said.

"How do you know?"

He pulled the door handle and let himself out. "We'll talk," he said.

He drove home to Gooseberry Lane. His house was a simple two-story place that, with his wife and the kids and the dog, had always felt comfortably full. Now there was only him and the dog. Trixie had spent the day in the backyard, tethered to a line that was connected to her own little doghouse and that let her roam without running loose. When she saw Cork, she greeted him with barking and eager leaps and a tail that beat like a metronome gone wild.

"Hey, girl," he said, "bet you're famished. Makes two of us. Let's see what we can rustle up."

He poured dry dog food into a bowl, and Trixie plunged her muzzle in and chomped away greedily. Cork opened a can of tuna taken from the pantry shelf, mixed in some mayo and pickle relish. He sliced a tomato and washed a large leaf of lettuce. He pulled a slice of Swiss cheese from a package in the refrigerator and layered all the ingredients between a couple of pieces of wheat bread. A handful of potato chips and a cold bottle of Leinenkugel's finished the preparations. He sat on the patio as evening settled over Aurora, and he ate alone and tasted nothing.

It was twilight when he finished, and he took Trixie for a walk. He passed houses he was almost as familiar with as his own, where people lived whom he'd known his whole life. He walked to the business district of Aurora, two square blocks of storefronts and enterprises. Gerten's Travel, Bonnie's Salon, The Enigmatic Gnome, the Tamarack County Courthouse, Pflugleman's Rexall Drugs, Johnny's Pinewood Broiler. It was early summer, and the town was full of tourists. Unlike that of Gresham, Aurora's economy was solid, booming even. Five decades he'd walked these streets. Now they felt different to him. With Jo gone and the kids away, what held him to this place was history. And what was history but memory? And of what value, in the end, was a memory? A man's life needed to be made of stuff more immediate and substantial. Cork wondered what that was for him now.

"Mr. O.C.!"

He turned and found Ophelia Stillday limping toward him from the door of Pflugleman's drugstore. In the blue light of dusk, her face was dark and serious.

"What's wrong?" Cork said.

"I'm glad I caught you." She petted Trixie, who danced all over the sidewalk at the attention. "I've been thinking about Lauren," she said. "I know I gave you a hard time this morning, but I'm worried about her. Have you found out anything?"

"Yeah," he said.

"Really? What?"

He nodded toward the steps of the courthouse half a block away. "Let's sit down." When they had, he said, "I'm going to tell you something, but you need to promise me that you'll keep it to yourself for a while."

"Sure."

"I mean this absolutely."

"Cross my heart," she said, and did.

He told her what he'd found that day in the Vermilion Drift. He didn't describe the state of Lauren Cavanaugh's body, but Ophelia looked stricken nonetheless. Her mouth hung open in a silent O of surprise and shock. Her eyes were full of horror.

"I'm sure the body we found is Lauren Cavanaugh's, but it hasn't been officially identified yet, and that's why it's imperative that you keep this to yourself. Do you understand, Ophelia?"

"Yes," she said. "Absolutely." Then she said, "Oh, Jesus," and buried her face in her palms. "Oh, Christ." She dropped her hands and looked at him, confused but also, he thought, angry. "Who would do that?"

"I don't know. And the reason I've told you about this is that I'm hoping you might have an idea who."

"Me? No. Why would I?"

"Someone from the investigation will interview you and ask that same question. So take a while to think about it. Is there anything important you know that might help?"

"No," she answered, shaking her head. "No." But even as she said it, Cork saw a light come into those brown Ojibwe eyes.

"What?" he said.

She frowned and struggled a moment with her conscience. "We're in trouble financially."

"The center?"

She nodded. "Since Lauren's been gone, I've had to tackle some areas that typically she handles. Mr. O.C., we owe a lot of money to people. Money that, as nearly as I can tell, we don't have."

"Her brother tells me that he's been picking up the bills for the center."

She looked down, troubled. "Not for a while. Lauren was supposed to find her own support for the center. She hasn't been successful. Some of the correspondence I've gone through in the last couple of days has been from creditors. Some pretty threatening letters."

"That's important, but I'm not sure it's enough to kill for."

"What would be?" she asked. She was serious.

"Murder, generally speaking, is a crime of passion. It can be about money, but not usually about money owed. Unless the mob's involved. If it's money, it's usually about greed. If it's not money, then it's love or anger or revenge. Do any of those fit?"

She thought for a while, shaking her head the whole time. "She was so loved by everyone. She was such a remarkable person. I don't know why anyone would want her dead."

"Probably there's a lot about her you didn't know. People hide things. Think for a minute. Anything come to mind? Derek, for example."

"Derek?"

"That handsome young artist at the center."

"I know who Derek is."

"I got strange vibes from him today. Is it possible there was something between him and Lauren?"

The features of her face squeezed up, as if Cork had offered her something foul. "That's impossible."

"Is it?" Cork asked. "Lauren was a beautiful woman, unattached, as nearly as I can tell. Derek's a nice looking kid. And he didn't strike me as the shy type."

Ophelia shook her head adamantly. "What happened to Lauren definitely has nothing to do with Derek."

There was no reason for Cork to convince her otherwise, so he said, "All right, let's try something else. She has her own wing at the Parrant estate. Sorry, the center. It has an entrance of its own?"

"Yes."

"And she's created that little getaway for herself in the boathouse. Have you ever seen anyone come or go using her private entrance, or visit her at the boathouse, particularly at night?"

"No." She raised an eyebrow. "But I'm not usually there at night."

"Which is when someone who didn't want to be seen visiting would probably visit. Who is there at night?"

"Joyce, our housekeeper. She has a room down the hall from my office, but she's never at the center on weekends."

"Still, someone should talk to her."

"Why not you?"

"Because I'm not part of the official investigation."

Although he could be, if he wanted. All he had to do was accept the sheriff's offer. The idea was beginning to have its attractions.

Ophelia said, "Jenny told me once that her mom hated you being sheriff."

"With good reason."

"But you could help out this one time, couldn't you? I mean, this is in a good cause, right?"

"That's exactly what I used to tell Jo," Cork said. "And her response was always that, when the bullets start flying, a good cause is a poor shield."

"You think there could be flying bullets?" She seemed caught by surprise.

"That's the problem with business like this, Ophelia. You never know." Cork pointed to the courthouse behind them. "The clock on that tower. The hands are stuck."

"I know this story," she said.

Hell, everyone in Aurora probably knew the story, but Cork repeated it anyway.

"That clock was hit by bullets during an exchange of gunfire between my father and some men who'd just robbed the bank. My dad was fatally shot during that exchange. The hands of the clock haven't moved since. People around here think of it as a kind of fitting memorial. For me, it's a reminder that, when guns are involved, people you love can be lost forever."

"Jenny told me you stopped carrying a gun. So, if bullets start flying, what do you do?"

"Duck and run, Ophelia. Duck and run."

TEN

A few minutes before ten, Cork headed to Sam's Place to give a hand with closing. Judy Madsen was a terrific manager, but she never closed. She didn't like being out after dark, so Cork usually made sure he was there to supervise.

It was a Monday night, not particularly busy. Judy had put Kate Buker and Jodi Bollendorf, two great kids, on the schedule. They were Anne's friends, who'd worked for Cork during their high school years and who, home from college for the summer, were putting in time again. They both wanted to be lawyers. *Just what the world needs,* Cork thought dismally, *more lawyers.* But everyone had to have a dream, no matter how misguided.

He'd parked his Land Rover and was just about to head inside when Max Cavanaugh pulled up in his Escalade and got out.

"Got a minute, Cork?" he said.

"Sure, Max."

Mounted on a tall pole above the parking lot was a yard light so bright it made the gravel look like dirty snow. Cavanaugh stood in the glare, clearly troubled. He glanced toward Sam's Place, then at the dark along the shoreline of Iron Lake.

"Over there," he said.

Cork followed to the old dock he maintained for boaters who wanted to come off the lake for a burger and needed a place to tie up. Cavanaugh strolled to the end. Another step and he would have been in the water. He stood looking down the shoreline toward the lights of town. In the right mood, he might have understood, as Cork did, how lovely it was: the black surface where the lights danced; the sky above salted with stars and hung with a crescent moon thin as a clipped fingernail; the quiet in which, if Cork listened closely, he was sure he could hear the earth breathe.

"I just came from Nelson's Funeral Home," Cavanaugh said, his back to Cork.

Nelson's was where the autopsies for Tamarack County were performed. For a long time, Sigurd Nelson had been the coroner and did the job himself. In one of his last battles as sheriff, Cork had convinced the county commissioners to hire a certified medical examiner. Now Dr. Tom Conklin, a retired surgeon, handled the function. But the funeral home was still where the job was done.

Cork said, "I'm sorry, Max."

Cavanaugh hunched his shoulders, dark against the broader dark of the water. "The sheriff wanted me to identify my sister's body. How could I identify that? Christ, how could anyone?"

There wasn't much to say to that. Rhetorical, Cork figured. Frustrated, angry, devastated, and rhetorical.

Cavanaugh turned back to Cork. "You found her." It sounded a little like an accusation.

"Lou Haddad and I."

"The authorities don't know anything. Or wouldn't tell me. Which is it?"

"A little of both, I suspect," Cork replied.

Cavanaugh took a step. Not threatening. "What do you know?"

"That I can tell you?"

"You're working for me, remember?"

"Technically, Max, my job is finished. Your sister's been found."

Cork didn't have to see the man's face to sense his rage.

"I want to know everything you know," Cavanaugh said. "God damn it, I'll pay you."

"It's not about money, Max. In a situation like this, there are good reasons for not making everything public."

"My sister's dead. I have a right to know things."

"And you will. It'll just take some time."

Cavanaugh was silent. Although Cork considered the man his friend, he knew that Max was used to being obeyed. Perhaps in a mine or in a boardroom his silence might have had the desired effect, but Cork simply held his ground and matched Cavanaugh's silence.

Cavanaugh broke first. "They asked me questions, as if I was a suspect. Am I a suspect, Cork?"

"More likely a person of interest. At this point, pretty much everyone in Tamarack County who knew her is a person of interest. It's not personal, Max. Did you give them a formal statement?"

"No. I'll go in tomorrow morning."

"I'd advise you to take legal counsel with you. I know how it will look, but it's the prudent thing to do."

Cavanaugh turned slowly, like a windmill adjusting to a change in the direction of the wind. He stared across the empty lake, where the distant shore was marked by solitary pinpricks of light from cabins hidden among the pines.

"You had someone you loved die this way, Cork. You've got to understand what I'm feeling."

Cavanaugh was probably talking about Cork's wife, Jo. But he might also have been speaking of Cork's father. Either way, the answer was yes, Cork understood.

For the briefest moment, he thought about telling Cavanaugh that it was likely one of the old bodies in the Vermilion Drift was his mother. And that he knew what that was like, too, having someone you love disappear and a very long time later learning their true end.

Instead he waited and listened in vain to hear the earth breathe.

Cavanaugh straightened. "I'd like you to continue working for me."

"In what capacity?"

"I want to know who killed my sister."

"There are a lot of very capable law enforcement personnel who'll be investigating."

"I want someone working on it just for me."

"Believe me, Max, the resources they have available to them are light-years beyond anything I could bring to the table."

"You know this town, the people in it. You don't have to walk a thin legal line and go by the book."

"You mean I can twist arms and bust faces? I don't work that way.

The sheriff's people and the BCA are the best there is. I've worked with them for years."

"And if you were me, would you trust them or you?"

A complicated question, not just because of the convoluted syntax. Cork thought a lot of his own abilities, and the truth was that in an investigation he had certain advantages over those who were uniformed and badged. Which was one of the reasons Marsha Dross had already sought his help. And that was part of the complication. If Cork agreed to hire on with Cavanaugh, he couldn't also agree to sign on with the sheriff. Conflict of interest.

He felt for Max Cavanaugh. He understood the man's grief, his confusion, his frustration, his desire to rip away the veil of mystery surrounding his sister's death and, although Cavanaugh didn't yet know it, his mother's death as well. Because Cork thought he had a better chance of making that happen working with the sheriff and the BCA, he said, "No, thanks, Max. But if you're bound and determined, I can recommend a couple of good investigators."

The old dock groaned under Cavanaugh's weight as he brushed past Cork, wordless, and returned to his Escalade. In the quiet by the lake, Cork could hear the angry growl of the engine for a long time after it had disappeared into the night.

ELEVEN

The next morning Cork was up before sunrise and running.

Years earlier, he'd been a smoker and enough overweight to worry about it. When he hit forty-two, his life went into a meltdown. He lost his job as sheriff, lost a lot of his self-respect, nearly lost his family. Part of pulling himself together involved getting comfortable in his own skin, and running helped him do that. He discovered that when he ran all the tight screws in his head loosened, and he seemed to think a little clearer.

That morning he had a lot to think about.

He jogged easily to Grant Park, which was situated along the shoreline of Iron Lake, a quarter mile south of Sam's Place. He spent ten minutes stretching, then began his run in earnest. He headed north along a trail that followed the shoreline, past the poplars that hid the old foundry, past Sam's Place, past the abandoned BearPaw Brewery. He curved into town and then out again, to the end of North Point Road, where the old Parrant estate stood. This was a halfway point, and he stopped to watch the sun rise over the lake.

In Cork's experience there was nothing to compare with sunrise in the North Country. Across any lake on a calm morning, the crawl of the sun played out twice: first in the vault of heaven and again on the surface of the water, which was like a window opened onto another heaven at his feet. Five decades of life and he could still be stunned to silence by such a dawn.

The old Parrant estate sloped down to the shore. As Cork stood and watched the sun bubble red out of the horizon, something startling occurred. The brick from which that great house was built turned scarlet, and the walls began to melt, and rivulets of blood ran red across the emerald lawn. Cork stood mesmerized and amazed, but it wasn't the first time he'd had a discomforting vision involving this particularly cursed piece of real estate. Half a dozen years earlier, shortly before he'd discovered the murder-suicide there, he'd observed a sea of black snakes churning in the yard, snakes seen by no one but him.

He blinked his eyes, and the morning was again as it had been, and the Parrant estate was solid brick, and its broad lawn was clean and green.

Mudjimushkeeki, he thought. Bad medicine.

The tall, lean figure of Derek Huff came from the back of the big house. He was dressed only in a bathing suit. As he headed toward the lake, he cast a shadow that followed him, long and black, like one of those snakes in Cork's vision years before. He reached the dock, dropped the towel he'd carried over his shoulder, and dove into the lake.

Cork drank water from the bottle he carried, and he stretched some. His muscles were a little sore. Lately he hadn't been running as regularly as he would have liked. Despite his best intentions, life often got in the way.

As he prepared to resume his run, he looked back at the lake, where Derek Huff stroked easily away from shore, leaving a wide, undulating wake behind him that rattled the reflection of heaven.

When he'd finished the run and had showered and dressed, Cork composed and sent e-mails to his children. He didn't tell them about what he'd found in the Vermilion Drift. He told them he was busy, happy, missed them. The Vermilion Drift would come up sooner or later, he knew. He wanted it to be later.

He headed to Johnny's Pinewood Broiler for some breakfast. He could have eaten at home, but he needed to talk to Cy Borkman, and Borkman always breakfasted at the Broiler.

He found Borkman sitting on a stool at the counter, already doing major damage to a platter of eggs over easy, link sausage, hash browns, and toast. An empty juice glass sat off to one side, and coffee steamed in a cup within easy reach. Borkman had been hired as a deputy when Cork's father was sheriff of Tamarack County, and he was still a deputy when Cork held that office thirty years later. He'd always been a big man, always overweight, but with retirement from the Tamarack County Sheriff's Department he'd edged more and more toward the girth of a walrus, and the little stool he sat on seemed hard put to keep from buckling.

"Morning, Cy," Cork said and gave Borkman a hearty slap on the back as he sat down beside him.

"Hey, Cork." Borkman spoke around a mouthful of breakfast, and it came out something like, "Hey, Hork."

It was a busy morning at the Broiler. Kathy Lehman was waitressing the counter. She was blond, fortyish, a transplant from Wisconsin, but nice as they came. She stopped as she hurried past with three plates balanced on her right hand and forearm, shot Cork a smile, and said, "Coffee, hon?"

"Thanks, Kathy."

"Be right back." And she was gone.

Borkman put down his fork. He grabbed his napkin and, with a quick swipe, cleaned hash browns and ketchup from his chin. "Say, what was all that commotion at the Vermilion One yesterday? Everybody's talking about a convoy of official vehicles that trucked in there. The protest getting out of hand?"

"Nothing like that, Cy."

"Me, I didn't have these bum legs, I'd be walking that protest line myself. Say, heard you're working for the mine." It wasn't the most friendly tone he'd ever used.

"Security consult," Cork said. "Some threats have been made."

"Now that's a shocker." Borkman laughed and gulped coffee.

"Cy, you remember the Vanishings? Back in 'sixty-four?"

"Hell, yes. Strangest damn case my whole time on the force. We never solved that one."

"Three women, right?"

"Yep. Two from the reservation and Mrs. Peter Cavanaugh. Now there was a looker. That daughter of hers?" He shook his head and lifted his fork again. "Like I'm staring at a picture of the mother."

"You never had a suspect in the case, right?"

"Not officially."

"How about unofficially?"

He grinned and his face was all folded flesh. "The priest."

"Priest?"

"Yeah. The priest at St. Agnes. Your church."

"Why him?"

"For one thing, he was a young guy. Macho for a priest. Weight lifter. Big muscles. Me, I like my clergy kind of soft like bread dough, you know?"

"What else?"

"We got an anonymous tip about him. Said he—" Cy broke off and eyed Cork suspiciously. "I don't know if I should be telling you this. It's a cold case. File's still open."

"As a favor between old friends?"

He thought a moment. "What the hell. It'll never be solved. This tip said that the priest liked to masturbate while listening to confessions."

"Jesus."

"Tell me about it."

Kathy Lehman breezed up with a cup of coffee in one hand and her order pad in the other. She slid the coffee onto the counter in front of Cork, snatched a pencil from where she'd stuck it in the hair above her ear, and said, "What'll it be, hon?"

"Oatmeal, raisins, brown sugar."

"Coming up." She whirled and was gone again.

"Did you follow up on it?" Cork asked.

"Yep. Priest denied everything. But guess what we found stuffed behind the confessional. Delicates."

"Delicates?"

"Women's underwear, stained with semen."

"I don't remember any of this."

He shrugged. "It was never made public. That was your dad's

doing. The confessional was open to anyone. No way to prove the priest put those things there. No way in those days to prove the stains were his. We didn't have anything else on the guy. Your father was able to keep it all out of the papers. We could do that back then. But the bishop got involved and yanked the priest, sent him off to Siberia or someplace. And then Mrs. Cavanaugh disappeared. Because the priest was long gone, we pretty much wrote him off as a suspect. And after that the Vanishings stopped. End of case."

"FBI and BCA involved?"

"Yep. Baffled them, too."

"Was there ever any word on other missing women?"

"We watched things in the county and adjacent counties pretty carefully. Followed up real seriously when we got a report of a runaway or missing person. Nothing ever came of it."

"Any speculation on disappearances that came before the first victim was reported and that might have been related?"

Borkman chewed thoughtfully and finally shook his head. "Not that I recall. What's the big interest in an old case?"

"Just wondering. You know how it goes."

"Yeah. I like retirement, but I miss being involved in the action. I think about old cases a lot. It was a good job, a good life. And your old man, he was a hell of a cop to work for."

TWELVE

Cork found Marsha Dross in her office at the sheriff's department. She looked ragged at the edges, and it was clear she hadn't slept much. She cradled a cup of coffee and eyed him over the rim as he sat down on the other side of her desk. It was a lovely morning, and her office windows were open. Cork could hear a cardinal calling in the maple tree outside. Sunlight plunged through the eastern window like a gold sword stuck in the floor.

"All right," he said. "Count me in."

She put her coffee down. "In?"

"I'll consult on the case. I'll interview anyone on the rez you'd like me to interview. I'll also interview anyone else I think might be able to help. I'll keep you apprised of everything I learn. But I want something in return."

"And that would be?"

"I want to know everything you know about the bodies in the Vermilion Drift."

"Everything I know now?"

"Now and as it's revealed."

"Full access to everything?"

"That's the deal."

She frowned, thinking. "All right. But I want two more things from you."

"Name them."

"First of all absolute silence. Whatever you learn on the reservation, whatever you learn from me, it stays between us."

Cork opened his mouth to say fine, but she held up her hand.

"I know you, Cork. I know that being part Ojibwe sometimes pulls you in a direction counter to the interests of this department. I have to believe absolutely that in this you're with me. You understand?"

"I understand. And the second thing?"

"Everything you find out that pertains to the case you share with me. You don't hold anything back. You don't protect anyone. This goes right back to my concern about your Ojibwe ties."

Dross was right. This had been a problem in the past, and so Cork had to think before he answered.

"It's a deal," he finally said. "What do you know about the bodies so far?"

"Not much. We got all the skeletal remains bagged and they've been taken to the BCA lab in Bemidji. Agent Upchurch is working on them now. The preliminary autopsy report on Lauren Cavanaugh indicates death from a single gunshot wound to the chest. The bullet pierced her heart. Luckily, it stayed in the body, and wasn't badly deformed, so Simon's people can run ballistics on it."

"Any indication of sexual assault?"

"No."

"Okay, go on."

"One of the skeletons also shows evidence of a gunshot wound, probable cause of death."

"What evidence?"

"Agent Upchurch found a bullet lodged in the spine," Dross replied. "She's not able at the moment to say anything about the other victims. Our crime scene techs did a good job of clearing the area. We have clothing fabric still intact. We'll get good dental impressions. If some of the remains are from the Vanishings, we'll know."

"Time of death for Lauren Cavanaugh?"

"Tom Conklin's put that at approximately a week ago. He's still trying to nail it down more specifically. The last recorded call on the victim's cell phone was Sunday night at eleven-eleven P.M. Nobody's seen her since that night. In their canvass of the neighborhood, one of Ed's guys talked to Brian Kretsch."

"Lives in that sprawling house across the road from the Parrant estate, right?" Cork asked.

"That's him," Dross said. "He recalled hearing squealing tires a little before midnight. Odd, because North Point Road is usually so quiet. He was just locking up for the night and looked out his picture window, but he was too late to see anything. We haven't found anyone who saw Lauren Cavanaugh the next day or anytime after. So at the moment, we're operating on the theory that she was killed that Sunday night sometime after eleven-eleven P.M. and before midnight."

"Did Kretsch hear a shot?"

"Nope. Apparently he was watching a Jackie Chan DVD. Lots of gunplay and explosions, I guess."

"What about the two bodies we can't account for, what do we know about them?"

"Not much. You seem to think they're Ojibwe. Any way you can be certain?"

"I'm headed out to check on that now. What about you?"

"At the moment, I'm trying to keep a lid on what we've found. I'd like to get a few more answers before we have the media hopping all over this."

"All right." He stood up and started out.

"Cork?" Dross called.

He turned back. She had pushed away from her desk, and the sun through the window had settled on her lap like a sleepy yellow dog. She was as fine a woman as he'd ever known and as skilled a cop as he'd ever worked with. "It's good to have you on the team again," she said.

He nodded, and, though he didn't tell her so, he liked being there.

Cork broke from the thick pine of the Superior National Forest and stepped onto Crow Point. On the far side of the meadow, smoke rose from the stovepipe atop the cabin of Henry Meloux, and even at a distance Cork could smell cinnamon and baking dough, which made him realize he was hungry. He had no idea what the old man was cooking up, but whatever it was, he knew Meloux would share, and his mouth watered in anticipation.

Crow Point was an isolated finger of land that poked into Iron Lake many miles north of Aurora. Meloux lived there alone, his only companion an old yellow mutt named Walleye. He had no running water, no electricity, and did his business in an outhouse thirty yards from the cabin. He was a member of the Grand Medicine Society, one of the Midewiwin, a Mide. He was old, well past ninety. He'd been a friend as far back as Cork had memory. Twice Meloux had saved his life. On more occasions than Cork could recall, Meloux had advised him in a way that untwisted a knot Cork could not undo himself. Meloux offered this gift to many people, not just to Cork, and not just to the Ojibwe.

It had been a long winter and a cool spring. The green of the poplars and birch that edged the shoreline of Crow Point was so new it was still thin and pale. Many of the wildflowers that should have been in bold color were only just now peeking out from the tall meadow grass. Under the warm morning sun of that June day, Cork threaded his way along the narrow path to the cabin door, drawn both by his desire to talk with his old friend and by the tantalizing aroma wafting from the cabin. He knocked and was surprised when the door opened, for it was not Meloux's face that appeared there.

"Who are you?" he asked.

"Right back at you," the woman in the doorway said.

"Where's Henry?"

"Who wants to know?"

"My name's Cork O'Connor. Henry's a friend."

She looked him up and down and seemed disappointed. She appeared to be Cork's age, more or less. Her hair was long and black but with a wide gray streak running through like a glacial stream. White flour smudged her left cheek, and, as she stood there, she wiped flour from her hands with a dish towel. She might have been pretty, Cork decided, if she'd smiled, even a little.

"So you're the famous Cork O'Connor," she said.

"I don't know about famous."

"I've been hearing stories about you for years from my uncle."

"That would be Henry?"

"He's my great-uncle actually. My grandmother's brother."

"You must be Rainy Bisonette. I've heard about you, too." But not from Henry. Other people on the rez with relatives who were Lac Court Oreilles in Wisconsin talked about her. "You're visiting?"

"Learning."

"The way of the Midewiwin?"

She didn't deny this, but neither did she confirm it.

"Is Henry here?"

"Not at the moment. But he's expecting you."

This didn't surprise Cork. Meloux had a way of knowing these things. Over all the years of their friendship, Cork had come to take it for granted.

"He's waiting for you," she said.

"Where?"

"I don't really know. He said to tell you to follow the blood. Do you understand what that means?"

"I think so."

He looked past her into Meloux's one-room cabin. "Smells good."

"Enjoy your visit," she said, stepped back inside, and closed the door.

Cork returned the way he'd come, through the long meadow and into the pines, and soon came to a small stream that flowed west toward Iron Lake. Because of its color, white folks called it Wine Creek, but the Ojibwe called it Miskwi, which meant "blood." He turned east and followed upstream. It took him only a little while to see that he was on the right track. He found the imprint of a dog's paw in the soft earth at the edge of the stream. It was a recent print he suspected had been left by Walleye, pausing to lap from the cool water. For nearly half an hour more he shadowed the creek, finally squeezing through a narrow cleft in a rock ridge and emerging into a clearing that lay in the bottom of a natural bowl formed by rugged hills.

Though it had no real name, Cork thought of it as Blood Hollow.

A remarkable event had taken place there several years earlier. A young man accused of murder, a man named Solemn Winter Moon, had received a vision of Jesus. Although many people knew about the vision, only Meloux and Cork knew the location of its occurrence, a remarkable place, filled with an abundance of wildflowers, which were much larger and bolder in color than those on Crow Point and which Meloux often gathered for the healings he offered.

The old Mide was there all right. Cork spotted him sitting next to the stream near the center of the hollow, his back against a tree stump, almost invisible amid the tall grass and the flowers. His eyes were closed as if in sleep, and he didn't seem to be aware of Cork's approach. Walleye lay at his side, his forepaws pillowing his old yellow head.

"I've been expecting you," Meloux said without opening his eyes. "Sit down." He sounded irritated, as if Cork had missed an appointment.

Cork did as he'd been told, but for a minute or more Meloux seemed to pay him no heed. Finally the old Mide opened his eyes and, much to Cork's relief, smiled. Cork pulled out the tobacco pouch he'd brought as an offering. He gave it to Meloux, who opened it, pinched tobacco from inside, sprinkled a little to the four corners of the earth, and then let some fall in the center. From a pocket of his overalls, he pulled a book of matches and a small pipe carved of red stone. He filled the pipe, struck a flame, set an ember burning, and drew on the pipe stem. He passed the pipe to Cork. They sat a long time in this way, smoking silently.

Meloux's hair was long and white and fine as spider silk. His face looked as if it held a line for every year he'd lived. His eyes were warm and inviting, little brown suns. He wore a blue denim shirt, old denim overalls, and moccasins he'd sewn himself. He wore no hat, and the breeze in the hollow ran through his hair. The long white filaments quivered and glowed as if electrified. Cork noticed that the old man's hands, whenever they held the pipe to his lips, trembled, something Cork had never seen before, and though he mentioned nothing to his friend, he was concerned.

Finally Meloux said, "Isaiah Broom has you in his sights."

"Isaiah and I have been exchanging fire since we were kids."

"An angry wind, that man. From a child."

"Has he ever come to you asking help?"

Meloux shook his head. "His anger blinds him."

Walleye lifted his head briefly, blinked at them, then went back to resting.

"When he was a boy too young to remember, he was brought to me," Meloux said. "His father was dead in Korea, his mother gone in the night. He was a child abandoned and wrapped in a blanket of pain. I tried to help him, but he was not ready for what I offered. In his anger, he has been a strong voice for The People. So maybe that was what was meant for him all along."

"Henry," Cork said, changing the subject, "I had a vision today."

The old man looked at him closely. "Your face is troubled."

Cork described the blood running from the house across the lawn of the Parrant estate. "It's the second vision I've had there, Henry. The second disturbing one."

Meloux's eyes took in the sky. "Everything is alive, Corcoran O'Connor. And everything alive can become ill. That is a diseased place, I think."

"Can it infect those who live there?"

"That is the nature of disease."

Cork thought about Ophelia Stillday working at the center, and the situation concerned him.

"This vision is not the cause of the trouble I see in your face," Meloux said.

"No, there's something else."

Cork told him about the grisly discovery in the Vermilion Drift. "If it's the Vanishings, Henry, then two of the unidentified bodies are definitely Ojibwe. One of the others is probably Monique Cavanaugh. But that leaves two we don't know about. I'm wondering if there were any other disappearances of women from the rez back then. Someone gone but never reported."

"Not all The People love this land, Corcoran O'Connor. There have always been those who abandon it, and sometimes they do not say a word to anyone. They just go."

"That's not an answer, Henry."

The old man looked down where his hands quivered on his lap. "Talk to Millie Joseph."

"Because her memory is better than yours?"

"Because you are a man who is happy asking questions and she is a woman happy to answer. Go to Millie. Ask questions. It will make you both happy."

"Henry, did you know about the wildcat mine pit sunk on rez land?"

"There's not much about this reservation I do not know."

"Who else knew?"

"A long time ago, probably many. Now?" He gave a shrug.

"Henry—"

"It is time you talk to Millie Joseph."

It was clear to Cork that was all Meloux was going to say on the subject. He stood up to leave. "By the way, I met Rainy. She says she's here to learn from you."

"That's not the only reason she's here," the old man said unhappily.

Cork glanced toward Meloux's trembling hands. "You'll get back to your cabin okay?"

"Walleye and me, we'll take our time. That is something we both still know how to do well."

"*Migwech*, Henry," Cork said. It meant "thank you."

Cork started away through the tall meadow grass, but Meloux called his name and he turned back.

"I will say one thing, and then I will say no more." The sun was behind the old man, and his face lay in shadow. "Your father was one of those who knew about that pit. Your father knew there was another way into that mine."

THIRTEEN

Millie Joseph had a room in the Nokomis Home, which was an assisted living facility that had been built by the Iron Lake Ojibwe in the town of Allouette, on the reservation. She'd been married three times and had outlived all her husbands. From these marriages, she had eight children. Six were still alive. Only one resided on the rez. The others had scattered to the four winds.

Millie Joseph had been Cork's mother's best friend. She'd also functioned as a kind of unofficial historian for the rez. She'd kept papers and documents and had recorded oral histories. Most of her collection had gone to the Iron Lake Historical Society, which she had helped form. Now she suffered from dementia. Although she was still gifted with periods of extreme lucidity, particularly about details of her past, about other things her mind was often as clean as a freshly laundered sheet. She'd always been a pleasant woman, and her dementia had not yet changed that. When Cork found her in the dayroom of Nokomis Home, she was sitting alone in her wheelchair, staring through the window at the blue stretch of Iron Lake. She was smiling and seemed lost in reverie.

"*Boozhoo*, Aunt," Cork said, using the familiar Ojibwe greeting and calling her by the relational name he used for most reservation women her age, regardless of actual blood connection. He leaned and kissed her wrinkled cheek.

"Hello, there," she replied, as if Cork were a stranger, but a welcome one.

"It's a beautiful day," Cork said, looking with her through the window.

"When I was a girl, I used to swim in that lake every morning."

"You were a good swimmer, I've been told. Better than most boys."

She laughed. "My mother told me it wasn't good for a girl to beat boys, but I didn't care. I was fast as an otter."

Cork knelt beside the wheelchair. "Millie, there's something I want to ask you."

She smiled at him, expectantly.

"Many years ago my cousin Fawn disappeared. Do you remember that?"

Her smiled melted, and a wariness came into her eyes.

"Another young Ojibwe woman also vanished. Naomi Stonedeer. Do you remember?"

She looked away from him, and although her eyes settled again on the lake, Cork suspected it was a different vision she was seeing. "Fawn liked to swim, too."

"I know," Cork said. "She was a good swimmer, like you."

"They said the lake took her." She shook her head. "It wasn't the lake."

"Did others disappear, Millie?"

"Naomi Stonedeer and Fawn."

"Yes. I know about them. But were there others?"

She frowned, thinking, and her eyes seemed more focused. When she spoke, there was gravity in her words. "Hattie's girl ran away about that time. Seems to me Hattie never heard from her again. A wild child, that one. Didn't surprise me that she'd run off without a word."

"Hattie's girl?"

"Abbie."

"Anyone else?"

She thought a moment. "Yes, seems to me before that Leonora Broom had took off. She just up and left her boy. Now that was a shame."

"Isaiah?"

She nodded. "Oh, he was an angry little boy."

"So, Leonora Broom first and then Abbie Stillday. Anyone else?"

She thought some more, and while she thought, her tongue lapped idly over her lower lip. "Not then."

"What do you remember about then?"

She turned her face to him and she smiled. "It was so long ago. But sometimes, when I read your mother's poems, I remember. Your mother, she was a beautiful writer."

"Yes."

"She wrote the loveliest poems. She could have been famous, I bet, if she'd wanted to be. And her journals. She gave them to me before she died. I used to read them. I don't read much anymore."

He had forgotten about his mother's writing. "Did you pass them on to the historical society?"

She shook her head. "Kept those for myself."

"Where are they?"

"In my room. Push me?"

He wheeled her out of the dayroom, past two old Shinnob men playing checkers and an old woman nodding in front of the television. Her room was on the first floor. It was small but pleasant. She pointed to the closet. "In there."

Inside, Cork found an old steamer trunk taking up much of the floor space. Beside it were stacked four cardboard boxes. One was marked "Allouette" and one "Brandywine," the names of the two communities on the rez. On the other two were written his mother's name: Colleen O'Connor. He lifted the first two boxes, set them on the trunk, and pulled free those below that bore his mother's name. They were sealed with tape.

"Take them," Millie Joseph said at his back. "I don't need them now. I can't read anymore."

"*Migwech*, Millie," Cork said.

"She could have been a famous author, I bet," she said again. "Are there any famous Ojibwe authors?"

"A few," Cork said.

"Good," Millie Joseph said and smiled.

* * *

He'd loaded the boxes in his Land Rover and was heading back toward Aurora when his cell phone rang. It was the sheriff's office.

"We have some preliminary information from the crime scene if you want to stop by," Dross said.

"I'm on my way. I've got some information for you, too."

She was in her office, with Ed Larson and Simon Rutledge. They appeared to have been waiting for him.

"What did you find out?" Larson asked.

"And good morning to you, too, Ed," Cork said.

"Sorry," Larson said. "A little eager."

There were no chairs available, so Cork leaned against one of the file cabinets. "I've got two possible names for the additional bodies in Vermilion One."

Larson had his small notebook out in an instant, pen poised above a clean page.

"Hattie Stillday's elder daughter, Abigail, who was believed to be a runaway. And Leonora Broom, Isaiah Broom's mother, who everybody thought simply abandoned him. Check the community clinic in Allouette. There may be dental records for both women available through the Indian Health Service."

"I'll get right on that," Larson said.

Dross asked, "Did you find out if anyone knew about the sink on reservation land?"

"I didn't get a satisfactory answer to that particular question," Cork replied. He knew he was spinning out the thinnest thread of truth, but at least it wasn't a lie. "What did you get from the crime scene?"

"Something we don't understand," Rutledge said with a wistful, unruffled look. Not much ruffled Rutledge. It was one of the things Cork liked about him. "The bullet pulled from Lauren Cavanaugh during the autopsy and the bullet Upchurch found lodged in Monique Cavanaugh's spine were both thirty-eight caliber. Although they were deformed by impact, both stayed in one piece and our techs were able to examine the rifling impressions pretty clearly. Get this, Cork. Both bullets were fired from the same weapon."

"What kind of firearm?" Cork asked.

"Because of the right-hand twist to the striations, we're thinking Smith and Wesson, a thirty-eight."

A .38 Smith & Wesson was a firearm with which Cork was eminently familiar. He owned one himself and had worn it when he was sheriff of Tamarack County. Forty years before that, the gun had belonged to his father.

It wasn't an uncommon weapon, yet the coincidence made Cork uncomfortable, and he knew that, as soon as the meeting was over, there was something he had to do.

"Anything else from the mine?" he asked.

Larson glanced up from his notebook. "Yes. Beneath the older victim with the bullet in the spine we found a gold wedding band. There was an inscription on the inside surface. 'My Unique Monique.'"

"Monique Cavanaugh," Cork said.

"We can't say a hundred percent at this point, but it's sure looking that way."

"Anything useful on the other victims?"

"Clothing remnants still clinging to bone on three of the victims, which may indicate that the other two were nude when they were put there. I can't imagine the clothing will be much help with IDs at this point. We'll check dental records at the Indian Health Service, and if the victims are the other vanished women, maybe we'll get lucky and find matches."

"It's the Vanishings, Ed. I'm sure."

He could see that Larson was certain, too, but the opinion of the sheriff's chief investigator would be an official and quoted one, and so, good cop always, Captain Ed Larson was cautious in his speculations. "We'll see."

Rutledge eyed Cork with arched interest and asked, "What do people on the reservation remember about the Vanishings, Cork?"

"I've only talked to one person, Simon. An old woman named Millie Joseph. Her memory's pretty hit-and-miss."

"But you'll talk to others?"

"Of course."

"Of course," Rutledge said and smiled enigmatically.

Cork shoved away from the file cabinet, preparing to leave.

Dross stood up. "Cork, we've been able to contain most of the information about what we found in the mine. But as soon as this story breaks, it's going to break big and the media will descend like locusts."

"Maybe that's not such a bad thing," he replied.

"How do you mean?"

"The Vanishings are decades old, probably as cold a case as you're likely to find here. Maybe someone will come forward with new information. It happens."

"Don't hold your breath," she said.

FOURTEEN

Cork's father had left a legacy that included a lot of intangibles. The idea that justice was an imperative. That you made commitments in life and, come hell or high water, you stood fast by them. That loyalty was the lifeblood of friendship. That the love of family was the deepest root that tapped your heart.

But he'd also left material things, among them, the house on Gooseberry Lane, his sheriff's uniform with its bloody bullet hole through the pocket over the heart, a fine basket weave holster, and a .38 caliber Smith & Wesson Police Special revolver.

In his own time as sheriff, Cork had proudly worn his father's sidearm. He'd kept it cleaned and well oiled, and it fired perfectly. Three years earlier, after a bloody incident that had turned his stomach against their mindless potential, he'd divested himself of his firearms and had given them into the keeping of Henry Meloux. What the old Mide had done with the firearms, he'd never said. Cork had never asked. But as he sped north along the back roads of Tamarack County toward Crow Point with mounting concern, that's exactly what he intended to do.

He parked his Land Rover near the double-trunk birch that marked the trail to the old man's cabin. He walked quickly, going over and over in his head thoughts and questions that plagued him.

Meloux, in his parting words the last time they'd met, had revealed that Liam O'Connor knew about the sink on reservation land, about the other way into the mine. Cork's father, better than anyone, was in a position to thwart a criminal investigation. His father owned the same kind of weapon that had killed Monique Cavanaugh. What the hell had gone on forty years ago? And what the hell was going on now?

With an angry bound, he leaped Wine Creek and, a few minutes later, broke from the pine trees into the meadow, where he fixed his eyes on the solitary cabin ahead.

"Stop!"

He spun to his right, startled by the woman's voice.

She knelt among the wildflowers and, like them, seemed to grow up out of the earth itself. She wore a straw hat with a wide brim that shaded her face. She'd braided her long hair, and it hung over her left shoulder and fell between her breasts. She glared at him from the shadow of her hat.

"My uncle is resting. He shouldn't be disturbed," she said.

"I'll talk with Henry," Cork replied and started forward again.

"Are you always this rude?"

"Visiting your uncle was a hell of a lot easier before you arrived."

"That's one of the reasons I'm here."

Cork altered his course and waded through the meadow grass to the place where she knelt. Despite the rising heat of the summer day, she wore a long-sleeved shirt of thin cotton embroidered with tiny flowers around the cuffs and collar.

"What exactly is going on with Henry?" he asked. "Is he sick?"

"I don't know. He doesn't either."

"The shaking?"

"It began a month ago. It's getting worse."

"Parkinson's?"

"Maybe. Without tests, it's hard to know."

"And he won't be tested?"

"No." She looked toward the cabin. "He tires easily these days."

"He's within a stone's throw of having lived a hundred years. Maybe he's entitled to a little fatigue."

"This isn't just age," she said. "This is something else."

"Did he ask you here?"

She plucked a wildflower, a touch-me-not, and dropped it in a basket woven of reeds. "I came under the guise of wanting to learn more about his healing techniques. The family sent me. We're all worried."

Cork almost smiled. "And you think Henry hasn't seen through you?"

"I'm sure he has. But he hasn't objected."

"He wouldn't." Cork glanced toward the cabin. "I need to talk to him. It's important."

She considered him and finally stood. She lifted the basket, which contained many gathered wildflowers. "Very well," she said and led the way.

She quietly opened the door. In the cool inside, Meloux lay on his bunk. Walleye was sprawled on the floor nearby. They both turned their heads as Cork entered with Rainy. Walleye's tail wagged sluggishly across the floorboards. Meloux simply smiled.

"Two visits in one day. I am a blessed man, Corcoran O'Connor." The old Mide rose slowly and swung his feet over the side of the bunk. "My niece is going to make blackberry leaf tea, I think. Will you have some?"

"*Migwech*, Henry."

Rainy went to the old stove, opened the door, and threw in a few sticks of wood to stoke the fire. The old man stood up and said to his niece, "We will be by the lake."

Cork walked beside his old friend down a path that threaded between two great rock outcroppings. On the far side, very close to the shoreline of the lake, lay a circle of stones that contained the deep black char of many fires. Sectioned tree trunks had been placed around the circle for seating. Meloux eased his old, narrow butt onto one of these, and Cork sat next to him. Meloux's breathing was rapid and shallow, and he seemed exhausted. Cork thought about commenting on this but figured if Henry wanted to discuss it he would.

Meloux stared at Iron Lake. There was no breeze, and the surface of the water lay flat and silver. The air near the fire circle smelled of the ritual burning that was often a part of the old Mide's work.

It was a long time before Meloux spoke. "You visited Millie Joseph?"

"Yes," Cork replied. "She was helpful."

The old man nodded.

"Henry, I need to know what you did with my revolver."

Meloux turned his face to Cork. His eyes were brown and watchful. "I put it with your rifle in a safe and sacred place."

"Where?"

"A place I do not think even you know, Corcoran O'Connor. It is a place remembered by only the oldest of The People, a place of *bimaa-diziwin*."

Bimaadiziwin. Cork translated the word in his mind: *a healthy way of life.*

"It is a place where things that have blocked the way of our people, the path toward wholeness, have been put aside for good."

"I want to see the revolver, Henry."

The old man seemed puzzled. "Do you need it?"

"No, I just need to know that it's still there."

"Why would it move?"

"Humor me, Henry. Just tell me how to find it."

While Meloux considered this request, Rainy appeared, carrying three white ceramic mugs, which she brought to the stone circle. She handed one to Meloux, one to Cork, and kept the other.

"Shall I stay?" she asked her uncle.

Which seemed to Cork clearly her intention, considering the cup she'd brought for herself.

"For a few minutes," the old man said. "Then you will show our guest something."

Cork glanced up at her. She seemed as surprised by this as he.

She sat down. Her presence felt awkward, and Cork was reluctant to continue the discussion. But perhaps as far as Meloux was concerned the discussion was finished anyway. They sat for several minutes in an ill-fitting silence. Cork was used to silence; the Ojibwe were quite comfortable with saying nothing for a long time. But the woman struck an alien chord in him. He wanted to be rid of her. Meloux seemed blithely clueless. He drank the tea, which smelled both sweet and pungent, and contemplated the silver lake. For her part, Rainy did the same.

"The home of Judge Parrant," Meloux finally said. "It is a place of bad medicine. There are many diseased places, but there are also those places of healing, places of *bimaadiziwin*."

"*Bimaadiziwin,*" Rainy responded. "The healthy life."

"Do you remember where the blackberry bushes grow? I showed you."

"Of course. East along the lakeshore about a mile. On top of a cliff."

The old man gave a nod. "There is a cave in that cliff. The opening is small and hidden by blackberry brambles. What Corcoran O'Connor is looking for, he will find in that cave. Will you take him there?"

"Of course, Uncle."

"I would go myself, but I am tired."

"Would you like to walk back to the cabin?" she asked.

"No. I will stay here and finish my tea. You go with Cork. Go now. I think today he is a man in a hurry."

She stood up, walked to where the path threaded between the out-croppings, and glanced back impatiently, as if she were the eager one and Cork the laggard. He pulled his butt off the stump and said to Meloux, "*Migwech*, Henry."

At the cabin, Rainy paused only long enough to put their mugs inside, then walked briskly east. She led him through a dense stand of paper birch, then across a small marsh on a narrow spine of solid ground he would never have found on his own. He followed her up a face of rock colored and lined like a turtle shell and topped with as-pens. They wove among the aspens, which were pale green with new leaves, and when they broke from the trees they stood atop a cliff with Iron Lake stretching below them. All along the edge of the cliff grew blackberry bushes. "This must be it," Cork said. "Where is this place of health?"

"You know as much as I do. Uncle Henry asked me to bring you to the top of the cliff, and here we are."

Cork eased his way between the thorny blackberry brambles and carefully peered over the side of the precipice. The lake lay a good hun-dred feet below. The water was clear, and he could see perfectly the dark contours of the rock that had broken from the cliff face and now lay jag-ged on the lake bottom. Just above the waterline, seeming to cling to the very rock itself, was another long line of blackberry bramble.

"I can't see any way down," he said.

"Maybe down isn't the best way to approach," Rainy suggested. "Maybe up from the water."

"Henry didn't offer us a canoe."

"You can't swim?"

He gave her a cold look and walked farther east, where the land sloped in a gentle fold. At the bottom was a small creek that fed into the lake. Cork followed the creek to its mouth, where he sat on the trunk of a cedar that had long ago toppled. He untied his laces and removed his boots. He pulled off his socks and stuffed them into the boots. He unbuttoned his blue denim shirt and shrugged it off. He tugged off his T-shirt. Finally he began to unbuckle his belt.

Rainy, who'd followed him, watched all this with deep, silent interest.

"The pants are coming off," he warned her.

"Boxers or briefs?" she said.

He hesitated. "It's been a long time since I took off my pants in front of a woman. I'm not real comfortable with this."

"For heaven's sake, I'm a public health nurse. Believe me, I've seen it all."

He skinned the jeans from his hips and drew them off.

"Black boxers," she said. "Interesting."

He ignored her, folded his pants, and laid them atop his other things.

"Are those bullet holes?" she asked.

"Yes."

"It's hard to believe they didn't kill you."

"At the time, I was pretty sure they would."

"Luck?"

"Henry, I think, would say destiny. You coming?"

"Are you kidding? That water's freezing. I'll wait here, make sure no one steals your clothes. Enjoy your swim." She smiled with wicked delight.

She was right. Although it was mid-June, the lake water was still frigid. In the North Country, the cool nights would keep the water temperature challenging until well into July. Cork plunged in, and the icy water gripped him like a fierce, angry hand. He considered with amazement the mining engineer, Genie Kufus, who claimed to swim in the lake regularly. *You're a better man than I am, Gunga Din,* he thought as he swam feverishly away from shore and circled back to the cliff.

In the middle of the gray face of rock, beginning just at the waterline, he found natural steps. He quickly climbed from the lake and immediately the sun began to warm him. Barefooted, he carefully mounted the rock, working his way toward the line of blackberry bushes. Although from the lake the opening of the cave couldn't be seen, from his current vantage, Cork could clearly make out the small black hole Meloux had mentioned. He eased behind the bramble, knelt in the mouth of the cave, crawled inside, and waited while his eyes adjusted slowly to the dim light.

It was cool and dry. The floor sloped toward the entrance, so that any water that might have found its way in would have quickly drained. The chamber was small, the size of a five-man tent, and edged with rock shelves. On the shelves lay many items, some looking quite ancient. Cork could see no rhyme or reason to what had been placed there: a bow made of hard maple with a deer-hide quiver full of arrow shafts whose featherings had long ago turned to dust; a colorfully beaded bandolier bag; a rag doll; a muzzle-loader with a rotted stock and beside it a powder horn, still in good condition; a woven blanket; a coil of rope. There were knives and a tomahawk and what looked to be a collection of human scalps. And there was a bearskin that belonged to Cork, in which he'd wrapped his Winchester rifle and his .38 Smith & Wesson Police Special when he'd handed them over to Henry Meloux. He pulled the bearskin from the shelf, set it on the floor, and unrolled it. The Winchester was still there. The .38 was gone.

FIFTEEN

Meloux seemed puzzled but not disturbed.

Cork strained to control his anger. "Henry, why didn't you keep it here with you? Why put it somewhere someone might find it?"

"I do not lock my door, Corcoran O'Connor." The old man shrugged. "Here, too, someone might find it."

"Don't blame my uncle," Rainy said. "Why didn't you disable the weapon before you gave it to him? Remove the firing pin or something? You can do that, right?"

It was late afternoon. They sat at the table in the cabin on Crow Point, Cork on one side and Meloux and his niece on the other. Rainy angled her body toward Cork in a threatening way, and, if her eyes had been fists, his face would have been bloody.

"You come here, ask my uncle for help, and when he gives it to you, all you can do is criticize. He's told me of your good friendship. Frankly, from what I've seen so far, I have trouble believing it."

"Niece," Meloux said gently. "Your tongue is a knife. If I need a knife, I have my own."

Cork said, "Henry, you know things you're not telling me."

"What I know is that you are looking for a truth I cannot give you now."

Cork bent toward the old Mide. "A woman is dead, shot with the same gun that over forty years ago killed her mother. It's the same kind of gun you put in the cave and is now missing. I'm hoping against hope that they're not the same weapon. I can't even guess how that could be possible. But I gotta tell you, Henry, I don't like the feel of it, not one bit. I need to know everything you know."

Meloux's face was a blanket of compassion, but there was no hint that he was going to offer Cork anything more.

"Do you know if it was my father's revolver that killed Monique Cavanaugh?"

Meloux's expression changed not at all, and again he didn't reply.

"At least tell me this," Cork said, his voice pitched with frustration. "Who else knows about this place of *bimaadiziwin*?"

Meloux thought a moment. "It has always been a secret and sacred place. The Mide have always known, but most have walked the Path of Souls. I do not know who knows and has not yet walked that path."

"So only you and the dead know? Christ, Henry, that's not true. Someone very much alive and kicking took that gun." Cork rose and towered over the old man. "If you know who that is, Henry, for God sake tell me."

But it was like throwing punches at the wind. The old Mide looked up at him and said quietly, "You are a man on a journey. And all the while you stand here, your feet are idle."

Fire flared in Cork's brain. "God damn it," he said and spun away and headed toward the door.

Rainy followed him outside. "When you come again, if you ever do, will you bring something with you?"

"What?" he snapped at her.

"Manners." She turned, went back inside, and shut the door.

His only food that day had been the oatmeal he'd ordered for breakfast at the Pinewood Broiler when he talked with Cy Borkman. He was starved, and he headed to Sam's Place. He parked in the lot, went into the old Quonset hut, and apologized to Judy Madsen for having been absent all day. She glanced at his face, and what she saw there caused her obvious concern. "You look like you swallowed a cockroach. The kids and me, we've got this covered. You worry about your other business."

Judy fixed him a Sam's Super with the works and a large basket of fries. He took his meal in the rear of the Quonset hut.

Sam's Super was the hallmark of Sam's Place. It had been Sam Winter Moon's pride. Sam had believed in a quality burger. He never used frozen patties. Every day, first thing in the morning, he took twenty pounds of lean ground beef and rolled it in his hands into quarter-pound balls, which, order by order, he placed on the hot grill, pressed flat with his spatula, and seared to juicy perfection. The patty was topped with good Wisconsin cheddar, freshly sliced tomato, a large frond of leaf lettuce, a thin slice of Walla Walla sweet onion, and Sam's own special sauce, whose recipe was a closely guarded secret. Every time Cork bit into a Sam's Super, he tasted a heaven of memories.

He was almost finished eating when his cell phone chirped. "O'Connor," he answered.

"It's Marsha Dross, Cork. We have a situation here. Can you come to my office right away?"

The instant he walked into Dross's office, he could feel the tension in the air. Dross was at her desk. Rutledge was standing at the window. Ed Larson was sitting with Lou Haddad and his wife. All eyes swung toward Cork.

"Come in," Dross said, rising. "You know Sheri?"

"Of course. How are you?" he asked.

Haddad's wife smiled bravely, and her hand lifted a little in a half-hearted greeting.

"Sheri got a note," Dross said. "Same message Lou and the others received, but with a twist."

Dross indicated a sheet of paper on her desk. Cork walked over and took a look but didn't touch. There was a trifold, just as there'd been with the others. The note had been printed on paper that Cork was pretty sure had no identifying watermark, and the same blood-dripping font—From Hell—had been used. The message was almost the same as before, but, as Dross had indicated, it was different and in a terrifying way: *We die, U die. Just like her.*

"Just like her?" Cork said.

"We're assuming it refers to Lauren Cavanaugh," Ed Larson said. "Which is interesting. As far as we know, only those of us associated with the investigation knew that Lauren Cavanaugh was one of the victims in the mine."

"Not true," Cork said. "The person who put her there knew."

"Exactly," Larson said. "We're taking this very seriously."

"Where did you get this, Sheri?"

"It was under the windshield wiper of my car."

"Have Max Cavanaugh or Genie Kufus received anything more?" Cork asked Dross.

"We contacted Cavanaugh at his house this afternoon. He's got nothing more."

"And Kufus?"

For a moment, they all appeared to be frozen, a tableau of awkward concern. Then Dross said, "She seems to be missing."

SIXTEEN

Genie Kufus wasn't at her hotel, nor was she answering her cell phone. Her car was gone. None of her team from the DOE knew where she was.

"When was the last time anyone saw her?" Cork asked.

"She met with her team over lunch, then she returned to her room to work. None of them have heard from her since, and none of them saw her leave the hotel."

"Have you checked her room?"

"Of course," Dross said. "She's not there."

"You went in?"

"Yes. With the manager."

"Any sign of a struggle?"

"No."

"Anything appear to be missing?"

"That's hard to say without knowing what should be there."

"You put out a BOLO?" Which was shorthand for Be on the Lookout.

Dross nodded. "She's driving a rented cherry red Explorer. Not easy to miss."

"You mind if I have a look at her hotel room?"

Dross shot glances toward Larson and Rutledge. They both gave nods. "Under the circumstances, I'm going to say okay. But I'd like to be there with you."

"Of course." Cork stood up and smiled at Haddad and his wife. "I think you should go somewhere safe. When was the last time you two took a vacation together?"

* * *

The room Genie Kufus occupied at the Four Seasons overlooked Iron Lake and the marina. It was a lovely view of white-masted sloops and powerboats set against dark blue water.

Dross said, "My guys have already been here, Cork. What are you looking for that they didn't see?"

"I hope I'll know it when I see it."

He turned from the windows and scanned the room. Kufus was neat, well organized. Either she traveled a great deal and had the process down or this was who she was all the time. Nothing looked out of place, and that was helpful to Cork. He walked to the desk. Her laptop was closed. He opened it.

"Don't turn that on," Dross warned. "Until I've determined that she's officially missing, we're on thin ice just being here."

She was right. Cork glanced through the documents that lay stacked next to the computer. They all appeared to be technical papers dealing with the mine and mining in general. He went to the closet. Dresses and slacks were hung with care; shoes had been set on the floor like soldiers in formation. He went to the dresser and opened the top drawer. Lingerie, scented with lilac from a little pouch of sachet. Which seemed odd for a woman in town on business. The rest of the drawers held other, less interesting, clothing: folded tops, sweaters, shorts.

He entered the bathroom, where he found the towels racked with measured precision. Not even an errant hair on the sink.

"Interesting," he said.

"What?"

"Kufus is a swimmer, but I don't see a bathing suit anywhere. Why don't you call the front desk, make sure none of the staff saw her go out for a swim this afternoon."

"We already did that."

"Never hurts to double check."

She looked ready to offer a reply, probably not a pleasant one, but instead moved to the phone to make the call.

Cork went back to the desk. The charging cord for the woman's cell phone was still plugged in, but the phone was gone. Next to the cord was a small pad of notepaper supplied by the hotel. There was a clear indentation from a note that had been written and then torn from the pad. Cork lifted and turned it so that the white paper caught the light through the window just right, and the faint grooving of Kufus's handwriting was legible. He put the pad back down as Dross hung up the phone.

"She usually takes a swim in the afternoon, but, as we've already been told, no one saw her go out today," Dross reported.

"All right," Cork said. "I'm finished here."

"Wasted trip," she said.

Cork chose not to contradict her.

It was dusk when he headed out of Aurora, south along the shoreline of Iron Lake. He passed the Chippewa Grand Casino just outside of town, where the parking lot was three-quarters filled and still filling. The casino had been a godsend to the Iron Lake Ojibwe, whose profits had underwritten more improvements on the rez than Cork could count. Over the years, however, the casino had also delivered its share of difficulties, but that evening when he passed, he wasn't thinking about the pros and cons of Indian gaming. He was thinking about the words Kufus had written on the sheet of notepaper she'd torn from the pad in her room: Moon Haven Cove.

Four miles south, Cork turned off the highway onto Moon Haven Drive. The road narrowed to a slender thread of black asphalt weaving among a thick stand of red pine. He didn't have to think about where the road led. There was only one home on Moon Haven Cove, and it belonged to Max Cavanaugh.

He could have told the sheriff what he'd found, but the note had satisfied him that the disappearance of the DOE's mining consultant probably wasn't cause for alarm, and he'd decided that it would be better to pursue the lead quietly on his own. If, as he suspected, Kufus's visit had nothing at all to do with mine business, a sudden appearance by the authorities had the potential for being embarrassing for all involved.

Of course, the whole question could have been easily answered with a phone call, but Cork had a gut sense—and he was nothing if not a man who followed his gut instincts—that something very interesting might result from seeing to this personally.

He drove slowly as he approached Cavanaugh's lake home. It was a behemoth of a construction. All the homes that went up on the lake these days seemed to be that way. When Cork was growing up, a place on the lake still meant a modest cabin or a small house with a screened porch that may or may not have been insulated for winter occupancy. There was often a tiny dock, where a boat with a reasonable outboard or a little skiff with a mast for a single sail was tied up. The woods drew close around those old places, and they shared the shoreline together in comfortable intimacy.

No one built small anymore. Certainly not Max Cavanaugh. And the woods stood back from his opulent construct, as if drawing away, repulsed.

The great home lay in deep purple cast from the evening sky. The wide lawn appeared to be an inlet of a wine-colored sea. The black asphalt gave way to a circular drive made of crushed limestone bordered with flowers. Parked in the drive, near the front door, was the red Explorer that Kufus had rented for her time in Aurora. Cork pulled up behind her vehicle, turned off his Land Rover, and stepped out onto the drive. He saw immediately that the Explorer's tires were flat. On closer examination, he discovered they'd been slashed, all four. He also discovered that an envelope had been slipped under the windshield wiper on the driver's side. On the face of the envelope, printed in the dripping red font called From Hell, was Kufus's name.

When he reached the porch of Cavanaugh's house, he wasn't surprised to find another envelope, this bearing the name of Max Cavanaugh, printed in From Hell. The envelope had been pinned to the door with a hunting knife that would have been perfect for gutting a moose or slashing tires.

He rang the bell, twice. No one answered. He began a slow circumnavigation of the property, checking the windows as he went, unable to see anything because the curtains were all drawn. From the back of the house came the sound of soft jazz playing over good speakers. Rounding the rear corner, he saw the great bricked patio, the table and wine bottle, the two chairs with towels folded over the back of each, but he saw neither Cavanaugh nor Kufus. The music came from an opened patio door.

Cork was just about to head that way when he caught sight of the dock on the far side of the back lawn where it edged the cove. Cavanaugh and Kufus were there. Cavanaugh wore red swim trunks. Kufus wore a swimsuit, a black one-piece that looked designed more for exercise than for showing off at the beach. They stood close together, and, as Cork watched, Kufus put her arms gently around her companion. Behind them in the late dusk, the surface of Moon Haven Cove was a perfect mirror of the plum-colored sky.

Cavanaugh spotted him and pulled away. He said something to Kufus, and they both turned toward the house. They spoke a moment more, then walked the path to the patio.

"My, my," the woman said, taking one of the towels from the back of a patio chair. "You do get around."

"I rang the bell," Cork said. "No one answered."

"Can't hear much from down there," Cavanaugh said, indicating the dock. He had a body taut and sinewy but also scarred in a number of places. In the shower after one of the basketball games the Old Martyrs had played, he'd told Cork they were all the results of his mine work over the years. He'd said he liked the danger of the job. "What's up?"

Cork said, "Ms. Kufus, did you know the whole county is worried about you?"

"It's Genie, and whatever for?"

"Some more threats have been delivered. As a matter of fact, you have one waiting for you on your car. And, Max, there's one for you."

Cavanaugh looked confused. "What are you talking about?"

"Why don't we all go to your front door and I'll show you."

Cavanaugh led them into the house, leaving a gray trail of water droplets on the white carpeting all the way to the front door. When he saw the envelope, he reached for the knife that pinned it.

"It might be better to wait, Max," Cork said. "The sheriff's people will want to go over it for prints."

Cavanaugh ignored him, tugged the knife blade free, and opened the envelope.

We die. U die. Just like her. In dripping red From Hell.

He held it out for Kufus to see. She read it, and her response surprised Cork.

"Fuck them," she said. She looked beyond Cavanaugh to where her rental was parked. The envelope was clearly visible on the windshield, a white rectangle against the reflection of a bruise-colored sky, and she said again, low and hard, "Fuck them."

Azevedo was the deputy dispatched on the call. When he arrived, he told Cork the sheriff wanted to see both Kufus and Cavanaugh at the department as soon as possible. Cavanaugh stayed while the deputy filled out an incident report, but Cork offered to drive Kufus into town immediately. Cavanaugh told her to go ahead. He'd be in touch. Azevedo put the notes, the envelopes, and the knife into evidence bags and gave them to Cork to deliver to the sheriff. Then Cork and a taciturn Kufus took off for Aurora.

Dark had fallen, and a mist of stars covered the sky. Kufus sat silently on the far side of the Land Rover, and Cork could feel her anger.

"Mind if I ask a question?" Cork said.

"Would it matter?" Clearly she was still pissed. Maybe about the threats. Maybe about Cork's intrusion. Maybe about having to be chauffeured back to Aurora by a guy she didn't particularly like.

"What is it between you and Max?"

She looked out the window and up at the stars. "He knows I'm a swimmer, and he invited me out to swim in the cove."

"And to talk about mine business?"

"Yes," she said. "Mine business."

"That's why you were holding each other? Mine business?"

"It's not what you think."

"I haven't told you what I think."

"You're a man. I've spent my whole life in a business dominated by men. I know what men think."

"Men like Max Cavanaugh?"

"Max is different."

"How?"

She looked at him. "Are you really trying to get me to open up to you? Because if you are, you're doing a shitty job."

He kept his eyes on the road ahead, but he could feel her glare.

"Hell," she finally said, settling back. "Are you married?"

"I was. My wife died."

It had been well over a year, but the actual words still felt alien to him, and every time he was forced to say them, he wondered if they would ever come easy.

"I'm sorry," she said, her voice softening just a bit.

"Gauging by the rock and the gold band on your finger, I'd say you're married."

"To a wonderful guy named Steve, whom I love very much. Given what you're clearly assuming about me, you may not believe that."

"I don't know you well enough to assume anything about you."

Cork swerved to avoid a deer lurking at the edge of the road.

"Look, Max speaks highly of you, so I'm going to level," she said. "I knew him a long time ago. Before Steve. We were in graduate school together at Carnegie Mellon."

"You knew him well back then?"

"Very well."

"The one that got away?"

"I let him go. He made it clear from the beginning that he had no intention of ever settling down, having a family. And those were things I wanted very much."

"For two people who let go of each other a long time ago, you looked pretty cozy on the dock."

"We've stayed in touch over the years, okay? He needed to talk to someone about Lauren. It's tearing him up, and he doesn't have anyone here he feels he can confide in."

Cork said, "I appreciate what you're telling me."

"And I'd prefer it wasn't something you share with people."

"Worried about conflict of interest where Vermilion One is concerned?"

"The appearance of it. In my mind, there is no conflict of interest."

"Folks around here would give a whole lot to know your thinking about the mine right now."

"I still have a lot of mine to look at. I'm excellent at what I do. And fair. If it's a good site for nuclear storage, I'll say so." She was quiet again, then: "I have children, Cork. I have a home I love. I understand how people here must feel."

"But in the end, you have a job to do?"

"In the end, don't we all? And isn't a part of who we are about the integrity we bring to our work?"

It was a tough point to concede, but Cork understood exactly where she was coming from.

He delivered Kufus to the sheriff's office, along with the evidence bags. He stayed while Dross and Larson and Rutledge interviewed her.

As the two men drew their questioning to a close, Dross signaled Cork to follow, and they exited the interview room.

In the hallway, Dross said, "We got a preliminary indication from Agent Upchurch this evening. All the skeletal remains are female and, except for one, appear to be Native American. The one that isn't was the one with the bullet in her spine."

"Monique Cavanaugh," Cork said. "Mother and daughter killed with the same weapon. Curiouser and curiouser."

Cork escorted Genie Kufus back to her hotel. He walked her to her room, where she opened the door and allowed him inside to check the safety of her lodging.

"Lock your door," he said as he prepared to leave.

"See? Just like a man. Of course I intend to lock my door."

"Sorry," Cork said. "Habit."

"Are there any women in your life?"

"A couple."

"They haven't taught you anything, have they?"

"They've tried. Night," Cork said.

"Good night." Then she added, though it seemed to go against her better judgment, "Thank you."

She closed the door behind him.

He waited in the hallway until he heard the lock click.

SEVENTEEN

Much earlier that night, when he saw how things were going, Cork had called Judy Madsen and asked her to supervise the closing of Sam's Place. She'd agreed, though reluctantly, and had said, "You know, if I were a bona fide partner in this enterprise or, heck, owned the whole damn thing, I'd feel a lot better about this."

Cork had never before seriously considered taking her up on her offer, but that night he thought the unthinkable. He thought, *Maybe.*

At the house on Gooseberry Lane, he fed Trixie and walked her. Afterward he carted in the boxes he'd taken from Millie Joseph's room. He carried them to the office on the first floor, the office that had, for nearly twenty years, been his wife's, and he set them on the floor next to the desk. Then he stopped, caught in one of those moments that still ambushed him sometimes. He reached out and ran his hand along the polish of the desk, recalling the day Jo had bought the old antique. He remembered the overcast sky, the farm where the estate sale had been held, the look on his wife's face when she'd seen the desk that had been stored in the barn, covered with dust and strung with cobwebs. Somehow beneath that thick skin of neglect, she'd been able to see the beauty waiting to be rediscovered. She refinished the piece herself, over the course of the summer that she'd been pregnant with Stephen, and now, sometimes, when Cork's hand touched the wood, it was as if he was touching Jo's hand as well.

The moment set him to wandering. He left the office and walked the first floor, encountering apparitions. Trixie followed him, but only Cork saw the ghosts, which were the memories that haunted him and made him happy. They were his memories of being a father and husband. Memories of his children and Jo and him gathered around the dining room table for the pleasure of a thousand meals he'd thoughtlessly taken for granted. Of the games they'd played in the living room—Operation, Monopoly, Risk! Of wrestling with the kids when they were small enough and the girls not so worried about being girls. Of Jo and him on the sofa together in that quiet hour after Jenny and Anne and Stephen were asleep and before they themselves, wearied, had trudged upstairs to bed. Often in that sofa hour, Jo would slip her feet, cold always, under him for warmth.

So small and so precious, the moments lost to him now, lost to him forever except as the ghosts of memory.

He realized that he'd forgotten to eat, a chronic occurrence since Stephen had been gone and Cork had become responsible for feeding only himself. In a saucepan, he stirred together milk and Campbell's tomato soup, and when it was hot he crumbled in some crackers. He grabbed a cold beer to wash it down.

He returned to the office and ate at the desk while he checked his e-mails, hoping for word from his children. He wasn't disappointed. Jenny had sent him a short note updating him on a home painting project she and Aaron had undertaken. Anne had sent him a longer note. Her work in El Salvador was hard and the conditions were difficult and she was tired. But the bottom line was that she was doing what she felt she was meant to do and was happy. Nothing from Stephen. No surprise. Stephen was too busy having fun being a cowboy.

At last he turned to the boxes from Millie Joseph, boxes that contained more ghosts. Ghosts, Cork would discover, that he could never have imagined on his own.

He began to read his mother's journals.

July 22, 1946

I wasn't excited about the reunion in Chicago. My father's family are ruffians, for the most part, and I'm amazed that Mother seems to enjoy herself in their company. They call her "their darlin' squaw." If it were said by anyone else, Mother would lash them and not just with her able tongue. She calls them "ignorant Micks," an epithet that would land most folks

*flat on their back with a bloodied lip. But the men laugh and
toast her, and I have heard them say to my father that she's
the prettiest and smartest bit of skirt they've ever laid eyes on,
and how the hell did a four-eyed bookworm covered in chalk
dust ever manage to land such a prize?*

*Tonight at dinner a guy sat across from me. A little older
than me, I suspect. His name is William, although he goes
by Liam, and he's an O'Connor, too, the grandson of my
grandfather's brother, I've learned. I'm still trying to figure
out what iteration of relation that makes us. He said nothing
to me during the meal—it would have been hard, anyway,
to be heard above the hubbub—but his eyes kept finding me
and later he caught me outside, alone, enjoying the dusk.
He introduced himself and I was about to offer my name in
return when he said it wasn't necessary. He already knew
all about me. Attending teacher's college in Winona—on
scholarship, he said. I couldn't tell if he was making fun of that
or if it was something he saw as admirable. I told him he had
me at a disadvantage. He said, rather pleased, "Then I'm a
mystery to you." And I said, "Not so much as you imagine." I
looked him up and down and said, "You're a policeman. New
to the force. You have very little money and you live with
your parents. On Friday nights, you drink with your bachelor
friends. On Saturday, you play baseball. And on Sunday, you
go to Mass and pray that a pretty young colleen will be swept
off her feet by your blarney and favor you with a kiss." He
laughed and said, "And, sure, you're the answer to my prayer."*

*He is a handsome man, much too sure of himself. But
then, he got his kiss.*

The books were covered in leather, black or brown or red or green,
and the spaces between the printed lines were small, perfect for the
tight, precise script that filled them. The dates that headed all the entries began the year his mother had entered Winona Teachers College
in Winona, Minnesota. The first entry was simple:

September 14, 1943

*Away from home, at last! I feel like Dorothy at the door
to the farmhouse, with Oz awaiting me outside. Homesick?
A little. But I know that will pass. My roommate is named
Gloria O'Reilly. She's from St. Paul. Big city girl. We'll be the
best of friends, I can already tell.*

Mingled with the journal entries were poems, generally brief.

*The river bends to the strength of the hill
But does not from the conflict resign.
It shapes the rock with persistent will.
In both forces, beauty. In both, the divine.*

She had graduated in the spring of 1947 and taught sixth grade
for a year in Kittson County, in far northwest Minnesota, one of the
flattest places in the world. She'd been fond of saying that it may not
have been the end of the earth, but you could see the end from there.

In 1948, her father had become ill, very ill, and she'd returned to
Aurora to help with his care. In returning, she discovered that the
place she'd fled had changed, or that she had, and what she saw in the
North Country was both beautiful and divine. After her father passed
away, she stayed on with her mother in the small house in Allouette,
living with her mother's people and teaching in the one-room schoolhouse on the reservation that her parents together had founded.

In all that time, she'd been courted by the cheeky policeman from
Chicago named Liam O'Connor.

November 24, 1949 (Thanksgiving)

*Liam is asleep on the living room sofa. As I lie in my
own bed, I can hear his deep breathing. A gentle sound, but
with just a little forcefulness. That is Liam, yes. He's asked
again for me to move to Chicago. How can I? I find it an
odious place, full of noise and stockyard smells and too many
people living too closely together. I ask him, What's wrong
with Aurora? And he laughs. Backwater, USA, he calls it.
Hayseed City. But I know he likes it here. He gets on well*

with my mother's people, my people. He adores their humor.
They make light fun of him. "City boy," they call him. He
and Sam Winter Moon have become fast friends. They both
share a passion for baseball. Liam has told Sam if he ever
gets down to Chicago, they'll see the Cubs play.

In the spring of 1950, Liam O'Connor got a job as a deputy with the Tamarack County Sheriff's Department. He was one of a force of four. In August of that year, he married Cork's mother. With the G.I. Bill and his savings from his years as a bachelor cop in Chicago living with his parents, he made a down payment on the house on Gooseberry Lane. A little over a year later, Cork was born.

January 30, 1952
    Corcoran is a fussy baby, colicky. Liam's mother has told
me that Liam was that way, too. She advised putting him in a
basket and setting the basket on top of our washing machine
and letting the machine run. We did not have a washing
machine, but Liam bought one, used. And his mother was
right. It calms Corcoran immensely. Liam is a wonderful
husband. And even when Corcoran has been screaming for
hours, Liam doesn't lose his patience. He says it's the result
of years of having drunks and street punks scream at him in
Chicago. He says it reminds him of home. (Ha, ha.)

The journals were not in any order, and Cork spent a good deal of time organizing them chronologically. He'd meant to locate immediately the journal or journals written during the period of the Vanishings, but every time he opened one of the volumes, he discovered his parents and rediscovered his childhood.

November 16, 1956
    Cork's fifth birthday today. Mom baked Indian fry bread
and Sam Winter Moon supplied a venison roast. Henry
Meloux came and said that a naming ceremony was long
overdue. Hattie Stillday clicked away on her camera. Maybe

we'll end up in National Geographic, *alongside the giraffes
and emus and other exotics. Lots of friends from the rez, and
from town, too, though the two groups don't mingle well.
Liam, ever the grand host and proud father, was everywhere
with Cork on his shoulders, telling stories that kept our guests
in stitches. Everybody says that someday he should run
for office. Cork is a quiet boy, thoughtful. He watches, sees
everything, but he isn't a talker like his father. Liam was called
away in the middle of festivities. A bad accident on Highway 1
due to ice. I prayed for him and for those on the road.*

There were photographs slipped into the pages with this entry, clearly the work of Hattie Stillday. They were black and white, but not like the Kodak box photos his parents shot. They were taken with an eye that understood the nuances of light and shadow, that divined the drama of a human look. Cork was in one, a small child off to the side, watching a group of adults who surrounded his father. His little face was turned upward, hopeful, it seemed. But hopeful of what, Cork could not now say. There was another, of his mother, a beautiful woman whose hair was long and black (though he remembered that in the proper light you could see the scarlet tint that was a bit of her father's Irish red), caught leaning against a doorjamb with a cigarette in her hand and a laugh on her lips. Cork didn't remember his fifth birthday at all.

He glanced at the clock on Jo's desk—his desk now, he reminded himself—and was surprised to see that it was after midnight and he still hadn't found the journal entries that were of particular interest to him. He opened volume after volume and finally found one whose dates were promising.

June 15, 1964
   *Mom told me that Hattie Stillday's daughter, Abbie, has
run off and Hattie is heartbroken. Alcohol, Mom says. Hattie
tried to get her to Henry Meloux, but she refused to be
helped. And now she's gone. Where, no one knows. The Twin
Cities probably. Hattie's afraid Abbie will end up a prostitute
on Hennepin Avenue. She's called friends down in the Cities,*

asked them to keep an eye out for her daughter. So many are lost to us. So many.

June 26, 1964

Naomi Stonedeer has vanished. Simply vanished. Mom says she went to practice the Jingle Dance at the community center and never came home. Liam has begun an official investigation, though he believes she probably ran away, which is what some of the men on the reservation believe, too. I don't believe this, nor does Mother, nor does Becky Stonedeer. Naomi's only thirteen. She has no reason to run. Men are blind sometimes. Worse, they're stupid. And even worse, they don't listen to their hearts. In my heart, I know that Naomi is in grave danger. Cork is sick with worry. He's so fond of Naomi. And he's angry with Liam for suggesting the girl has run away. He's vowed that if Liam doesn't find her, he will.

July 10, 1964

It's been two weeks and Naomi is still missing. Liam has called authorities in the adjacent counties and in the Twin Cities. He's gone to Crosby to question Naomi's father, Corbett, whom we all called Fisheye when he was a kid because of his bulgy eyeballs. He's turned into a hard-drinking man, and he claims ignorance and innocence. Liam doesn't trust him, but he can't break Fisheye's story. I think Liam still believes that Naomi simply ran away, but he's doing his best, what he calls "due diligence," to make sure he's covered every possibility. A lot of white folks in Tamarack County think he's on a wild-goose chase and wasting both his time and public funds. He may be blind sometimes and stupid in the way of men, but he does listen to his heart. And in his heart he's committed to being a good and fair officer of the law, and that means doing everything he can to give Naomi Stonedeer a chance to be found.

Cork remembered that time. He remembered it differently, though. In his own recollection, his father was too cautious, too lax. Cork wanted him to crack someone's head, Corbett Stonedeer's for sure, to get answers. He recalled that, when his father finally brought an official end to the search, there'd been an angry confrontation. It was in the evening, on the front porch, when, long after dinner had gone cold, his father returned from the last day of that futile effort. Cork didn't recall now his exact words, but in no uncertain terms, he'd called his father a fraud. Liam O'Connor had stood there, taller by two heads than his son, and heard him out. And when Cork's frenzied sputtering had come to an end, his father had said—this, Cork remembered icy word for icy word—"I've done my level best. That's all I ask of anyone. That's all I expect anyone to ask of me." He'd moved toward the door, but Cork had blocked his way. His father had reached out, firmly threw his son aside, and gone in. For days after, they barely spoke to one another.

July 17, 1964

It hurts them both, I know, this silence. They walk past each other like strangers. Worse, like enemies. I've tried to mediate, but they hold to their anger fiercely. Liam refuses to discuss it with me. Cork listens but doesn't really hear. He's still a child, and his silence is understandable. Liam's refusal, that's just plain stubbornness. But, oh, he cares about his son's opinion of him. He loves Cork so much.

Cork put down the journal and stared at the far wall. Of course his father loved him. He knew that. And he'd loved his father. Their anger had passed eventually. Hadn't it?

August 12, 1964

Fawn is missing. We're all frantic. God, what's happening here?

That was the final entry of that particular journal volume. One line on the page, and when Cork turned that page, there was nothing more. But at one time, something more had been there. There'd been more pages. It was clear from the neat slivers left attached to the binding that someone had, very carefully, cut those pages out.

EIGHTEEN

Cork rummaged through the journals until he found one that began with the earliest date following the final entry of the volume whose pages had been removed.

> *September 17, 1964*
> *Fall is here and everywhere I look I see blood. It's in the color of the sumac and the maple leaves and the sky at sunset and at dawn. Henry Meloux is helping Hattie and Ellie and Mom and me. Liam walks like a man made of stone, cold and hard. Cork, ever the quiet, watchful child, sees and wonders but does not ask. Thank God.*

Cork scanned the other entries for September of that year. No mention of the missing five weeks between August 12 and September 17. No indication of what had occurred in that time, though he knew of two things from his own recollection and from the collective recollection of Tamarack County. The search for Fawn Grand was futile. And another woman had vanished, a white woman: Monique Cavanaugh.

It was nearly 2:00 A.M., and he was tired and confused. He turned out the lamp on the desk and headed for the door. Trixie rose from the carpet where she'd been sleeping and followed him upstairs. He readied himself for bed, laid himself down, and stared at the ceiling where light from the streetlamp outside, shattered by the leaves of the elm on his front lawn, lay scattered like shards of broken glass. His mind was a muddy swirl of too little information and too many questions.

He was afraid he wouldn't be able to sleep. But before he knew it he was dreaming.

His father stands at the edge of the flat rock, and behind him is the thunder of water. It seems familiar, this landscape. Mercy Falls, Cork thinks, watching from only a few feet away. There's laughter at his back. A party perhaps. He considers turning to see, but he can't take his eyes off his father, whose own eyes are locked on Cork. Is it anger in them? Disappointment? Confusion? Cork can't tell. His father opens his mouth as if to speak and at the same moment steps backward, losing his balance. He flails his arms, fighting to right himself, and Cork, in a terrible panic, reaches out for him, but his arm is not long enough, and his father plummets, vanishing into the gray mists of the falls.

And then it happens again. The whole scene replays. Only this time Cork stands outside the dream, watching himself in it as it unfolds. He sees, as he always does in this nightmare revisited, that his father does not simply lose his balance. He sees that it is his own small hand, reaching out, that pushes his father backward, sending him—surprised? disappointed? angry?—stumbling over the edge into oblivion.

The next morning, he was waiting at the door to the Aurora Public Library when it opened at 9:00 A.M. Maggie Nelson swung the door wide and greeted him with a smile. He went immediately to the cabinets that contained the microfilm archives of the *Aurora Sentinel*, which was the town's weekly newspaper. They also contained archived material from the *Duluth News Tribune* and several newspapers from the Twin Cities. He spent the morning reading every account about the investigation of what the reporters had dubbed "the Vanishings."

The reportage was basically the same in all of them. The Tamarack County Sheriff's Department was stumped. They'd asked for assistance from the BCA and later the FBI. The authorities believed—were certain—that foul play was involved, but they couldn't find any evidence. The victims had simply vanished, as if into thin air. There was no mention of the priest at St. Agnes and, except for Corbett Stonedeer, no indication of any suspects or persons of interest. The families were interviewed extensively, and their pain came through. Until Monique Cavanaugh disappeared, the white community of Tamarack County had been concerned mostly about the money and resources the sheriff's department was expending on the search for the two Ojibwe girls. The predominant white sentiment seemed to be that most likely the girls had simply fled the abominable conditions of the Iron Lake Reservation. The Ojibwe community was more tight-lipped, but those who spoke for the record had nothing good to say about Cork's father, whom they accused of being less than diligent in his investigation of the missing girls. Cork recognized the names of those quoted. Percy Baptiste. Bob Fairbanks. Arthur Skinaway. Shinnobs for whom, no matter what a *chimook* did, it was no good. The way the news stories were structured, however, made it sound as if the whole of the Anishinaabe people were aligned against Cork's father.

Once the white woman—a rich white woman—vanished, the white community's concern over misused law enforcement resources seemed to vanish as well.

Cork didn't know much about Monique Cavanaugh or the specifics of her disappearance, nor was he able to glean much from the newspaper coverage.

Monique Cavanaugh had been the only child of Richard and Agnes Goodell, wealthy Bostonians. She'd been raised much abroad and was well educated. She had apparently met Peter Cavanaugh in Boston while she was briefly home visiting her parents, and Cavanaugh was conducting business with Richard Goodell on behalf of the New York City office of Great North. They married a very short time later. They'd had two children, Max and Lauren. When Thomas Cavanaugh, Peter Cavanaugh's father, fell ill, the son moved his family from New York to Minnesota in order to assume the reins of Great North. Before their arrival, Thomas Cavanaugh built an elaborate home for his son on North Point. A year later, Thomas Cavanaugh died, and less than a year after that his daughter-in-law disappeared.

Cork paused. Judge Robert Parrant had lived on the North Point property so long that everyone called it the Parrant estate. But it had actually belonged to the Cavanaughs first. Cork had forgotten that little piece of history.

He read on.

By all accounts, Monique Cavanaugh had been an extraordinary woman: a wonderful hostess; an accomplished musician; a generous benefactor of numerous social causes, including the Ojibwe of the Iron Lake Reservation; a devout member of the St. Agnes parish; a loving wife; a doting mother.

On the night she disappeared, she'd gone to Duluth to attend a gala fund-raising event for a hospital charity. She'd left the event alone shortly after 10:00 P.M., intending to drive the two hours to Aurora rather than spend the night in a hotel in the port city. She never arrived home. No trace of her or of her automobile had ever been found.

Plenty of photographs of Monique Cavanaugh accompanied the news accounts. Hers was a face the camera loved. Cork found it uncanny how much her daughter, Lauren, resembled her.

His cell phone vibrated, and he picked up the call. It was Sheriff Marsha Dross.

"Are you available to come to my office now?"

"Sure. What's up?"

"You'll see when you get here."

NINETEEN

W hen he arrived at the Tamarack County Sheriff's Department and County Jail, Cork understood what Dross had meant with her cryptic parting comment. The parking lot was full of news vans. Clearly, the story of the bodies discovered in the Vermilion Drift had broken, and, like crows flocking to a carcass, the media had descended. Cork made his way inside and was buzzed through the security door. He found Dross, Larson, and Rutledge in council in the sheriff's office. Agent Susan Upchurch, the BCA's forensic anthropologist, was with them.

Cork took the only empty chair. "So," he said. "They know."

Dross gave a philosophic shrug. "We've been able to keep a lid on things for almost two days. I knew that sooner or later this would happen. I've scheduled a news conference for noon. Simon and I will handle it. But before we go in there, I'd like to know exactly where we stand with everything. Ed?"

Larson wore spectacles and was fond of sport coats with leather patches. His hair was neatly cut and just beginning to silver. He spoke in considered tones and had always reminded Cork of a college professor. He removed his spectacles and began cleaning them with a handkerchief he'd pulled from his back pocket.

"Using dental records, we've been able to establish the identity of all but one of the older victims," he said. "They are Monique Cavanaugh, Abigail Stillday, Fawn Grand, and Naomi Stonedeer. We believe, based on what Cork's found out, that the final victim is Leonora Broom, but we haven't been able to confirm it yet. The most recent victim has been positively ID'd as Lauren Cavanaugh. The medical examiner has determined her death was the result of a gunshot wound to the chest. We believe her mother, Monique Cavanaugh, was also the victim of a gunshot wound. Simon's forensic people have told us that the bullets that killed both women were fired by the same weapon. In the case of the daughter, powder tattooing on the skin indicates that the firearm was discharged at nearly point-blank range. We believe the murder took place somewhere else and the body was transported to the Vermilion Drift site, where it was hidden with the others. So far, we've been able to find no witnesses to Lauren Cavanaugh's murder. We can't find her car. We have no idea where the actual murder might have taken place. Currently, we have no suspects in any of the killings." He paused, thought a moment, then said, "I guess that's it for me."

Dross looked to BCA Agent Rutledge. "Simon?"

"I don't have anything to add," he said. "I'll defer to Susan."

All eyes settled on the forensic anthropologist.

"I haven't had time to do anything except a cursory examination of all of the remains," Upchurch said. She spoke slowly, and her words were drawn out slightly with her Alabama drawl. "With only bone left to us, it's difficult at this stage to speak with any certainty about cause of death. None of the victims show evidence of blunt trauma, nothing broken. Except for Monique Cavanaugh, all of them show clear evidence of sharp force trauma—bone cuts—that appear to be incised wounds, but the locations vary from victim to victim."

"Incised wounds?" Dross said.

"These would be from cuts or incisions rather than stab wounds. These marks tend to be longer than they are deep. But we have to be careful, because sometimes the teeth of scavengers leave the same kind of mark."

"Is there a reason why you believe these are from cuts and not from scavengers?" Dross asked.

"Scavengers large enough to leave marks would probably also have spread the bones around. The skeletons were all intact."

"Okay, so what would these wounds indicate?"

"If they are, in fact, knife wounds, then torture, perhaps. Or maybe something ritualistic. Two of the victims show cuts consistent with stab wounds on the left side of the thoracic cage, which might indicate a knife thrust to the heart." She paused and thought a moment. "That's really all I can say for sure at this time."

"Thanks, Susan," Dross said. "Cork?"

He could have told them that his father, the man responsible for the investigation of the Vanishings more than forty years earlier, knew about the hidden entrance to the Vermilion Drift. He could have told them he had an idea about the weapon that had been used to kill both mother and daughter, that there was a very good possibility it had once been his father's sidearm and had been his, too, but now it was missing. He could have told them that he'd found journals that should have contained a full and personal account of the final days of his father's investigation but someone had removed the pertinent pages. But how could he explain any of this?

He said, "Nothing to add, I guess."

"Any speculation on the connection between the Ojibwe women who were the early victims?"

Cork shook his head. "Leonora Broom and Abigail Stillday weren't identified as victims during the investigation in 'sixty-four, so they wouldn't necessarily have been missed. Most folks on the rez thought they'd simply run off. The vanishing of Naomi Stonedeer was the first to raise concern. She was a very young woman, well known, whose absence would be quickly noticed. The final Ojibwe victim, Fawn Grand, was a girl of simple mind and simple understanding—these days we'd call her challenged—and was probably way too trusting. She could easily have been enticed by almost anyone. But her disappearance certainly wouldn't have escaped notice. So, I haven't seen anything that ties them together, except their heritage."

"Someone who had a significant prejudice against the Ojibwe?" Larson asked.

"Maybe. But then how do you explain Monique Cavanaugh?"

"Exactly," Dross said.

"Has anyone looked at the old case files?" Upchurch asked.

"I'd love to," Larson said. "But we don't have any. The sheriff's department used to be housed in the courthouse. Back in 'seventy-seven there was a fire, destroyed a lot of our records. Right after that, the county built this facility."

"The BCA was involved though, right?" She looked to Rutledge. "You probably have files."

Rutledge looked a little sheepish. "I'll see what I can find."

"Finally," Dross said, "what's the connection between Lauren Cavanaugh and the Vanishings in 'sixty-four?"

"Why does there have to be a connection?" Larson asked. "The notes that Haddad's wife and Genie Kufus and Max Cavanaugh received pretty much indicated she was killed because of the mine."

"Or someone wants us to believe that's why she was killed," Rutledge said. "Whoever killed her knew about the other bodies, and the other bodies were there long before anyone proposed schlepping nuclear waste into Vermilion One."

Quiet descended. Through the opened window came the sound of media vehicles continuing to arrive for the news conference at noon.

Cork said, "Maybe Lauren knew something."

"Knew what?"

"Something about the Vanishings."

"How could she?"

Cork said, "The Parrant estate belonged to her father before it belonged to Judge Parrant. She spent some time there when she was a child."

"So?"

"I don't know. Maybe she found something when she moved back in. Or returning to the old place caused her to remember something."

"You're suggesting she was killed because of what she knew?"

"Just throwing mud against the wall to see what sticks, Ed," Cork said.

"All right. We need to interview her brother again with that possibility in mind," Dross said. "If she knew something, maybe he knows the same thing."

"Okay if I take that interview?" Rutledge asked.

Simon Rutledge was well known for his interviewing ability, especially when it came to coaxing a confession from someone. Among Minnesota law enforcement agencies, the particular effectiveness of his technique was known as "Simonizing." On a number of occasions during his time as sheriff, Cork had seen hardened criminals slowly bend during Simon's interviews and finally break.

"That's fine," Dross said. "Would you like one of my people with you?"

"I can handle it by myself, Marsha."

"He knows his mother was one of the victims in the Vermilion Drift?" Cork asked.

"Yes," Dross said. "I spoke with him at his home earlier this morning."

"How'd he take it?"

"Surprised. Stunned, actually. But not emotional, really. It was a long time ago."

"And Hattie Stillday?" Cork said. "Does she know about her daughter?"

"I've tried to reach her several times," Dross said. "Until I do, we'll refrain from making Abigail Stillday's name public. Same with the others."

"Mind if I track her down and deliver the news myself?" Cork said. "She's a family friend."

The sheriff thought it over briefly, then said, "I sent Azevedo out this morning to request her presence in my office, but he couldn't find her. If you can, and you're willing to deliver the news, all right. Just let me know when you've connected."

"She'll probably want to claim what remains of her daughter."

Dross said, "That'll be up to the BCA and Agent Upchurch."

Cork gave the agent a questioning glance.

"I can't say at this point. A week, maybe two," Upchurch replied.

"I'll tell her," Cork said. "What about Isaiah Broom?"

"What about him?" Larson said.

"His mother was probably one of the victims. He ought to know."

"When we're certain of that, we'll make sure he's informed. In the meantime, it would be best if you kept it to yourself."

"Sure," Cork said. "Are we done here?"

Dross waited for someone to say otherwise. "For now," she said. "By the way, Cork. Lou Haddad and his wife have taken a little vacation, and Kufus and her team are gone. The DOE pulled the plug on their assessment until all this gets sorted out."

"But Max Cavanaugh's still around?" Cork asked.

"Last time we checked," Rutledge said.

TWENTY

On his way to the rez to see Hattie Stillday, Cork made one stop first, at St. Agnes Catholic Church. He found the young priest in his office there, reading a baseball book, *The Boys of Summer*.

"When I was a kid," Father Ted Green said, marking his place with a strip torn from an old Sunday bulletin, "I wanted two things: to pitch for the Detroit Tigers and to win the Cy Young Award."

"What happened?"

The priest touched his collar. "Got called to play for another team with a manager you can't say no to. That, and I never could deliver a fastball worth squat. What can I do for you, Cork?"

Ted Green was a lanky kid, half a dozen years out of seminary. He'd taken a while to get his feet firmly on the ground with the parishioners of St. Agnes but had proven to be an able administrator, preached a pretty good homily, and represented the Church well in a time when much of the non-Catholic world was suspicious of the Vatican and its clergy. Cork quite liked the guy.

"I'm wondering how difficult it might be to track down one of the priests assigned to St. Agnes years ago, Ted."

"If he's still a priest, not hard."

"If he isn't?"

"More difficult but not impossible. Care to tell me who?" The priest arched an eyebrow and added, "And I wouldn't mind knowing why."

* * *

Hattie Stillday was famous and could have been wealthy, except that all her life she'd held to one of the most basic values of the Anishinaabeg: What one possessed, one shared. Hattie was a generous woman. Long before there was a Chippewa Grand Casino bringing in money to underwrite education for kids on the rez, she'd established the Red Schoolhouse Foundation, which helped Shinnob high school grads pay for college. She'd helped build the Nokomis Home and had begun the Iron Lake Indian Arts Council. She lived with her granddaughter, Ophelia, in the same small house in which she'd resided when her alcoholic daughter, Abigail, had run away four decades earlier and had never come home. Except that Abbie hadn't run away. Or if that had truly been her intention, she hadn't gone far.

Hattie had decorated her yard and home with artwork by other Indian artists, which she'd acquired over the years. On her lawn, never well kept and chronically crowded with dandelions, stood a tall, rusting iron sculpture meant to represent a quiver full of arrows. There was a chain saw carving, a great section of honey-colored maple topped with a huge bust of *makwa,* a bear. There were odds and ends that dangled and glittered and made music in the wind.

Cork knocked on the door and got no answer.

"Hey! Cork!"

He turned and spied old Jessup Bliss crossing the street. Because of his arthritic knees, Bliss walked slowly and with a cane.

"Lookin' for Hattie?" Bliss called out.

"I am, Jess."

Bliss walked up Hattie's cracked sidewalk.

"Sheriff's car was here earlier, looking for her, too, I guess."

"You tell them anything?"

"Cops? You kiddin'?"

"Know where she is?"

"Sure. Went over to see Henry Meloux, way early this morning. Ain't come back. Say, true what I heard? Buncha bones in that mine over to the south end of the rez? Buncha dead Shinnobs buried there?"

"It's true."

"Son of a bitch." Bliss spit a fountain of brown tobacco juice into the profusion of dandelions that yellowed Hattie's yard. "When'll white folks learn?"

"Learn what, Jess?"

"Us Indians are like them dandelions there. Don't matter what you do to get rid of us, we just keep comin' back."

Cork cut across the rez on back roads and parked at the double-trunk birch that marked the trail to Meloux's cabin on Crow Point. Hattie Stillday's dusty pickup was parked there, too. He locked the Land Rover and began a hike through the pines. He'd been down this path so often and was, at the moment, so lost in his thoughts that he didn't see the beauty of that place. Thin reeds of sunlight plunged through the canopy of evergreen, and if Cork had taken even a moment to see, he would have realized they were like stalks whose flowers blossomed high above the trees. A moment to listen and he'd have heard the saw of insect wings and the cry of birds and the susurrus of wind, which was the music of unspoiled wilderness. A moment to feel and he'd have been aware of the soft welcome of the deep bed of pine needles beneath his feet. But all the confusion, the bizarre nature of the puzzle he was trying to solve, made him deaf and blind.

Then he stopped, brought up suddenly in the middle of a stand of aspens by the intoxicating fragrance of wild lily of the valley, a scent that reached beyond his thinking. In the mysterious and immediate way that smell connects to memory, he was suddenly transported to a summer day nearly fifty years in the past.

He was walking the trail with his father, headed toward Meloux's cabin, feeling happy and safe. He recalled his father's long, steady stride. He remembered watching that tall, wonderful man float through shafts of sunlight, illuminated in moments of gold. And he remembered how his father had stopped and waited and lifted him effortlessly onto his broad shoulders, and they'd moved together among the trees like one tall being.

As quickly as it had come, the moment passed, and Cork found himself once again a man older than his father had ever been, alone on the trail. He stood paralyzed, wracked by terrible uncertainty. How could the man in that moment of golden memory have been the same man who knew about the hidden entrance to Vermilion One, whose sidearm had been a murder weapon, and yet who'd claimed bafflement at the Vanishings? How could he be the same man whom Cork, in his nightmares, had pushed again and again to his death?

Meloux wasn't at his cabin, but Rainy Bisonette was. She came to the door holding a book in her hand. She didn't seem particularly happy to see him. Meloux, she said, was with someone at the moment and couldn't be disturbed. Cork looked toward the rock outcroppings near the shoreline of Iron Lake and saw smoke rising beyond them. Without another word, he started in the direction of the smoke.

"Wait!" Rainy called. "Damn it, come back."

He found Hattie Stillday and Meloux sitting at the fire ring, burning sage and cedar. At his approach, they looked up, but neither of them showed any emotion.

"I'm sorry, Uncle Henry," Rainy said at Cork's back. "I couldn't stop him."

"Let him come," Meloux said. "What is it that cannot wait, Corcoran O'Connor?"

"I have something I need to tell Hattie."

"Then tell her."

Cork walked forward and knelt before the old woman. "Hattie, they've been able to identify most of the remains found in the Vermilion Drift. They're certain one of the victims is your daughter, Abbie."

Her look didn't change, not in the least. No surprise, no shock, not even the specter of sadness. And Cork realized that she already knew. How? Had Meloux, in that inexplicable way of knowing, understood the truth and revealed it to her? Had the news somehow reached the rez telegraph and traveled, as it often did, with unbelievable speed? Or—and this came to Cork in a sudden rush that nearly knocked him over—had she known from the beginning? Had Meloux?

"What's going on, Hattie?" She didn't answer and Cork addressed Meloux. "What the hell is going on, Henry?"

"You are intruding here, Corcoran O'Connor."

"I need answers."

"No, you want answers," Meloux said. "Need is a different animal."

"What are you hiding? What are you all hiding?"

Their eyes lay on Cork like winter stones.

"I'll find the truth, Henry, wherever it's hidden."

"The truth is not hidden, Corcoran O'Connor. It has never been hidden. You simply are not yet ready to see it."

"Jesus Christ. For once, can you cut all the mystic bullshit, Henry, and just tell me straight-out what's going on?"

"Leave," Meloux said, firmly but without harshness. "Your anger disturbs this place."

"Anger, Henry? You haven't seen my anger yet." Cork turned and began to march away.

"I have seen your anger," Meloux said at his back. "More than forty years ago I saw it in another man who was not yet ready to understand the truth."

Because he didn't care what Meloux had to say, Cork gave no sign that he'd heard. He walked away from the circle of stones, from the fire at its heart, from the cleansing smoke of the cedar and sage, and from the man who held to the truth like a miser to his money.

TWENTY-ONE

It was nearing sunset when Cork pulled into Ashland, Wisconsin, an old port city on Chequamegon Bay, a deepwater inlet of Lake Superior.

He parked in the lot of the Hotel Chequamegon and headed to Molly Coopers, the hotel's restaurant and bar. On the deck, which overlooked Lake Superior and was nearly empty, he spotted a man wearing a dark blue ball cap and a T-shirt that stretched tightly over twenty extra pounds of belly fat.

"Father Brede?"

The man looked up and smiled. "It's been just plain Dan Brede for more than four decades. You O'Connor?"

"Yes." Cork shook the man's hand and sat down. "Father Green didn't have any trouble locating you."

"I haven't tried to hide. From what Ted Green told me, you have some questions about the Vanishings. Nobody's asked me about the Vanishings in over forty years."

"But you haven't forgotten."

"A thing like that never leaves you."

"Then you wouldn't mind talking to me."

"I didn't say that."

"Did Father Green tell you that the women who vanished have been found? Or what remains of them."

"He told me."

"And did he tell you that there's been another, recent murder, and that the woman's body was hidden with the others?"

"Yes."

"And you don't want to talk about that?"

"I didn't say that either."

"What are you saying?"

"Have a beer," Brede said, signaling the waitress, who was already coming their way. "And then you can tell me about who you are."

Cork ordered a Leinie's and watched a big motor launch back away from its slip in the marina behind the hotel, swing around, and head north up the deep blue bay.

When his beer was delivered, Cork said to Brede, "You knew my parents, Liam and Colleen O'Connor."

"I remember them. And I remember you, too."

For Cork, the memory of the priest was fuzzy. He recalled a young man with a great deal more hair, and it hadn't been gray. Brede had been thin then, Cork remembered.

"In the year I knew you, you were a lot of trouble," the ex-priest said.

"Trouble?"

"You have any idea how much your mother prayed for you? And your father?"

This caught Cork off guard. He didn't remember being a problem to them at all. "Not really."

Brede smiled and shrugged. "Doesn't surprise me. Kids, teenagers especially, are clueless."

"You work with kids a lot?"

"Over the years. And I have two of my own."

"You said you haven't been Father Brede for over forty years. You stopped being a priest not long after the Vanishings then."

"A year after I was yanked from St. Agnes."

"Yanked?"

"The Church reassigned me. To a little parish in southern Indiana where nobody cared or really even knew about the Vanishings. Two things about it bugged me. That I was found guilty without a trial and without any chance to defend myself. And that, finding me guilty, they simply reassigned me. I'm not sure which trespass of conscience I objected to more."

"Will you tell me about the Vanishings, what you remember?"

"Why are you interested? I understand that you were a cop once, like your father, but you're not anymore. Ted Green said that you're a private investigator. Who are you working for?"

"The Tamarack County Sheriff's Department. As a consultant."

"They know you're here?"

"Is that important?"

He laughed. "People who have something to hide often respond to a question with a question. What is it that you're hiding, O'Connor?"

"There are aspects of this case, old and new, that are very personal for me. Although I intend to share everything I find with the sheriff and her investigators, I need to put a few things in perspective for myself first. I think my father knew more about the Vanishings than he officially revealed."

"I know he did. For one thing, he knew about me."

"Why didn't he say anything?"

"Most people who know about his silence believe it was out of loyalty or respect for the Church."

"But it wasn't?"

He shook his head. "He knew I was innocent."

"How?"

"Your father was an astute judge of character."

"That's it?"

Brede laughed and took a swallow of beer. "You're a cop all right. You require evidence."

"My father was a cop, too. A good cop. I'm sure he asked for evidence."

"He did. And I explained to him that I knew who'd planted the items that had incriminated me but that I couldn't reveal the name."

Cork said, "Because it was something you'd learned in confession?"

"The sanctity of which I firmly believed in then."

"And now?"

"Now I'm a Methodist," he said.

Cork drank from his own glass and waited. The ex-priest eyed the still water of the bay for a minute, then told his story.

At first the woman came to him in the normal way, confessing sins he'd heard before and for which he was fully prepared emotionally. An unclean thought. A coveting. A harmless lie to her husband.

Hail Marys, he instructed her, and to pray for strength to resist these small temptations. He knew full well who she was. In a small parish, he knew the voices of all those who entered the confessional. As time went on, the sins she confessed began to change. They became darker, more disturbing. Sex with men other than her husband. Sex with women, too. Sometimes with both at once.

"Did you believe her?" Cork asked.

He didn't know what to think. Surely there was no reason to lie about these things, especially for a woman in her particular position. He took her seriously and advised her to pray and to seek God's guidance, and when that didn't work, he urged her to seek professional help. She laughed at him, laughed seductively. And then she began the overtures. She often thought about them together, she said. She fantasized him forcing himself upon her in ways that disgusted him. He instructed her to banish such thoughts, but she swore she couldn't. The images overwhelmed her and she masturbated thinking of them. This was beyond his ability to deal with, spiritually and emotionally.

The priest looked into the empty distance above the lake and shook his head. "The oddest part of it was that I saw her every Sunday in church, and she spoke to me cordially during our social hour afterward, and it was as if she'd never said any of those foul things to me in the confessional."

Then she threatened him. She said if he didn't have sex with her, she'd make him sorry. And very soon after that, the anonymous phone call had been made, and the incriminating items had been found. Although he couldn't prove it was her, he knew that it was. Everything that had gone on, however, had been framed within the context of the confessional and her confessions, and he truly believed that he was bound to a sacred vow of silence. And the woman, if her name were made public, was so well thought of that he couldn't be certain anyone would even believe him. So he'd said nothing. Yet Cork's father had somehow divined his dilemma and had done his best to manipulate the public information so that the priest was never a part of the official investigation.

"How did he know?" Cork asked.

"Got me. He never said. But he saw to it that I was removed from the parish. Which," Brede added philosophically, "was better for everyone in the long run."

Cork said, "You've carefully avoided telling me the name of the woman."

"I thought you might have guessed by now."

Cork said, "A woman in, as you said, a particular position. Someone well thought of. Someone relatively new to the parish, I'm guessing. Young, intelligent, devious and deviant but able to hide it well, so probably sociopathic or maybe even psychopathic. Someone who, apparently, caused no problem for the priest who replaced you, Father Alwayne, who everyone said looked like Cary Grant. Which means that either Cary Grant wasn't her type or she ended her behavior toward priests or, most likely, she herself was removed from the scene. Given all that, Monique Cavanaugh would be my guess."

The former priest lifted his beer and said, "Cheers."

TWENTY-TWO

Cork reached Aurora shortly before midnight. During the three-hour drive from Ashland, he'd examined everything he knew so far.

More than forty years earlier, four Ojibwe women had been abducted and murdered and their bodies concealed in an abandoned drift of the Vermilion One Mine. Monique Cavanaugh had also been abducted and murdered, and her body had been hidden in the drift with the others. Some Ojibwe undoubtedly knew about the secret entrance to the drift. According to Henry Meloux, Cork's father also knew.

Two of the Ojibwe women were eager to leave the rez, and that may have contributed to their abduction. Two of the Ojibwe were quite young and vulnerable, and their naïveté might have allowed them to be easily duped. The white woman was an outlier. So far as Cork knew, she was neither eager to quit Tamarack County nor naïve. But she was abnormal, to say the least, in her behavior. And it was the kind of abnormal that could easily have put her at risk.

Because he was a cop, Cork's thinking had been shaped in a way that made him skeptical of coincidence and always on the lookout for connections, no matter how thin they might appear to be at first. As a result, he found himself considering another possibility where Monique Cavanaugh was concerned. She'd been a woman with bizarre sexual proclivities. Worse than bizarre. Her behavior with the priest had been not only heartless but criminal as well. Could her appetites have been even more unsavory? Given the timing, could she also have been somehow involved in the Vanishings?

Cork let himself think along this line for a while and saw a problem. Although he couldn't say about the first two victims, the second two—Naomi Stonedeer and Fawn Grand—had disappeared from the rez itself. If Monique Cavanaugh had been on the rez, trolling for vulnerable young women, she'd have been seen. A beautiful, rich white woman would have stood out like a polar bear. So how could she have snatched the girls without raising an alarm?

The only answer that made sense to Cork was that if Monique Cavanaugh was, indeed, involved, she wasn't working alone. Whoever took the girls was probably someone who would have gone unnoticed on the rez.

Cork thought about all the people he knew on the Iron Lake Reservation, and that was almost everyone. He couldn't think of many he'd call saints, but he also couldn't think of anyone alive at the moment and old enough to have been involved in the Vanishings who struck him as deeply predatory. He didn't know the history of the rez well enough to be able to finger a suspect from the past.

But there was someone he did know who, in his consideration of all the possibilities, he couldn't overlook. And that was his father.

Liam O'Connor had been a regular visitor to the reservation, most often as a relative or friend rather than in his official capacity as sheriff. He could easily have come and gone without much notice at all. The priest had said that Cork's father had somehow intuited his dilemma. Perhaps an intuitive understanding wasn't the reason. Maybe the reason stemmed from his father's deep involvement in the Vanishings. Involvement with Monique Cavanaugh herself, perhaps. It was, after all, probably his weapon that had killed the woman. Was it possible that, in the way she'd tried to seduce the priest, Monique Cavanaugh had succeeded in casting her seductive net over his father?

Cork arrived home thinking all these things and hating himself for it.

He took Trixie for a long overdue walk under a moon that was waning. And as they walked in the night shadows, he kept circling the facts in his head, jabbing at them, hoping he could get them to reveal the truth.

His father knew about the second entrance to the Vermilion Drift. His father had the unique ability, because of his position as sheriff, to make certain that any investigation could be thwarted. Someone had torn important pages from his mother's journal. Henry Meloux and Hattie Stillday held some damnable secret. Someone was being protected, it was clear. Or the memory of someone.

For most of Cork's life, his father had existed as a memory, an accumulation of memories. But memories were unreliable. Cork understood well that, although they came from the fabric of fact, more often than not his own were a weave of the way things had been and the way he desired them to be. His father had died in the fall, not long after the Vanishings had ended. Cork was only thirteen years old. Was the man he had always believed his father to be simply the construct of a boy's desire and a boy's imagination?

When he pulled the box from the attic, it was layered thinly with dust. He took it to the office downstairs, switched on the desk lamp, and sat down. He removed the lid. Inside, jumbled without any order, were dozens of family photographs his mother had kept with the idea that someday she would organize them into scrapbooks. She'd never quite gotten around to it, and, after her passing, they'd fallen to Cork. It had been a good long while since he'd handled the photos, always a nostalgic experience. This time he was concerned that the experience would be different.

His father hadn't been a handsome man, but in the photographs he was always smiling and there was something boyishly charming in his aspect. Cork picked up a photo of his father in his youth in Chicago, a black-and-white of a boy, maybe nine years old, squinting into the sun and grinning big, with a ball glove on his right hand. In the background was a vacant lot and in the distance, miragelike, the city skyline. Cork recalled his father talking about his boyhood, and although it had been in the days of the Depression, he'd spoken of that time with warmth. There was a photograph of his father in an army uniform. He'd served in the 82nd Airborne Division and had been wounded at the Battle of the Bulge. He'd kept the Purple Heart in the top drawer of his dresser. There was a photo of him holding a baby who was Cork. Although memory could lie, photos seldom did, and it was abundantly clear how proud and happy a father he was. There were photos with his deputies and his friends on and off the rez. There were photos with Cork's mother and with Cork—camping and fishing and picnicking. In them all, his father was a man clearly happy with his life and surrounded by people who looked on him with admiration and love.

Could the man in those photographs have fooled his family and his friends all his life? Could there have been a dark depravity to him that he ably hid? Cork tried very hard to accept the possibility, but it simply didn't fit. It felt so god-awful wrong, not only in his own memory but in all the evidence he had from the memories of others and from the photos in the box.

His father had not been the one responsible for the abductions of those young women from the rez almost fifty years before, but there was something about his father's involvement in the Vanishings that was necessary to keep hidden. What could that have been?

And if his father had not made those women vanish, who had?

TWENTY-THREE

Max Cavanaugh agreed to see him, and, at 9:30 the next morning, Cork was shown into Cavanaugh's very large office by an administrative assistant, a young man whose round glasses made him look like Harry Potter. Cork shook hands with Cavanaugh, who turned to Harry Potter and said, to Cork's great amusement, "Coffee for both of us, Harry."

"Is that really his name?" Cork asked after the young man had left.

Cavanaugh shook his head. "It's Howie, but no one calls him that. He's okay with the Potter thing. Sit down."

They took cush chairs near the window, which overlooked the great red wound that was the Ladyslipper Mine. Cork began with a condolence, sympathy over the news that Cavanaugh's mother was one of the bodies found in the Vermilion Drift.

"It was a long time ago," Cavanaugh replied. "But it does answer a question left hanging in the air all my life."

"What do you remember about your mother?" Cork asked.

"Not much. I was only five when she disappeared." He caught and quickly edited himself. "When she was murdered."

"Do you have any early impressions?"

"Of course. But why are you asking?"

"I'm just trying to build a profile of all the women involved in the Vanishings. The more we know about the victims, the better chance we have of understanding the crime." He wasn't proud of himself, stringing Max along this way, but he also knew he couldn't simply blurt his suspicions.

Cavanaugh thought a moment. "She was beautiful. Smart. Vivacious."

Which were things people said about her, but was that the way a five-year-old would have remembered her?

"Was she an attentive mother?" Cork asked.

"Attentive?"

"Do you have a lot of memories of doing things with her?"

"Not really. But as I said, I was only five. And she was a very active woman in community affairs."

"That was certainly true in Aurora. What about before you moved here?"

"I don't remember anything before Aurora."

"Your parents lived in New York City after they were married, is that right?"

"My father was an attorney for the Great North office there. It's where I was born, and Lauren. When my grandfather became ill, we moved back here."

"What about after your mother's disappearance? Where did you go?"

"My father returned to New York City and raised us there."

"And turned management of Great North over to others?"

"Yes, it ceased being the family-run operation my grandfather had hoped to continue. It wasn't at all a bad decision. From New York, my father helped expand Great North into a global concern."

"Why New York City? Couldn't he have accomplished the same thing here?"

"Although he was born on the Range, he didn't really feel at home here. He was a city guy at heart."

"What about you, Max? You've worked mines in India, South Africa, Australia, Germany, Chile. You feel at home here?"

"The truth is I never feel at home anywhere except in a mine. I love the work of mining, Cork. It's a battle of sorts, and involves all kinds of strategy to get the rock to release what it holds. Done well, it's an art."

"From what you've told me, you don't spend much time in the pit these days," Cork pointed out. "Why'd you come back here to take an office job? I mean why now?"

"The economy," he said with a shrug. "It's lousy, and making this mine profitable—hell, making any mine on the Range profitable these days—is a challenge, but it's one I'm good at. Second, when I learned that the DOE was interested in Vermilion One, I figured I wanted to be here to oversee that process personally. Honestly, I felt I had an obligation to do what I could to discourage the government. The Range has been good to my family. And I feel my family has an obligation to the people here. I don't want what we created with Vermilion One to end up the death of this place or these people. Literally."

"What about your sister?"

"What about her?"

"Did she love mining?"

Cavanaugh looked surprised at the question. "She knew absolutely nothing about mining."

"But as nearly as I can tell, she followed you everywhere, to every mine location, and finally here. Any particular reason?"

"We were close all our lives," Cavanaugh said. "Neither of us were married, and really we only had each other."

It was a closeness that seemed more than a little unusual to Cork, but he let it go.

"Did your father ever talk about your mother?"

"No. At least not that I recall."

"Did that trouble you?"

"Why should it?"

"No reason. Did he remarry?"

"No."

"He was still a young man, relatively speaking, when he lost your mother, yet he went the rest of his life without marrying again. Any reason that you're aware of?"

There was a knock at the door, and Harry Potter returned with coffee: two white mugs on a tray with a small container of cream, a little bowl of sugar, some packets of Splenda, two spoons, and a couple of napkins.

"Thank you, Harry," Cavanaugh said, and the young man left.

Cavanaugh handed Cork a mug, then stirred cream and sugar into his own coffee.

"What do you know about my father, Cork?"

"I'm beginning to think not enough."

"For starters, he wasn't exactly the son my grandfather wanted."

"Why not?"

Cavanaugh sipped his coffee, then said casually, "For one thing, he was homosexual."

Cork didn't bother to hide his surprise.

"I'm not telling you any secrets. Most people who knew him in later life were well aware of it. But he hid it well in his early years here. Hell, he probably didn't even acknowledge it to himself then. The war broke out and he enlisted, and after that he went to college, Yale and then Harvard Law, and by that time his life and what he was willing to accept had changed, I guess. New York City was a reasonable place to be gay in the fifties. But he still needed a good cover for the sake of business and my grandfather. My mother gave him that cover."

"She knew?"

"Of course."

"But they had children."

"To keep the families happy and at bay and to maintain the façade."

"Did you always know?"

"No. They had separate bedrooms, but I was a kid then, and what did I know? They also had very separate lives, but I don't suppose that was unusual either. My father was a good man, Cork, and a good father. He loved Lauren and me tremendously."

"And your mother?"

"Love wasn't at all what their relationship was about."

"I meant did she love you."

"I think we were like expensive vases in the living room, something for people to look at and admire, part of a perfect life. Or the image of a perfect life."

"But it wasn't perfect?"

"What I remember wasn't awful. It was just"— he thought a moment —"a vacancy. Air where a mother should have been. But why all these questions about my parents? That's ancient history. What about Lauren? Shouldn't you be asking questions that will solve her murder?"

"Your mother and your sister were killed with the same weapon. That would tend to suggest they were killed by the same person. So, if we could solve the earlier murder we might solve your sister's murder as well. Theoretically."

Cork didn't necessarily believe his own logic, but he hoped it sounded plausible and would keep Cavanaugh answering the questions that concerned him most at the moment.

"Do you have any family memorabilia from that period?" Cork asked. "Photographs, letters, journals?"

"What good would that do?"

"I won't know until I've had a chance to see the things," Cork replied.

"No," Cavanaugh said firmly. "Nothing."

"What about from the time before your folks moved here?"

"Not then either."

"After?"

Cavanaugh said, "I have some things in storage at home. I suppose I can look and see what's there."

"So these would be items your father kept after your mother disappeared?"

"That's right."

"He kept nothing from before that, from his time in Aurora and all the earlier places?"

"Not that I'm aware of."

"Wedding photos?"

"I told you, nothing."

"Even though it wasn't a marriage in the usual sense, Max, doesn't that seem odd to you?"

Cavanaugh considered Cork's question and appeared to be surprised. "You know, I never thought about it. Or if I did, I suppose I just figured that it was all too painful and he simply wanted to forget."

"So he never talked about her and you never asked?"

Cavanaugh folded his arms on his desk and leaned toward Cork. "My father was in the war, World War Two. Whenever I asked him if he'd killed any Germans, he would always reply, 'I shot at a lot of them.' It was clear he didn't want to talk about it. Whenever I asked him about my mother, he'd say, 'Why try to remember what's best forgotten?' In its way, it was, I suppose, the same response." Cavanaugh sat back and said with a sigh, "I'll look through the things I have and see what I can come up with, all right?"

"I'd appreciate it, thanks." Cork put his mug down. He realized he hadn't taken a single sip. "Max, your sister's death has opened a lot of wounds. I'm sorry that it seems like all I do is pour in salt."

Cavanaugh turned away, swiveling in his chair, and stared out the window toward the great wound that bled iron. He was quiet a long time, and Cork realized it was because he simply couldn't speak. The weight of Cavanaugh's sadness was undeniable, as if every breath the man exhaled filled the room with suffocating grief.

"You want to know the truth, Cork?" His voice broke as he spoke. "I feel as empty as that hole out there. I didn't know anything could hurt so much."

"I understand, Max. My own experience has been that, as cliché as it sounds, time will help you heal."

Cavanaugh swung back to him. "First I need to know who killed her. Then I can start healing."

Millie Joseph sat in her wheelchair on the porch of the Nokomis Home with a lap blanket spread across her knees. From there, she could see much of Allouette, the town where she'd lived all of her eighty years, and beyond Allouette the wide, cool blue of Iron Lake, sparkling under the noonday sun. The air was full of the scent of late-blooming lilac, and Millie Joseph looked perfectly content and seemed absolutely delighted to see him.

"It's been a long time, Corkie." Like Hattie Stillday, she called him by the nickname all his mother's friends had used.

Only two days, Cork thought, but it was obvious that his last visit wasn't there at all in the perfectly clear sky of her memory.

"Millie, I'd like to ask you some questions about my mother's journals and about the people on the reservation many years ago."

"When I was a child, the government didn't want us to speak our own language here. Did you know that, Corkie? But your grandmother said hogwash. And she taught Ojibwemowin to the children in her school. Your grandmother was a strong woman."

"Yes. And a woman much loved." Cork leaned against the porch rail. "Someone cut out pages from my mother's journals, Millie. Do you know who?"

"Oh, Corkie, I know I should have looked at everything she gave me, but I never had the time. If something's missing, well, I suppose it was your mother's doing. Everybody's got things in their past they don't want folks to know, don't you suppose?"

"I suppose," Cork agreed. "Millie, was there someone on the reservation when you were a young woman who was not so well loved? Someone you were warned against?"

"Mr. Windigo," she said darkly and without hesitation. "Oh, I used to be scared of him. We were always warned about Mr. Windigo."

She was speaking, Cork assumed, of the creature out of Ojibwe myth. In the stories the Ojibwe told, the Windigo was a cannibal giant with a heart of ice. It had once been a man but had become a monster that loved to feast on the flesh of the unwary—children especially. It was often used in much the same way white people employed the bogeyman, to frighten children into obedience.

"Was there a man or a woman that people on the rez stayed away from?"

"We didn't like everyone, but we were all Shinnobs and neighbors and got along. Some people were afraid of Henry Meloux. They called him a witch. The government doctors tried to tell us that. Henry a witch," she said with a dismissive laugh.

Meloux. He knew he should be talking with Henry, but his old friend had made it clear that Cork was on his own.

"And Mr. Windigo, of course," the old woman added. "There were all kind of stories about Mr. Windigo snatching kids."

"When Fawn disappeared, did my mother or my aunt talk to you?"

"Your mother always talked to me."

"Did she talk about Fawn?"

"Of course." Millie Joseph smoothed her lap blanket. "And she talked about Mr. Windigo."

"Did she think the Windigo had something to do with the Vanishings?"

"She knew he did."

Cork was confused. Why would his mother blame a mythic beast for a real disappearance?

"She was awfully sad, your mother. Your aunt, too. We all were. And scared, because who would be next?"

"But the next to vanish was a white woman. And she was the last."

"Oh, we were all very happy about that."

"That the white woman vanished?"

"That she was the last Mr. Windigo took."

"Did you know her, the white woman the Windigo took?"

"Sure. From St. Agnes."

"Did you know her well?"

"Not well, no."

"What did you think of her?"

"She was rich." Which clearly was not a good thing to Millie Joseph. "Your mother knew her better."

"What did my mother think of her?"

"Your mother used to say that she was a woman like a snowshoe rabbit. In the winter, she would be white, in the summer dark."

"What did she mean?"

"A woman who was two women, I guess."

And one was light and one was dark, Cork thought.

"After the white woman vanished, what did my mother say?"

Millie thought awhile and her hands twitched. "Why, I don't think she said anything, except what the rest of us said. That it was good Mr. Windigo wasn't lurking around the rez anymore."

An old pickup cruised past on the street and the driver, Ben Cassidy, lifted his hand and called out, "*Boozhoo,* Millie! Cork!"

She waved back and said, "We found his truck."

"Whose truck?"

"Mr. Windigo. We found it half-sunk in a bog way south on the rez."

"The Windigo drove a truck."

"You keep saying 'the Windigo.' I'm not talking about the Windigo. I'm talking about *Mr.* Windigo."

"He was a man?"

"Of course he was a man. His name was Indigo. That's how he got the name we called him."

"Tell me about him."

"He was tall and thin like a broomstick. Had eyes like black fire. Whenever he looked at me, I burned and got cold at the same time. I didn't like that man."

"Was Indigo his only name?"

"No, he had a last name. It was perfect for him, because it was exactly what he looked like, a broomstick. His name was Indigo Broom."

TWENTY-FOUR

He found Isaiah Broom among the protesters at the gate to the Vermilion One Mine, although, in truth, Broom wasn't exactly "among" the protesters. He'd separated from them and stood blocking the progress of a huge pickup truck that belonged to Great North Mining Company and that was trying to reach the gate. Cork pulled off the road, parked, and, as soon as he got out, he could hear the heat of the discussion.

"You're women, but you work for a company that rapes the earth," Broom challenged.

"You're a man, but you're going to be dickless if you don't move out of our way" came a reply from inside the cab.

That was followed by another from the cab: "Hell, he's probably already dickless, Bobbi."

Cork knew the voices. The Noon sisters, two women no man in his right mind would cross. Not only was Broom in contempt of the restraining order, but he was baring his chest to she wolves.

Before Cork reached the pickup, the women had opened their doors and stepped out. Kitty Noon held a baseball bat. Bobbi Noon gripped a tire iron. They both were dressed basically the same: faded jeans, work boots, ball caps, and denim shirts with the sleeves rolled high enough because of the heat to show impressive biceps. In the glare of the midday sun, they faced Isaiah Broom, a wall of a man.

"We're just a couple of peace-loving females, Broom. And right now we'd love nothing more than a piece of you," Bobbi said.

Broom didn't give an inch, and Cork had to admit those dark Shinnob eyes showed no glimmer of fear. In Broom's place, Cork would've been thinking about the state of his health plan.

"Lunch is just about over," Kitty said. "A couple of minutes from now, we've got to punch back in. Got work to do on the other side of that gate. Every second we're late you pay for, Broom, one way or another."

"Hey, Kitty. Broom doesn't get out of our way, what do you say we make him our afternoon work? Maybe use him as fill for a pothole or something."

The two sisters laughed.

Broom said, "You can do violence to me. That would be a small crime. But the violence to Grandmother Earth is another kind of crime. And the violence a nuclear waste dump would do to generations after us, that's the greatest crime of all."

Kitty laid the bat over her shoulder and looked like a hitter waiting her turn at the plate. "We're not arguing your point, Broom, just your tactic. You're not winning yourself or your cause any friends by keeping a couple of breadwinners from jobs that put food on the table."

"You got a problem with dumping nuclear waste here, fine," Bobbi said. "The idea doesn't exactly make me do somersaults. But our work has nothing to do with that. So kindly step aside and let us pass."

Broom stood his ground. "If not us, who?" he said, more to the crowd than to the sisters. "If not now, when?"

"You know, you're beginning to piss me off," Kitty said and unshouldered her bat.

The gathering of protesters clearly didn't know which side to root for: Broom, big as a bear, or the two women, tornadoes in tight jeans.

Cork approached on foot and said, "Isaiah, you don't stand aside, you're in contempt of the restraining order."

"And who'd blame us for kicking your ass?" Bobbi said.

Broom crossed his arms over his chest. "I'm willing to be arrested for doing the right thing."

"Nobody doubts that, Isaiah," Cork said. "But why not save that move for when the big trucks roll up carrying the nuclear waste? It'll get a lot more play in the media than a confrontation with two women."

Kitty turned on Cork. "You saying we don't count?"

Bobbi said, "Relax, Kitty. He's on our side."

Cork said, "I'm not taking sides here. I'm just saying consider which battles you fight, Isaiah. You really want the news story to be that you got knocked around by a couple of working females just trying to put food on the table for their families?"

"Let 'em pass," one of the protesters hollered.

Broom held his ground for a moment more, then lowered his arms and stepped out of the way.

The two sisters started back to the pickup.

"Thanks, Cork," Bobbi said.

Kitty still looked pissed. "You ever insinuate that women don't count in a confrontation, I'll shove this ball bat up your ass, understand?"

"I read you loud and clear, Kitty."

"Good," she said. She opened the driver's door, threw the ball bat inside, and said over her shoulder to Cork, "Next time we see you at the Buzz Saw, your beer's on us."

The sisters slammed the doors shut. The engine kicked over, and the big pickup rolled through the front gate.

"Got a minute, Isaiah?" Cork asked.

"Fuck you, O'Connor." Broom started back to join the other protesters.

"I have a question about one of your relatives. Indigo."

That stopped Broom in his tracks. He turned to Cork and, for a Shinnob, showed an unseemly amount of emotion.

"Why the hell are you asking about *him*?"

A car approached on the highway where the two men stood. It gave a little warning honk.

"Let's talk over there." Cork pointed toward his Land Rover.

They cleared the asphalt, and the car drove past. The protesters settled back into their canvas chairs or returned to quiet conversations in small groups. Cork walked to his Land Rover with Broom fuming at his side.

"You ever mention that name again and I'll beat you within an inch of your life," Broom swore.

"He was a relative of yours, right?"

"My mother's cousin. What's it to you?"

"According to Millie Joseph, he disappeared about the same time the Vanishings ended."

"So?"

"Just wondering if there might have been some connection."

"Between him and the Vanishings?" Broom seemed genuinely surprised but not offended.

"Isaiah, has the sheriff talked to you about the remains they found in the Vermilion Drift?"

"What about 'em?"

"They've positively identified all but one of the bodies. The one still remaining? I think there's a good chance it's your mother."

"My mother?"

"Millie Joseph told me your mother disappeared just before the Vanishings began. Everyone thought that she'd taken off, abandoned you. I believe that wasn't true. I believe she was one of the first victims. And I believe that Indigo Broom may have had something to do with it."

Broom was stunned to silence. He stood there, a big man with his mouth open.

Cork went on. "Millie Joseph called Indigo Broom 'Mr. Windigo.' She told me he was a man folks on the rez avoided. Did you know him?"

Now Broom's mouth closed and his eyes became hard as fists. "I knew him," he said, his lips barely moving.

"What happened to him?"

"He left."

"And went where?"

"I didn't care."

"Did anyone ever say?"

"No. And no one gave a shit."

"Not even his family?"

"Family? He fed on family."

"What do you mean?"

Broom looked at Cork. "We called him Mr. Windigo, too."

"Was he the kind of man who could have made those women disappear?"

Broom said, "I've talked enough." He turned his back on Cork and began to walk away.

"Isaiah," Cork called after him. "Are you responsible for the graffiti in the mine?"

Broom stopped and turned back.

Because the second entrance to the Vermilion Drift was on the rez, Cork had felt strongly from the beginning that a Shinnob was responsible. Although Cork's question had been a shot in the dark, Broom's reaction made him think he might have hit the mark.

"Which would mean you knew about the other way into the mine. Did you know about the remains?"

Broom walked slowly back and stood looking down into Cork's face. The big Shinnob cast enough shadow that it completely swallowed Cork.

"I know nothing about those bodies down there. As for the graffiti, if I had anything to do with it, which I didn't, I'd know that tunnel was about the most evil place on earth."

Broom left, taking his huge shadow with him.

TWENTY-FIVE

Given what Cork now knew, he believed that Isaiah Broom's long-lost relative, Indigo, was a very likely suspect in the disappearance of the women on the Iron Lake Reservation more than forty years earlier. It struck him as odd that Indigo Broom's name had never been mentioned during the investigation Cork's father had conducted. Cork had made the connection with relative ease. Why hadn't his father? Or the other people on the rez?

He thought about these things as he drove back to Aurora, and before he reached the town limits, he'd arrived at some very speculative conclusions.

Indigo Broom and Monique Cavanaugh had disappeared at approximately the same time, and the Vanishings had stopped. Broom was a man of desires dark enough to be feared, even by his own people. Cork might have suspected that Indigo Broom was responsible for the fate of Monique Cavanaugh except for one salient detail: his father's .38 Smith & Wesson Police Special may well have been the weapon used to kill her. He knew, too, that Cavanaugh was a woman of dark desires and devious motives, which she'd hidden well from others, but not from the priest and probably not from her husband, who refused to speak of her once she was gone. Could she, too, have played some part in the Vanishings?

It was entirely possible, probable even, Cork concluded, that the Anishinaabeg of the Iron Lake Reservation had not been as ignorant as the official reports of the investigation seemed to indicate, nor had his father.

But why had they all lied?

And how had a bullet from his father's gun come to be lodged in the spine of Monique Cavanaugh? If he knew that, maybe Cork would know how a bullet from the same weapon had found its way into the body of her daughter.

As he pulled into town, his cell phone rang. Sheriff Dross. She told him that she'd scheduled another news conference for the afternoon. She wanted everyone in her office beforehand, at 2:00 P.M., so that she knew where all the parts of the investigation stood.

Cork stopped by home, grabbed a quick bologna sandwich, and took Trixie for a short walk. Then he headed to the Tamarack County sheriff's office. He was the last to arrive. In addition to Dross, there were the other usuals: Captain Ed Larson, Agent Simon Rutledge, and Agent Susan Upchurch. Once again, there weren't enough chairs, so Cork leaned against a wall.

"Susan," Dross said to the BCA agent, "why don't you give us an update on what you've found so far."

"All right. Remember the marks on the bones that I indicated earlier could have been made by incisions or by the teeth of a scavenger? I've pretty much concluded that they're the result of a knife blade. I also believe they were delivered perimortem."

"Perimortem?" Cork asked.

"At or very near the time of death."

"What makes you believe that?" Larson said.

"In perimortem wounds, the edges of the bone along the incision often curl, like if you'd cut into a live branch that you've pulled off a tree."

"So the victims may well have been alive when these cuts were made?"

"Yes. But it's also possible the cuts were made immediately after death."

"To what purpose?"

"They might be ritualistic. They might have been the result of some kind of homicidal frenzy, I suppose. But you also sometimes find this same kind of mark on victims of cannibalism."

"Cannibalism?" Dross looked aghast.

"I'm not saying that's what occurred, just that the marks are consistent with a number of possibilities, and that's one of them."

"Great," Dross said. "The media will love that, I'm sure."

Cork asked, "Did Monique Cavanaugh have any of these marks?"

"No. We've found no knife marks on the remains of the Cavanaugh woman, no evidence of knife wounds."

"So cause of death was probably the bullet lodged in her spine?"

"That's the best speculation at the moment."

Cork looked at the sheriff. "Anything more from the Lauren Cavanaugh autopsy?"

"Yes," Dross said. "In addition to the bullet wound to her chest, Tom Conklin found a superficial wound on her right side, just above her hip."

"What kind of wound?"

"Tom thinks it's a bullet graze."

"The killer missed the first time around?"

"We couldn't say that officially, but that would be my current speculation. Ed, tell Cork what you've got."

"We've gone over the old Parrant estate," Larson said. "We didn't find anything of particular value in the big house. But in the boathouse, which Ms. Cavanaugh had renovated into an additional private living area for herself, we found two things. First, between the floorboards, we discovered traces of what we believe to be blood. Simon's people are analyzing the samples now."

"What do you think?"

"Well, the M.E. believes she died quickly from the gunshot wound. The blood covered a significant area, so I think Lauren Cavanaugh lay facedown after she died, lay there quite a while so that gravity pulled a lot of blood out the chest wound. It looks to me like someone eventually tried to clean things up and, except for what seeped between the boards, did a pretty good job."

"What was the other thing?" Cork asked.

"We got really lucky. We pulled a fingerprint from the back of a table lamp. A bloody fingerprint. Simon's people are analyzing that blood, too, and trying to match the print."

"You're pretty sure she was killed in the boathouse?"

"Like Marsha says, I wouldn't state that officially, but that's my current speculation."

"So killed in her boathouse, taken to the Vermilion One Mine, and sealed up with the other bodies in the drift," Dross summed up.

"Anybody at the Northern Lights Center hear or see anything?" Cork asked.

"The current residents didn't arrive until the next day, and all the staff had gone home by then," Larson said. "The only person who might have heard was a guy named Huff. He's a long-term resident. But he wasn't at the center in the time frame we believe the killing took place. He was out drinking and has someone who backs up his story. So basically nobody's been able to give us anything."

"I'll give you something," Cork said. "Huff was quite comfortable in Monique Cavanaugh's private area. You might want to lean on him a little, see what gives."

"And you know this how?"

"I was there a couple of days ago, talking with Ophelia Stillday. Just an observation I made."

"All right." Larson jotted a note in his little book.

Simon Rutledge eyed Cork, and there was an enigmatic expression on his face. He said, "I have a little something to add about the earlier killings. The priest assigned to St. Agnes in those days was accused of masturbating in the confessional. Shortly after that, some women's panties were found hidden there, stained with semen. The investigating officer apparently didn't feel the situation was such that the priest should be looked at as a viable suspect in the Vanishings, but the Church yanked the guy."

"Jesus, where'd you get that information?" Larson asked.

"You said the files had been destroyed, but I knew that one of your retired deputies, Cy Borkman, had been with the department back then, so I talked to him. Then I tracked down the priest. It was basically the same thing Cork did."

Dross leveled a cold eye on Cork. "You knew about this?"

"Yes."

"And you were going to tell us when?"

"As soon as I had a few more things worked out."

"Like what?"

Cork said, "Simon, did the priest tell you about Monique Cavanaugh's sexual proclivities?"

"Reluctantly."

"What do you think?"

"If it's true, she wasn't exactly Snow White."

Dross leaned forward, and, even across the room, Cork thought he could feel the heat of her rising anger. "What are you two gentlemen talking about?"

"According to the priest, Monique Cavanaugh propositioned him several times," Cork replied. "She finally threatened him. And that was followed by an anonymous call to the sheriff's department that resulted in the aforementioned soiled intimate items coming to light in the confessional."

"She set the priest up?"

"That's certainly what he believes."

"That doesn't mesh at all with the image everyone has of her," Larson said.

"You need to press her son a little more on the subject of his mother, Ed. You may discover that he doesn't consider her Snow White either."

"Is there anything else you know but haven't told us?" Dross asked.

"I saw Isaiah Broom today," Cork replied. "I told him I was pretty sure the unidentified body was his mother."

"Jesus Christ, what were you thinking?" the sheriff cried. "We haven't positively ID'd the final remains. If this gets out and you're wrong . . ." She took a moment to rein in her anger, and the whole time the smolder of her gaze was directed at Cork. At last she said, "What's done is done. That's all for now, gentlemen."

The normal tourist traffic had swelled with the influx of folks curious about the grisly discovery in the Vermilion Drift, and Sam's Place was doing a land-office business. Judy Madsen, Jodi Bollendorf, and

Kate Buker had the situation under control when Cork checked in. He promised to be there early that night to close and left things in their capable hands.

He returned home, gathered the boxes that contained his mother's journals, and took them out to the patio in the backyard. Trixie jumped up and ran to greet him. He released her from the tether that held her, and she bounded to the far corner of the yard and snatched a dirty tennis ball in her teeth. Cork threw it a few times, then told her gently he had work to do. He grabbed a cold Leinie's from the refrigerator, settled into a patio chair, and took out the journal that contained the entries immediately following the missing pages that would have chronicled the time of the Vanishings.

September 17, 1964

   Fall is here and everywhere I look I see blood. It's in the color of the sumac and the maple leaves and the sky at sunset and at dawn. Henry Meloux is helping Hattie and Ellie and Mom and me. Liam walks like a man made of stone, cold and hard. Cork, ever the quiet, watchful child, sees and wonders but does not ask. Thank God.

Does not ask, Cork thought. Well, he was asking now.

He scanned other entries, looking for anything that might be a clue to the missing days.

September 21, 1964

   The first day of fall officially. Usually a glorious time, but this year we all mourn. Winter is already in our souls. Liam grows more distant. What has been asked of him is great, and he struggles. He is not one of The People. If he were, he might understand and better accept how things must be. There is friction between us. This I can live with. For now. What hurts is seeing how Liam has distanced himself from Cork as well. He's short with his son. And the Irish in Cork flares up and he lashes back. They battle these days. Except that Cork has no idea of the true enemy here.

September 29, 1964

Cork has been suspended from school. He got into a fight with another boy. Over what neither of them would say. Liam is furious. Nothing new. He's angry all the time now. I've asked him to talk to Henry Meloux. He refuses. Cork sits in his room, staring a hole through the wall. My heart is breaking.

October 16, 1964
Liam my beloved Liam is dead.
Dear God why?

TWENTY-SIX

In October 1964, the Summer Olympics were held in Tokyo. In that same month, Dr. Martin Luther King, Jr., received the Nobel Peace Prize. The St. Louis Cardinals became World Champions, beating the heavily favored New York Yankees in the seventh game of the World Series. China detonated its first nuclear weapon. The Star of India was stolen from the American Museum of Natural History in New York City. Nikita Krushchev was removed as leader of the Soviet Union.

And in October 1964, Cork O'Connor lost his father.

In his memory, his life until then had been happy. But one cool fall day, when the oak leaves were a stunning russet against a startling blue sky, when the cry of migrating Canada geese chorused over Iron Lake, when the evening air was full of the scent of woodsmoke curling from the chimneys of Aurora, everything changed. Changed over the course of a few hours. Changed, in fact, in a single instant. Changed forever with the final beat of his father's heart.

It had begun with a shoot-out. Cork's father and a deputy had responded to an alarm at the First Citizen's Bank, where three inmates who'd escaped from Stillwater Prison were attempting a robbery as they fled toward Canada. During the exchange of gunfire that erupted, a deaf old lady, a cantankerous woman notorious for yelling at children trespassing on her precious lawn, wandered into the line of fire outside the bank. Cork's father left the cover of the Buick that shielded him to pull the old woman to safety. In those few moments of exposure, a bullet from a stolen deer rifle pierced his heart.

He didn't die immediately. He lingered for several hours, unconscious, with his wife and son at the side of his hospital bed. The doctor, a good man named Congreve, didn't have the ability to mend a heart torn by a bullet designed to bring down a deer and gave them no hope. Cork's mother had prayed, prayed desperately. Although Cork had said prayers with her, they were empty words. As soon as the doctor had proclaimed that there was no hope, young Cork O'Connor had closed his heart in the way he might have closed a door to an empty room.

It took him a while to absorb the full impact of his father's death. He was numb for days, numb during the funeral, numb at the site of the open grave, numb to the words of consolation, numb to his mother's grief. For a long time he felt nothing, neither joy nor sadness nor fear nor hope.

That year in mid-November, he helped Sam Winter Moon close up Sam's Place. The trees by then were bare things, wet, black skeletons in the drizzle of the bleak season. Sam had been his father's good friend, and as he and Cork put plywood over the serving windows of the Quonset hut, he talked about Liam O'Connor.

"You know," Sam said around a nail gripped in his teeth, "that man could outfart a draft horse. Hold your side up a little higher, Cork." He took the nail from between his teeth and positioned it.

Cork thought it a little unseemly, speaking of his father that way, but he held his tongue.

"We were canoeing once up on Angle Lake. Came around a point, headed for the next portage. There 'not five feet away was a bull moose, munching on lakeweed. We startled him as much as he startled us. That animal lowered his head and was about to do real damage to our canoe and probably to us in the bargain. Your father, he farts and it's like cannon fire. Echoes off the trees. Sends a tidal wave across the lake. Scares the crap out of that bull moose. The critter turns and hightails it." Sam was laughing hard enough that he couldn't hammer. He leaned against the Quonset hut for support and finished, breathless, "And then your father, he says, 'I just hope we don't run into a bear, Sam. I'm clean outta ammo.'"

Cork stood holding up his side of the plywood, watching Sam Winter Moon laugh heartily.

"It's okay, Cork," Sam said. "It's okay to laugh. It was something your father loved to do."

And Cork did laugh. He laughed so hard tears began to squeeze from his eyes, and before he knew it, he was crying. Sam Winter Moon laid his hammer down and took Cork's hands from the plywood, wrapped his big arms around the weeping boy, and held him.

December 24, 1964
Christmas Eve. We went to the candlelight Mass at St.
Agnes. A lovely service. Walking home, snow began to fall.
I took Cork's hand and he let me. He's a somber young man
these days. He misses his father. As I do. Henry Meloux
says that what we feel, this incredible emptiness, is like a
held breath. He says the heart is wise, and if we listen to it,
we will understand how to breathe again. I hope Meloux is
right.

Cork put down the journal he was holding and thought about that dark time. He'd grieved for a year, and in the fall of 1965 he'd hunted a bear with Sam Winter Moon, an enormous black bear that Sam had tried to capture with a log trap. The log was heavy enough that it should have broken the back of any normal black bear, but the animal had shrugged it off. Sam, fearing the great creature might be injured and suffering, had gone after it, and Cork had gone with him. It was a journey far different from anything either of them had imagined, a journey that involved a brush with a Windigo and that resulted in the largest black bear pelt anyone in Tamarack County had ever seen, a journey that finally brought Cork out of his grieving.

January 1, 1965
We didn't celebrate the beginning of this new year. We
have no reason to celebrate. My husband is dead. My niece
is dead, killed by a madwoman and an Ojibwe majimanidoo.
And we who are left abide with our guilt, an uncomfortable
companion in all our hours. I miss Liam so much. I will miss
him forever.

Cork paused and reread.

My niece is dead, killed by a madwoman and an Ojibwe maji-manidoo.

Majimanidoo. Evil spirit, Cork translated. Devil. Indigo Broom.

A madwoman? Monique Cavanaugh?

His mother had known.

We abide with our guilt.

What the hell did that mean?

The summer solstice was only a couple of days away, and as Cork headed to Sam's Place that night to close up, a narrow strip of sky along the western horizon was still lit with a pale yellow glow. Jodi Bollendorf and Kate Buker had shut the serving windows. They looked beat, and Cork told them to go on home, he'd take care of the cleaning and would close up himself. They agreed without argument.

He emptied the deep-fry well, scraped the grill, wiped the prep surfaces clean with a mix of water and bleach, washed the serving utensils, and mopped the floor. He took the cash from the register and went to the rear half of the Quonset hut to do the daily count.

All the while his brain was working on the mystery of the Vermilion Drift.

His mother knew about Monique Cavanaugh and about Indigo Broom. Probably his father had known, too. If so, why hadn't he arrested them, done his duty as an officer of the law? Was it possible that, in the extraordinary circumstances of forty years ago, he'd seen his duty differently, and that was why a bullet from his revolver had ended up lodged in Monique Cavanaugh's spine?

The more Cork thought about that last consideration, the more he thought about the image of Liam O'Connor which had emerged from his mother's journals. A man, at the end, dark and distant and brooding. What had happened to make him so? What had been done that was so difficult for him to accept that it ate at him constantly?

Cork had finished the daily count and was preparing for a night deposit when his cell phone rang.

"O'Connor," he said in answer.

"Cork, it's Rainy. You've got to come out to my uncle's place. You've got to come out now."

"Why? What's going on?"

"It's Isaiah Broom. He's going to kill Henry."

TWENTY-SEVEN

She called him again just after he'd parked his Land Rover at the trailhead to Crow Point. The moon was up but on the wane and offered only enough light to give definition to the larger particulars of the forest. Cork carried his Maglite. He paused and slipped the phone from his pocket.

"Where are you?" Rainy demanded.

"On the trail. I'll be there in ten minutes."

"My god, it's taking you forever."

In fact, he'd practically flown. But Cork knew that the kind of tense situation in which Rainy had found herself caused every minute to drag on forever, and he let her censure slide off his back.

"What's going on?" he asked, moving ahead as quickly as he could, using the Maglite to illuminate his way.

"Broom's barricaded the door. It won't budge. And it's quiet in there now."

"Will either of them respond when you call?"

"No. But I think I can hear voices."

"Don't try to force your way in, Rainy. Wait for me. I'm coming as quickly as I can."

He leaped Wine Creek and a few minutes later neared the edge of the woods. Before he left the cover of the trees, he killed the beam of his flashlight and silenced his cell phone. He knew the dark would afford him an opportunity to assess things as he approached, and if all his years in law enforcement had taught him anything, it was the wisdom of caution. In the drift of soft light from the gibbous moon, Meloux's cabin was a dark shape rising on the far side of the open meadow. No light was visible inside. The trail across the meadow was dimly discernible, and he kept to the path most of the way, bent low, moving swiftly. Fifty yards from the cabin he paused, listened, heard nothing. Rainy was nowhere to be seen.

He crept left and circled behind Meloux's outhouse to come at the cabin from behind. When he reached the back wall, he paused, heard a small muffled cough, then heard Broom whisper, "Shut up."

"I didn't . . ." It was Rainy's voice.

"Shut up." A few moments passed, then Broom whispered, "Where is he?"

"You know everything I know." Her voice was a knife honed sharp with anger.

"Christ, if you screwed me, I swear I'll kill you and the old man both."

"I've done everything you asked. You've heard everything I've said to him." Then, much to Cork's dismay, she added, "Asshole."

Cork inched to the end of the wall and peered around the corner. The cabin blocked what little light the moon offered, and Cork saw only darkness. He had no way to assess the situation. If he came at Broom quickly, he might be able to surprise the man, but at what cost? If Broom had a firearm pointed at Rainy, it could easily discharge in the fracas, maybe on purpose, maybe accidentally. Cork ran quickly through his options as he saw them and made a decision. He retraced his steps to the outhouse, crouched, and loped far out into the meadow, where he laid himself down in the tall grass.

"Isaiah!" he called.

Broom made no response.

"If you think I'm coming up there, Isaiah, think again."

"I've got the woman and the old man, O'Connor."

"So?"

"I'll kill 'em."

"So?"

Broom was quiet.

Cork said, "What is it you want from me, Isaiah?"

"I want to know what you know about the Vermilion Drift. I want to know what the old man knows."

"You could ask."

"He's saying nothing."

"Maybe he doesn't like being threatened. Look, Isaiah, you've got good reason to be pissed, but that doesn't give you license to threaten folks. You want to talk, I'll talk. I can pretty much guarantee that Meloux will talk, too, if you approach him reasonably."

"He's drunk, Cork," Rainy called. "And he's got a rifle."

"Shut up!"

Cork heard the woman grunt.

"Rainy, you okay?"

"Yes. But I'll have a hell of a bruise in the morning."

"Look, Isaiah, I give you my word that I'll tell you everything I know if you just step away from all the threats."

"What about the old witch man?"

Old witch man? Broom evidently saw Meloux in the way many modern Shinnobs did: an anachronism. An old man of the old ways, a witch. Unfortunate because Broom might have been easier to deal with if he respected Meloux in the way Cork did.

"Just ask him, Isaiah. Ask him without the rifle."

There was only silence from Broom's direction. Then Cork saw movement in the dim moonlight that fell on the ground in front of the cabin. He made out Broom, pushing Rainy ahead of him to the cabin door. He heard the squeak of hinges, but no light came from inside. Then the door squeaked shut. A moment later, behind the curtain of a front window, a faint orange glow appeared. One of Meloux's oil lamps had been lit.

Cork stayed where he was, hoping reason had prevailed.

The door opened, and Broom stood silhouetted against the light. A stupid move, if Cork had been armed. Cork could see the black outline of Broom's rifle still held in his right hand.

"Okay, O'Connor. The old man says he'll talk. Come on up."

"Not until you put that rifle down, Isaiah."

Broom leaned to his right, and when he came back up, his hand was empty.

Cork stood, slipped his Maglite into his back pocket, and walked to the cabin. Broom stepped away from the door, and Cork entered. Inside, he found Meloux bound to a chair next to his table. Rainy sat across the room on her great-uncle's bunk. Cork turned back to Broom just as the big Shinnob pulled a target pistol from under the shirttail at the small of his back.

"Ah, shit," Cork said. He glanced at Rainy. "You told me he had a rifle. You didn't say anything about a handgun."

"If I'd known I would have told you," she replied drily.

"Sit down, O'Connor." Broom waved him toward an empty chair.

Cork did as he was told and took stock of Broom. The smell of whiskey was strong off him. His eyes were heavy and red, and he was unsteady in his movements. He was a huge Shinnob. To stagger the way he did, he must have consumed a lake of alcohol. On the other hand, Broom wasn't a man with a reputation for being fond of liquor, so maybe he simply had little tolerance for drink but a lot of motivation that day for drinking.

"I want to know everything you know, everything the old man knows," Broom said.

"All right, Isaiah. Where do you want me to start?" Cork replied.

Broom didn't answer. He turned his attention to Meloux. "Was it my mother in that tunnel?"

Meloux said, "No. Your mother long ago walked the Path of Souls."

"Don't play games, old man. Was that my mother's body?"

"It was her body," Meloux acknowledged.

"How'd it get there?"

"Like the others."

"How'd they get there?"

"*Majimanidoo,*" the old Mide said.

Broom thought a moment, swaying like a tree in a strong wind. "Evil spirit?"

"Indigo Broom put them there," Cork said.

The big Shinnob stared at him, red-eyed. "He killed my mother?"

"I think so. Her and the other women whose remains were in the Vermilion Drift."

Broom fell silent. His legs looked as if they were becoming more wobbly by the moment. "It was him," he said with certainty.

Meloux spoke quietly. "He showed you the tunnel, didn't he? A long time before he put the bodies there."

Broom lifted his eyes to Meloux.

"I know what he did to you in that tunnel, Isaiah Broom. Things only a man of evil spirit would do."

Broom seemed angered by Meloux's knowledge. "I never told anyone."

"You never told anyone," Meloux agreed gently. "But your mother knew."

"No," he said. Then: "How?"

"That was a thing a small boy could not hide from a mother who loved him. She wanted to kill Indigo Broom, but she vanished."

"Loved me? You're a liar."

"A very long time ago, I tried to guide you to the truth, but your heart was hard, and your spirit was all fire. I could not help you. You are a man now, and I am offering you the truth again."

Broom looked suddenly sick. He turned, threw open the door, and rushed outside. From the dark came the sound of retching.

Cork took the opportunity to grab Broom's rifle. He checked the chamber. It was empty, and the magazine, too, which probably meant Broom intended to use the weapon only to frighten. Rainy went to her great-uncle and untied the rope that bound him to the chair.

In the light of the lantern on Meloux's table, they waited. Broom didn't return. Cork finally lifted the lantern and went to the door. The big Shinnob lay on his back at the edge of the meadow, passed out.

"What do you want to do with him, Henry?" Cork asked.

"Let him sleep for a while. Then I will talk with him."

"He may be just as belligerent when he wakes up," Cork said.

Meloux replied, "He would not have been a problem except my niece was less than hospitable. She spoke to him harshly."

"Jesus, Uncle Henry, a drunken maniac breaks into your cabin waving a rifle and you treat him like an honored guest."

"It is my cabin. If I choose to treat him that way, it is my right. And, Niece, until you spoke, he did not point his rifle at anyone."

"Oh, Christ," she said and turned away.

Meloux asked her, "Will you build a fire in the ring? Corcoran

O'Connor will help you. If Isaiah Broom wakes, I will bring him there."

Rainy stormed down the path toward the fire ring at the edge of the lake. Cork took the Maglite from his back pocket.

"I think it would be safer if I stayed here with you," Cork said.

"I am not afraid of Isaiah Broom."

"It's not Broom that has me worried, Henry." He glanced down the path where the angry woman had gone.

In the dark, he saw the old man smile.

TWENTY-EIGHT

He offered his flashlight. She refused.

"I don't need your help," Rainy said as she gathered cut wood from a box near the ring. "I know how to build a fire."

"Fine," Cork said. "I'll just stand here and watch."

The moon gave only a faint definition to things. The tall outcroppings that isolated the ring were the color of pencil lead. The ground was a gray pool of bare dirt, the fire ring a black hole of ash. The lake a dozen yards away was like mercury, a dark liquid silver. The woman, as she moved from the woodbox to the fire ring, was an angry obsidian blur.

Cork said, "He can be hard to understand sometimes, but in my experience, he's usually right."

She dropped a load of wood inside the ring. "Jesus, the man was drunk. He was waving a rifle, for Christ sake. And I'm supposed to say 'Mi casa, su casa'?"

"Henry's casa actually."

She bent and spent a minute arranging the wood. Cork could hear the snap of kindling.

"Damn it," she said.

"What?"

"I didn't bring any matches."

"Me either."

"I need to go back to the cabin."

"Why don't you relax for a little bit? That was pretty intense stuff back there."

She stood a moment, outlined against the dark silver of the lake, then sat on the ground not far from Cork.

He studied the stars and let a minute pass.

"Why did Broom come to Henry?" he asked.

"People come to Uncle Henry all the time. They think he knows everything that happens on the rez."

"He probably does. Why did you come to Crow Point?"

"I told you. The family's worried about Uncle Henry."

"No, I mean why you? Of all the family, why you?"

"For one thing, I'm a public health nurse."

"Summer off?"

"Funding cut. I'm between jobs at the moment."

"For another thing?"

"My children are raised and gone. I have no one who depends on me being there every day."

"Not married?"

"Divorced. A long time ago. Are you always this nosy?"

"Inquisitive. Goes with my job."

"And your nature, I'd say."

Cork heard the flap of big wings overhead. Rainy looked up startled.

"An owl," Cork said. "Should I be worried about Henry?"

Rainy didn't answer immediately. She continued to look up where the owl had flown and where the stars were legion.

"The shaking? The tiredness? They're symptoms," she said. "Of what, I can't say. There are dozens and dozens of diseases or conditions that could cause it. If it were something like multiple sclerosis, I'd expect to see problems with his vision and maybe numbness or tingling in his limbs. He claims to be fine. If it's the result of a stroke, then it was a mild one. But even so, I'd expect to see, oh, I don't know, muscle weakness or numbness or maybe some disorientation. Maybe it's simply a neurodegenerative situation of some kind. Old age, basically. But he's not showing any other symptoms, so I don't know. Whatever it is, he doesn't seem much concerned." A loon called from the lake, and Rainy turned her head. "It's lovely here," she said.

"Not a bad place for a man to live. And to die, when that time comes."

"That time will not come soon, Corcoran O'Connor."

owls fly silently

They hadn't heard the old Mide's approach, but Meloux stood not ten feet away. He came now and sat with them.

"I thought you were going to build a fire, Niece."

"I didn't have matches, Uncle Henry."

"Just as well," Meloux said. "I think Isaiah Broom will not wake until morning. And I think I need to sleep. Thank you for your help," he said to Cork.

"You want me here when Broom wakes up?"

"He will wake in sunshine and hungover. He will not be in the mood for confrontation. He will want to be quiet, and I think he will listen."

"What will you tell him?"

"What I tell him will be for his ears only, Corcoran O'Connor."

In the dark, Cork leaned nearer the Mide. "I've found a few answers, Henry, but I still have a lot of questions. I think you can help me."

"Tell me what you know."

"All right. Forty years ago, it went like this. I think that the Vanishings began with Leonora Broom. I think she confronted Indigo about what he'd done to her son and Broom killed her and put her body in the Vermilion Drift. Maybe he'd killed before or just had the deep desire to kill, I don't know, but murdering Isaiah's mother set him off that summer for sure. Next it was Abbie Stillday, a girl everybody knew was leaving the rez sooner or later. And then it was the vulnerable ones, the ones easily preyed on. Somewhere along the way, Broom brought Monique Cavanaugh into it. Or maybe it was just the evil of these two people that somehow brought them together. Broom snagged the victims and he and Monique Cavanaugh both . . ." Cork searched for the right word.

Meloux supplied it. "They fed."

"Fed?" Rainy said, aghast. "You don't mean they cannibalized their victims?"

"Do you know the story of the Windigo, Niece?"

"A monster with a heart of ice. A cannibal."

"They were both Windigos," Meloux said. "They did not start out that way, but they did not start out as whole human beings either. They were born with something missing. They did not have souls."

"Everyone has a soul, Uncle Henry," Rainy said.

"What is a soul? I believe it is our connection with the Creator and our deep awareness of our connection with all things created by him. And this is what they did not have. Some people who have souls make choices that lead them to evil. These two did not have a choice."

"*Majimanidoo.* That's what you called Broom. Evil spirit. He was simply born that way? But why would the Creator do that, Uncle Henry?"

"I have lived a very long time, Niece, and I have seen many things I do not understand. I only know they are so."

"If Broom and Monique Cavanaugh didn't start out as Windigos, Henry, what happened?" Cork asked.

"A small evil is like a shadow. It follows us but it has no effect. But when evil finds evil, it can become a different creature, Corcoran O'Connor. It can become huge and monstrous. When those two soulless people met, something worse than what they had been before was created. They fed on their own evil and then they fed on The People."

"Why The People?"

"Because if the Ojibwe disappeared, who would care? Only the Ojibwe and we were few and powerless."

"How did these two find each other, Henry?" Cork asked.

"I do not know."

"My father knew about them, didn't he?"

"He knew."

"What did he do about it?"

"Your father was a good man. One of the best I have ever known. But he was not one of The People."

"What does that mean?"

"You are not yet at the end of your journey, Corcoran O'Connor. When you have reached the end, you will understand and my answers will not be necessary."

"It was my father's gun that killed Monique Cavanaugh, wasn't it, Henry? Explain that to me."

"You still ask in anger. The end of your journey is a place without anger. Come to me when you have reached that place." Meloux slowly stood. "I am going to bed now."

Cork watched the dark between the outcroppings swallow his old friend.

"Shit," he said under his breath.

Rainy said, "He can be hard to understand sometimes, but in my experience, he's usually right."

"Oh shut up," Cork said and got to his feet.

TWENTY-NINE

He dreamed his father dying.

And he woke anxious and angry.

Clearly, he was nowhere near the end of the journey Meloux had referred to.

But he had an idea, which he wanted to pursue, and he got up quickly and prepared for the day.

Before he headed out, his phone rang. A call from his daughter Jenny.

"Dad?" She sounded worried.

"Hey, sweetheart, what a nice surprise."

"I just heard about what's going on up there in the Vermilion One Mine. Jesus, Dad."

"Yeah, pretty crazy stuff."

"On CNN, they reported that you found the bodies. Is that true?"

"Afraid so."

"My God. Are you all right?"

"Me? Fine."

"Are you . . . involved?" She phrased it much the way her mother might have, her words both a question and an admonition.

"Just happened to be at the wrong place at the wrong time. No need to worry."

"Just happened? Right."

"Look, sweetheart, I'd love to talk to you, but I have some pressing business—"

"Does it have to do with—what are they calling it—the Vanishings?"

"I'm just going over to the rez to visit Millie Joseph. You remember her?"

"Old and a little senile, but nice."

"That's her. I try to visit whenever I can these days. So don't worry about me, okay?"

"I can come up if you need me."

"No, sweetheart, I'm fine. Give that boyfriend of yours my best."

When he hung up, he wasn't proud of himself, but at least he'd avoided actually lying to his elder daughter. He had enough to worry about without being concerned about her worry.

When he reached the Nokomis Home, he found Millie Joseph rocking in the porch shade. It was morning and still cool, and she had a knitted shawl around her shoulders.

"*Boozhoo*, Corkie," she said with a smile so huge it nearly made her eyes disappear. "How come you never visit?"

Cork let her question slide and pulled up a chair next to her. "A beautiful day, Millie," he said, looking toward the steely blue of the lake.

"At my age, Corkie, every day you wake up is beautiful."

"Millie, could I ask you a question?"

"Sure. But it will cost you."

"What's the price?"

"Today's Friday. Sarah LeDuc over at the Mocha Moose makes fry bread on Fridays. I'll answer your question if you bring me back some fry bread."

"It's a deal," Cork said.

"Ask away."

"Indigo Broom—" Cork began.

"Oh," Millie said, and her face changed. "Not him."

"I just want to know where Indigo Broom lived."

"Why do you want to know that?"

"Do you want fry bread?"

She weighed her craving against her reluctance to answer and gave in. "He lived way over south on the reservation. An old logging road off Waagikomaan. He had himself a little cabin there. But you won't find it now."

"Why not?"

"Burned down."

"When?"

"Long time ago. About the time he left, I think."

"You mean disappeared."

"He didn't disappear. He left the reservation, and good riddance."

"How do you know he left?"

"Sam Winter Moon said he got word from relatives somewhere. I don't remember where. I just know I felt sorry for those people whoever they were."

"This old logging road, do you recall where it cut off from Waagikomaan?"

"West of Amik, I believe. But why do you want to go there? It's a bad place."

"Why do you say that?"

"Everyone on the rez knows it's a bad place."

"Because Broom lived there?"

"Maybe the place is bad because Broom lived there, maybe Broom lived there because the place is bad. Doesn't matter. People with any sense know better than to go there."

"Nobody ever accused me of having much sense, Millie. *Migwech*."

"My fry bread, Corkie?"

"Back in ten minutes."

And he was.

Waagikomaan was an Ojibwe word that meant "crooked knife." It was a good name for the road on the rez, which cut a winding path through aspen and then into marshland and finally into timber. Cork reached Amik, which was the Ojibwe name for a lake the whites called Beaver, without spotting any cutoff. He turned around and drove back more slowly. It had been a good seventy-five years since any significant felling had been done in the area, and a logging road gone unused for that length of time would probably have been reclaimed by the wilderness. Hell, it was enough time for a whole new forest to grow. Still, he eyed the pines carefully, and about a quarter mile west of Beaver Lake he spotted an unnatural break in the tall timber. He pulled the Land Rover to the side of the road, parked, and got out. He waded through the wild grass at the shoulder of the road and reached the edge of the trees, where he studied the vegetation. He laid his cheek to the earth and eyed the contour. Finally he ran his hand over the ground itself and was satisfied that there were still ruts, the faintest of scars, leading into the trees. He stood and followed them in.

Cork believed that a forest was a living thing and that people who paid attention heard its voice and smelled its breath and knew its face. He realized very quickly that Millie Joseph had been right. In that place, the forest was sick. Not with blight caused by beetle or fungus, but suffused with a sense of malice.

Mudjimushkeeki, he thought. Like the Parrant estate, this was a place of very bad medicine. Although he couldn't remember ever having been there, the way seemed oddly familiar to him, and the deeper he went into the trees, the more powerful became his own sense of resistance.

After fifteen minutes, feeling far weaker than the distance and the effort should have made him, he came to a place almost devoid of undergrowth. It was backed by a ragged wall of bare, slate-colored rock. The place was dead quiet. He couldn't hear the call of a single bird among the trees or see the dart of a single insect in the air. He felt a little nauseated and realized that his stomach was knotted in a way that usually only happened when he was very afraid.

What was there to be afraid of?

Cork stood momentarily paralyzed. He thought about the fact that he'd spent a good deal of his life in places where great trauma or tragedy had occurred, arenas where death was a regular contender. Yet he'd never before felt what he felt from the clearing in which he now stood, where even the sunlight seemed sucked dry of its energy.

He started toward the rock wall and within moments saw the outline of a cabin foundation in the dirt, a black rectangle of half-buried, charred logs. A dozen yards to the north was the foundation of another burned structure, much smaller than the cabin. Cork paused before he crossed the boundary of the cabin logs. He fought against the urge to turn and run. Finally he stepped inside the rectangle.

The ground was bare, with a deep covering of soil dry as ash. Cork's boots left clear impressions as he walked. He wasn't sure what he was looking for but wished he'd brought a shovel or something suitable to turn the dirt, to sift the past. He could tell the basic layout of the cabin. One large room, two smaller rooms. Beyond that, the ruin told him very little. He knelt, lifted a handful of the dry earth, and let it slide between his fingers. It left a gray residue that Cork wiped on his pant leg. He stepped out of the outline of the cabin and went to the smaller structure. A storage shed perhaps? A garage? The ground there was ash-dry as well, and Cork saw boot tracks. They were clean, the edges still well defined. Not much time had passed since they'd been made. He turned in a circle, scanning the trees around the clearing, the top of the rock wall. He didn't see anyone, but that didn't mean he wasn't being watched. He realized his gut had knotted even more. He didn't like this place, didn't like it one bit.

But he'd come for a reason, and he turned back to his purpose. He began to kick through the layer of dry soil in the smaller ruin, searching for a clue to the purpose of the original structure. The toe of his boot hit metal. Cork bent, felt in the dirt, and his fingers touched rusted iron. He dug and got a grip and pulled from its grave a long and heavy chain with an open iron cuff at each end. He rose slowly and realized he was holding a set of manacles.

He laid the piece down, knelt, and began to scrape through the dirt, using his fingers as a rake. It took him five minutes before he came across the bones.

There was nothing large, only chips and fragments. And a tooth. He knew that fire burned flesh and muscle and cartilage completely, but even a crematorium couldn't get rid of all the bone in a body or any of the teeth. Who'd died in the fire here almost fifty years ago? Indigo Broom? Was this the reason for his disappearance? And if so, who was it that caused him to disappear in this way?

He was so engrossed in his thinking that he didn't hear until it was too late the soft patter at his back of someone in a rush. He tried to turn, but not quickly enough, and the morning exploded, brighter than sunlight, followed by a darkness more than night.

He came to feeling as if his skull had been split open across the back. His right cheek pressed against the ground, and the taste of dirt was in his mouth. He lifted himself slowly, waiting a moment on his knees for everything around him to stop spinning. He spit wet, black grit and wiped his lips with the back of his hand. He tried to stand, returned to his knees, gathered himself, and finally came to his feet. He realized he was no longer inside the foundation of the smaller structure. He'd been dragged outside the ruin. Inside, the ash-dry dirt carried rake marks. The whole area had been carefully gone over. He checked his watch and realized that he'd been out for nearly two hours. He could have dug some to check for anything that might still have remained, but he doubted he'd find anything. Besides, he wasn't seeing particularly well at the moment and was worried about the pain in his head. He turned and stumbled away, eager to be clear of the sickness of that place.

THIRTY

Whe they heard how long Cork had been unconscious, the ER staff at Aurora Community Hospital immediately took X-rays and then did a CT scan. The results showed no fracture and nothing more serious than minor swelling to the area outside the skull where the blow had landed. They were frankly amazed.

"My hard Irish head," Cork joked.

They wanted to keep him overnight for observation; he told them no, he had things to do. They argued, but in the end sent him home with lots of Tylenol and a printed sheet of symptoms that might indicate more serious developments later. He stripped his clothes off and showered the dirt from his body, fixed a grilled cheese sandwich and, against medical advice, popped the cap on a cold bottle of Leinenkugel's beer.

He sat on the patio, where he tossed a tennis ball for Trixie to chase, nibbled on his sandwich, drank his beer, and tried to figure who'd blindsided him.

When Jo was alive, he'd often consulted with her, tossed questions and speculations her way to get her response. She'd had a fine mind and was somehow able to think logically without losing sight of the human element and its unpredictability and to remember always the need for compassion in any of Cork's considerations. Left to himself, Cork tended to be easily influenced by his prejudices and selfish concerns, and he wasn't certain he could trust any of his own conclusions.

But there was no other option, so he thought alone through the things that troubled him.

Someone had been there ahead of him. The boot tracks inside the smaller foundation told him that. How long before his own arrival, he couldn't say, but it was entirely possible that, whoever it was, his coming had surprised them, and they'd slipped into the trees and simply waited for their chance to bushwhack him. He'd seen no other vehicles on Waagikomaan. Did that mean they'd hiked in, or they'd parked somewhere out of sight? And what were they after? Cork hadn't known exactly what he'd find, but his assailant had brought a rake and so must have had a pretty good idea of what was there. Bones and teeth. They could have been from additional victims of Broom's savagery, or they could have been the remains of Broom himself. Because he hadn't learned of anyone else who'd gone missing over forty years earlier except those discovered in the Vermilion Drift, and because the burning of the cabin coincided with the disappearance of Indigo Broom, Cork was inclined to think they belonged to the man Millie Joseph had darkly referred to as "Mr. Windigo."

Who would have known about Broom's death?

Sam Winter Moon must have known because the story he'd spread about Broom leaving the rez to be with relatives somewhere else had clearly been a lie.

Did Cork's mother know? His father? Henry Meloux? And if they knew, what had been their part in getting rid of Broom? if any.

The night before, after the nightmare of his father dying, he'd lain awake thinking about what Meloux had said, that Indigo Broom and Monique Cavanaugh had behaved like Windigos, cannibalizing their victims. Which was probably the reason for the cuts Agent Upchurch had found on the bones from the Vermilion Drift. But something that gruesome had to be well hidden, carried out in great secrecy, and where could that have been? Which had got Cork to wondering about where Indigo Broom had lived. When Millie Joseph told him it was a cursed place, he'd been almost certain he had the answer he was seeking. And when he'd found the manacles, he knew absolutely it was a place of horrific incident.

Cork sipped his beer and watched Trixie romping in the afternoon sun, and he puzzled over Broom and Monique Cavanaugh, who came from two very different worlds but in the darkness of their souls were united. How did they connect? How did evil find evil?

The Internet might have been a way, but 1964 was decades too early. A personal ad in the *Aurora Sentinel*? Cork could just imagine: *MWF with bloodlust seeks like companion*. Finally Cork decided there might have been another way, an age-old way of connecting.

He went inside and looked up a telephone number in his address book, then dialed.

He ordered Leinie's for them both, and when the beers came, he slid one of the frosted mugs over to Cy Borkman.

"Thanks, Cork. Been too long since we tipped brews together." Borkman tapped Cork's mug, then took a long draw from his own and wiped foam from his upper lip. "How's the investigation going?"

"Plodding along," Cork said.

"Yeah, after you talked to me, Simon Rutledge looked me up, covered the same ground about the priest. You guys really ought to coordinate better."

"We're trying, Cy. Which is one reason I called."

"I figured." Borkman smiled. "What do you need?"

They sat at the bar of the Four Seasons with a view of the marina through a long bank of windows off to their right. When Cork was a kid, the Four Seasons hadn't been there and the marina had been a simple affair with three short docks where maybe a dozen boats were tied up at any given time. Now it was a forest of masts with sailboats too numerous to count, a summer port to ostentatious powerboats and small yachts that often sat idle in the water for weeks on end, playthings for the rich who looked on Aurora as a place of diversion and looked with thinly veiled disdain on those who called the town home.

Cork said, "Back in your early days with the department, was there a bar somewhere that had a particularly unsavory reputation? Someplace that catered to, I don't know, a clientele like the Hells Angels maybe? The kind of place prone to trouble but the owner maybe preferred to handle it on his own."

"Here in Aurora?"

"Probably not. Maybe not even in Tamarack County, but close enough that someone from Aurora could patronize it if they wanted to."

"Oh, sure. Used to be a place like that in Yellow Lake. Jacque's. Christ, there was a dive. Story was that the guy who built it was descended from one of the Voyageurs and his ancestor's name was Jacque something or other. Pretty quiet in the winter, but come summer that place really jumped. Full of loggers and miners, big guys who could get pretty mean when they were drinking. A magnet for lowlifes, too, troublemakers of every kind. Bikers. Indians. Prostitutes. The joint had a little postage stamp of a stage and a strip show. Guy who owned it last, let's see, his name was Fredricks or Fredrickson, something like that, he used to keep a loaded Mossberg behind the bar. Discharged that bad boy on a number of occasions, never at anyone, just to, you know, get everybody's attention. That was when Hal Sluicer was chief of police in Yellow Lake. He never seemed to take much notice of what went on down at Jacque's. Turned out Fredrickson, or whatever his name was, was paying Sluicer off. Eventually Sluicer got his ass fired. Yellow Lake went for a spell without a regular police presence and contracted with the Tamarack County Sheriff's Department for law enforcement during that time."

"You ever get a call down there?"

"Oh, yeah. That place kept us plenty busy."

"Ever run into an Indian there name of Indigo Broom?"

"Broom? From the rez? Sure, Broom was right at home."

"How about Monique Cavanaugh?"

Borkman seemed surprised. "What would a woman like her be doing in a place like that?"

"I don't know."

"That lady had class. No way she'd be caught dead in a joint like that."

"Maybe if she wore a wig and called herself something else?"

"Why would she do that?"

"I don't know. Forget it."

"Naw, you asked. Why?"

"The truth is, Cy, that I'm thinking there was some connection between Monique Cavanaugh and Indigo Broom. But they moved in such different circles, I can't figure out how they would have stumbled onto each other. I thought a place like Jacque's might have provided the opportunity."

"A woman like her with a guy like Broom? That doesn't make any sense."

"You're right. It doesn't. Forget I said anything."

Borkman sat quietly for some time sipping his beer. Cork watched a sailboat back from its slip, come around, and head out into the lake under the power of its engine. When it cleared the marina, a sail went up, an explosion of white against the blue of the sky, and the vessel tilted in the grip of the wind and glided east across the water.

"Jesus," Borkman said. "Oh, Jesus."

Cork turned on his stool. "What?"

Borkman looked at him, and his eyes were big circles of wonderment.

"What is it, Cy?"

Borkman didn't answer immediately. Cork could tell he was working through something in his head.

"Your father was a good man," Borkman finally said, but so softly that Cork had to lean to him. "But he wasn't a perfect man."

"What do you mean?"

"Christ, I shouldn't be telling you this, you of all people."

"Don't crap out on me now, Cy."

"It was decades ago, so I suppose . . ." Borkman gripped his beer with both hands, as if the mug was all that anchored him. "Look, your father was seeing another woman."

"What?"

Borkman said, "It wasn't that he didn't love your mother. It's just that sometimes a man, well, you understand."

"No, Cy, I don't. Enlighten me."

"Look, the Vanishings had him all twisted up. He was going crazy. And frankly, your mother was riding him hard, because it looked like her people were the ones being targeted. He wasn't sleeping. He wasn't particularly eager to go home at night. And, hell, you were being a little shit."

"What do you mean?"

"You were a teenager, and, hell, teenagers are always difficult. And because the investigation took your dad away a lot those days, I suppose you were the one helping your mother through what she was dealing with and saw mostly her side of things. Anyway, you did nothing but give him grief and push him away, and I got the sense your mother was doing the same. He ended up getting pushed into the arms of a woman."

"What woman?"

"I didn't know who it was, but he met her at Jacque's. And it wasn't about love, Cork, I can tell you that."

"What was it about?"

"Look, it happened like this. We got a disturbance call. Your father and me, we both responded, arrived in our cruisers about the same time. A couple of guys in the parking lot were beating the hell out of each other over a woman. A skanky looking thing, a peroxide blonde in a skirt that barely covered her ass. We broke up the fight. Didn't book anybody, but the woman claimed she was afraid, so your father offered to give her a ride. He was gone a long time, longer than necessary, and when he came back into the department, there was something different about him. The kind of different easy to spot. Wouldn't look me in the eye. None of my business, so I didn't push him. We were in the middle of the investigation of the Vanishings, so he was out a lot anyway, but after that, sometimes when he was gone, I figured it had nothing to do with the job."

"How'd you know?"

"A feeling. I knew your old man pretty well. Anyway, after the Cavanaugh woman disappeared, I didn't see any more of that behavior from him."

"And you're saying what?"

"You were the one who said the Cavanaugh woman could've worn a wig and called herself something else. It's pretty coincidental that after Monique Cavanaugh disappeared, your old man settled back down. And you know as well as I do that coincidence is never coincidence."

Cork looked outside at the lake and tried to think clearly through a spin of unpleasant images.

Borkman said, "You asked about Monique Cavanaugh and Indigo Broom, so you must know something about her I don't. Was she the kind of woman who could've got her jollies disguising herself and slumming it at Jacque's? And if she was, was she the kind of woman who'd make your old man the kind of offer he couldn't refuse?"

Before Cork could answer, his cell phone rang. Sheriff Dross.

"Cork, I wanted to let you know. That bloody fingerprint we found in Lauren Cavanaugh's boathouse? We finally got a match."

"Who is it?"

"Hattie Stillday. We just brought her in."

THIRTY-ONE

Sheriff Marsha Dross looked tired but relieved. She wore her khaki uniform, something she usually did only when she had to face the media and wanted to be certain that the impact of her authority came through in every way possible. Agent Simon Rutledge sat in a chair in a corner of the office. He wore a tan sport coat, white shirt, and yellow tie. The knot on his tie was pulled down a comfortable few inches, and the collar of his shirt was unbuttoned. He was working a Rubik's Cube and seemed to be paying very little attention to the conversation between Cork and the sheriff.

"When we showed up at her home to interview her, she took one look at us and told us everything," Dross said. "We brought her back to the department. She refused an attorney and then repeated everything on videotape for us. She seemed happy to get it off her chest."

"You believe her confession?" Cork sat on the far side of the sheriff's desk, trying not to pay too much attention to the pounding in his head, which, despite the Tylenol, threatened to crack his skull wide open.

"The evidence is all there," Dross said. "In the back of her pickup we found a canvas ground cloth with bloodstains on it. She claims she wrapped Cavanaugh's body in it. Simon's people are taking it down to Bemidji to analyze the stains. And she certainly knows things about the murder that we haven't made public."

"Like what?"

"That Cavanaugh was killed with a thirty-eight."

"Does she have the weapon?"

"She claims she threw it into the lake."

"Where?"

"Somewhere along the eastern shoreline, near the rez. She doesn't remember exactly where."

"What about the details of the shooting itself? Lauren Cavanaugh was shot twice, right? The graze and the fatal wound. What did Hattie have to say about that?"

"She was unclear about the number of shots she fired."

"Unclear?"

"She said she fired once. I didn't press the issue. But she told us other things only the killer would know."

"Like what?"

"She claimed to know precisely the location of Lauren Cavanaugh's car."

"Which is where?"

"Sunk in a bog half a mile from the entrance you and Haddad found to the Vermilion Drift. Ed Larson and his crew are out there right now checking on it."

"What was her motive for the killing?"

"She argued with Lauren Cavanaugh over payment for some photographs. She didn't mean to kill her, just to threaten her. Things went south. An accident."

"What was the deal with the photos?"

"Cavanaugh bought them but kept sidestepping the issue of payment. Finally Stillday demanded they be paid for or be returned. Cavanaugh flat-out refused, so Stillday confronted her in the boathouse with the gun. Bang."

A diseased place, Cork thought. Meloux had been right.

Dross glanced at Rutledge, intent on his Rubik's Cube, then said, "It makes sense, Cork. People get crazy when money's involved."

"And she put the body with the others already in the mine?"

"Yes."

"How did she know about the Vermilion Drift?"

"On that subject, she's saying nothing."

"For now," Rutledge said without looking up.

Cork thought that before too long Hattie Stillday would be "Simonized."

"Did she say where she got the murder weapon?"

"Claims she's had it for years. Came down to her from some dead relative on the reservation."

"Does she know the thirty-eight was also the weapon that killed Monique Cavanaugh?"

"She didn't offer any information that would indicate she did. Like I said, she wasn't inclined to talk about the Vanishings."

"What about the threatening notes Max Cavanaugh and the others have received?"

"She says she doesn't know anything about those. And she finally refused to answer any more questions without an attorney."

"Has she retained one?"

"She called Oliver Bledsoe's office."

Bledsoe ran the Office of Legal Affairs for the Iron Lake Ojibwe.

"The counselor was down in Duluth for a hearing, but he's on his way back," Dross continued. "Should be here in an hour or so."

"Did she say when the killing took place?"

"A week ago Sunday."

"That's right in keeping with the M.E.'s assessment," Cork agreed. "Did she give you a time?"

"Apparently there was some kind of meeting at the center that night. Hattie says she waited outside until it was over and Lauren Cavanaugh went to the boathouse, where she confronted and shot her."

"Mind if I talk to Hattie?"

"I guess not. Provided she's willing. Okay with you, Simon?"

"Sure," Rutledge said in a distracted way.

"I'll have her brought to the interview room," Dross offered.

"Thanks."

Rutledge held up the Rubik's Cube, solved. "I hear you've got yourself quite a headache, Cork."

"Where'd you hear that?"

"Around. What happened?"

"My best guess is that someone on the rez isn't particularly happy with my investigation."

"Any idea who?"

"Still working that one out, Simon."

"And you'll be sure to let us know when you do?"

"Absolutely."

Rutledge gave Cork a Mona Lisa smile and started undoing the puzzle he'd just solved.

Hattie Stillday sat with her old hands folded on the tabletop in the interview room.

"This is serious, Hattie," Cork said from across the table.

"I know that, Corkie."

"Have you ever been in jail before?"

"Hell, yes. In Youngstown, Ohio, back in 'fifty-two when I was shooting photos of the steelworkers' strike. And again in Pittsburgh a few days later. Now that was a fine time in labor history. And two years ago during the vigil at Fort Benning. I've always been rather proud of my incarcerations."

"That's good, Hattie, because if your confession stands up, you'll very likely finish your life in prison."

"I didn't mean to kill that woman, Corkie."

"But kill her you did."

"Intent matters," she said, as if she knew the law. "And what do you mean if my confession stands up?"

"There are things about this killing that you don't know."

"I know everything about this killing. I was there."

"How many shots were fired from your gun, Hattie?"

"I don't remember exactly."

"You just told me you knew everything."

"This old brain of mine doesn't always remember all that it should. And it wasn't exactly like I was playing mah-jongg."

"You told the sheriff you killed Lauren Cavanaugh over money. Is that true?"

"I said it, didn't I? That woman was a cheat."

"You killed her because she was a cheat? We have courts to help people get what's rightfully theirs, Hattie."

"You think a court is going to side with an old Shinnob woman over a rich white woman like Lauren Cavanaugh?" She laughed, as if the idea was absurd.

"So you killed her?"

"You keep coming back to that. Yes, I killed her. I'd kill her again."

"You said it was an accident."

"Doesn't mean I'm unhappy with the outcome."

"Do yourself a favor, Hattie. Don't say that to anyone. By the way, where did you get the gun you used?"

"Oh, I've had that for years."

"Who gave it to you?"

"I don't remember exactly. A cousin or something."

"What did you do with it?"

"Threw it into the lake."

"But you don't remember where?"

She tapped her head. "Like I said, rusty thinking sometimes."

"You waited outside the Northern Lights Center until the meeting was over and everyone had left, then you followed Lauren Cavanaugh to the boathouse. Is that how it happened?"

"No. That's just how I got to the boathouse. How it happened involved pulling a trigger, Corkie. I'm tired. I think I'm all done talking for now." She moved her chair back and made ready to stand.

"Does Ophelia know you're here?"

"I don't think so," Hattie said.

"Would you like me to tell her?"

"Would you?"

"Sure." He stood, crossed to the button near the door that would call for the jailer, but hesitated before pressing it. "Hattie, is this why you were with Henry Meloux last night? Was this what you were planning?"

"You've always been a curious person," Hattie replied. "Like your father. Always asking questions. I hope the answers, if you find them, make you happier than they made him."

Cork buzzed, and a moment later Dross opened the door, accompanied by a matron who took Hattie Stillday away.

"Did she tell you anything more?" the sheriff asked.

"Nothing you didn't already know."

Dross nodded and said, "Ed Larson just called. He found Lauren Cavanaugh's car exactly where Hattie Stillday said it would be."

THIRTY-TWO

Ophelia Stillday bent toward the camera mounted on a tripod on the back lawn of the old Parrant estate. Even though it was called the Northern Lights Center for the Arts, Cork never thought of it that way. "The old Parrant estate" inevitably came to mind, a name that called up all the darkness of that diseased place.

Ophelia was intent on her photography, a shoot that, as nearly as Cork could tell, was focused on Iron Lake. It was late afternoon, and the sunlight was the soft color of goldenrod. The lake was beautiful, but he'd seen so many photographs of it over the years that even to his pedestrian eye the subject seemed a little tired.

He coughed as he approached, a subtle announcement of his presence. Ophelia straightened up and turned to greet him.

"*Boozhoo,* Ophelia," he said.

She smiled pleasantly. "Hello, Mr. O.C."

"Beautiful day for a shoot."

"My grandmother says there's no such thing as a day unsuited to photography. She says the eye of the artist should always be able to discern the opportunity in any circumstance."

"It's your grandmother that brings me here," Cork said. "Did you know she's in the Tamarack County Jail at the moment?"

"Grandma Hattie? What for?"

"She confessed to killing Lauren Cavanaugh."

Ophelia looked genuinely stricken. "I don't believe it."

"It's true. She claims the killing was an accident and that it was all about payment for some photographs. Do you know anything about that situation?"

Ophelia didn't respond. She seemed overwhelmed with trying to wrap her thinking around her grandmother's situation.

"Ophelia?"

"Yes," she said in a dazed way. "I knew about it. I told you the center was in financial trouble. But Grandma Hattie would never kill someone over something like that."

"What would she kill someone over?"

That snapped her awake, and she shot Cork an angry look.

"I'm sorry," he said. "That was uncalled for. The truth is I'm having trouble buying her confession, especially considering the motive she's given. I've known your grandmother all my life. She's never cared anything about money. Whenever she's had it, she's given it away. So I'm thinking either she's not telling the truth about killing Lauren Cavanaugh or she's being untruthful about her motive."

"She didn't kill Lauren Cavanaugh," Ophelia stated with absolute certainty. "Grandma Hattie couldn't kill anybody. I need to go to her. Will they let me see her?"

"You can always ask."

She turned and started away, then spun back. "My cane," she said.

Cork picked up her cane from where it lay on the lawn near the tripod and handed it to her.

"Thanks," she said and hobbled quickly toward the big house.

When he was alone, Cork headed to the boathouse where Lauren Cavanaugh had probably been killed. The door was barred with crime scene tape. He tried the knob. Locked. He walked the perimeter, peering in at every window, recalling that the boathouse had been remodeled into what was essentially a large boudoir, which made him think about the morning he'd been there with Ophelia and then Derek Huff had walked in.

He recrossed the lawn and came to the tripod and the camera, which Ophelia Stillday in her haste had left behind. It looked like an expensive piece of equipment with a powerful telescopic lens affixed. He thought he'd best take it into the big house, but before he did, he bent and squinted to look at the image she'd been framing for her shot. He almost laughed. Iron Lake hadn't been the real subject of her interest. Brought marvelously close by the power of the lens was the image of Derek Huff, swimming laps far out in the lake. With every stroke, his great swimmer's hands flung droplets of water into the air, where they arced, sparkling like diamonds.

Simon Rutledge was sitting in the swing on Cork's front porch when Cork returned from walking Trixie that evening. Trixie bounded up the steps, jumped on the swing, and greeted the BCA agent with little woofs and a wagging tail. Cork wasn't as enthusiastic.

"Evening, Simon," he said.

"Cork," Rutledge replied.

"Come on, Trixie," Cork said, calling the dog to his side. "What's up, Simon?"

Rutledge took a moment, as if composing himself, and began in a tone that was clearly part of an architecture of diplomacy. "We've known each other a long time, Cork. We've worked a number of difficult cases together. I've thought of us as friends as well as colleagues. The thing is, I think I can read you pretty well. And what I'm seeing right now concerns me."

"What are you seeing?"

"Mist."

"Mist? Is this a riddle, Simon?"

"Definitely. And the answer to the riddle is whatever is behind the mist, whatever it is that you're trying to keep us from seeing."

"You think I haven't been honest with you?"

"Maybe. Or maybe it's just that you haven't been completely honest. I get the feeling that you're throwing us bones, Cork, and keeping the meat for yourself."

A fair reading of the situation, Cork decided. In truth, he appreciated that Rutledge was approaching him this way rather than in some kind of confrontation with Sheriff Dross or Captain Ed Larson present.

"What would you like from me, Simon?"

"How about a name?"

"What name?"

"I think you know a lot more than you're telling about the Vanishings. I think you might even have a suspect in mind."

"What makes you think so?"

"Ah, you see? You didn't say I was wrong. Give me a name."

"Not yet."

"Why?"

"I need a little more time."

"You're asking a lot."

"Not really. What went on over forty years ago is ancient history, Simon. For those involved, it's over."

"Not quite over. There's Lauren Cavanaugh."

"Did you Simonize Hattie yet?"

Rutledge smiled at the reference to his interview technique. "I questioned her. Her attorney was present."

"What did she tell you?"

"I think that's something I'll hold on to."

"I'll make you a deal. I'll give you a name if you tell me what Hattie Stillday said when you questioned her."

Rutledge thought it over for a second. "Deal. You first."

"Indigo Broom," Cork said.

"What's that?"

"The name of a man reviled by the Ojibwe on the Iron Lake Reservation more than forty years ago."

"Responsible for the Vanishings?"

"I believe so."

"How do you know this?"

"I've asked a lot of questions and put the answers together. That headache you heard about. Someone coldcocked me this morning when I was at the site of Indigo Broom's cabin."

"What were you looking for?"

"I didn't know exactly. I just wanted to see where he lived. The cabin burned to the ground around the time the Vanishings ended, and Broom disappeared the same time. Word on the reservation was that he'd left to visit relatives and never returned. I think that wasn't true. I think he was burned along with his cabin. And one more thing,

Simon. I found manacles in the ruins. My guess is that's where the victims were killed."

"Where is this place?"

"A couple of miles north of the entrance Haddad and I found to the Vermilion Drift. I'll draw you a map. Now, what about Hattie Stillday?"

"One more question first. Do you have any idea who cold-cocked you?"

"Not at the moment. Like I told you this afternoon, I'm still working that one out. Honest."

"All right." Rutledge got up and stood at the porch railing. He looked across the quiet street, where rooftops half hid the setting sun. "Hattie Stillday definitely had something to do with the murder of Lauren Cavanaugh, but I haven't figured out what exactly. She knows some things, she hedges on others, and to some of my questions she gave the wrong answer."

"Like what?"

"Her story is that when she confronted Cavanaugh the woman went berserk. Began throwing things. Stillday moved to avoid one of the items and the gun went off. I asked her how far away from Cavanaugh she was at that point. She said a few feet. But according to the medical examiner, the powder burn indicates the shot was fired point-blank. Another thing. I asked her about the murder weapon, the thirty-eight she claims she's had forever. I asked her if she ever cleaned the weapon. She said she did. I asked her how she went about it. She couldn't answer."

"What did she have to say about getting rid of the body?"

"You've been thinking about that, too?" Rutledge smiled, as if it made perfect sense to him. "Her story is that she panicked, drove back to the rez, thought better of it, and came back to the center to clean things up and get rid of the body. I asked her how she managed to drive her truck, with Cavanaugh's body wrapped in a tarp, out to the rez and also get Cavanaugh's car out there. She wouldn't answer me. She's a tough lady, but I saw worry on her face, Cork."

"What did she say about the Vermilion Drift and the bodies there?"

"Absolutely nothing. When I tried to take the questioning in the direction of the Vanishings, she clammed up. Her attorney wouldn't let her answer any questions about the old killings. I got the feeling that, even if Oliver Bledsoe hadn't been present, Hattie Stillday would have told me squat about what happened over forty years ago. Is it possible she threw in with Broom back then?"

"Absolutely not, Simon. Hattie lost a child to the Vanishings. If it was Indigo Broom behind those killings, and I'm almost positive it was, the business Hattie had with him was a different kind of business entirely."

Rutledge stared at Cork for a moment. "You said Broom was burned along with his cabin. An accident?"

Cork shook his head. "I'd say justice."

The two men both stared toward the sunset, where the sky was going red.

"Simon, Hattie insists that she had nothing to do with the second set of threatening notes. Do you believe her?"

"Yeah, I do. Why would she confess to the killing but lie about that?"

"You know what it means?"

Simon's face was a red mask reflecting the vermilion sky. "It means we're still in the dark in a lot of ways."

"And," Cork added, "it means people associated with Vermilion One might still be in harm's way."

THIRTY-THREE

After Rutledge had gone, Cork got out the box given to him by Millie Joseph that contained his mother's journals. Since his conversation with Cy Borkman that afternoon, he'd been chewing on questions for which he had no answer. Had Borkman read the situation right? Had his father really been involved with another woman? If so, could that woman have been Monique Cavanaugh? Did his mother know?

He took the box to the patio and, in the warm blue of summer twilight, sat down and began to read.

> *January 1, 1965*
>
> *We didn't celebrate the beginning of this new year. We have no reason to celebrate. My husband is dead. My niece is dead, killed by a madwoman and an Ojibwe majimanidoo. And we who are left abide with our guilt, an uncomfortable companion in all our hours. I miss Liam so much. I will miss him forever.*

His mother had known about Monique Cavanaugh's involvement in the Vanishings, and something had happened in all that terrible, chaotic time that left her with guilt, *an uncomfortable companion in all our hours.* Was it something to do with Monique Cavanaugh's death? Was it guilt over having driven her husband away, driven him into another woman's arms? Guilt because there'd been no reconciliation before he died? But the guilt was some kind of collective guilt as well: *. . . we who are left.* Had she meant Cork, who, according to

Borkman, had been party to driving his father away? Or had she meant someone else?

He read entry after entry with no indication of remonstration against his father for unfaithfulness. Yet Borkman had been certain of the infidelity, uncertain only of the true identity of the woman his father had picked up at Jacque's.

Cork closed his eyes, trying hard to remember those days. He blanked. He recalled clearly the hospital vigil he'd kept with his mother while Liam O'Connor lay dying, but before that so much was missing, which was something he'd never really thought about before. Memories were always spotty at best, snapshots put together to create the sense of a more detailed whole. But the summer of 1964 was different. It wasn't just that there were no snapshots; it was a sense that, like those missing pages of his mother's journal, something important had been torn out.

It was nearly dark when he put the journals back into the box and went inside. He took the Rolodex from the desk in his office and flipped to a number he hadn't called in quite a while. He got voice messaging.

"This is Dr. Gray. I can't take your call at the moment. Leave a message and I'll get back to you as soon as I can."

Cork waited for the beep. "Faith, it's Cork O'Connor. I know you get this all the time, but here goes. I need your help and I need it now."

A summer storm moved in after dark, bringing a steady rain. Cork was preparing a night deposit slip at Sam's Place when Dr. Faith Gray returned his call. It was 10:45 P.M.

"You sounded pretty desperate," she said. "Are you all right?"

"Not really."

"I'm at home if it's an emergency."

"I'd appreciate talking to you."

"Come on over. I'll leave the porch light on."

Faith Gray lived four blocks from the O'Connor house, in a rambler painted light blue with yellow trim. She was a quirky homeowner, with no particular love of lawns. Her property was given over to hostas and planter boxes and rickety-looking trellis affairs without any apparent master plan. Sun catchers and medallions and odd, glittery bits hung on ribbons from the low branches of her trees. Here and there she'd stuck signs amid the foliage. The signs changed from time to time, depending upon the political season and the affairs of the world beyond Aurora, but they tended to praise peace and advocate justice and, in general, exhort people to follow a reasonable and compassionate path through the minefield of life.

Her porch light was on, as promised, and when Cork came out of the rain and mounted the front steps, she was already waiting at the door.

"Come in," she said with a gracious smile.

She was tall, solid, big-boned, with lovely, long gray hair, a plain, angular face, and eyes the welcoming green of ivy leaves. "I'm having chamomile tea. Would you like some?"

"No thanks."

"Suit yourself. Have a seat."

Her living room contained almost as much foliage as her yard, and Cork took an easy chair next to a healthy rubber tree plant.

"You look nice," he said.

She sat on the sofa, which was backed by a shelf of ferns. "A date."

"Do I know her?"

"This is about you," she said. "Talk to me."

"I need to remember some things, Faith."

"Okay."

"Things from my past. From my childhood. I try to reach back, and it's like everything is there except the one thing I'm trying to remember."

"That's not unusual. Our memories are protective that way."

"It's important that I remember this period."

"Why?"

"Is this confidential? Doctor-patient?"

Faith Gray was a psychologist. During his tenure as sheriff of Tamarack County, Cork had brought her on as a consultant to work on psychological assessments of new hires and to help establish guidelines and regulations concerning such things as treatment for deputies involved in officer-related shootings. He liked her. More important, he trusted her.

"I'll consider it so," she replied. "And I'll bill you for this session. I ought to warn you, I charge overtime." In response to his blank stare, she offered a smile. "That's a joke, Cork."

On the street outside, a car went past, and the sound of tires on the wet pavement was a long, heavy sigh. Faith Gray waited.

Cork gathered himself and said, "It's about the Vanishings."

He didn't tell her everything. He left out the parts that might incriminate anyone, and focused on those elements that were about his family, particularly Borkman's accusation concerning his father's infidelity. As evidence that there were things hidden, he also told her about the missing journal pages. He asked if she could maybe hypnotize him in order to help him remember what happened in the late, fateful part of the summer of 1964.

"I don't hypnotize people, Cork. But what I can do is guide you through some relaxation techniques that may help you retrieve the memories yourself."

"What do we do?"

"Why don't you start by lying down?"

They exchanged places, and Cork, once he'd laid himself on the sofa, could smell the hot chamomile tea in the cup on the end table.

"Close your eyes, and listen to my voice. What I'm going to do is offer you some suggestions meant to help your body and your mind relax. They'll all be very simple and very safe, all right?"

"I'm ready," Cork said.

She began in a soft voice and had him focus on his toes, on being aware of each of them. Gradually she moved up his body, toward the top of his head, but as she was leading him ever so gently through the relaxation of his eyes, Cork suddenly found himself in the middle of the nightmare, watching his father fall to his death.

He jerked awake.

"What is it?" Gray asked.

"Sorry. I must have fallen asleep."

"That happens sometimes."

"I was dreaming. A nightmare."

"Want to talk about it?"

He sat up and shook his head. "It was just a normal nightmare."

"One you've had before?"

"Yes."

"Often?"

"They began a little over a year ago."

"Is it the same nightmare every time?"

"Not exactly."

She sat patiently. Outside the window, rain dripped off the roof and hit the leaves of her yard plants with steady little slaps. Finally Cork told her. About how, when his father fell, it was in different ways, and how the nightmare repeated itself, and how, the second time around, he stood outside and watched himself push his father to his death.

"Just a normal nightmare?" she said. "Cork, dreaming that you had a hand in killing your father isn't exactly your usual thing-that-goes-bump-in-the-night nightmare."

"All right, what is it?"

"What kind of relationship did you have with your father?"

"He was a terrific father. I loved him."

"Yet time and again you push him to his death."

"Not because I didn't love him."

"Why then?"

"You're the mind reader. You tell me."

"Any conflicts with him?"

"Not that I remember. Although people I talk to lately tell me differently."

"What do they tell you?"

"That I was kind of a shit toward him."

"But you don't remember that?"

"No. It's part of all that stuff I can't recall."

"How old were you when he died?"

"Thirteen."

"It could be Oedipal," she said.

"What? I wanted him out of the way so that I could sleep with my mother? Right."

She shrugged. "I'm not a big fan of Freudian interpretations either."

"So what else?"

"How did he die?"

Cork explained the shoot-out at the bank and the vigil at the hospital.

"You were with him when he died?"

"Yes. My mother was there, too. Praying her heart out."

"What about you?"

"What do you mean?"

"Were you praying your heart out?"

He shook his head and realized the headache he'd had most of the day was coming back, big-time. "I knew it was hopeless."

"Why?"

"Because the doctor said so."

"Is that the only reason?"

"Probably not. I wasn't happy with God at that point."

"Oh?"

"Didn't believe him."

"Any particular reason?"

"I've always thought it was my age."

"Do you think it might have made a difference if you'd prayed?"

"Maybe. I suppose I've always wished I had."

"So do you think it's possible the root of the nightmare might be that you interpret not praying as pushing your father into his death?"

"I don't need a nightmare to tell me that. I've always felt guilty and always wondered if I'd prayed like my mother would it have made a difference. I thought nightmares were about things you didn't want to know about consciously."

"Nightmares can be complicated and about more than a single thing. Our minds are pretty complex, and connections can be intricate. You told me that the nightmares began a little over a year ago. That would be shortly after your wife died, yes?"

"Yes."

"Sometimes, Cork, when we see someone fall in our dreams, it may have to do with our own belief that we're lacking an essential quality they possess or that we've let them down somehow."

"But it was Jo I lost, not my father."

"Do you believe your father would have saved Jo?"

"What kind of question is that?"

"Just a question. But I think it's a relevant one, considering when the nightmares began."

"Nobody could have saved Jo."

"You sound a little angry."

"There's a lot going on. I'm kind of wound up."

"I understand."

She waited and watched him, and when she didn't offer anything further, he blurted, "Look, it's not about Jo, okay?"

"If you say so."

He pulled himself back, tried to quell his inexplicable anger, and said, "So what else could it be about?"

"It's possible the nightmare has to do with something very particular, something you don't remember from that time you can't recall."

"If it is, what do we do about it?"

"The truth is that nothing is ever lost. It's all in there somewhere," she said, tapping her head. "It could take a long time to crack that nut, Cork, but I'm willing to help you try. If you call my office tomorrow, I'll see when I can work you in."

"A long time?" Cork closed his eyes and rubbed his throbbing temples. "I'll think about it. Do I still have time on this hour?"

"Sure."

"What do you know about psychopathy?"

"That depends on what you're interested in."

"Can it be inherited?"

"There's a lot of research that points toward a genetic component."

"People can be born bad?"

"'Bad' is a judgmental term. But I believe people may be born without a conscience, yes. Environment also plays an important part in shaping psychopathic behavior. What you're talking about is generally referred to these days as dissocial or antisocial personality disorder, and psychopaths are generally referred to as antisocial personalities."

"A rose by any other name," Cork said. "They're good at hiding who they really are, right? Like Ted Bundy?"

"They can be very good. They're often bright, and although they don't feel remorse or guilt or empathy the way most people do, they know how to mask that. There have been a number of famous cases in which serial killers were able to hide their activities from wives or husbands or parents. But just because someone might be diagnosed with this disorder, that doesn't mean they're dangerous like Ted Bundy was dangerous. These traits can make them very successful in competitive environments, like business or politics."

"Are you saying our politicians are psychopaths?"

She smiled. "Some of them, probably. As were some of the great robber barons and industrialists, certainly."

"But they didn't kill people, at least not outright, not like Bundy or John Wayne Gacy. What makes someone do that?"

"We're outside my comfort zone of knowledge here, Cork. If you'd like, I'll do a little research on the subject. I know a couple of colleagues who are better versed in psychopathic behavior than I am. I'll be glad to talk to them."

"Thanks, Faith." He stood up, prepared to leave.

"You'll call tomorrow, make an appointment?"

"I'll think about it seriously."

But what he was really thinking was that he needed answers sooner than Faith Gray was going to be able to supply them.

It was still raining when he got home. As Cork stepped from the garage, Trixie poked her nose out the door of her doghouse and woofed. He freed her and let her in the house, gave her a fresh bowl of food and fresh water, took some Tylenol for himself, went out to the front porch, and sat on the swing. A few moments later, Trixie scratched at the screen, and Cork let her out so that she could join him.

They sat together while rain made everything that was illuminated by the streetlamps look liquid. The swing had been an important part of Cork's life. He and Jo used to sit in it after the kids had finally gone to bed, and they'd talked about the things that parents and married people and longtime lovers discuss in quiet voices meant not to be overheard. He missed that. Missed Jo. Although his deep grieving had long ago ended, he still sometimes found himself feeling terribly sad and abandoned. His children were gone, establishing their own lives, and that was only natural. But where did it leave him? What was the road ahead for a man who was no longer a husband and was a father mostly at a distance?

Thinking of all these things brought him back to the question Faith Gray had posed earlier: *Did he think his father might have saved Jo?* It seemed like a question out of left field, but it had stung him, and he wondered now where his anger had come from. He wasn't angry at Jo. He didn't believe he was angry at his father. And although he'd snapped at her, he hadn't been angry at Faith Gray.

"So who am I pissed at?" he asked aloud, putting the question to Trixie, who only looked up at him with her brown eyes and then nudged his hand to be petted.

At long last, Cork went back inside and headed upstairs to bed, where his only company for a long time had been his nightmares.

THIRTY-FOUR

Cork slept surprisingly well and woke with several ideas rolling around in his head, knocking together like ball bearings. He was eager to get some of them out of there.

His first stop that morning was the sheriff's department. Marsha Dross was at her desk, sipping from a big coffee mug. She had a thick folder open in front of her and was so intent on what it held that she didn't notice Cork's arrival. His "Good morning" startled her, and she spilled coffee over the documents and swore. She looked for something to wipe up the mess, had nothing at hand and, when Cork offered a clean handkerchief, accepted it, almost grudgingly.

"Sorry," he said.

"I didn't expect to see you so early." She handed his handkerchief back, damp and stained.

"You look like you could use a couple more hours of sleep."

"I could use some sleep period," she said.

"A case like this, a lot of monkeys on your back, I imagine."

"You don't know the half of it."

"I sat in that chair for seven years. Believe me, I do."

"Oh, is that so?" She stood up and leaned toward him, not in a friendly way. "You ever have an old serial killing and new murder dovetail? You ever have the newspapers call the department, and I quote, 'rural and rudimentary'? You ever had the entire board of commissioners visit you at ten P.M. on a Friday night to insist that you do more to, and I quote again, 'resolve this unfortunate situation before Tamarack County becomes the new Amityville Horror'?"

"Not really," Cork said. "Guess I must've been a better sheriff, huh?"

She gave him a hostile stare, then took stock of his smile, and finally let her body relax. "Have a chair," she said. When she'd retaken her own, she asked, "So what brings you here too early on a Saturday morning?"

"A few questions about your confessed murderer, Hattie Stillday. I'm not convinced you're getting the true story there."

"Nor am I. Rutledge said he filled you in. She knows things only the killer would know, but she's also wrong on some pertinent facts. She's involved, I'm just not sure in what way exactly."

"Are you going to hold her?"

"It's the weekend, so we can hold her without charges until court opens on Monday. I'm hoping we can use that time to work loose some better answers and maybe get some disturbing loose ends tied up. I'd hate to have someone of her reputation falsely charged. Definitely wouldn't look good for this 'rural and rudimentary' department."

"Did you do a follow-up interview with Derek Huff at the Northern Lights Center?"

"Ed Larson took that."

"And?"

"Huff and Lauren Cavanaugh were involved sexually. That's all there was to it, he insists. Sex. He was pretty open and nonchalant about it. Made it sound like not an unusual thing for a California kid, having sex with a woman twice your age."

"Kind of makes me wish I'd grown up out there." Cork smiled briefly.

Dross leveled a sober look at him, then went on. "If Hattie Stillday is right about the time of Lauren Cavanaugh's death, Huff has an alibi. He was out drinking with Sonny Gilroy. Larson confirmed that."

"Did he talk about the nature of the sex with Lauren Cavanaugh?"

"What do you mean?"

"I've got my suspicions that Cavanaugh was not exactly the lady she led people to believe she was. Bed is a place where masks get dropped pretty quickly."

"Maybe I'll have Ed talk to the kid again, push that issue," Dross said. "Have you come up with anything more in your own investigation?"

"You mean besides the probability that a Shinnob named Indigo Broom was responsible for the Vanishings and that he probably tortured and cannibalized his victims?"

"For God sake, don't say that to anyone with a pen and pad in their hand. Rutledge is in Bemidji this morning, discussing that possibility with Agent Upchurch."

"I'm pretty sure she'll confirm it."

"If it's true, we'll probably have to make it public at our press conference this afternoon. As for the possibility that Broom was burned along with his cabin, Ed and his guys are out there this morning, sifting through ash, looking for evidence. Depending on what they find, that could open a whole other can of worms on the rez. Cork, you're getting some good information out there, but I'll need to know names at some point."

"I understand." He stood up. "If I come up with anything else, I'll let you know. You'll do the same?"

"That's our deal, isn't it?"

They both smiled.

There was a program in progress at the Northern Lights Center, a showing. The lawn, still sparkling from the rain the night before, was set with easels displaying pieces by the current residents, who stood or sat next to their work. A long table had been set with refreshments and with a stack of brochures about the artists and the center in general. Cork ate a mini cinnamon roll and watched people milling about, moving from easel to easel, pausing, nodding, talking with the artists. Near the boathouse was a larger display, several easels with work clearly by the same artist, the featured artist, Derek Huff, who stood bathing in the glory offered him by the people of that rural and rudimentary county.

It was Ophelia Stillday whom Cork had come to talk to. He

wanted to know if she was aware of the relationship between Derek Huff and Lauren Cavanaugh. But Ophelia was nowhere to be seen.

He wandered onto a large, recently constructed flagstone patio and walked through French doors into the house. It was quiet, and the enormous place felt empty. He made his way to Ophelia's office, where he found the door closed but unlocked. He swung it open and was surprised to find Max Cavanaugh seated at Ophelia's desk, intent on the contents of a file folder opened in front of him.

"Max?"

Cavanaugh looked up, startled. "Hey, Cork."

"What are you doing here?"

Cavanaugh sat back and shook his head. "Battling, in a way."

Cork came into the room and approached the desk. "What do you mean?"

"I never come here. I hate this place. When I was a kid, for years after we moved away, I had nightmares about it."

"Lauren didn't feel the same way, apparently."

"Christ, I tried to talk her out of buying the estate, but she had her heart set on it. I knew nothing good would come from her being here." His face contorted in a way that made Cork wonder if he was ill. "Can't you feel it? This place is evil."

"*Mudjimushkeeki*," Cork said. "An Ojibwe word. It means 'bad medicine.'"

"It's certainly been bad medicine for my family."

"So if you hate this place, why are you here?"

"You asked me for information about my parents during the time my mother was alive. I thought maybe Lauren might have something. She always had a fascination where our mother was concerned."

"She was pretty young when your mother died."

"Too young to remember her at all. Maybe the reason for the wonderment."

"Have you found anything?"

"No."

Cork nodded toward the folder opened on the desk. "Those look like financial documents. Anything to do with your mother?"

Cavanaugh closed the folder. Cork saw that on the outside someone had doodled a figure that looked like a dog or a wolf. "They deal with the center. As long as I was here, I thought I'd check on the financial mess Lauren left behind."

"They're holding Hattie Stillday for her murder. You've heard?"

"Yeah. I got a call. I was always afraid that Lauren's shenanigans would get her into real trouble someday. I just never figured they would get her killed."

"You think Hattie's guilty?"

"I don't know Ms. Stillday well enough to say one way or the other. But the sheriff told me there's a lot of evidence pointing her way. And, hell, she confessed."

"Yeah," Cork admitted. "There's that."

Cavanaugh stood up, took the folder to one of the file cabinets, and slipped it into a drawer. When he turned back, he looked drained. "I've got to get out of here. This place is killing me."

"I understand."

Cork walked him to the front door, where Cavanaugh said, "You coming?"

"No, I'm here for the art show. Think I'll stroll around some more. Take care of yourself, Max."

Cavanaugh looked at him with eyes still sunk deeply in sadness. "You told me the other day, Cork, that time would heal. How much time does it take?"

Cork put his hand on Cavanaugh's shoulder. "More," he said.

After Cavanaugh had gone, Cork returned to Ophelia's office and pulled open the file drawer in which Max had put the folder. He thumbed through until he found the one with the canine doodle on the front. The folder was marked "Stillday, H."

Cork opened it and found several invoices for artwork. A yellow Post-it was affixed to the first invoice. On it was a handwritten note: *Pay this, you stinking whore!*

Hattie's writing? Cork wondered.

He put the folder back in the drawer, left the office, and headed down the hallway toward the north wing, which had been Lauren Cavanaugh's private residence. The door to the wing was unlocked. He retraced the steps he'd taken only a few days earlier, when he'd first been hired to find Max Cavanaugh's sister: through the study, the parlor, the dining room, the bedroom. As he went, he noted again the artworks that hung on every wall. Some were paintings, oil and watercolor and other media he couldn't even guess at. Many were photographs, a lot of them by Hattie Stillday but a few by Ophelia as well. The approaches of both women were similar, though Hattie clearly had the more seasoned eye. Her nature photographs didn't just frame a scene, they evoked atmosphere and mood and texture. They suggested story. He wondered which of the photographs were those Lauren Cavanaugh had purchased but never paid for, photographs important enough that Hattie claimed she had killed for them.

He sat on Lauren Cavanaugh's bed, wondering if this was where she'd had her romps with Derek Huff, or had she used the bed in the boathouse for that? He opened the drawers of her dresser again and went through her vanity. He checked her closets. He returned to the study and rifled the drawers of the desk. He came up empty-handed, even though he hadn't really known what he was looking for. He sat in an easy chair in the parlor and stared at the east wall, which was hung with an arranged display of photographs of the North Country. Three of the photos together formed a long panoramic view of a dramatic shoreline. They'd been shot in black and white, an odd choice, Cork thought, when the subject in reality was so vivid in its color—Iron Lake, which would have been hard blue against the powder blue of the sky, the face of a rock cliff, probably the gray of wolf fur, topped with aspens whose trunks were ivory and whose leaves would have been pale jade. He'd never understand art or artists, he decided, and got up and started away.

He'd reached the French doors and was about to step outside when it hit him. He turned and hurried back to the parlor and stood in front of the three photographs. The reason he'd been able to visualize the colors of the scene so well, he realized, was because he knew the place. A place of *bimaadiziwin*. It was where Cork's revolver had been hidden but was no more.

Although he could already tell who'd taken the photos, he leaned close and read the artist's tag to be absolutely certain.

Ophelia Stillday.

THIRTY-FIVE

H e asked at the refreshment table if anyone knew where Ophelia Stillday was. They pointed him toward the dock behind the boathouse, and he found her there, sitting by herself on a bench with her cane at her side. She stared out at Iron Lake, where a few sailboats clipped across the water, the triangles of their canvases like white knives cutting the air. She didn't hear him coming.

"Ophelia?"

Though he spoke gently, she looked at him with surprise and, he sensed, a little bit of fear.

"Okay if I join you?"

She didn't invite him immediately. She had to think it over.

"I guess," she finally said.

He sat next to her on the bench.

"You look worried," he said.

"About Grandma Hattie," she replied and returned to watching the sailboats.

"You know what I think about Hattie, Ophelia? I think she didn't do what she says she did."

Ophelia stared hard at the sailboats.

"I think she's covering for someone else. It must be someone she loves a lot, don't you think?"

"I wouldn't know," she said without heart.

"I think you would. Ophelia, tell me about shooting Lauren Cavanaugh."

When she finally looked at him, it was with something like relief. "How did you know?"

"Because I know where you got the gun. It's a place on the rez, a place of *bimaadiziwin*, of healing. How did you learn about it?"

"Grandma Hattie," Ophelia said. "She's shown me a lot of places sacred to our people. She never photographs them herself, but she said if I thought I could do them justice and be respectful that it would be all right."

"You went into the cave?"

"Yes. That wasn't part of what Grandma Hattie had in mind, I know, but I wanted to understand the full importance of the place, of *bimaadiziwin*."

"You took the gun?"

"Not then, but I knew it was there. When I finally understood Lauren, the real evil in her, I went back. But I only wanted to threaten her with the gun, not kill her."

"When you took it, the gun wasn't loaded, Ophelia."

"I bought cartridges. I went to a store in Eveleth so no one would recognize me."

"Most people when threatened with a firearm wouldn't know whether it's loaded. The firearm itself is usually enough to scare them. Putting bullets in, Ophelia, that makes me wonder."

She looked back at the sailboats, then up where an egret flew above them, white and elegant. "I don't know. Maybe I did want her dead. She was an awful person."

"Tell me about her."

She sighed deeply. "She wasn't anything like she made people believe. I mean she was smart and charming and all that, but it was all surface. Below that everything about her was dark. She lied. She connived. She manipulated. She had no sense of decency. But unless you were around her all the time, like I was, you wouldn't know because she was so good at keeping it hidden."

"Why didn't you leave her when you discovered what she was really like?"

"She promised to make sure the right people saw my work."

"That's it?"

She looked away.

"What else, Ophelia? It's all going to come out anyway, so you might as well tell me."

She laughed, but it was a sound without joy. "What was it you told me on the courthouse steps? The reasons people kill?"

She swung her eyes toward Cork, her young, pained eyes, and he understood.

"You loved her," he said.

"And I thought she loved me. She told me this leg of mine, this ugly, crippled thing, didn't matter to her. She told me she saw something beautiful in me and in my work." She was crying now, softly. "And I believed her."

"Oh, Ophelia," he said and took her in his arms and let her cry.

To love and to be loved, he thought. Oh, God, who didn't want that? And what parent didn't want this simple blessing for his child?

"It's all right, Ophelia," he cooed. "It's all right." As her sobs subsided, he asked gently, "So there's nothing between you and Derek?"

She shook her head. "I hated him at first. I thought he took Lauren from me. Then I realized Lauren simply used people and threw them away. But she didn't let go of them until she was ready, and I realized Derek was a prisoner just like me."

"What do you mean?"

"He wanted out of it. She wouldn't let him. She told him if he left her, she'd ruin him. She'd see to it that no one paid any attention to his work."

"The night you shot her, would you tell me about that?"

She wiped her eyes, then folded her hands and stared at them awhile, gathering herself before she began.

"We'd met with some of the center volunteers to talk about the new group of resident artists who would be arriving the next day. It was a kind of a cocktail thing. Lauren had a little too much to drink. After everyone left, she went to the boathouse. She called Derek from there and said she wanted to see him. He came down from his room angry. I was finishing up some work in my office. He stormed in and told me he felt like a servant being called to a duty. He basically said to hell with her and went into town instead to drink with Sonny Gilroy."

Gilroy was a local wildlife artist, a guy who liked his Johnnie Walker and painted great ducks.

"After he'd gone," Ophelia went on, "Lauren called me, demanded I get Derek out there. I'd had the gun for a while. I'd been imagining what it would be like to confront her with it. I don't know why exactly, but that night I decided it was time to find out. Maybe I'd had a little too much to drink, too. The truth is that I hated her. I hated what she'd done to me and I hated what she was doing to Derek. Everything in me just . . . hated her. So I loaded the gun with the cartridges I bought and went to the boathouse. I knocked. She told me to come in, and when she saw that it wasn't Derek, she went crazy, screaming at me all kinds of obscenities. I pointed the gun at her. Honest, I didn't really know what I was going to do. But it was like she didn't even get it. She screamed something like, 'Oh just give me that thing, you stupid bitch.' She started throwing stuff at me, whatever she could put her hands on. I tried to jump out of the way." She stopped, thought, then finished, "And the gun . . . just went off."

"How many times?" Cork asked.

"Once."

"You fired the revolver only once?"

"Yes."

"You're sure."

"I'm positive. I was horrified. I mean, oh, God, I couldn't believe what I'd done. I turned and I ran."

"Did the bullet hit her?"

"I guess. She fell back anyway."

"Did you take the gun?"

"When I got back to my office, I didn't have it. So I don't know, I must have dropped it. I was, like, in shock. I didn't know what to do. I left the center."

"And drove home to your grandma Hattie?"

"Yes."

"What did Hattie do?"

"Everything. She heard me out, and then we drove back to the center in her truck. There was Lauren lying dead on the boathouse floor. Grandma Hattie told me to help her, and we wrapped the body in a canvas tarp and put it in the back of the pickup. We cleaned up all the blood. Then I took Lauren's keys and got her car and followed Grandma Hattie out to the rez. She showed me where to ditch the car, and she drove me home and dropped me there. She said she'd take care of the body. She made me swear that I wouldn't say anything to anyone, that I would just pretend I knew nothing. And that's what I did."

"When Lauren's body was found with the others in the Vermilion Drift, did you ask Hattie about that?"

"Yes."

"What did she tell you?"

"Nothing. She said I should never ask about that again, ever, and I haven't."

"Okay, back to the shooting in the boathouse. How far away was Lauren when you shot her?"

"I don't know. Ten feet."

"You're sure?"

She thought a moment. "Yeah, pretty sure."

"Did she fall down?"

"Yes."

"Straight down, or did she fall back?"

She thought a moment. "She kind of stumbled back, like she was surprised or something, and then fell down."

"On her back?"

"I don't know. I don't remember."

"When you returned with Hattie, how was Lauren lying?"

Her brow furrowed, and she worked at remembering. "Facedown. I know because, when we lifted her up, there was blood all over the front of her dress and on the side of her face that had been on the floor."

"What time was this?"

"After midnight, maybe twelve-thirty."

"How long were you gone to Hattie's?"

"Maybe an hour and a half."

"So you shot Lauren at what time?"

"It was a couple of minutes before eleven when Derek left. I went to the boathouse a few minutes later, and I wasn't inside more than a minute when it all happened."

"When you left to go to Hattie's, did anybody see you?"

"I don't think so. Except for my office, the lights in the center were off. All the volunteers who'd had cocktails with us had gone home. The house staff were off for the weekend." She reached out for her cane. "I need to go now. I need to get Grandma Hattie out of jail."

Cork reached out and put a gentle restraining hand on her arm. "I'd like you to wait on that, Ophelia."

"Why?"

"Your grandmother can't be arraigned until Monday, but I suspect that our county attorney might be reluctant to charge her with anything. There are too many discrepancies in her story. I understand why now. Before you say anything to anyone, I'd like to do a little more investigating. I think I'm close to some answers, and I need a little more time."

"Answers? I gave you the answers."

"This is more complicated than you imagine, Ophelia. And Hattie's a tough old girl. She can take a day or two behind bars, especially because she's doing it for someone she loves. All right?"

She didn't seem entirely convinced, but she said, "Okay, Mr. O.C. If that's what you want. But will you do me a favor?"

"Sure, what is it?"

"When I finally do go in to talk to the sheriff, will you go with me?"

"Kiddo, I'll be right there holding your hand."

THIRTY-SIX

When Cork returned to the sheriff's department, Ed Larson was back from the site of Indigo Broom's burned cabin. He looked up as Cork walked into Marsha Dross's office, and he shook his head.

"Nothing?" Cork said.

"My guys are still out there sifting dirt, but it's not looking fruitful. Those manacles you mentioned to Rutledge? Not there. No bone fragments either. We didn't find anything but scraps of metal and broken glass and broken crockery, all of it showing char. Oh, Azevedo got excited about finding a nineteen twenty-five Peace silver dollar, whatever the hell that is."

"Did you see the rake marks?"

Larson nodded. "Somebody went over that area pretty carefully. After you got clobbered, how long were you out?"

"A couple of hours."

"That might have been enough time to clean that small area. Bottom line is that, at the moment, we don't have a thing to support any allegation against this Indigo Broom."

"It appears that somebody's protecting him. Which is odd," Dross said to Cork, "if what you've told us about him is true."

"I'm only repeating what I heard."

"Heard where?" Dross said.

"I can't divulge that at the moment."

"If you did, we might be able to twist some arms legally."

"They'd be Ojibwe arms and you'd get nothing. Ed, did you talk to Max Cavanaugh about his mother?"

"Yes. He claims he doesn't remember much about his mother, but what he does remember is all good, warm, motherly stuff."

"He said that?"

Larson pulled out a small notepad from his shirt pocket, flipped a couple of pages, read a moment, and said, "Yep."

The sheriff and Larson both looked at Cork with blank faces.

"I can't give you any more than I already have," he told them.

Dross sat back in her chair and crossed her arms. "Because there's no more to give or because you're just not willing to give any more? Or am I being too pushy here?"

"I told you about the Ojibwe, Marsha. You can't twist arms. What they give me, they give in their own time and in their own way."

"Which is exactly how you give it to us," she said.

Cork said, "Any chance I could get my hands on the M.E.'s final autopsy report for Lauren Cavanaugh?"

"What do you want to know?" Larson asked.

"Tom Conklin said he found two wounds. One of them appeared to be superficial, right?"

"That's right," Larson said. "A graze on her left side below her rib cage."

"Fired at close range or from a distance?"

"No tattooing, no singeing, so probably from a distance. Why are you asking?"

"Just collecting pieces of the puzzle, Ed. You checked out Derek Huff's alibi, that he was drinking with Sonny Gilroy, right?"

"Gilroy confirmed it."

"How long did they drink together?"

"Until about midnight."

"Then Huff went back to the center?"

"That's what he said."

"To bed?"

"I didn't ask him that." Larson studied him a moment. "You like Huff for the shooting?" Larson shook his head. "He was at the Black Bear with Gilroy when Cavanaugh was killed."

"That's true only if Cavanaugh was killed when Hattie said she was. But we all know there are holes in Hattie's story."

"Maybe, but she sure as hell hauled the body away and dumped it.

Look, Cork, I know how you feel about Hattie Stillday, but you're wasting your time with Huff, I can guarantee it."

At the moment, there was no reason for Cork to argue.

Dross said, "The pieces of this puzzle that you're collecting, Cork, if you put them together, you'll let us know, right?"

"I'll do that, Marsha."

"And not on Ojibwe time," she added.

"One more thing," Cork said. "Any chance you'd let me talk to Hattie again?"

Dross looked at Larson, who voiced no objection. "I'll have her brought to the interview room," the sheriff promised.

"Mind if I take her a cigarette?"

"Be my guest."

Hattie Stillday listened impassively while she smoked the Marlboro that Cork had brought her. When he finished talking, she said, "You think you've been a pretty good father, Corkie?"

It was a question that caught him off guard, but he answered honestly, "I think I've done my best, Hattie."

"You probably have." She sat back, tired. "I was a shitty mother. My girls were less important to me than my photographs. I was tramping all over hell and gone, making a name for myself when I should've been home. Couldn't keep a husband. Let my mother raise my girls. They were little hellions, of course. Into all kinds of trouble. When Abbie disappeared, I figured she'd just run off, which, in its way, was what I'd done. Janie, that was Ophelia's mother, she couldn't wait to get away. Ended up dying in a rat's nest of a place in Los Angeles, heroin overdose. Which was how I ended up with Ophelia. You shoulda seen that little girl when I went out to L.A. to get her. Broke my heart. I swore I'd take care of her better than I did her mother. And I have, Corkie. Hell, life's not been kind to that girl, but she never gives up."

Hattie Stillday let out a trickle of smoke that climbed her cheek, where it met a little stream of tears.

"I lost two daughters because of my selfishness. I've always looked on my granddaughter as a way to make amends. I swear I've done my best by Ophelia. I'll die, yes, I will, before I see that girl lost to me." She gave him a look that was iron hard and at the same time full of soft pleading. "You can't tell them. Promise me you won't say a thing about Ophelia. Promise me, Corkie."

"I'll make a deal with you, Hattie. Tell me how you knew about the bodies in the Vermilion Drift and I promise I won't say a thing about Ophelia."

She drew back, drew herself up. "You got no idea what you're asking."

"That's the deal I'm offering."

She stared at him, the cigarette idle in her fingers, a snake of smoke coiling between her and Cork. "Would you really break my heart? I'm asking you—begging you. If someone has to pay for what happened to Lauren Cavanaugh, Corkie, let it be me."

He could have played her longer, played her harder, but he didn't have it in him. He said, "I don't think Ophelia killed Lauren Cavanaugh, Hattie."

She looked startled, then disbelieving. "Is this some kind of trap?"

"I think the bullet your granddaughter fired only grazed the woman. After Ophelia left for the rez, someone else came to the boathouse."

"Who?"

"I don't know yet."

"Did you say anything to the sheriff?"

"No. It would have required explaining about Ophelia."

"When are you going to tell them?"

"Not until I have a few more answers."

"Answers that will keep my granddaughter's name out of all this?"

"It's like how I raised my children, Hattie."

"What do you mean?"

"I'll do my best."

*　*　*

Cork left the sheriff's department and drove back to the Northern Lights Center for the Arts.

It was just after noon, and the day was growing hot and humid. The gathering had thinned as people began to think about lunch. Each of the artists displaying work had been given a deli box, and they were all relaxing at the moment, eating sandwiches. Derek Huff sat apart from the others, alone on the grass that edged the shoreline of the lake.

Cork stood between Huff and the sun, in a way that made the young artist squint as he looked up. "Remember me, Derek?"

Huff smiled, a genuinely friendly gesture, and Cork could see why women would fall for the kid. He was good looking, with blond hair that tickled his shoulders, a deep tan, the build of a swimmer.

"I'm afraid I don't," Huff said.

"My name's O'Connor. I'm working with the sheriff's department on the Lauren Cavanaugh murder investigation."

Recognition lit Huff's eyes. "You're the guy who found Lauren's body in that mine tunnel."

"I'd like to talk to you about your relationship with her."

"I already talked with somebody from the sheriff's office."

"Captain Ed Larson," Cork said. "I'd like to ask a few questions he didn't."

Huff shrugged easily. "Sure."

Cork glanced around, saw an empty folding chair, grabbed it, and set it next to Huff. "Derek—you mind if I call you Derek?"

"Go ahead."

"Derek, we know you had a sexual relationship with Lauren Cavanaugh. From what I understand, it wasn't exactly a healthy kind of thing."

Huff looked uncomfortable. "What do you understand?"

"She did a lot of threatening."

"That's true."

"Pissed you off, I understand."

"So?"

"Maybe enough for you to kill her?"

"Hey, I was drinking with an artist friend when Lauren was shot. Ask that other guy, Larson. He knows."

"You left the bar around midnight. What did you do then?"

"Came back here, went to bed."

"You didn't stop by the boathouse?"

"Are you kidding? Lauren was in a mood. I didn't want to have anything to do with her."

"What happened in your relationship?"

Huff put his half-finished croissant sandwich back in his deli box and set the box on the grass. "Look, I know my way around women, okay? Lauren was like no woman I'd ever come across."

"How so?"

"She was one thing at first, then she turned into something else. You know *The Wizard of Oz*? She started out all Good Witch of the North, but ended up Queen of the Flying Monkeys."

"Tell me about it."

Huff actually looked pained as he recalled. "At first, it was pretty normal, then things began to get too weird. She'd, like, want to tie me up, which I would have been okay with except I got really uncool vibes from her. Get this, man. A week ago she pulls out a gun, puts the barrel inside her, and tells me to pull the trigger."

"By 'inside her' you mean . . . ?"

"I'm not talking about her mouth, dude. But, look, it wasn't just the strange sex stuff. She was always making promises she had no intention of keeping. She was going to make my name huge in the art world. She was going to introduce me to important gallery owners. She didn't do any of that. And when I got pissed because of it, she threatened me. And not only that, man, she was really cruel to Ophelia sometimes."

"Did she behave bizarrely to anyone else?"

"Naw, with everybody else she was all sugar and spice."

"Did you tell any of this to Captain Larson when he interviewed you?"

Huff shook his head. "I didn't think he'd believe me."

"I believe you. But I also think you might have killed her."

"No way. I told you, I was drinking with Gilroy. Besides, Ophelia's grandmother confessed."

"I don't think Hattie's confession is going to stand up, and I don't think Lauren died when Hattie said she did. I think there was time for you to have come back and visited the boathouse and shot her."

The kid looked scared now. "Jesus, I told you. I went straight to bed. Look, I can prove it. I keep a video diary. It's up in my room. Every night when I go to bed, I record something. I'll show you."

Huff got up and led the way back to the big house and upstairs to his room, which was at the end of the south wing. He went to the desk, where a laptop sat open. He sat down at the desk and worked the touch pad.

"It's got a built-in webcam," he said.

In a moment he brought up a piece of video that carried a time-date stamp in the lower right-hand corner. The date was the Sunday that Lauren Cavanaugh died, and the time was 12:17 A.M.

Derek Huff stared out from the screen of the laptop. For a long time he said nothing, just sat looking hollow-eyed and drunk. When he finally spoke, it was three sentences full of despair.

"Tomorrow I tell Lauren to go to hell. I miss the ocean. And I hate the fucking smell of pine trees."

THIRTY-SEVEN

Although Derek Huff's video diary proved absolutely nothing, the feel Cork got from the kid—that he didn't kill Lauren Cavanaugh—was genuine. He was also thinking about the squealing tires Brian Kretsch had reported on North Point Road well before Huff returned to the center. He didn't write the kid off completely, but when he left Huff's room, he turned his thinking to other possibilities.

He drove to his house on Gooseberry Lane, had some lunch, and afterward took Trixie for a midday walk. While he walked, he thought.

If not Ophelia, if not Hattie, if not Huff, then who?

He didn't get much further before a black Tahoe pulled to the curb beside him, with a familiar Shinnob at the wheel. Tom Blessing leaned across the seat and hollered out the passenger window, "Hey, Cork! Somebody on the rez you need to talk to."

"Mind if I bring my dog?"

"No problem. Hop in."

Cork opened the passenger door, and Trixie, who hadn't learned and probably never would learn to distrust strangers, eagerly leaped in ahead of him.

"I tried your home phone and Sam's Place," Blessing said, pulling away from the curb. "Didn't have your cell number, so I finally decided to come into town and see if I could track you down."

"What's up?" Cork asked.

"You'll see when we get to Allouette."

Blessing headed out of Aurora, around the southern end of Iron Lake, and back up the eastern shoreline. He drove with the windows down, something Trixie thought was heaven. She sat on Cork's lap with her head outside, blinking against the wind.

"Heard that with all the crap that's happened in the Vermilion One Mine the government's going to look elsewhere to store all their nuclear junk," Blessing said. "True?"

"As far as I know, all they've done is pull the survey team back. They haven't crossed the mine off their list yet."

"But they're thinking about it?"

"That's my hope. A lot of bad publicity so far, and the worst is yet to come. But it's the government, and you know how deep bureaucratic stupidity can run."

"What do you mean the worst is yet to come? What's worse than a bunch of bodies stuffed in a mine tunnel?"

What happened to those bodies before they got there was what Cork thought but didn't say.

Instead he replied, "I'm just thinking there's no chance they can spin any of this in a good way, Tom."

"Are you kidding? They sold an entire nation of Christian folk on the idea of killing most of us Indians. If there's a way to make radioactive drinking water sound like Kool-Aid, the federal government'll find it."

A few miles outside Allouette, Blessing got on his cell phone. "We'll be there in ten minutes," he said. "You still got him? Good." He snapped the phone shut and slipped it back into his shirt pocket.

They entered Allouette, pulled onto Manomin Street, and swung into the parking lot of the community center.

"How long will this take, Tom? I'm wondering if I should leave Trixie in the truck."

"Bring her in. Elgin'll watch her."

Inside the center, they walked down a long hallway, past the open doors to the gym, where Ani Sorenson was running some girls from the rez basketball team, the Iron Lake Loons, through drills. They passed the door to the administrative wing, where all the tribal offices were situated, and they took a right toward the room where Blessing did his work.

Tom Blessing had been a hard case. He'd been a leader in a gang of Ojibwe youths who'd called themselves the Red Boyz. As a result of a remarkable and deadly firefight on the rez, he'd experienced a radical transformation. Now he was deeply involved in the Wellbriety Movement, helping troubled Ojibwe kids find their way on a healing path using the teachings of elders and based on ancient wisdom and natural principles.

On his door hung a poster of a white buffalo. Inside his office, the walls were plastered with photographs of Blessing and some of the other former Red Boyz, along with a lot of kids doing a lot of things—learning to make birch bark canoes, harvesting wild rice, boiling down maple sap into syrup, playing softball, serving fry bread at a powwow, preparing for a sweat.

Elgin Manypenny, who'd also been one of the Red Boyz, sat on Blessing's desk. In a chair shoved against one of the walls slumped a teenage kid. Cork knew him. Jesse St. Onge. His uncle Leroy stood next to him.

"*Boozhoo*, Elgin, Leroy," Cork said and shook each man's hand in turn. "*Boozhoo*, Jesse."

"*Anin*," the kid replied respectfully.

"Shake the man's hand," St. Onge said.

The kid reached up and did as he was told.

"Sit down, Cork," Blessing said. "Elgin, mind taking Trixie for a walk?"

"Happy to." Manypenny slid from the desk. "Come on, girl. Let's go play."

Trixie didn't hesitate a second.

Blessing sat in his desk chair and nodded to Leroy St. Onge, who held out a folded piece of paper toward Cork.

"Found that in my nephew's coat pocket this morning," he said.

Cork unfolded the paper. Printed inside in the bloody From Hell font were the words *We Die. U Die.*

"Jesse got one of these threats?" Cork asked.

"Not exactly," Leroy St. Onge said. "Go on, Jesse. Tell him."

The kid focused on his hands, which were folded in his lap. He didn't say anything at first.

"Jesse," his uncle said.

The kid gathered himself and mumbled, "Okay, I did the throw up in the Vermilion One Mine."

"The throw up?" Cork asked.

Blessing explained. "When a piece of graffiti art is done fast, it's called a 'throw up.'"

"It was you? How did you get into the mine?"

"Through the entrance on the rez that the cops got all taped up now."

"How'd you know about that entrance, Jesse?"

The kid got quiet again.

"Go on," his uncle said sternly.

"Isaiah Broom."

"Did he go into the mine with you?"

"No, just showed me the way. He wouldn't, you know, go in himself."

"Why not?"

Jesse shrugged.

Everyone waited.

Finally Jesse said, "I got the feeling he was scared."

"But you weren't?"

"No." The kid straightened up in a display of bravado.

"You went in alone?"

"Yeah. I took a flashlight and my paint cans and this printout Isaiah gave me of what he wanted me to do."

"Did you notice anything strange in the mine?"

"Yeah, the smell. Like something dead. I understand now, but I just thought, you know, that maybe an animal got stuck in there and died. I didn't think . . . you know."

"Sure, Jesse," Cork said. "Tell me about being in the mine."

"Well, I went in like Isaiah showed me, and it was real dark and spooky. I had a flashlight but it wasn't much and going into all that dark was like pushing through mud. I went all the way to the end of the tunnel. There was a wall and I couldn't go any farther. I went back and told Isaiah, and we left and went to his place, and he got some stuff, power tools, you know, and we came back. This time he came in with me."

"He went all the way in?"

"Yeah, but he was all jumpy, like the place was full of ghosts or something. We got to the wall, and Isaiah cut through it, and we crawled in and kept going to where the elevator shaft was. I was going to do my piece there, but Isaiah said we should go down farther so they wouldn't know how we got in. So we climbed down this ladder that was, you know, next to the elevator. Isaiah showed me where he wanted me to work. Me, I wanted to do something I'd be proud to tag, but he wanted it done just like he'd printed out and he wanted it done fast."

"It was Isaiah's design?"

"I guess. I'm all like, hey, man, it's not aesthetic. But it was what he wanted, so I just did the throw up, and we left."

"Why?"

The kid stared at Cork. "What do you mean?"

"Why did you agree to do what Broom asked?"

"You mean his design?"

"No, the whole thing in general. It was pretty risky."

"I don't want all that radioactive stuff here," Jesse said, as if it should have been perfectly obvious to anyone. "It was a way of fighting back. The warrior's way," he added proudly. "Isaiah, he's been sort of leading the protest, and when I told him I wanted to help, he said The People could use my talent. See, on the rez I've got kind of a rep for my work. Isaiah said he had an important job for me."

"'We Die. U Die.' What did that mean?"

"Just, you know, that if the junk they put in there leaks, we're all dead. Even the assholes who are responsible."

"Who would those assholes be?"

"I don't know. The guys who make the decisions, I guess."

"Names?"

"I don't know."

"Max Cavanaugh? Lou Haddad? Eugenia Kufus?"

"I don't know who those guys are."

"Some of the people making the decisions. They all got notes saying 'We Die. U Die.' Do you know anything about that, Jesse?"

"No, nothing. I just did the throw up in the mine."

"We Die. U Die. Who came up with that?"

"Me, sort of. When I was on the protest line in front of Vermilion One, I said we should have a sign that read something like 'This won't kill just us. It will kill everybody.' Isaiah liked it, but he shortened it for the throw up."

Leroy St. Onge asked, "What kind of trouble is he in, Cork?"

"Trespass with criminal intent, maybe. Vandalism." He leveled a long look at Jesse. "His heart was in the right place, and I think even the people who own the mine aren't excited about the prospect of dumping nuclear waste there, so I'm guessing that, when the whole story's known, no charges will be brought. That's certainly the recommendation I'll make to the mine people and the sheriff."

St. Onge said, "I think I need to have a talk with Isaiah Broom."

"Get in line, Leroy," Cork said.

"Can we go now?" Jesse asked.

"As far as I'm concerned," Cork told him. "Look, I'll do what I can to make things easy for you, Jesse, but the sheriff's people will want to talk to you."

He made a sour face. "Ah, man."

"I'll be there with you," his uncle said and put his hand on the boy's shoulder.

"Mind giving us a few minutes alone, Cork?" Blessing asked.

"No. I need to go outside and make a call on my cell phone anyway. Meet you at your truck?"

"Fine."

Cork left the way he'd come. Outside, he could hear Trixie barking in the park next to the marina a block away, and he saw Manypenny throwing a Frisbee, which Trixie was having a great time chasing down. He plucked his cell phone from its belt holster, pulled up the number from which Rainy Bisonette had called two nights earlier, and punched redial. While he waited, he watched Trixie having the best time she'd had since Stephen left for West Texas. He made a mental note: *Play more with the dog.*

Rainy answered, her voice distant and impersonal. "Yes, Cork?"

"*Boozhoo,*" he said, trying to be cordial.

"What do you want?"

All business, this woman. *All right then,* he thought, and got down to it.

"What time did Isaiah Broom leave Crow Point yesterday?"

"Early. Shortly after sunup."

"Any idea where he was headed?"

"He didn't say."

"Is Henry there?"

"No. He's out gathering."

Herbs, Cork figured.

"How did Broom seem when he left?"

"Hungover. Worried."

"Did Henry talk to him?"

"Not really. Broom hurried off like a man on a mission. Uncle Henry couldn't persuade him to stay."

"Thanks, Rainy."

"For what?"

He meant to say for the information she'd just given him. But what came out was "For taking care of Henry. I love that old man."

Her end of the line was quiet. "So do I," she finally said, speaking more gently than she ever had to Cork.

When he hung up, he headed immediately back into the community center. He ran into Blessing outside the open gym doors and spoke over the squeak of rubber soles on urethane.

"I need a favor, Tom."

"Ask."

"I need to borrow your truck for a little while."

Blessing reached into the pocket of his pants, pulled out his keys, and handed them over.

"Is it okay if Elgin plays a little longer with Trixie?" Cork asked.

"How long will you be?"

"Not long if I can find the man I'm looking for."

"Broom?" Blessing guessed.

"Broom," Cork said.

THIRTY-EIGHT

Isaiah Broom lived in a cabin of his own design and making. It stood at the end of a short stretch of dirt track in a small clearing a couple of miles east of Allouette. Where the track split from the asphalt of the main road, Broom had pounded a post and hung a sign from it: *Chainsaw Art.*

As Cork drove into the clearing, he spotted Broom in front of the cabin, shirtless, a big Stihl chain saw in his hands, working on a section of maple log that stood six feet high. The noise of the saw drowned out the sound of Blessing's truck, and Broom didn't notice Cork's approach until the vehicle pulled to a stop in a shroud of red dust.

Broom shut off the chain saw and watched Cork come. He didn't put the Stihl down. In the heat of the summer afternoon, his powerful torso dripped with sweat.

"Isaiah."

"What do you want, O'Connor?"

"How's the head?" Cork asked.

"Huh?"

"Heard from Rainy that you were a little hungover the other day. I know how that feels. You okay now?"

"My head's fine," Broom said.

"Aren't you going to ask about mine?"

"Why should I?"

"Somebody whacked me good yesterday. Right here." Cork pointed toward the back of his head. "Still a little tender, but I'm okay. Thanks for your concern."

Broom finally lowered the chain saw to the ground, where it sat amid chips and sawdust. "What's your game, O'Connor?"

"Looks like it's going to be twenty questions. What did you do with the things you raked up at your uncle's cabin?"

"I don't know what you're talking about."

"I was out at Indigo Broom's yesterday morning. Just wanted to see the place for myself. Or what remained of it, which wasn't much. I stumbled onto a couple of items that made me believe some of the things I've been thinking lately about your uncle are true. Then I get hit on the head, and when I come to these things are gone, along with anything else that might incriminate your uncle."

"I wouldn't go spreading rumors about my family if I was you, O'Connor."

"See, right there, that's the point."

"What point?"

"I can't think of anybody who'd care what I said about Indigo Broom except you. And I know you were no fan of the man. So the only thing that makes sense to me is that you're trying to protect your family and your family's name. You don't want it associated with the kinds of things your uncle did. Considering the monster he was, if I was you, I wouldn't want that either. Family's important, Isaiah, and should be protected. I get that."

Broom's hands drew themselves into fists. "Get out of here, O'Connor."

"So the first thing I want to say is that my head's all right, and, all things considered, there's no need for you to apologize." Cork gave him a quick smile, then went on. "Now we come to the part that's more troublesome. I just had a long talk with Jesse St. Onge. I know you put him up to the graffiti in the mine. I know you showed him the way in and you cut through the wall in the Vermilion Drift and led him to the place you wanted him to put his throw up."

"His what?"

Cork laughed. "Yeah, sounds funny, doesn't it? His art, Isaiah. Except that it wasn't really his art. It was yours. Exactly the same design that was on the threatening notes a bunch of folks in Tamarack County got. You sent those notes."

Broom's fists relaxed, then balled again, and Cork wondered if the man was aware at all of his body language.

"I don't know what you're talking about," Broom said.

"Oh, I'm certain you do. And when Jesse tells his story to the sheriff's people, they'll be certain, too. The thing I don't understand is why you killed Lauren Cavanaugh."

"I killed Lauren Cavanaugh? What the hell are you talking about?" Now his hands went limp, as if they'd just let go of something.

"The second set of notes. The ones you sent to Haddad's wife and put on the windshield of Genie Kufus's car and stuck to Max Cavanaugh's door with a hunting knife. See, whoever wrote that second set of notes knew Lauren Cavanaugh was dead. That was something known only to the authorities and to those of us on the inside. And, of course, the killer."

"Second set of notes? Look, O'Connor, I don't know anything about a second set of notes. Yeah, I went into the mine with Jesse and we put up the warning. And, yeah, I sent some threats to Haddad and Cavanaugh and that Kufus woman. Just to scare them. But I didn't have anything to do with those other notes you're talking about. And I sure as hell had nothing to do with killing Lauren Cavanaugh. Why would I kill her? I didn't even know her. My only concern in all this is to keep nuclear waste away from our land, to protect Grandmother Earth."

"Where did you get the font you used for the notes?"

"Off the Internet. You can get any damn thing off the Internet."

"Mind showing me?"

Broom looked at Cork as if the request was crazy.

"The police will be asking you to do the same thing, Isaiah, after Jesse talks to them. If I get a jump on things, maybe I can help protect your family's name."

Broom eyed Cork, made a sound like he'd just forced something odious down his throat, and turned to his house. Cork followed him inside.

Broom was a man who'd never married, and his place showed no evidence of a woman's influence. It was cluttered with papers and magazines. Broom subscribed to a lot of publications across a broad spectrum of interests. *American Indian Culture and Research Journal. American Indian Quarterly. Anishnabeg Mom-Weh Newsletter. The New Yorker. The Wall Street Journal. Time. Mother Jones. National Geographic.* And others sitting in stacks around the living room and dining area. The floor hadn't been swept since the Ice Age, and from the mess he could see through the doorway to the kitchen, Cork was very glad Broom would never invite him to lunch.

Broom went to a desk in a corner of the living room where a computer tower and monitor and DSL modem had been set. On a cart next to the desk was an ink-jet printer. He plopped down in the desk chair and brought the machine out of hibernation. With a couple of clicks of his mouse, he was on the Internet. Cork watched over Broom's shoulder as he hit the drop-down box in Google search, checked his search history, found a website with the URL http://www.eyepoppingfonts.com, and clicked on it. Once the website came up, Broom navigated quickly to the font called From Hell.

"There." He shoved away from the desk.

"You did that pretty quickly," Cork said.

"Any idiot could do it quickly," Broom said, then gave Cork a cold look and added, "Even you."

They went back outside and stood near the sculpture, which was barely begun and showed no sign yet of what it would become. Cork touched the rough-cut wood. "What's it going to be, Isaiah? An eagle?"

"*Animikii.*" A thunderbird. "What happens now?"

"You'll get a visit from the sheriff's people, I imagine. But it would probably be best if you visited them. It would look better. And you'd also have high ground for any activist statements you might want to throw in. But take a lawyer with you."

Broom bent and lifted his chain saw. His face was like the wood of the sculpture, hard to read.

"Isaiah, there's no way I can keep your uncle's name out of this. We both know what he did."

Broom gave the chain saw cord a yank. The roar of the motor would eat anything more Cork might have had to say, so he simply turned and left.

THIRTY-NINE

It was midday and hot under a cloudless sky when Blessing dropped Cork and Trixie back at the house on Gooseberry Lane. Cork tethered his dog to her doghouse and prepared to head to the sheriff's office to report what he'd learned. He was two steps from his Land Rover when Simon Rutledge drove up in his state car, parked in the driveway, and got out. He was wearing a gray sport coat and blue shirt, no tie. In his right hand he held a six-pack of cold Leinenkugel's.

"Got a minute or twelve?" Rutledge asked, lifting the beer toward Cork as enticement.

"Depends on what you've got on your mind, Simon."

"Beer. What else do you need to know?"

Cork waved him to the front porch, and the two men settled in the swing. Rutledge handed Cork a bottle, then took one for himself. They unscrewed the caps and sat for a minute, letting the brew wash their throats.

"Nothing better than a cold beer on a hot summer afternoon," Rutledge said.

"Agreed."

Two boys of maybe ten or eleven rode by on bicycles, carrying tennis rackets, heading, Cork figured, to the courts in Grant Park.

"You know, tomorrow's my son's birthday," Rutledge said.

"Yeah? How old?"

"Thirteen."

"Teenager. Tough times ahead."

"He's a good kid. I'm not worried. I'd love to be there."

"Why can't you?"

"Because we're close to an end here. I can feel it. I don't want to leave until I know we can shut the lid on this one."

"This isn't just one thing, Simon. It's a whole bunch of things."

"Yeah, but they're all tied together somehow, Cork. And you know what?" He laid his arm on the back of the swing and gave Cork a long look. "I think you've got an idea how."

Cork smiled despite himself. "Gonna Simonize me?"

"I was kind of hoping the alcohol might loosen your tongue."

Cork laughed. He heard Trixie barking and said, "Be right back, Simon." He went through the house and out the patio door to where he'd tethered Trixie. He freed her, and she followed him eagerly to the front porch. She jumped on the porch swing beside Rutledge and nuzzled his hand.

"You spend a lot of time with this dog," Rutledge noted.

"Nobody else around to see to her these days. Same goes for me." Cork sat on the swing, so that Trixie was between him and Rutledge. He patted her head gently. "This isn't exactly how I'd envisioned spending my time once the nest was empty, Simon. I figured Jo and me, we'd do the things we were always talking about doing. She wanted to spend a month in Italy, rent a villa in Tuscany, you know? Me, I never had much interest in Italy, but if that's what she wanted." Trixie looked up at him with affectionate brown eyes. "What do you say, girl? Want to go chase some Italian rabbits one of these days?" He glanced at Rutledge and apologized. "Sorry. Off topic."

"No problem," Rutledge said quietly.

Cork told him much of what he'd learned that day, including his speculation that someone other than Hattie Stillday had killed Lauren Cavanaugh. He kept Ophelia's name out of it. For the time being.

"Okay," Rutledge said, nodding tentatively. "So who did kill Cavanaugh? What about Broom?"

"He's copped to the graffiti and to the first notes but swears he had nothing to do with the murder or the second round of notes. If he's telling the truth, then someone else sent them."

"You believe him?"

"I do, but that doesn't mean I haven't been fooled."

"Okay, if not him, then who?"

Cork sipped his beer and stared at the shadow on his lawn cast by the big elm. "I've been thinking about the timing of Lauren Cavanaugh's murder. Someone visited her after Hattie left and before she returned, and that person probably killed her. So was this person's visit an unfortunate accident? Or did this person know an opportunity existed and took it?"

"How would they know?"

"A couple of possibilities. Either they responded to the shot fired by Hattie or they came because Lauren Cavanaugh called them."

"Maybe she had another appointment that evening?" Rutledge offered.

"I don't think so. According to Ophelia, she was all set to spend the night with Huff, but he crapped out on her."

"So," Rutledge said, clearly skeptical, "you're saying she'd been grazed by a bullet and was still looking for someone to sleep with?"

"More probably someone to take care of her, to bind her wound, to sympathize."

"Who would that be?"

"Didn't Ed say that the last call from her cell phone was made a little after eleven?"

"That's right," Rutledge replied.

"Do you know who she called?"

He shook his head. "We can phone Ed and find out. But what about the possibility that someone heard the shot and used the opportunity?"

"It would most likely have been someone at the center, but the center was empty that night. All the staff had gone home, and the new residents didn't come until the next day."

Rutledge thought it over. "All right. What say we find out who she called before she died?" He set his bottle on the porch and pulled his cell phone from the pocket of his sport coat. He tapped in a number, put the phone to his ear, and waited. "Ed. Simon here. A question for you. Who did Lauren Cavanaugh call the night she died?" He listened. "Uh-huh. That's it? Just the one call, you're sure? Thanks, Ed." Rutledge slipped the phone back into his coat pocket. He reached down, picked up his beer, and took a long draw.

"So?" Cork said.

Rutledge ran the beer around in his mouth, then swallowed. He looked at Cork and said, "Her brother."

FORTY

Dross sat at her desk, listening, her face unreadable. Larson leaned against a wall, arms crossed, expression neutral.

"Think about it," Cork said. "It fits. The second round of threats referenced his sister's death. He was the only one outside of our investigators who knew that his sister was among the bodies in the Vermilion Drift."

"Why the second round of threatening notes?" Larson asked.

"To throw us off, maybe. Make it look like her death was about the mine stuff, not about—hell, whatever it was about."

"What was it about?" Dross said.

"I don't know. I do know that he was bleeding money to support his sister and the Northern Lights Center."

"Money?" Larson said. "You really think he'd kill his sister over money? He's a very rich man, Cork. And I suspect anything he loses to the center is simply a tax write-off."

Dross got up, walked to a window, and stood looking out with her hands clasped at the small of her back. "You found the second *We die. U die.* notes shoved under the Kufus woman's windshield wiper and pinned to Cavanaugh's door. How did he do that, with the woman there?"

"Slipped away from the dock while she was swimming in the cove," Cork said. "Maybe he went inside, ostensibly to get drinks or to use the head, and he did it then. It wouldn't have been that difficult. If we can get a look at his computer, we can check to see if he's accessed the website for the From Hell font. That would be pretty damning."

Larson shook his head. "Not necessarily. He could simply have wanted to check it out for himself once he knew where the font had come from. At least that's how I'd argue it if I were his attorney."

"We have to walk carefully here," Dross said, not turning from the window.

"We come back to why," Larson said. "Why would a man kill his sister?"

Simon Rutledge, who'd been sitting quietly, said, "In many of the homicide investigations I've been involved in, Ed, it's ended up being about family."

"There's a big problem with thinking of Cavanaugh as a suspect," Larson responded. "He was at a reception for Genie Kufus and her team the night his sister was killed."

"You confirmed that with Kufus and the others?"

"Not Kufus, but Lou Haddad, who was there, too."

"The reception was at the Four Seasons?" Cork asked.

"Yeah."

"Which is five minutes from the center. Is it possible Max left and came back? Said he was going out for a smoke or something?"

Larson said, "I'd have to look at my notes. But I've got to tell you, it feels like a stretch."

"Did you ask him about that final call from his sister?"

"Of course. He said she often called at the end of a day, just to talk. They were close. The phone records bear that out."

"She said nothing about being shot?"

"I think he would have mentioned that, don't you?"

"I agree with Ed, Cork," Dross said. She faced them. "We need something substantial, and, until we have it, I'm not going to harass Max Cavanaugh." She rubbed her forehead in a tired way. "You'll have to bring me more."

Larson pushed away from the wall. He arched his back. "Christ, I'm beat. I'd love to go fishing tonight, clear my head."

Dross said, "I think we could all use an evening to ourselves." She glanced at Rutledge. "You're dying to be home for your son's birthday tomorrow, Simon. Why don't you go now?"

"What about Cavanaugh?" Rutledge asked.

"Let's all give our brains a break," Larson suggested. "Maybe we'll come up with a bright idea."

Rutledge seemed about to object, and Cork said, "Cavanaugh isn't going anywhere, Simon. There's always another day."

Rutledge gave in. "You know how to reach me. Good luck with your fishing, Ed."

They separated, all going their own ways. Cork walked to his Land Rover in the parking lot. He understood everyone's exhaustion. He was tired, too. He was glad Simon Rutledge had decided to go home for his son's birthday. A festive family affair, he imagined.

Cork headed home, too. Home to his big, empty house and to the only female in his life these days, a little spotted mutt who was always glad to see him.

FORTY-ONE

He unscrewed the cap on one of the Leinie's Rutledge had brought earlier that day and checked the clock on the wall. Nearing five. He thought about heading to Sam's Place to give a hand with the dinner rush but instead went out to the patio in the backyard, and drank the beer and threw the ragged tennis ball for Trixie. It was a pattern he'd followed since Stephen had left, and he was getting sick of it. He thought about calling one of his friends, or maybe doing a little fishing or, hell, even going out to the Pinewood Broiler for dinner. Nothing appealed to him. He felt stuck. Part of it was the general realization that as his children left he would have to redefine himself and his life, and he wasn't even sure where to begin and the idea was overwhelming. But a part of it, too, was that he simply felt weighted by the burden of all the events of the past week and the questions about his own past that those events had raised and that still remained unanswered.

So mostly he just felt like getting drunk.

When the beer was empty, he went back inside. Instead of going to the refrigerator for another bottle, he went to the office and checked his e-mail. He was pleased to find messages from both his daughters. He read Annie's first.

Dad,

I got a note from Jenny saying that some pretty horrible things have been happening back home. Bodies buried in a mine. Is that true? She said the press is speculating that it was the work of a serial killer a long time ago. Is that true, too? She also said that you're involved in the investigation. I was like, duh. Can you tell me anything?

Buried bodies. Hard to imagine in Aurora. But that's something people here in El Salvador are familiar with. During the civil war in this country, a lot of families had loved ones who disappeared in the night. Just disappeared. Whole villages vanished, too, I've heard. People still stumble onto mass graves in the jungle. Here, it's about politics and economics. And the crimes are committed by the kinds of people you pass on the street every day. It's easier to think that kind of atrocity is only committed by crazed serial killers. If it were only so.

Jenny says she's coming home for a few days just before the Labor Day weekend. I'd like to be there, too. Will Stephen be back from camp? And could Aunt Rose and Mal come, too? It would be wonderful to have us all together, even if for only a few days.

Love and peace,
Anne

Cork sat back and stared at the screen. Without realizing it, Annie was keeping him grounded to the reality of the world. Which was that, as bad as things seemed in Aurora, in the world at large, these events were next to nothing. Death on an enormous scale was as common as rain.

A depressing thought, so he considered instead the enticing possibility of all the O'Connors being together for a little while at summer's end, and that cheered him.

Jenny's e-mail queried him further about what the hell was going on in Aurora and why hadn't he called her back? For the moment, he held off replying. He didn't want to think about it.

It was late afternoon, and dark was still a long way off. He took Trixie for another walk, and although he tried to keep his mind away from the investigation, his thinking kept coming back to Max Cavanaugh and the reception at the Four Seasons the night his sister was murdered.

Larson had said he'd questioned Lou Haddad, who'd confirmed that Cavanaugh was at the Four Seasons until after midnight, beyond the time Lauren Cavanaugh had been murdered. If that was true,

Cavanaugh was off the hook. But if Ophelia was correct about the time of her own encounter with Lauren Cavanaugh, then Max had talked to his sister on the phone after she'd been shot. And what woman, having been grazed by a bullet, wouldn't say something to her brother about it? Her silence made no sense. What made a great deal more sense was that Max Cavanaugh had lied to Larson about the content of that final conversation.

When he returned home, he went straight to the telephone in his office and punched in Haddad's cell phone number.

"Lou, it's Cork O'Connor."

"Hey, Cork, what's up?" What sounded like jazz was playing in the background.

"I just wanted to check to make sure you and Sheri are okay."

"We're fine. Down in the Twin Cities, staying at a fancy hotel, eating fancy food in fancy restaurants. Listening to some great jazz at the moment and drinking some good wine. And get this. Max told me all expenses are on the company. This has turned into a great getaway."

"I'm glad."

"Look, Cork, I know you didn't call to chat."

"Could I ask you a couple of questions, Lou?"

"Sure. About what?"

"The night of the reception for Kufus and her team."

"Fire away."

"What time did the reception at the Four Seasons break up?"

"Officially at around ten-thirty. But several of us headed to the bar and hung out there until after midnight."

"Max Cavanaugh?"

"Yeah, he was with us."

"The whole time?"

"Pretty much."

"What do you mean by 'pretty much?'"

"We all took trips to the head now and then. Alcohol does that, you know."

"Did Cavanaugh take any long trips?"

"To the head? Nothing unusual, seems to me. He stepped outside for a smoke a couple of times."

"Was he gone long?"

"Five, ten minutes, I think."

"That's all? You're sure."

"Honestly, I wasn't keeping track. By that time, I'd had a few my-self, and we were all having a pretty good time."

"So he could have slipped away for longer than a few minutes and you might not have noticed?"

"Yeah, I suppose. Just a minute," he said. He covered the mouth-piece for a few seconds. "Sheri says he went out for a while."

"Does she remember when?"

Cork heard Haddad pose the question to his wife. Her reply was too faint to hear.

Haddad said, "A little after eleven o'clock. She remembers because he got a cell phone call, just as she was getting ready to call our baby-sitter and let her know we wouldn't be home until after midnight."

"Does Sheri remember how long he was gone?"

Haddad asked, then relayed the reply, "Twenty minutes, maybe."

"Thanks, Lou. You guys just go on having a good time, okay?"

"What's up with the investigation?"

"We have answers to some of the questions, but we haven't nailed down a suspect in Lauren Cavanaugh's death yet."

"Is that why you're asking about her brother?"

"No comment, Lou. Like I said, you guys just have a good time. And tell Sheri thanks for the information."

He'd put the phone down and was a few steps away when it rang: Lou Haddad calling back.

"Cork, Sheri has something you might be interested in." He gave the phone over to his wife, who said, "I don't know if this is important, Cork, but I thought you might want to know. It was noisy in the bar at the Four Seasons, so I went outside to make my call to our babysitter. I saw Max leave the parking lot in his Escalade. And another thing. That evening he'd been wearing a knockout blazer. Armani, de la Renta, some expensive designer thing, I'm sure. Anyway, when he came back and joined us at the bar, he didn't have it on anymore. He didn't stay long, mostly just said good night, and went home."

"How did he seem when he came back?"

"Distracted, I thought. I figured he'd had a bit too much to drink and he was a little, you know, distant. Maybe fuzzy-headed. Which was different from the way he'd been before he left. He was all charm then."

"Anything else, Sheri?"

"Not that I can think of. Does this help?"

"A lot. Thanks. But, Sheri, why didn't you tell someone all this before?"

"Nobody asked me," she replied, a little curtly.

Haddad came back on the line. "Cork, you want us to come back and give statements of some kind, we'll be happy to."

"If that's necessary, Lou. I'll let you know."

"All right, then. You take care."

In Cork's thinking, you needed three things to hang a crime on someone: opportunity, evidence that placed the suspect at the scene, and motive. Cavanaugh had left the bar around the time of the killing. So opportunity. When he returned, he'd removed his expensive blazer, perhaps because it was covered with bloodstains. If he was smart, he'd gotten rid of the blazer, but maybe there was residue on some of the other clothing he wore that night, or on his shoes. And maybe he still had the shoes and the other clothing. So physical evidence. But what about motive? That was the tough thing. Why would Cavanaugh kill his sister? From all indications, he'd taken care of her all his life. What happened that night that made a difference?

That was something only Max Cavanaugh knew.

FORTY-TWO

Cavanaugh was clearly surprised to find Cork at his door. He also didn't seem pleased, but he was cordial.

"A business call, Cork? More questions?"

"Just something I need to get off my mind, Max. May I come in?"

"Be my guest." Cavanaugh stepped aside.

The house was cool, and from another room came the sound of sitar music, something Cork hadn't heard since the seventies. A glass of red wine sat on a table near the front door, and Cavanaugh lifted it as he passed.

"Can I offer you something to drink?" he asked.

"No thanks, Max. Okay if I sit?"

"By all means."

Cork took one of the two wing chairs in the living room. It was upholstered in a green fabric soft as doe hide. Cavanaugh took the other.

"Ravi Shankar?" Cork said, with a slight nod toward the music.

"Nikhil Banerjee. I became familiar with his music while I was working in the Great North's bauxite mine in central India. He's dead now. This is a rare recording. Did you come here to talk music?"

"I came here to talk about Hattie Stillday."

Cavanaugh nodded and looked concerned. "I've been thinking about her, too. What she did, it was so needless. Christ, there was plenty of money. I was angry with Lauren, I mean all the mismanagement, but I'd have given her what she needed to pay off Stillday."

"Do you know Hattie?"

"Just her work."

"A fine woman. Very Ojibwe in a lot of respects, especially in her disregard for the value of money. She didn't think much of it, except for the good it could do others."

"Apparently she thought enough to murder for it." His tone had turned cold.

"See, Max, I have a problem with that. I don't think Hattie did it."

"She confessed. From what I understand, she knew everything about the murder."

"Not everything."

"Well, I suppose where murder's involved a person's thinking might not always be clear."

"My sentiment exactly. You know, Max, you've always seemed to me to be a fair man."

Cavanaugh didn't respond. He swirled red wine in his glass and watched Cork.

"I'm wondering if you really intend to let Hattie Stillday go to prison."

"That's not my call, is it?" he said.

"Oh, but I think it is. Hattie Stillday didn't kill your sister, and you know it."

Cavanaugh said, "I do?"

"Max, I'm not here in any official capacity. I'm here to give you a chance to do the right thing, before it all turns ugly. And it will. All the dirty secrets will get dragged out, and the press will have a field day with you and your family."

"You're talking in riddles, Cork."

"Am I? Let me tell you how it went down that night. A few minutes after eleven, you received a call from your sister. She was upset. She'd been shot, but not seriously. She wanted you, needed your comfort, your protection, which you'd given her your whole life. You left the gathering at the Four Seasons, drove to the Northern Lights Center, and found her in the boathouse. There was a gun there, left by the person who'd shot her earlier. A kind of accident, really. You had an exchange with Lauren, a fight maybe. And you took the gun and killed her. When you realized what you'd done, you ran. You went back to the Four Seasons, spent a few minutes with the people you'd left, then you made your excuses and went home.

"I'm guessing," Cork continued, "that you expected to hear about your sister's death the next day, but that didn't happen. Nor the next. And when it became clear that Lauren's body wasn't anywhere to be found and that her car was missing and there was no evidence of your crime, you were surprised and probably scared. What the hell happened to Lauren? And that's where I came in."

"I loved my sister," Cavanaugh said.

"I'm not hearing you deny you killed her. What I don't understand is why, Max."

"I don't have to sit here and listen to this." But he made no move to end it.

"I'm telling you things I shouldn't, because I really don't believe you're the kind of man who'd let Hattie Stillday take the blame for something you did. And I'm doing it because, if I were you, I'd be eaten up inside by guilt. Everything will come to light sooner or later. Rutledge and Larson will be out with a search warrant. You've left tracks. Like you said, where murder's involved, you don't think straight. And don't bother trying to figure out what tracks I'm talking about. We know too much. Come back to Aurora with me, Max. Talk to the sheriff. Get it all off your chest and be done with it."

Cavanaugh stared at Cork, then said coldly, "You sound just like Lauren. Next you'll be telling me I've got no other friend in the world but you."

"Believe it or not, I am your friend. Come back with me, and I'll stand by you, I promise."

"I'm not going anywhere with you, Cork. You're going to leave and I'm going to finish my wine and have some dinner and a good soak in my tub and go to bed. And I think I'll call my lawyer while I'm at it."

"The longer you string this out, the more it will twist your gut. I'm just trying to help."

"Your kind of help gets people hanged."

Cork stood up. "Think about it. If you want to talk, call me." He took a card from his wallet and held it out to Cavanaugh, who didn't even look at it. Cork put the card on the coffee table and headed out the door, leaving Max Cavanaugh alone in the cool dark of his big house, listening to music played by a dead man.

FORTY-THREE

Marsha Dross lived alone on Lomax Street, in a little house with flower boxes on the front porch and green shutters on the windows. Her pickup was in the driveway when Cork pulled up and parked at the curb. Smoke drifted from the backyard, and the breeze carried the delicious aroma of barbecue and sizzling fat. He walked across the lawn and around to the back, where he found the sheriff on her patio, dressed in khaki shorts and sandals. She was turned away from him, and she had a beer in her hand. She wore earbuds that snaked up from an iPod cradled in the pocket of her khakis, and she was doing a line dance move as if the smoking Weber grill with its rack of ribs was her partner. Ed Larson fished to relax. Cork walked his dog. Marsha Dross, apparently, danced.

He hated what he had to do to her.

"Yo, Marsha," he said, but not loudly enough, because she kept on dancing. "Marsha," he said again.

This time she heard.

She had never been what most people would call pretty, and Cork seldom gave it much thought, but turning to him, she looked, for an instant, happy and relaxed, and Cork could see a kind of beauty in her that was common and good. When she saw his face and understood that she was probably not going to like what he had to say, she changed. She became, in the blink of an eye, the law.

She pulled off the earbuds and reached down to turn off the iPod and said, with a little brittleness, "What did you do now?"

"You could offer me a beer."

"Tell me first, then I'll decide about the beer."

"Want to sit?"

"For Christ sake, just tell me."

"I was out at Max Cavanaugh's place. I told him I thought he killed his sister."

"You did what?" She put the beer bottle down on her patio table, hard enough that a bit of the brew splashed out the longneck.

"Before you toss me on that grill with those ribs—which, by the way, look pretty good—just listen a minute."

"This is what I get for bringing you in on a case. Jesus, it's always the same. You never do things the way I ask or that you promise. You just go off and do whatever comes into your head. You're not the sheriff anymore, Cork. Christ, you haven't been in, like, forever."

"I know. But just give me a minute to explain."

"God, I thought for a little while, just a little while, I could relax."

"He did it, Marsha. He killed his sister, and I can almost prove it."

"Almost? Oh, that'll sound good to a grand jury."

"Hear me out."

She huffed an angry breath, crossed her arms, gave him a killing look, and said, "All right, I'm listening."

"I talked to Lou Haddad and Sheri this afternoon. Sheri told me that Cavanaugh got a cell phone call at the Four Seasons, after the official reception, when they were all gathered in the bar."

"We know this already."

"He went outside, and Sheri did, too, so that she could make a cell phone call to her babysitter. She saw Cavanaugh take off in his Escalade."

Her eyes changed, the anger transformed in an instant to interest. "He left the Four Seasons?"

"He sure did, and we have a witness to that. According to Sheri, he was gone twenty minutes, enough time to drive to his sister's boathouse and kill her. And get this: When he came back, he wasn't wearing the designer blazer he'd worn all evening. According to Sheri, he seemed distant. 'Fuzzy-headed' was how she put it. He didn't stay long."

"Why did he take off his blazer?" she said. Then answered herself, "Bloodstains."

"A pretty good speculation."

"Did he get rid of the clothes, do you think?"

"A search warrant would answer that question."

She sat down at the table, looking troubled. "Here's one a search warrant won't answer: Why?" She picked up her beer and idly sipped.

Cork sat down with her. "It was a risk talking to Max. I knew that, Marsha. But the truth is he's not a bad guy. I think that what happened wasn't premeditated. And I was hoping that when he understood what I suspected, he might want to talk about it. A thing like that, it's got to weigh on his conscience. When I left, he looked pretty dismal."

Dross thought for a while in silence. The fat from the ribs fell onto the coals and sizzled. Finally she stood up.

"I'm going to see if I can't get a search warrant. It's all pretty thin, but I'd like to try. Ed's fishing at his cabin on Emerson Lake. He told me he was leaving his cell phone at home."

"He usually fishes from his dock. I'd be glad to head over and give him the word."

"Thanks."

"Sorry to interrupt your evening, Marsha."

"If it means I can sleep tonight, I'll forgive you."

She took a long set of tongs, lifted the ribs off the grill and put them on a waiting platter, then headed inside to start making phone calls.

FORTY-FOUR

He was halfway to Emerson Lake when Max Cavanaugh called. Cork pulled over to the side of the road and answered his cell phone.

"I want to talk," Cavanaugh said. "But only to you. Come alone. You've got twenty minutes."

"Your place?" Cork said.

"No. I'm at the Ladyslipper Mine."

"All right."

"Twenty minutes," Cavanaugh said. "Alone."

"Max—" Cork began. But Cavanaugh had hung up.

He swung his Land Rover around, called Dross, and told her what was up.

"I'll meet you there," she said.

"He said alone, Marsha."

"Fine, you meet with him alone, but I'll be lurking in the general vicinity."

"That'll do."

"Just before you have your talk, call me on your cell and leave the phone on, okay? I'd like to hear what he has to say."

"Kind of like wearing a wire?"

"Make sure you get close to him."

It was late, and the sun had set. From the eastern horizon a red smear was spreading across the sky, and the clouds that hung there became like bloodstained cotton. At the gate to the mine, the guard directed Cork to follow one of the roads into the great pit.

"Mr. Cavanaugh went down there himself maybe forty minutes ago." The guard gave Cork a map and outlined the way. "Mine operation's shut down for the night, so you don't have to worry about being run over by one of them monster trucks or blown up in the blasting."

Which was, in fact, a comforting piece of information.

Cork followed the road the guard had indicated. It was paved asphalt for a couple of hundred yards, then turned to hard-packed red dirt and curled south of the Great North office complex. It sloped into the pit and almost immediately cut sharply to the left, and Cork kept his Land Rover at a crawl as he negotiated the narrow switchbacks that angled toward the floor of the great excavation. Cork had seen the hole only from above; being inside was different. Above there was grandeur to the scale. Inside and up close, he could see the rugged scars of all the intimate battle that had taken place to open that great hole and tear the ore from the earth.

He turned the final switchback and came out onto the flat at the bottom of the mine, which was a broad plain of devastation as red and bare as Cork imagined the surface of Mars to be, and just as alien in its feel. Gargantuan machines stood idle amid great mounds of blasted rubble that lay waiting to be loaded and carried away. A quarter of a mile to the south, water had seeped in, and a small lake had formed in a depression there, a lake in which, Cork was pretty certain, nothing lived. He felt swallowed by the mine, dwarfed by the immensity of the excavation, and more than a little in awe of the enormity of the vision and enterprise necessary to create it.

He spotted Cavanaugh's Escalade parked a hundred yards ahead. He slowed and turned on his cell phone.

"Can you hear me, Marsha?"

"There's static, but I can still read you."

"All right. Going undercover now."

He slipped the phone beneath his shirt, where it lay cradled against the thin ridge along the top of his belt line.

"Can you hear me now?"

"Yes, and quit the clowning."

Cavanaugh had parked fifty yards from an enormous Bucyrus electric shovel. With its long neck and open-jawed bucket, the machine reminded Cork of a great dinosaur ready to feed.

He parked near the Escalade. Cavanaugh got out and met him halfway between the two vehicles. Cork closed to within two feet of Cavanaugh, who looked weary, like a man who'd run a thousand miles.

"I'm here, Max."

"You wanted to know why," Cavanaugh said.

"Everything else I pretty much understand."

Almost wistfully, Cavanaugh eyed the mine walls, which terraced toward the reddened evening sky. "My family made its fortune from this earth," he said. "I know that a lot of people look at the damage that's been done to the land here and judge us. Me, I look at this mine and I see the generations of families it's supported. I see the enterprise it's fed. I see the wars this nation fought and won because of it. It seems to me that sometimes you have to choose to do some harm in the hope—no, the belief—that it's for a greater good. That's how I've lived my life anyway, most of it in mines not much different from this one. That big shovel over there? I can work it. I can drive a truck that hauls three hundred tons. I've prospected and drilled and blasted. Mining's been my life, and it's been a good one."

"What about taking care of Lauren?" Cork said. "That's been a part of your life, too."

Cavanaugh eyed him dourly but didn't reply.

"It couldn't have been easy covering for her all these years."

"That's what you do when you're family."

"What kind of family was she, Max? Hard to love, I imagine."

"You're wrong. She was easy to love. Too easy. She walked into a room and she brought the sun with her. She was full of life, ideas, energy. Next to her, most people were like pieces of wood."

"Then why did you kill her?"

"I'm not entirely certain I did."

"Tell me about it."

"There are things you need to know first. Before he died, my father told me about my mother. Horrible things."

Cavanaugh fell silent and looked down at the hard rock beneath his feet.

"Was she involved in the Vanishings, Max?"

He gave his head a vague shake. "My father couldn't say for sure, but he suspected. She was capable of it, he believed. At least after they moved here."

"What made this place different?"

"She met a man, a truly evil man."

"Indigo Broom."

Cavanaugh lifted his gaze to Cork, apparently surprised that he knew the name. "Yes, Broom. My mother had had relationships before, a lot of them unconventional, but this was different. This was beyond bizarre. Where there'd been only, I don't know, narcissism in her, there was cruelty, brutality. The change in her frightened my father. He was preparing to go to the police with his suspicions when she disappeared and the Vanishings stopped. For him, it was like being freed from hell. My grandfather was long dead, every family tie here ended, and so we left Aurora and all the awful memories behind."

"But then you came back."

"The worst decision I ever made."

"Tell me about Lauren, Max."

Cavanaugh looked away, and his gaze ran across the whole devastated landscape around him. "On his deathbed, my father made me promise to be responsible for her because she was, in many ways, like my mother."

"What ways?"

"She was beautiful and smart, just like my mother, and just like my mother she had no heart. She loved no one."

"Not even you?"

"She needed me, needed me desperately. But love? I don't believe she understood the word. Not in the way you and I might understand it."

"What about you? Did you love her?"

"I'm not sure I can explain. We shared blood, history, a lifetime of memories. That was part of it. But more important, I understood that she had no choice in who she was. Some people come into the world missing a limb or without sight or hearing. We don't blame them for the way they're born. How could I blame Lauren because she came into the world without a heart? She was her mother's child."

"You're not like that."

"Luck of the draw. It might just as easily have been me. Or both of us. What a curse that would have been for my father." He let out a breath that may have carried a whisper of a laugh. "It was Dad who pointed out to me that I was the lucky one. He told me I had to share my heart with Lauren. And that's what I've tried to do. Pick up the pieces, fix what she broke, mend the wounds she delivered. Hers was a lonely existence, really. She used people and threw them away, and afterward she was alone. Always alone."

"Except for you. She came to you for companionship and comfort, yes?"

He breathed deeply, sadly. "She always came to me crying."

"Manufactured tears?"

"Real enough. But always for her, never for anyone else. In her world, there was no one else worth crying over."

"Not even you."

"Not even me."

"A hard love, Max. Is that why you killed her?"

"I told you. I'm not certain I did."

"What happened that night?"

"First you have to understand something. Lauren was always self-centered, and I'd come to expect that. But when she moved here and moved back into that awful place we'd lived as children, she began to change. I saw her becoming cruel. It wasn't simply that she didn't care about other people, she began to enjoy inflicting pain."

"Physical?"

"I don't know. Emotional pain, certainly. But because of what my mother was, I began to be afraid."

Evil finding evil, Cork thought.

"That night she called me at the Four Seasons, hysterical. I tried to calm her, but it was clear that she needed me. I left."

"Without a word to anyone."

"I thought a few minutes with her would be enough. Over the years, I've learned exactly what to say to her."

"Did you know she'd been shot?"

"She said something about it, but she often lied to be certain I'd come when she needed me. When I got there, I saw that it wasn't a lie. She'd bled, although she wasn't bleeding anymore. She told me what happened, told me in a fury, told me she was going to kill the Stillday girl. She was a mess. Partly hysterical with tears, partly in a hysterical rage. She was waving a gun around. She kept a small firearm somewhere, but this wasn't it. This one I'd never seen before. I had no idea where it came from. The gun scared me."

Cavanaugh stopped talking. The entire sky had turned vermilion, and everything beneath it was cast in the same hue. *If fire could bleed,* Cork thought, *this would be its color.*

"I couldn't get her to calm down," Cavanaugh finally went on. "And I was angry, too. Angry at the disruption of my evening, angry at Lauren because, hell, she probably had gotten what she deserved, angry at a whole lifetime of bending to her selfish whims and putting up with her crazy, selfish behavior. It seemed to me in that moment that two crazy people were in the room, and I said that to her. God help me, I said, 'We're both better off dead.'"

Recalling it, Cavanaugh seemed stunned, and he fell silent.

"What did she do, Max?"

"Stopped her raving," he said in a distant voice. "Walked to me. Walked to me with that gun in her hand. Pushed herself against my chest with the gun between us. Reached down and brought my hand up and put my finger over her finger on the trigger and whispered, 'Do you want that, Max? Do you?'"

Cork waited, then pressed. "What happened?"

"The gun went off." Cavanaugh turned his mystified eyes to Cork. "She looked up at me, and I couldn't tell if it was surprise or relief I saw. And then she dropped at my feet. Just dropped. I went down to her. I called her name and she didn't respond. There was blood all over her. I held her, but it was like holding a rag doll. I knew she was dead. I should have called someone, but instead I . . ."

By the end, Cavanaugh's voice had dropped to a desperate whisper. To be certain that Dross on the other end of the phone had heard clearly, Cork said, "You killed her, Max?"

Cavanaugh shook his head with sudden fierceness. "I don't know if I killed her. I don't know if I pulled the trigger or she did, honest to God."

"Then what happened, Max?"

"I went back and made excuses to the people at the Four Seasons and went home. I thought . . ." He hesitated, as if uncertain how to proceed. "I thought I would be free, but it didn't feel that way at all. Does that make sense? If you've walked bound all your life and suddenly the ropes are gone, is that freedom? I didn't quite know how to go on, Cork."

"Why did you hire me to find her?"

"When no one reported her dead, Jesus, I thought maybe she wasn't. Maybe she somehow pulled herself off that floor and went somewhere to recover and . . ."

"And what, Max?"

"And maybe she needed me." His face held a look of bewilderment. "How sick is that? I realized that in some twisted way I needed her, too. And I realized one more thing, Cork, maybe the hardest lesson of all. Dead isn't dead. The dead are always with us."

"The second round of threatening notes, 'We die. U die. Just like her.' That was you, wasn't it, Max?"

"After you found Lauren's body, I got worried, afraid you might look my way. It was simply misdirection." The tone of his voice indicated that to him it was a thing that hardly mattered now.

"Come back with me, Max. We can go to the sheriff, and you can explain."

Cavanaugh gave his head a slight shake. "I never married, Cork. Never had children. Do you want to know why?"

"Because you had your hands full taking care of your sister?"

"Because I might have had a child like Lauren. Or worse, like my mother. It's in my blood somewhere. But I'm the last of the Cavanaughs. When I'm gone, the blood curse is gone, too."

"Come with me, Max."

"You go on. I want to stay, keep company awhile with these rock walls. I feel comfortable here. You can tell the sheriff everything I told you. You will anyway, I suppose, and it's all right with me." He waited, and when Cork didn't move, he said, more forcefully, "Go on, Cork. I want to be alone."

"Max—"

"I can call a security person and have you escorted out."

"No need. I'll go." But he didn't, not right away. He said, "I'm sorry, Max."

"For what?"

"Those ropes you talked about, I guess."

Cavanaugh offered him a sad smile. "And I'd guess you have ropes of your own. Doesn't everybody?"

Cork walked back to his Land Rover and got in. He looked back and watched Cavanaugh return to his Escalade.

He slid the phone from under his shirt. "You get all that, Marsha?"

"Loud and clear, Cork. I'm at the front gate now. I'll pick him up when he comes out."

Cork swung his vehicle around and started toward the incline that would take him along the switchbacks to the top. He figured he'd join Dross and together they would wait for Max Cavanaugh.

He hadn't gone more than a hundred yards when he heard the explosion behind him, and the walls of the pit were lit as if by lightning, and he saw in the rearview mirror the Escalade consumed in an enormous blossom of red-orange flame.

FORTY-FIVE

He was home by midnight and in bed by one, but sleep stayed beyond his reach.

At three, he threw the covers back and went downstairs to check his e-mail, but there was nothing new from any of his children.

At four, he turned on the television in the living room and lay down on the sofa and surfed the channels, but nothing appealed.

At four-thirty, the birds began to chatter.

At five, he gave up, showered, dressed, and took Trixie for an early walk.

At six-thirty, he thought about breakfast but wasn't hungry.

At seven, he called Judy Madsen, told her he would need her to cover for him at Sam's Place for a while, got into his Land Rover, and headed to Crow Point to find Henry Meloux.

The dew on the meadow grass was heavy, and under the yellow morning sun Crow Point seemed strewn with sapphires. A breeze caught the smoke that rose from Meloux's cabin and thinned it quickly to nothing against the morning sky. The cabin door was open. Near it, Walleye lay drowsing with his head on his forepaws. Cork, as he approached, smelled biscuits baking.

Rainy Bisonette stepped outside, shaded her eyes, and watched him come.

"We got word early this morning that Max Cavanaugh killed himself and that you were there," she told him. "True?"

"I'm afraid so."

"Uncle Henry said you'd be here."

"Where is he?"

"Preparing for you. Have you eaten?"

"A little. But those biscuits smell good."

"I just made them. And I have coffee, if you'd like."

"Thank you."

They sat at the sturdy table Meloux had made for himself long before Cork was born. Cork looked around the simple, single room with affection and admiration.

"A person doesn't need any more than this," he said.

"Sometimes I think that, too. Other times, I'd kill for a lightbulb."

"Thanks for the biscuit. It's really good. Did you make this jam?"

"Yes."

"It's wonderful."

"Since the kids have grown and gone, I don't cook as much as I used to, or as much as I'd like. That's been one of the best things about being here with Uncle Henry. Someone to appreciate my cooking."

"How is he?"

"No worse. But I still haven't got a handle on what's going on."

"There's a pretty good hospital in Aurora. They could run tests."

"Uncle Henry won't go."

Cork nodded. It figured.

The light through the open door was blotted by a sudden shadow, and Meloux walked in. He moved slowly, bent and looking tired. He sat with them at the table, ate a biscuit with jam, drank some coffee, and said to Cork, "You are ready for the end of your journey?"

"There are things I've forgotten, Henry, things that I have to know. I can't sleep, I can't eat, I can't think. I've always been proud to say that I was the son of Liam and Colleen O'Connor, but now I don't know what that means. I'm not sure who they were, and I'm not sure anymore who I am."

"Are you afraid?"

"Yes. I think there must be a good reason I don't remember things, but I don't care what that reason is. I have to know the truth."

"Then I am ready to guide you to it. Niece?" He held out his hand, which trembled, and she helped him to his feet.

Every spring, in a small clearing on the eastern shore of the point, Meloux built a sweat lodge. The old Mide usually had help, Shinnobs from the rez, and some years Cork gave a hand. This year it had been mostly Rainy who'd assisted her uncle. They'd built the frame—a hemisphere eight feet in diameter and five feet high at the center—of willow boughs tied together with rawhide prayer strips, and had covered it with tarps overlaid with blankets.

When they reached the sweat lodge, Meloux turned to Cork.

"First you will fast," he said.

"How long, Henry?"

"A day. You will fast and ask yourself if you really want to know the truth, for that is the end of this journey. If you are thirsty, drink from the lake. If you feel the desire or need, bathe there, too. We will come at moonrise to see if you want to go on, and if you do, we will come again before the rise of the sun to build the sacred fire. Do you understand, Corcoran O'Connor?"

"Yes, Henry."

"Then sit here," Meloux said and indicated a bare area that lay between the sweat lodge and the lake, "and let it begin. Come, Niece. You, too, old dog," he said to Walleye, who'd padded slowly behind them from the cabin.

Meloux turned and headed back the way he'd come.

"Rainy?" Cork called.

She turned back. "Could you call John and Sue O'Loughlin? They live across the street from me. Tell them I might be a while and ask them to feed and, if they're willing, walk my dog until I get back?"

"I'll do that," Rainy promised.

Cork sat on the ground, crossed his legs, and waited.

The sun rose high and the day grew hot and Cork grew thirsty. He got up and walked to the lake, unsteadily because his legs had gone to sleep. As he knelt to drink, he saw a huge bird, a great blue heron, gliding over the lake, which was glass smooth and mirror perfect. The reflection of the bird crossed the reflection of the sky. Slowly, gracefully, the heron descended. In the mirror of the lake, its other self rose, and in a brief moment of rippling water, the two met. With a powerful sweep of wing, the great bird rose again and the other descended, and in a minute the sky and lake were clear again. The ripple of their meeting spread outward, however, and where Cork knelt at the lake's edge, the water undulated gently.

Sometime in the afternoon, a dark-colored snake shot from the grass that edged the cleared area around the sweat lodge. Cork had been drowsing, and the dart of the snake startled him, and he sat bolt upright. The snake stopped, tested the air with its tongue, and for a fatal moment lay there, a black crack across the bare dirt a dozen feet from Cork. In the next instant, a goshawk swooped down, snagged the reptile, and, effortless as dreaming, carried it away.

These sights, or sights like them, Cork had seen before in the great Northwoods, and he could explain them. But at dusk, he witnessed something that he'd never seen and for which he had no explanation.

The sun had set, and the lake had taken on the look of melted lead. The shoreline was drifting into darkness, and the tops of the pine trees formed a ragged black outline that reminded him of the sharp teeth of a predator. The night birds had begun to call, and the tree frogs were just starting to sing. At a place a hundred yards distant, where Crow Point met the shoreline in a curve of brush and timber, Cork spotted movement, a stealthy creep of pale white, which he realized was a wolf. Then he spotted another wolf, this one a mottled gray, which seemed to mirror the movement of the first. They circled, facing each other in a threatening way. Suddenly they lunged and met in terrible canine battle. The sound of their yips and snarls echoed off the trees, and the birds and the frogs fell silent. The wolves separated, circled, and lunged again, gnashing teeth and tearing through fur into flesh. They went on this way until it was too dark to see them, and then the noise of their struggle finally ended. Cork sat wondering at what he'd witnessed and wondering what it meant.

At moonrise, as he'd promised, Meloux returned. Rainy was with him.

The sky was black, and through it ran the pale river of the Milky Way. The gibbous moon, as it rose, cast a glow that pushed long, faint shadows across the ground.

"What have you seen today?" the old Mide asked.

"A bird descended from the sky, Henry, and touched its reflection and flew away."

"What else?"

"This afternoon, a snake crawled near me, and a hawk snatched it and carried it off."

"What else?"

"Something I didn't understand, and maybe didn't really see."

"What was that?"

"Two wolves fighting. Over there." Cork pointed toward the curve in the shoreline.

"Ah," Meloux said, as if this was important.

"What does it mean, Henry?" Cork asked.

"In every human being, there are two wolves. One wolf is love, from which all that is good in life comes: generosity, forgiveness, acceptance, peace. The other is fear, which creates all that is destructive: greed, hatred, prejudice, violence. These two wolves are always fighting."

"Did I really see them?"

"Really?" In the dark, the crescent moon of a smile appeared on the old man's face. "I don't know what that question means, Corcoran O'Connor. Are you willing to continue your journey?"

"I am, Henry."

"Then continue." He turned as if to leave.

"Wait, Henry," Cork said. "The two wolves fighting? Which one wins?"

But Meloux didn't answer. He walked away, and Rainy followed.

Just before sunrise, Meloux and Rainy came again, and Walleye came with them. They brought two folded blankets.

Cork hadn't slept, or been aware that he'd slept. The night had been long, and his thoughts had drifted widely.

"You are ready for the end of your journey?" Meloux asked.

Although he was weary, Cork replied, "I'm ready, Henry."

"Help me with the fire, Niece."

As Cork watched, Meloux and Rainy built the sacred fire, and when the blaze had produced a fine bed of glowing coals, the old man pointed Rainy toward a pitchfork that leaned against a nearby tree. Not far away was a stack of large rocks, which Cork knew were the Grandfathers, the stones that would heat the lodge. Rainy used the pitchfork to place the Grandfathers among the embers. Meloux burned sage and cedar in the fire and used an eagle feather to guide the smoke over Cork to further cleanse his spirit. He gave Cork tobacco, and Cork sprinkled it into the fire, asking the Great Spirit to guide him in his quest. Then Meloux told Rainy to put the blankets on the ground inside the lodge. When all was ready, he said to Cork, "It is time."

The old man stripped off his clothing, and Cork did the same. Meloux went first and Cork followed. When they were seated on their blankets, Rainy carried in the Grandfathers, one by one, cradled on the tines of the pitchfork, and laid the red-hot stones in the hollow in the center. She used a pine bough to sweep away any lingering ash or embers from the stones. Last, she brought in a clay bowl that held a small dipper and was filled with water. Then she retreated and dropped the flap over the opening, plunging Cork and Meloux into darkness.

During a long period of silence, Cork's eyes adjusted, and he saw Meloux reach for the dipper and pour water over the stones. Steam shot into the air, and Cork began to sweat, and the old Mide began a prayer, an Ojibwe chant whose words Cork didn't understand.

The heat increased, and Meloux sprinkled more water on the stones and continued chanting.

After a while, Cork relaxed.

His weariness overwhelmed him.

And he began to dream.

FORTY-SIX

What do you see, Corcoran O'Connor?
He was outside himself, seeing himself, and he said so.
How old are you?
Thirteen, he said.
Tell me what is happening.
And this is what he told.

He's lying on the sofa in the living room of the house on Gooseberry Lane. He'd thought he would watch television to take his mind off the worry that never left him these days, but he hasn't bothered to turn the set on. Instead, he stares up at the ceiling and wonders if his father will ever find his cousin Fawn or Naomi Stonedeer, and if he does, will they still be alive. They've been taken, abducted, everyone on the rez is sure, but no one has any idea who would do such a thing, and everyone is afraid. The Vanishings. That's what everyone is calling what's happened.

The house is quiet. He's alone. His mother is on the rez with Grandma Dilsey and Fawn's mother, Aunt Ellie. His father is . . . well, his father could be anywhere these days. He's gone a lot. During the day, he leaves in uniform. But at night he leaves in different clothing, and often he doesn't come back until early morning, when Cork is asleep. But his mother doesn't sleep, and his father's sneaking out is something that concerns her. Because of his mother's worry and because of his father's inability to find Fawn and Naomi and, most of all, because of his father's silence and odd behavior that clearly hurt his mother, Cork is angry with him, angry all the time. They barely speak these days. Sometimes Cork sees in his father's eyes something like regret. And sometimes he longs to tell his father that he's tired of his own anger and wants to let go of the worry and that all he really wants is for everything to be as it was before the Vanishings began.

He hears the kitchen door open, and a moment later he hears his mother's voice.

"Damn it, Liam, why won't you listen?"

"I have listened. To you and all your relatives and every other Shinnob on the reservation. And I understand your concern, and I wish to God that you'd trust me and let me do my job."

"You leave almost every night and are gone until almost dawn and you won't tell me where you go."

"That's the trust part, Colleen."

"Trust works both ways, Liam. Tell me what's going on. Trust that I'll believe you or forgive you or whatever it takes."

At first, his father offers only silence. Then he says, "Where's Cork?"

Cork lies still as death to be sure he can't be seen.

"I don't know," his mother replies. "Out, I suppose."

"Sit down."

Cork hears chairs scraping linoleum.

"A while back, Cy Borkman and I responded to a call from Jacque's in Yellow Lake."

"That's a vile place, Liam."

"Places like that are the reason I have a job," he says. "It was an altercation over a woman, the kind of woman who looked like she wasn't particular who shared her bed. I broke up the fight, and ended up escorting the woman to her vehicle. She made me the kind of offer an experienced streetwalker in Chicago might have come up with."

"Does that happen often?" his mother says, in a brittle tone.

"People try to negotiate with me using all kind of tender. This is about trust, remember?"

"I'm sorry. Go on."

"She called herself Daphne, and there was something familiar about her. Then it came to me. Beneath all that makeup and the wig and the slutty clothing was Peter Cavanaugh's wife."

"Monique?"

"Yep. Monique Cavanaugh."

"You must have been mistaken, Liam."

"No mistake. It was her."

"Did you let her know you recognized her?"

"No."

"Why not?"

"I was curious. What was a woman like her doing in a dive like Jacque's dressed like a prostitute and behaving like one? Since then I've been watching the place to see if she might come again, and to see if I could figure what she was up to. She's the wife of one of the richest men on the Iron Range, and I knew I needed to be careful in how I went about things. Last night, I saw her again. She was made up like Daphne, and she wasn't alone. She came with someone familiar to us both."

"Who?"

"Indigo Broom."

"Mr. Windigo? God, just thinking about him gives me the creeps."

"It gets creepier. I sit in my car in the parking lot most of the night waiting for them to come out. Finally Daphne does, but she's not with Broom. She's got a biker on her arm, some big, hairy ape of a guy who gets on his motorcycle and she gets on behind him. Before they take off, Broom comes out, gets in his truck, and when they leave, he follows them. I follow Broom. We end up at the North Pine Motor Court over on Long Lake. The biker and Daphne check in and take a room. Broom parks in the motor court lot, turns off his truck, sits. I park on the road and wait until almost dawn, then Daphne comes out. She gets into Broom's truck and leaves with him. I pull out my badge and buckle on my gun belt and knock on the door of the room she left. Nobody answers. I knock again, then try the knob. Door's unlocked. I go in. The biker's on the bed, naked, tied up with a woman's nylons and with a woman's panties stuffed in his mouth and looking like he's been attacked by a tiger, long bloody scratches everywhere. Bruises, too. I pull out the gag and cut the nylons, toss the guy his clothes, ask him what happened. 'Nothing,' he says. The badge gets me nowhere. I threaten to haul him in. He calls my bluff. The kind of guy who's dealt with uniforms a lot and doesn't scare. I tell him to get dressed, and I go to the motor court office, get us both some coffee, bring it back. He says he'll talk but off the record. There's something he wouldn't mind getting off his chest, but not to a lawman. So I say, 'Off the record.' He tells me that at one point when she's got him tied up, she pulls a knife from her purse, a switchblade, and says she's going to cut his heart out and eat it. He laughs, but then she puts the blade to his chest, and for a moment he thinks she's really going to do it. So I ask him, was it worth it? He says, 'Mister, even though I thought for a minute I might die, the way she made me feel I almost didn't care.'"

In the kitchen, it's quiet for a long time.

Then his father says, "I look at Indigo Broom and Monique Cavanaugh, who, as nearly as I can tell, are involved in some brutal and bizarre sexual behavior. I look at the Vanishings, and I get the feel of something brutal and bizarre there. Do you understand what I'm saying?"

"That they took Naomi and Fawn?"

"I can't say that. Not even unofficially. But there are connections. Broom knows the rez, knows the vulnerable girls, can move about without a lot of notice."

"And he takes Fawn and Naomi and then what, Liam?"

"I don't know."

"Oh, God, I hate to think."

Cork hears a kitchen chair slide back and hears his father pacing.

"Liam, how do we find out?" There is a different tone to her voice. Solid. Resolved.

"If I pull him in and interrogate him, I might lose the only advantage I have, which is that he doesn't know I'm looking his way."

"What about her?"

"Right. I haul in the wife of Peter Cavanaugh and interrogate her regarding the missing girls and mention the fact that she loves to dress like a whore and have kinky, dangerous sex with hairy bikers. That'll go over real big with my constituency. Hell, she wouldn't say a word to me without a lawyer there, anyway. And if I start asking her questions, I lose that same advantage I have with Broom, which is that she doesn't know I'm watching her."

"Have you told anyone else?"

"Just you."

"What are you going to do?"

"I don't know."

"Liam, let's talk to Sam Winter Moon and George LeDuc. And maybe Henry Meloux."

"To what end?"

"Maybe they can help."

"How?"

"I don't know. But they'll be more likely to believe you than almost any white person in Tamarack County."

"There's that," he says.

Where are you now?

At Grandma Dilsey's.

Who else is there?

You.

Who else?

Grandma Dilsey. My mother and father. Aunt Ellie. Becky Stonedeer. Sam Winter Moon. And George LeDuc.

He's supposed to be swimming in the lake, but he has sneaked back and is sitting against the side of the house below the kitchen window, and he can hear them talking inside.

"Never liked that man. Never trusted him," Sam Winter Moon says.

"Indigo Broom," Meloux says. "There is a powerful spirit there. Dark like bog water."

"I have no proof of anything," Cork's father reminds them.

"Proof? I know how to get proof," LeDuc says. "Liam, you know what the word 'Ojibwe' means? To pucker. We used to roast our enemies until their skin puckered."

"I hope you're joking, George."

"Our children are missing, Liam. About this, I don't joke."

"What do we do?" his mother asks.

"We go to his cabin, Colleen," LeDuc says. "If he's there, we talk to him. If he's not, we wait until he comes back."

"Talk to him?" Cork's father says. "Or pucker him?"

"Whatever it takes, Liam."

"I can't let you do that, George. That's not why I came here."

"Doesn't matter why you came."

"Now wait a minute," Sam Winter Moon says. "There's got to be something we can do short of torturing the man."

Grandma Dilsey says, "If we make him suffer and we're wrong, can we live with that?"

"Hell, I can," LeDuc says.

"Unless you silence him for good, George, he'll sue you for everything you've got."

LeDuc laughs. "That's the white man's revenge, Liam. On the rez, he'll just wait in the dark and slit my throat. I'm willing to take that chance."

"I think we should watch him," his mother says. "There are enough eyes out here that he can't hide. The moment he tries something, we grab him, and then, George, you can do all the puckering you want."

"What about the woman?" Meloux says.

"Would she do anything without Indigo Broom?" Becky Stonedeer asks.

"I don't know," his father replies. "Henry, these are not normal people. God alone knows what they will or won't do."

"Can she be watched?" Meloux asks.

"I can't put any of my men on her. I'd have to do some explaining, and I don't know how I'd do that. And I can't watch her myself night and day."

"I think," Meloux says, "that I would like to talk to this woman. Indigo Broom, I know. This woman is a stranger."

His father says, "Got any idea how I can arrange that, Henry?"

"I have an idea," his mother says. "She gives a lot of money away. What if Henry and I approach her about an Ojibwe charity?"

"What charity?" his father asks.

The kitchen is quiet. Then his mother says, "The Missing Child Fund."

Now? Where are you now?

It's night. Late. He has slipped from his house and ridden his bike ten miles to the southern edge of the rez. The moon is up, and Waagikomaan is a river of gray dirt winding among the trees. He knows from what he's overheard that Indigo Broom is being watched, and he's careful. There is only one way to Broom's cabin, and he's on it. He walks his bike and has tuned all his senses to the forest that presses in on either side of the road.

There are crickets and tree frogs, and then there is a deeper sound, unnatural, in the trees to his right. The sound, he realizes, of a man snoring.

He creeps past the sleeping man and, a hundred yards farther, re-mounts and rides to an old logging road that cuts south toward Mr. Windigo's cabin. He lays his bike at the side of Waagikomaan and starts up the logging road. The trees blot out the moon, and the woods are dark. He can barely see.

He's here because . . . because he's a boy on the edge of manhood, and he wants to be a part of this important effort to find his cousin and Naomi, to find the truth of the Vanishings, and he hopes that somehow in the dark of that night, or of another, he will find the way.

His whole life he has lived in the community of the great North-woods. He has spent nights alone in a tent or in a sleeping bag under the stars, and the darkness itself doesn't frighten him. But there is something about the place under his feet now that is different, that fills him with dread. There are no night sounds here. No crickets. No tree frogs. Only silence. It is a dead place, he thinks. And he thinks he should not be there.

But he forces himself to go on.

The cabin is a dark shape visible against a wall of stone that catches moonlight and seems to glow. There is another building as well, smaller and set off to one side and a little back from the cabin. There is a pickup truck parked near the second structure.

He goes to the cabin first, crouching in his approach, his Keds tennis shoes making no sound in the soft dirt. He peers carefully in at a window, cannot see a thing except his own faint reflection peering back. He circles the cabin, stealing a peek in every window, and in every window there is only his own, intense face. He lopes to the other building, which has no windows. He tries the door. It isn't locked. He opens it, and something—an ill wind, a malign spirit, a palpable evil—rushes out. He stands a moment, staring into the darkness, paralyzed by the malignancy he senses. He has brought with him a flashlight, which is clipped to his belt. He pulls the flashlight free, turns it on, and scans the interior of the small building.

At first, he thinks it is simply a toolshed. Many kinds of implements hang on the walls. Saws, axes, shovels, pry bars, a wheelbarrow, a coiled water hose. The beam, where it hits the wall, forms a round yellow eye, and he keeps it tracking to the right until suddenly in the middle of that eye is something he can't explain. A chain bolted to the wall with an iron cuff at each end. He creeps forward, circling a long, rough-hewn table in the center of the room, holding the light steady, more or less, on the chains. He reaches out and fingers a cuff. The metal is cold and, he thinks at first, rusted. Then he realizes the color is not from rust, and he yanks his hand back. His heart pounds furiously and his breath comes in shallow little gasps and he wishes he weren't there, but he is and he turns and the eye of the flashlight finds the tabletop and he sees manacles there, too, and dark mosaic stains soaked into the wood.

He hears a noise, a long intake of air, and shoots the beam of the flashlight toward the door where Mr. Windigo stands grinning.

FORTY-SEVEN

The old man touched his shoulder, and Cork came out of the dream to the wet heat of the sweat lodge on Iron Lake. He was tired beyond measure.

"I want to go on," he said to Meloux.

"First, we refresh. We cool ourselves in the lake." Meloux called to Rainy, who drew back the cover of the opening.

Sunlight cracked the dark inside the lodge, and Cork blinked at the sudden glare. He followed Meloux clockwise around the pit where the Grandfathers lay cooling. When he was outside, he saw that Rainy was standing ready with the pitchfork to remove the stones and replace them with others she'd set among the embers of the sacred fire to heat. Cork walked with Meloux to the lake and plunged in. The cold water was a slap and brought him fully awake and refreshed him.

When they came out of the water, the old man walked slowly, and Cork wondered about Meloux's strength.

"Henry, you don't have to go on," he offered.

"A long time ago I guided you from an evil place. I always knew that someday I would have to guide you back. We will go together."

They reentered the lodge. Rainy had removed the cooled stones. When the two men were seated, she brought in stones newly heated, filled the hollow in the middle of the lodge, and retreated, dropping the cover over the opening and plunging the inside of the lodge again into darkness. Cork heard the hiss of water as the old Mide sprinkled the Grandfathers. The steam rose, and Meloux began again a prayer chant, and in a few minutes Cork was overtaken again by dreaming.

* * *

He is alone in the dark of Indigo Broom's foul little structure, and the cuffs dig into his skin.

For hours, he's tried to pull himself loose, and his wrists bleed.

He's scared. Oh, God, is he scared. He knows now, knows with a deep, abiding terror the fate of his cousin Fawn and Naomi Stonedeer. And unless he can somehow free himself, he knows his own fate, too.

The door opens, and early sunlight, a kind of false hope, enters the room. With it comes Mr. Windigo. He's not alone. A woman is with him. A beautiful woman. They walk together, bringing with them the fresh scent of morning evergreen. It is the best thing he's ever smelled.

She touches his cheek gently with long, soft fingers. "What are you doing here?"

"I was just looking, that's all. Just looking."

"Curiosity?"

"Yeah. That."

"A child's simple curiosity. How convenient."

"He ain't no child," Mr. Windigo says.

Her hand drifts from his cheek, and a fingernail painted deep red traces a line down his throat, his chest, his stomach, his belt, to his crotch, which she cups in her palm. "No," she agrees. "Not a child."

She squeezes hard and it hurts and he cries out.

"Curiosity? Only that?" she asks calmly, not relaxing the vise grip of her hand.

"Please," he pleads.

She releases him, but the terrible ache between his legs is unrelieved.

"Keep him," she says. "When I'm back from Duluth tonight, we'll see."

"They'll miss him."

"They've missed the others. It hasn't mattered."

She kisses Mr. Windigo. Kisses him a long time and in a way that isn't about love. He knows no word for what that kiss is about.

"We'll have fun," she says and smiles. Her lips are deep ruby and frame the ice white of her teeth like two perfect razor cuts. She turns and leaves with Mr. Windigo at her side.

He left home without sleeping. It has been a long time since he's slept. There is a darkness before him so terrible that he can't begin to comprehend it, and his deep weariness and his deep desire to turn away from what he can't escape make his eyes too heavy to hold open and he sleeps.

He comes awake to the sound of something heavy thrown against the wall of the shed. In the next moment, the door flies open and sunlight blinds him. They have returned, he knows. Mr. Windigo and the woman with the razor cut lips. And he knows the business that he slept to escape can be escaped no longer.

"Jesus!"

He hears the familiar voice of Sam Winter Moon, and he cannot keep himself from crying with relief.

"You sadistic bastard." It's the voice of George LeDuc.

Something hits the wall again.

Sam Winter Moon lifts him, and the cuffs no longer cut into his wrists.

"Where's the key, Broom?" demands LeDuc.

"Peg. On the wall." Mr. Windigo sounds as if he's being choked.

In a moment, he can feel the cuffs released, and he falls into the good, safe arms of Winter Moon.

"Bring him out." It is the voice of Henry Meloux, calm and compassionate.

He's carried into the light.

"Are you hurt anywhere?" Meloux asks.

He shakes his head. He cannot speak, not yet. His throat is choked with gratitude.

"What about *him*?" LeDuc has a powerful arm around Mr. Windigo's throat, and the evil man's eyes look ready to pop from his head.

"Take him back inside," Meloux instructs.

Winter Moon helps LeDuc wrestle Mr. Windigo into the shed.

There are the sounds of a scuffle, of Mr. Windigo cursing, of chains rattling. Then the two men return.

"We've got him on the table, Henry."

Meloux nods and looks down at him with dark, somber eyes. "We have work. It is not work you need to see."

Finally able to speak, he says, "I'm not leaving." He sits up. "He killed Fawn and Naomi. Him and the woman."

Meloux asks, "You saw the woman?"

"Yeah."

"Do you know her?"

He shakes his head. "She looks pretty but she's not. Not inside."

"What did she say?"

"That she'd be back tonight. She's going to Duluth."

"He can't stay for this, Henry," Winter Moon says.

"I'm not leaving, Sam!"

Meloux considers. "He will stay. But he will not see." He points toward the wall of rock that forms a backdrop to the setting of the cabin and the shed. "Up there, Corcoran O'Connor. You will wait up there. You will give us warning if you see someone coming. Do you understand?"

"Yes, Henry."

"Good." Meloux helps him up. "Go now."

He makes his way to the top of the ridge, which places him fifty feet above the scene below. He can see the roof of the cabin, which is covered in black shingles and has no chimney, only a stovepipe. He can see the roof of the shed, which is cedar shake and slopes toward the rock wall where he sits. He can see the cut of the old logging road that divides the trees. And he sees his bicycle, which he'd laid beside Waagikomaan in the dark of the night before. Someone had found it, maybe the guy sleeping among the trees, and the men had come.

The cries, when they begin, startle him. Not only because of their wretchedness but because they are the only sounds in that vile part of the forest.

The cries go on and on.

At first, he doesn't mind. He's glad for the hurt being given Mr. Windigo.

But the longer the screams continue, the more they cut into his resolve. He wishes the sound would end. Finally, he puts his hands over his ears, but he can still hear.

And then the screams stop. Stop suddenly. But the silence that returns holds no relief. The echo of the screams goes on in his head.

The men step from the shed. They're carrying the water hose that had hung inside. They walk to a spigot that protrudes from the side of the cabin wall, connect the hose, turn on the water, and wash their hands and arms all the way above their elbows.

Meloux climbs the wall and sits beside him.

"Mr. Windigo is dead?" he asks the Mide.

"He was a thing incomplete, Corcoran O'Connor. A thing never really alive."

"He sure screamed like he was."

"Pain delivers us into this world. Pain is often the way we leave. That man—no, that half-formed thing—will not feel pain or give pain ever again."

"That's a good thing."

Meloux thinks on this. "It is a necessary thing."

"Henry," Winter Moon calls from below. "We need to talk about what now."

"Come."

Meloux rises, and together they descend. They join the others in front of the cabin. The men all look down at him.

"You understand, Cork, that nothing of this can ever be told," Winter Moon says.

He knows and shows them with a serious nod.

LeDuc eyes him with uncertainty. "I don't know, Henry."

"We will think about that later," the Mide advises. "Let us think about what is next."

"His folks are worried," Winter Moon says. "I'll send word he's with me and he's fine. I'll say that he was with me all night. A lie, but considering Liam and all, I don't know a way around it."

"His father needs the lie," LeDuc says. "But tell his mother to come to Dilsey's place. She'll understand."

Winter Moon asks, "What about the bodies Broom said they stuffed in the mine? We can't just leave them there."

"Their spirits have already walked the Path of Souls," Meloux says. "Moving them would be a dangerous thing. Broom told us what was done to them. For those who loved them, to look now on what is left, I think that would be too hard. The earth will take the bodies back. For that, one hole is as good as another."

"We just leave them?"

"We will honor their memory. But, yes, we will leave them."

"That doesn't seem right, Henry."

"In this business, what does?"

LeDuc says, "Cork said the woman will be coming here tonight. What do we do? Just wait?"

Meloux looks at the cabin and the shed and seems to listen to the dead silence of that evil place. "We burn," he says.

FORTY-EIGHT

She holds him a long time, and then she looks into his eyes, and her own eyes are brown flowers dripping dew.

"Oh, God," she says. "What he might have done to you."

"I'm fine, Mom."

"I know," she says. "I know."

"He killed Fawn, and he killed Naomi," he tells her.

"We've been to the mine tunnel," LeDuc says. "He killed more than just them."

His mother stands fully erect in his grandmother's living room and turns to the men. "Who else?"

"Hattie's girl Abbie. And Leonora Broom. Hell, we all thought they just ran off. Indigo Broom, that man was a monster. Christ. Him and the Cavanaugh woman."

"Windigos," Winter Moon says.

"We know how to deal with Windigos," LeDuc says.

Grandma Dilsey, who has seen much in her life, offers, "What we do, we must do carefully. There are laws not our own to consider."

They all look at his mother. It's clear they're thinking about his father.

"Liam can't know," she says. "What we've done, he won't understand."

"Or what we still have to do," LeDuc says.

She turns to her son. "What I have to ask, Cork, there's no way I can justify it. But it's the most important thing I've ever asked of you. You can't tell your father what happened at Indigo Broom's cabin. You can't tell him ever. Do you understand?"

"Yes," he says. And he absolutely does and has absolutely no intention of ever saying anything to his father.

"Good," she says. "It would be a disaster on so many levels." She turns to the others. "Where's Henry?"

"With Hattie Stillday. He wanted to talk to her himself," Winter Moon replies.

"What about tonight?" she asks.

"We have a plan," says LeDuc.

He came out of the dream on his own.

"You do not want to go on?" Meloux asked.

"The truth is I'm afraid," Cork replied.

"The truth is you have always been afraid. That is why long ago I helped you not remember."

"You?"

"I cannot explain. If you are to understand completely, you must remember."

"I have to go back?"

"You have to go back."

"Will you be there, Henry?"

"I have always been there."

It is night. He is at his grandmother's house with the others: Meloux, Winter Moon, LeDuc, Becky Stonedeer, Grandma Dilsey, Aunt Ellie, Hattie Stillday, his mother. The men have rifles. His mother is armed as well. She has brought his father's revolver, the .38 Police Special, which she took from the lockbox in their bedroom closet and has filled with cartridges. The firearm looks awkward in her hand. When Grandma Dilsey saw it, she'd questioned, "Do you need that?"

"I don't know what I need to kill a monster, but this is what I have."

She holds the gun at her side, so weighty that it seems to throw her body off balance.

He is in the back bedroom, where they made him go before they began their discussion. They closed the door. He's opened it a crack so that he can see and hear.

"I've checked," Winter Moon says. "This thing she's at in Duluth is supposed to finish up around ten. A couple of hours to get back here, and she should hit Broom's cabin around midnight."

"The remains of Broom's cabin, you mean," LeDuc says.

"We should be there early," Winter Moon advises.

"She comes," Hattie says bitterly, "and then what?"

"And then justice," LeDuc says.

"We just kill her?" Grandma Dilsey asks.

"She didn't just kill our children," Hattie says with acid bitterness. "She tortured them first."

"You're saying we should torture her, Hattie?"

"If you can't, I'll be more than happy to do it for you, Dilsey," Hattie replies.

Meloux says, "To end her life isn't a cruelty. Her life is an unnatural thing. But to drag out that end would be cruel."

"I'm just fine with that, Henry."

"Now, maybe. But your life will be long, Hattie, and someday you will regret your cruelty to this creature."

"I'm willing to live with it."

"Me, too," LeDuc throws in.

Meloux considers them, and his voice, when he replies, is a placid pool. "We must think with one mind, speak with one voice, act with one heart. If we are not together, we will crumble."

"I want her dead," Aunt Ellie says quietly, "as much as anyone here. But I don't want her to suffer. I don't want to become a Windigo, like her."

"To kill a Windigo, you must become a Windigo," LeDuc throws at her.

"And feed on her heart, George?" Grandma Dilsey replies. "There will be no satisfaction. That's the thing about a Windigo. It's always hungry."

"One heart, one voice, one mind," Meloux reminds them.

They stand in a loose circle. From where he watches through the crack in the door, he can see them eye one another, and although they don't speak, it's as if they're talking.

LeDuc finally says, "All right. We end it quickly. And do what with her body?"

"We put it with the bodies of those she's killed," Meloux says.

"No!" Hattie cries. "I don't want her anywhere near my Abbie."

"It will not be her. It will be only her flesh and her bone," Meloux replies. "Her deformed spirit will be on the Path of Souls."

Aunt Ellie offers, "Hattie, our girls will be like guardians. They won't let that monster harm anyone else."

"And she won't be found there," LeDuc adds.

Hattie lowers her head, considers, and says at last, "All right."

"We should go," Meloux tells them. "Prepare."

"Someone needs to stay with Cork," his mother says.

"I'll stay," Grandma Dilsey tells her. "But I won't let you leave with that gun, Colleen." She reaches out her hand. "There are guns enough already to do what must be done."

Into Grandma Dilsey's hand, his mother delivers the firearm. Grandma Dilsey walks to an old rolltop desk, slides open a drawer, and puts the gun inside.

FORTY-NINE

Grandma Dilsey is outside watching night push across the sky. She has been quiet and tense. He sits beside her on the porch steps, looking where she looks, but probably not thinking what she's thinking. He's thinking something else, he's pretty sure. When night has settled fully on both earth and sky, he says, "I'm tired. I'm going to lie down in the bedroom."

She puts her arm around him. Her face, dark from the blood of The People that runs through her body and darker still from the night, comes near his own. Her eyes are soft and full of pain. "I'm sorry, Mishiikens." She uses the Ojibwe word for "little turtle," an affectionate name by which she sometimes calls him. "These things, you should have been spared."

"I'm all right, Nokomis," he replies, using the Ojibwe word for "grandmother." "Just tired. I think I should rest for a while."

"Go," she says. "Lie down."

Inside the house he walks to the desk where Grandma Dilsey has put his father's handgun. Soundlessly, he slides the drawer open and removes the weapon. He goes into the bedroom and closes the door behind him. At the window, he takes off the screen. He's just about to ease himself through the opening when the door opens at his back and his father enters the room. Grandma Dilsey is with him. Her face is defiant and at the same time afraid.

"Where are you going, Cork?"

His father's voice is colder than he has ever heard.

"Nowhere," he replies.

"Give me the gun."

He walks to his father and holds the heavy firearm out to him. His father takes the weight from the small hand and fills the empty holster on his own belt.

"Where have they gone?" his father asks, his voice still like something frozen in winter.

He looks at his Grandma Dilsey and understands that she hasn't told. He wants to be like her, to hold his tongue even against the frigid power of his father. He says nothing.

His father reaches out and grabs his arm. His fingers are like the iron of the manacles in Mr. Windigo's shed. "You'll tell me what's happening. You'll tell me where they've gone. And you'll tell me now."

"Liam," Grandma Dilsey cries. "Don't hurt him."

"Then you tell me," he says, turning on the old woman.

"All right, all right. Just let him go."

The grip is released. And Liam O'Connor listens stone-faced as Grandma Dilsey tells him everything.

He stands there ashamed, knowing that, but for him, his grandmother would never have told. He hates himself and he hates his father and even when his father turns and something different is in his face now, something afraid, he goes on hating him.

"Stay here," his father says to him. His voice is stern but softer.

Grandma Dilsey stands barring the door. "Liam, it has to be done."

"Not this way, Dilsey. Not if I have anything to say about it." He shoves her aside, and his boots shake the floorboards as he leaves.

Grandma Dilsey follows, and he can hear her calling from the porch, "Liam, please understand."

He is alone and takes the opportunity to slip through the screenless window and drop to the ground, and as he sees the headlights of his father's car barrel into the dark, he lopes to a stand of paper birch thirty yards away and makes his way silently among the trees. He reaches the highway well out of sight of the house and heads south following where his father has gone, following toward Waagikomaan, toward the road the Cavanaugh woman must take that night to get to the place where Indigo Broom's cabin stands in smoldering ruin.

It's several miles, and he alternates between a brisk walk and a run. The night is quiet. The road is practically empty. Whenever he hears the approach of a vehicle and sees headlights, he slips among the trees and underbrush that edge the old potholed asphalt.

He is thinking: *They'll be at the place where the logging road to Mr. Windigo's cuts off from Waagikomaan. They'll be waiting for her, hiding in the trees there.*

He's not thinking what he will do when he gets there. He's simply thinking that it is because of him that his mother's people are in jeopardy now and he has a responsibility to them. And because of what happened to him in Mr. Windigo's shed, he has a right to be a part of whatever may occur.

He comes to the juncture, the place where the dirt and gravel of Waagikomaan branch off from the highway. The moon has risen by then. It's like a great hole in the dark sky that lets the light of some brighter place shine through.

He turns toward the full moon and has walked a hundred yards, heading in the direction he believes the others will be hiding and waiting, when a car whose engine is huge and quiet glides from the highway onto Waagikomaan and headlights brighter and harsher than the moon illuminate him.

He spins. The car stops in a little spray of dust. The headlights remain on. For a long moment, he's facing a beast with two glaring eyes and a low growl of a voice. Then the headlights blink out and the engine dies. The dark and the quiet of the night return. The door opens. She steps out.

She walks toward him in a way that makes him think of a sleek animal—a panther maybe—or maybe it's because she's wearing a sleek black dress. In the moonlight, her face is silver, and her hair, yellow in daylight, is now like a spill of angry white water. She stops two feet from where he stands. And she smiles.

"What are you doing here?" she asks in a friendly tone that suggests everything he believes about her is wrong. "Did you get away from Indigo? You naughty boy."

She reaches out a silver hand and ruffs his hair. Then her fingers become talons and her grip becomes a torture. She pulls as if to rip away his scalp.

"You goddamned little snot," she says through clenched teeth, bone white. "You could have spoiled everything."

"Let him go!"

It is his mother's voice, coming from the dark at the side of the road. She steps into the glare of the headlights and confronts the woman. Winter Moon is with her. Only those two. The others, he realizes, must be at the place where the road to Broom's branches off. Winter Moon is holding a rifle, which is pointed at the woman's breast.

The woman releases her hold.

Winter Moon lifts his rifle and fires a single shot into the air.

"Cork." His mother waves him to her side, and he obeys. His head hurts from the viciousness of the woman's grip.

The woman doesn't seem to be afraid. Instead what he sees in her face is anger. "What now?" she asks.

"We wait for the others."

The sound of vehicles comes from the direction of Broom's cabin, and she looks past them down the moonlit road at their backs.

"Indigo?"

"He won't be coming to your rescue," Winter Moon replies.

"Ah," she says. "Dead?" No one replies, and she gives a nod. "A little native justice? Is that what's in store for me?" She changes in an instant. Her body changes, becomes smaller somehow, fragile and vulnerable. Her face changes, becomes suffused with terror. And her voice changes, becomes such a desperate cry for pity that it's hard not to be moved. "Please, I haven't done anything, I swear. Please, don't hurt me."

She moves toward his mother, her hands out in supplication. "Oh, God, please. I'm a mother like you. I have children that I love and who need me." Tears run down her cheeks. "Please, just let me go back to my children."

The vehicles are close now, pulling to a stop not far behind him, their own headlights adding to the surreal brilliance in which he stands with Winter Moon and his mother and the woman who is suddenly too near. Her arm is like a whip, fast and deadly, and wraps itself around his mother and pulls her from his side. In the same instant, he sees the silver flash of a knife blade that has materialized in the woman's hand and is poised at his mother's throat. She draws back, pulling his mother with her and using her as a shield against Winter Moon's rifle.

"I'll kill her," she says calmly.

Doors slam behind him, and he hears the thud of boots on the packed dirt of Waagikomaan. The woman's eyes move there.

"I'll kill her," she repeats.

His father is suddenly, magically at his side. He steps toward the woman with the knife.

"If you kill her, you will yourself die," he says, matching her incredible calm. "What is it you want?"

"To go home."

"I'll come for you there."

"I think not," she replies slyly. "What I think is that you've all murdered Indigo and if I go to the gas chamber, you'll go with me. I think that if I make it home, I'm safe."

"As far as I'm concerned, Monique, you're safe now. I won't let anyone harm you, I promise."

His mother's eyes are wide and he can feel her fear and it hurts him as if the slash across her throat is already a real thing. He's paralyzed. He absolutely cannot move.

The woman edges her way toward her car, forcing his mother with her, foot by foot.

"This is the deal, Monique," his father says, matching her retreat with his own advance, foot by foot. "You release her unharmed, and I'll let you go. No one will touch you. You have my word." His hands are in front of him, held away from his gun belt in a way that makes it clear they're empty of both firearm and intention. "Not another step, Monique, until we have a deal."

"I have all the cards," she points out.

"You cut her throat and I kill you. I kill you here or kill you in your house or I kill you on the street, I still kill you. You let her go and I swear you go free. As you say, we have every reason to keep all this quiet."

"I'll keep her with me until I'm away, then I'll let her go."

"That's not the deal because I don't believe you."

"How can I believe you?"

"Because I've never broken a promise."

His father has said it, and the truth of it would be clear even to the worst lying snake that ever lived. He believes his father absolutely, and he prays the woman will, too.

Her eyes move past his father to the men at his back.

"I won't let them touch you, I promise. Let her go, return to your house, then leave this town forever. That's the deal."

"I can leave?"

"If you ever come back to Aurora, it will be your death, and that's a promise, too."

She considers, considers a long time. And in that time, which seems now to stretch into forever, something in him snaps. He is released from the moment. He can feel himself floating, drifting away, numbed, mercifully removed from the reality of what is occurring. The incredible brightness of all the headlights. The knife blade glinting fire against the skin of his mother's throat. His mother's face not her face but a mask unreal because he can't comprehend anymore what he sees there. It's all a dream. But even in that dream he is aware, vaguely, that he's wetting his pants.

The woman finally speaks, and he hears it as if across a great distance. "All right. We have a deal."

The knife slides from his mother's throat, and the woman steps away toward her car, still facing his father. So fast that it must be a part of the dream he's sure he's dreaming, his father's hand clears the gun from his holster and he fires once. The woman drops immediately in a heap, and, in the brittle light, the dirt on the road turns black with her blood.

In that same moment, he is in the dirt, too, staring up at sky whose stars he cannot see.

His mother kneels at his side.

"Cork?"

He hears but can't make himself reply, can't make himself turn his eyes to look into her face.

"Dead," LeDuc says, from where the woman lies.

"Henry, what's wrong with him?" his mother cries.

"Corcoran O'Connor?" The voice of Henry Meloux. It is a rope trying to pull him from the place where he can't move.

"Cork, are you all right? Why won't he answer me, Henry?"

"What do we do now?" Sam Winter Moon asks.

"What you were going to do all along," his father replies. His words are empty of feeling, his voice a ghost of a voice. "Put her where she'll never be found."

"What about Cork, Henry?" his mother pleads.

"I will talk with him," Meloux replies. "I will guide him."

"Where?"

"To a place where he won't remember."

"You can do that, Henry?"

"I can try."

"What about you, Liam?" Hattie says.

He stands above his son, but he isn't looking at his son. He's looking at the gun that is still in his hand. "I guess I'll have to live with this."

"What about Cork?" Hattie says. "He's just a child, and children don't keep secrets well."

"Henry, can you really make him forget?" his mother asks. She lowers herself and cups his face in her hands and speaks to him. It is like a mother in a dream speaking, a dream from which he would love not to wake. "Oh, Cork, can you ever forgive me? Can you understand?"

He doesn't. Not now. But his mind on some level is recording everything, though he's too numb to process or to respond.

"I don't want him to remember this, Henry." His father's voice is no longer empty. What fills it now is something like loathing. "I don't want him ever to know what I've done."

"Please make him all right, Henry," his mother pleads, holding him tightly. "Oh, please, Henry."

Meloux replies, "I will do my best."

It is dark and hot, and he is naked. His small body drips sweat. The air is pungent with the scent of sage and cedar. He can hear Meloux's voice chanting a prayer, a long invocation, which he doesn't understand. The Mide's voice rises and falls.

There is something inside his chest. It feels like a fist pressing against his breastbone. His ears take in the prayer and the old Mide's voice; his body absorbs the heat; his nose and mouth draw in the healing aromas. Ever so slowly, the fist opens. Ever so gradually, his eyes close against the dark. Ever so gently, he is drawn away from memory.

"He killed her."

"Yes," Meloux said.

It wasn't a hard thing to accept. Now.

"He saved my mother, but it went against everything he believed," Cork said.

"It was a sacrifice he made for those he loved. But it was also a wound, and it hurt him deep. It came between him and everything he believed and everyone he cared about. You, your mother, your grandmother, Sam Winter Moon, The People. If he had not been killed, the wound he felt would have healed eventually. He died too soon. It was left open."

"Left open in us all, Henry."

"Do you feel wounded now, Corcoran O'Connor?"

"No."

"Then it is finished."

The old man sounded exhausted. Cork helped him from the sweat lodge, and together they went to the lake and cooled and cleaned themselves there. Rainy had towels waiting, and they dried and dressed and walked slowly back to Meloux's cabin, where Walleye had been patiently waiting. The old dog rose to his feet and greeted them with a lazy wag of his tail.

"I need to rest," Meloux said. His hands shook worse than Cork had seen before.

They helped him to his bunk, where he lay down.

"*Migwech*, Henry," Cork said.

"I have something for you, Corcoran O'Connor. Niece?"

From the table, Rainy brought a small cedar box, opened it, and held it out to Meloux, who took from it an intricately beaded bracelet. He gave it to Cork, saying, "Your grandmother made this. She gave it to me when I thought I loved her."

Cork knew that long ago, when they were both very young, Meloux had courted Dilsey.

"I give it to you now."

"Thank you, Henry. But why?"

"To remind you. Like the beads of that bracelet, all things are connected. The past, the present, the future. One long, beautiful work from the hand of Kitchimanidoo. You, me, those who have gone before us, and those who come after, we are all connected in that creation. No one is ever truly lost to us." The old man lifted an arm weakly and waved him away. "Now go. It is finished." Meloux closed his eyes.

"One more question, Henry."

The old man's eyelids fluttered open. "With you, it is always one more question."

"The vision I had on Iron Lake? The two wolves fighting?"

"What about it?"

"You never told me which one wins. Love or fear?"

"It is the one you feed, Corcoran O'Connor. Always the one you feed." The old man closed his eyes again. In another moment, he was sleeping.

Outside, Cork stood with Rainy in the late afternoon sun. The wind blew across the meadow grass, bringing the scent of wildflowers and evergreen.

"This was hard on Uncle Henry," she said.

"You'll take care of him?"

"Of course." She smiled. Smiled beautifully. "I say that, but somehow I always end up feeling it's the other way around." She gave him an unreadable look. "I don't know what occurred in the sweat lodge, but you seem different. Better. Healed."

"The blessing of that old man in there." He looked away where the meadow grass rolled gently under the hand of the wind, then back at Rainy. "If that's one of the reasons you're here with him, I hope he passes his special gift on to you."

"That's one of the reasons." Rainy looked down for a moment. "I'm sorry I was so hard on you at first."

"I won't hold it against you."

Cork studied the bracelet Meloux had given him. All things connected. Of course.

"Could I tell you something?" he said. "It's something I would have told Jo if she were alive, something I need to share with someone."

"I'd be happy to listen."

"Ever since Jo died, I've been having nightmares about my father's death. I haven't understood why, but maybe I do now. A very wise woman recently suggested that the nightmares might have something to do with some essential quality in my father that I've felt was missing in me. I believe that's true. I believe that at some level I remembered what my father did in order to save my mother's life and to protect his friends. The behavior of The People during the Vanishings went against everything that as a lawman he embraced. But in the end, he did what was necessary for the woman he loved and for the people he cared about; it was a sacrifice, one that wounded him deeply, but he did it. I think maybe . . ." Cork faltered.

"You've been wondering if maybe you could have done something that would have saved her, some sacrifice you weren't willing to make?"

Cork looked into the warm brown of her eyes. "Yeah."

"You've been blaming yourself for your wife's death."

"I think maybe I have."

"And do you think it's time you didn't?"

"That might take some work."

"When you're ready, Henry's here. And so am I."

"*Migwech*, Rainy."

"Take care of yourself, Corcoran O'Connor." She took his hand, leaned to him, and lightly kissed his cheek. "Don't be a stranger."

FIFTY

Hattie Stillday listened, and when he finished, she said, "I'd kill for a cigarette right now, Corkie."

"Sorry, Hattie," Cork said. He leaned toward her across the table in the interview room of the Tamarack County Sheriff's Department. "All these years, you knew what happened, you and the others."

Hattie smiled gently. "We knew more than that. We knew what *would* happen. Henry said that someday the spirits in that old mine would reach out and herd you toward the truth. We all hoped it would be a time when you might be able to understand."

"For my sake?"

"Ours, too. Hell, wasn't any of us looking forward to what would happen if everything came to light. Some pretty dark doings."

"But you had nothing to do with them, Hattie."

"Wasn't by design. I was fully prepared to end that woman's existence. Your father just got there ahead of me. Ahead of us all. We were all guilty of intent."

She reached out and took his hands in her own, which were old but strong yet.

"Corkie, what are you going to do?"

"I have to tell them, Hattie."

"Why?"

"Because it's what happened. Because it's the truth."

She shook her head in mild disapproval. "You're so like your father. Except that everything he knew he took with him to his grave."

"He didn't die a happy man, Hattie."

"Maybe not. But he died a good man. The whites back then, they wouldn't have understood. The whites now, I don't know." She paused, and her dark, careworn eyes seemed to pierce him. "Do *you* understand, Corkie?"

He knew what she was asking. He thought about the men and women involved in bringing an end to the butchery of Indigo Broom and Monique Cavanaugh. He'd known them his whole life, known them as good people. The Vanishings had driven them to actions that most good people would have seen as unthinkable; yet he believed this hadn't changed who they were at heart. Max Cavanaugh probably had it right. Sometimes, for the greater good, you chose to do harm and hope that you could find your way to forgiveness. His mother and Sam Winter Moon and Henry Meloux and Hattie Stillday and the others, they'd found that way, and for the rest of their lives had chosen to feed a different wolf. His father had died too soon, died without coming to terms with what he'd done, with the things he thought too dark for his young son to have to deal with.

"Yeah, Hattie," he finally replied. "I do."

"Are you going tell them about Ophelia?"

This was a question Cork had considered long and hard, and there was no easy answer. There was the law, which he'd worked to enforce most of his life. And there was justice, which he believed in deeply. And there was what was right according to his heart. And these were not the same things. Any decision he made would not satisfy them all.

"No," he said.

"You can live with that, but you can't live with the truth of what your father did, is that it?"

"I know you don't understand, Hattie. But I think my father would."

She let go of his hands, sat back slowly, and Cork couldn't read the look on her face. "Yesterday, I had a visitor. Isaiah Broom."

"Broom came here? What did he want?"

"To talk to me about the Vanishings. And about his mother."

"He knows the truth?"

"Part of it. The part that will help him understand who she was and that she loved him and would never have deserted him. That was important for him to know. And something else, Corkie."

"What?"

"He told the sheriff he's known about the crosscut in the mine tunnel for years, ever since he was a kid. He told them he'd passed that information to me a good long time ago. They think that's how I knew where to put the woman's body."

"Did he say how he knew?"

"He told them about what happened to him down there with his uncle when he was a boy. A horrible thing to have to tell anyone, any time. He told them his uncle had showed him the crosscut tunnel, which wasn't yet full of bodies but would contain his if he ever told anyone what Mr. Windigo had done to him."

Cork said, "Did they believe him?"

"Apparently. Corkie, it explains a lot that you wouldn't have to."

Cork thought about Broom, and figured Isaiah, too, had decided to start feeding a different wolf.

"Hattie, what did you do with my father's gun?"

"Like I said, I threw it in the lake."

"And you honestly don't remember where?"

"Do you really want to go looking for it, Corkie?"

He didn't. Whatever part the firearm was meant to play in his life, he hoped it was finished.

"Look, I don't know for sure what's going to happen to you," he said. "But considering Max Cavanaugh's confession and his sister's eccentricities, I'm guessing they'll go pretty easy."

"As long as no one touches Ophelia, I can handle whatever they decide about me."

"Do one thing for me, Hattie, okay?"

"Anything."

"Get her out of there."

"The Northern Lights Center?"

"The old Parrant estate, yeah. It's a sick place."

She reached out and took his hands again and gave them an affectionate squeeze. "I don't pretend to understand you, Corkie, but so long as you keep her out of this, I'll do whatever you want."

* * *

Marsha Dross was waiting for him in her office. "You look rested," she said.

"You don't look so bad yourself. I heard Broom talked to you, told you what happened to him down there in the Vermilion Drift when he was a kid."

"Close the door," she said. "Sit down."

Outside a horn blared on the street and someone shouted. Dross got up and closed her window.

"A hard thing for him to tell, I imagine," Cork said.

"But it explained how Ms. Stillday knew where to dump Lauren Cavanaugh's body, which was something she was dead set against telling us herself." She sat down again and leaned back, relaxed. "Once I heard Broom's story, I understood. So long as he wanted it kept secret—and who could blame him for not wanting a thing like that known publicly—Hattie Stillday wasn't going to say anything. I can appreciate that."

Cork said, "I have a story you need to hear."

"I'm all ears."

He told what had come to him during the sweat. But with two exceptions. He left out Henry Meloux's hand in the fate of Indigo Broom, and he didn't mention Hattie Stillday at all. He saw no purpose in dragging his old friends into this business. When he was finished, Dross was quiet. She simply stared at him.

"You have any proof of this, Cork?"

"The bodies in that mine tunnel, aren't they proof enough?"

"Christ, if I told this story to the media, do you have any idea how crazy they would make it sound?"

"A guaranteed made-for-television movie," Cork said with a smile.

Dross got up from her desk and paced the room a few moments, finally ended up at the window she'd closed, and stood staring out. "A story remembered under the influence of a—forgive me, Cork—witch doctor. A story for which there is no proof."

"The bodies," Cork said.

"A bizarre mystery more than forty years old. Everyone associated with it dead. The media will keep poking, but I don't see any purpose in feeding their curiosity." She turned back to him. "I'm inclined to keep this to myself."

"I was witness to a homicide."

"A justifiable homicide," she said. "If what you've told me is the truth."

"There's also the murder of Indigo Broom," Cork said.

"Did you actually see what those men did to him?"

"No."

"Then you can't really say, can you?"

"I can't, no."

"We don't have a body. No witnesses. All the principals are dead." Dross came and stood over him. "We have Max Cavanaugh's confession, so we know who killed his sister. Hattie Stillday's part in it she'll have to answer for, but I don't think any judge or jury will go hard on her. As for the bodies placed there more than forty years ago, those are cold crimes. This department doesn't have the time or the resources to pursue that investigation. The media already think we're a hayseed operation. I can live with that. What I can't live with is the uproar that would be caused by your story, a story conjured up during some hallucinogenic Ojibwe ritual, being made public."

"Wait a minute, Marsha—"

"I'm not finished." She leaned down to him, very near and in a way not at all friendly. "The Great North Mining Company has deeper pockets than this county. Hell, probably deeper than this whole state. What if they chose to sue you or me or Tamarack County for libeling the Cavanaugh name with accusations of serial killings and cannibalism?"

He started up, out of his seat. "The law—"

She pushed him back down. "Screw the law. Let's talk justice. It seems to me that justice has already been served. Do you not agree?"

He sat, chewing on her question. Finally he said, "Yeah, I guess so."

"All right, then."

"It's not that simple," Cork cautioned. "You're taking a big risk, Marsha."

"There's a lot I admire about you, Cork, but you always make things more complicated than they need to be. You keep your mouth shut and let me worry about this, okay?"

For a moment, Cork held to an unrelenting sense of responsibility.

"Okay?" Dross said, more forcefully.

Cork finally let go, and that release felt very good.

"Okay," he said.

EPILOGUE

He still sometimes dreams his father's death.

As Dr. Faith Gray continues to tell him, the mind is complicated, and the connections between conscious understanding and subconscious beliefs are difficult to unravel and take patience to reknit.

Nights, when he's awakened by the nightmare, he often walks the quiet hallways of the house in which he has spent his life. It's comfortable territory, and although the place has seemed dismally empty since Jo left him—or he abandoned her; it's a connection whose understanding still eludes him and on which he's still at work—he knows that, in truth, he's surrounded by good spirit. It is as Meloux said: All things in Kitchimanidoo's beautiful creation are connected. Cork and his children and Jo. And also those who have come before and those who will come after.

And so, on those difficult nights, he will sometimes speak to the spirit of his father. He thanks him for saving his mother's life. He asks his forgiveness for not praying his young heart out when Liam O'Connor lay dying. And he assures him that he loves him.

But most important, he tells his father that he understands.